The Red Cobra

Rob Sinclair

First published in 2017 by Bloodhound Books

www.bloodhoundbooks.com

Print ISBN: 978-1-912175-11-6

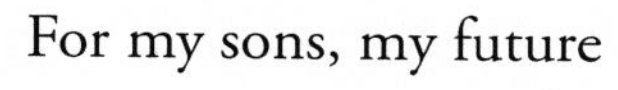

For my sons, my future

Chapter 1

She wiped clean the bloodied knife, sheathed it, then looked down at the two lifeless bodies. The man lay naked on the bed, his face twisted into an ugly grimace. Thick red blood smeared his flabby body; most of the blood his, some of it his wife's. Her lithe body lay haphazardly on the floor by her husband's feet. Her throat was open, the wound deep enough that the white of her spine was visible.

If only she'd stayed in the bathroom a few moments longer...

The man had been the target. It had taken just two days to track him down to the remote coastal house. One day later and he would have been smuggled safely out of the country.

Unfortunately for him, the assassin's hunting skills had been underestimated.

Killing the wife had been nothing more than a split-second reaction. It hadn't been the intention. If she'd simply been sleeping by her husband's side she may well have lived through the ordeal.

The killer wouldn't dwell. She spent a few moments satisfying herself that despite the impromptu second kill, the scene remained clean of her. Then she slipped out of the house, the many bodyguards stationed there to protect the dead man never once suspecting her presence.

She headed the half mile along the coastal road on foot to where she'd earlier parked her car. A chilling wind blasted off the nearby shore. It was dark outside, the time nearly two a.m. The closest town was over five miles away and there were no street lights here. With the sky overcast, the road was near black.

At least it was for the first five minutes of her walk. Then, out of the darkness, came the twin beams of a car's headlights, reaching out from behind the killer and slicing through the air ahead. She turned. The vehicle was only fifty yards away. She didn't panic, just kept on walking.

As the car neared, she held her breath. Her hand grasped the handle of her sheathed knife. The growl of the car's guzzling engine reverberated around her head, vibrations shooting through her as the vehicle crawled past. It came to a stop ten yards ahead.

The driver's door opened. For a brief moment, the car's dim interior light lit up the face of the man who stepped out.

She should have known it would be *him.*

He stood still, facing her. Now he was upright, away from the thin light seeping out of the car's windows, she could no longer make out his face.

'Why?' was all he said as he stood by the open door.

His hands hung casually by his sides. Was he armed?

'You know why,' she said.

'I can still protect you.'

'I never asked for protection.'

'No. You didn't. But you're going to need it now.'

She let his words sink in for only a second.

And then she ran.

She sprinted through the blackness, arms and legs pumping in a steady rhythm, her breaths deep and fast. Her heart soon pounded from adrenaline and exertion.

The darkness would help her, she knew, making her nearly invisible as soon as she was away from the faint glow of the car's rear lights. Still, she was surprised he didn't open fire on her. Perhaps he wasn't armed after all.

She heard nothing of him from behind and didn't once dare to look. Straining every sinew and muscle, she bounded across the soggy ground, headed directly for the steep cliffs that gave way to the thrashing sea below.

With each step she took, the roar of the crashing waves grew louder. Soon it filled her ears. On the distant horizon, the clouds began to part. A sliver of bright white light from the moon became visible. For the first time, she could see the endless expanse of inky water below. And the edge of the cliff just a few paces ahead.

She closed her eyes, preparing for the leap into the unknown...

The next second, she was shoved from behind. She lost her footing and ended up face down in the mud. Maybe he slipped too. Or maybe he'd simply thrown his whole body at her in order to bring her down. Either way, his big frame thudded onto the ground next to her.

In an instant, she turned onto her back, moving away from him, then leaped onto her feet. He did the same. She pulled out the long knife and swung it in a narrow arc as he raced toward her. She caught his arm and heard the slicing noise as the blade tore through skin and flesh.

He didn't cry out. Didn't even murmur.

He smashed into her. The knife flew from her grasp and they tumbled back to the ground, him on top, straddling her, pinning her arms with his knees.

Within seconds, two thick hands were wrapped around her neck, choking her. She rasped and gasped for breath.

The open wound on his forearm glistened in the moonlight. She reached out as much as his restrictive hold would allow, and dug her nails in. Dug deep. She squeezed as hard as she could.

Not so much as a flinch from him. It was like he wasn't even there. No humanity behind those pearly eyes. Just a... machine.

His strength, his determination, his focus, was too much. Her eyes began to bulge. The shadowy vision of him on top blurred.

But then she saw it. A faint sparkle in the darkness. Metallic. Not her knife. A gun. On the wet ground next to them.

He was armed after all. At least he had been.

She stretched out her hand, the pressure from his knees on her upper arms giving her little room to manoeuvre. She clawed at the soggy mud. Her fingertips were just an inch from the weapon. Her whole body strained...

She got it.

Grabbing the gun's barrel, she swung the grip toward his head. He never saw it coming. The thick metal handle crashed into his skull. He barely seemed to notice. She hit him again. Then a third time. Finally, the grip round her neck weakened. Slightly.

It was all she needed.

She bucked and pushed up with all the strength she could muster. His body gave a couple of inches. Enough for leverage. She swivelled and took him with her. A moment later, she was the one on top, the gun's barrel pressing against his forehead.

In the darkness, all she could clearly make out of him were his sparkling eyes. When she'd first met him she'd thought him handsome. Out in the cold, dark night, his penetrating gaze was sinister and unforgiving.

She stared down and he stared right back.

'If you were going to shoot me, you'd have done it already,' he said, still eerily calm and composed. A stark contrast to how she was feeling. 'Do it. Do it now. You won't get a better chance.'

Her finger was on the trigger. In fact, despite her hesitation, she was actually pushing down on the trigger as he made his move. He grabbed her wrist and pushed the gun up. She fired. Three times. The bullets sailed away into the night. The noise of the gun so close to her head was deafening. And disorientating.

The next she knew, he'd taken back the gun and was turning it round on her.

She was sure there would be no hesitation from him.

She was on her feet and hurtling to the cliff edge when he opened fire. A bullet caught her in the ankle. Then another in her side. As she leaped over the edge, a third bullet sunk into her shoulder.

She plummeted into the darkness below.

Chapter 2

Present day

'Mrs Walker,' the lady receptionist stated in her thick Spanish accent. She looked up over her computer screen into the waiting area where a handful of young women were sitting expectantly.

Kim got to her feet. She was alone. All the other women had husbands, boyfriends, or what looked to be their mothers, waiting with them. Kim didn't have a mother. Not one she'd known anyway. And her husband, Patrick, was as ever too busy to come with her.

That was fine. She could handle herself. She always had.

On the outside, Kim Walker was beautiful, radiant, confident and alluring. The type of person who made others feel happier. But then the world only ever sees what it wants to see. What lies underneath? Nobody ever really knows. Kim had always been an expert at masking her true self. That was the way it had to be.

The truth was she was wracked with nerves. As confident as she appeared, she always felt tense in the presence of someone of authority. They were just doctors and nurses here.

They weren't the police, the intelligence services or part of some secret and deadly government-sponsored murder squad. They weren't going to ask questions she couldn't or wouldn't answer.

They posed no real danger.

To them, Kim Walker was just another pregnancy, another statistic, and another set of forms to fill out. Albeit at thirty-six, she was certainly the oldest of the expectant mothers in the room.

Kim approached the receptionist, who indicated over to room number four. Kim headed to the door, opened it to reveal a darkened room, and spotted the young female doctor sitting in front of a bank of brightly lit monitors. The doctor looked up at Kim, an apology on her face.

'Mrs Walker, I'm Dr. Karmala. Please come, sit down.'

The doctor, as with all the other staff at the expensive private clinic in Marbella, spoke perfect English. Many of them *were* English, though the doctor's features and her accent suggested she was from somewhere on the Indian sub-continent.

'You can call me Kim. No need to be so formal.'

'Certainly, Kim.'

Kim shut the door and headed to the bed and sat, looking over the machines next to her with their myriad of knobs, dials, and lights. She felt a sickly sensation in the pit of her stomach. 'You have the results?'

The doctor hesitated, shifting in her seat, then looked down at the papers in front of her.

'Yes.' She paused, as if gathering her thoughts. Or trying to find the words. 'Mrs Walker–'

'Kim.'

'I'm sorry, Kim. As you know your pregnancy is considered more high risk because of your, urm, age–'

'Just tell me. Please,' Kim said, already preparing for the worst.

Tears rolled down Kim's face as she drove away from the clinic, back towards her lavish villa high up in the mountains overlooking the cool blue Mediterranean. She made no attempt to wipe at the salty streaks.

Perhaps this was nature's way of punishing her for what she was. She didn't believe in a god, about praying for a better life or for forgiveness for the bad things she'd done. Good and evil weren't concepts designed to test one's faith in a higher being, they were simply human nature.

Yet throughout her life, Kim had seen an element of karma; *that* she did firmly believe in. What goes around comes around. Or maybe it was just pure shitty luck.

Either way, deep down, Kim felt *she* deserved it. But how the hell was she going to break the news to Patrick?

They'd been together for over five years, married for four. He'd long wanted children. She'd always been more hesitant. Because of her own painful childhood, she was fearful of the world she would be bringing a child into. What if it suffered as she had? Even worse, what if it turned out to be just like her?

But slowly, as the years wore on, her natural mothering instincts had won out. Patrick had never pressurised her. She'd loved him even more for that. Of course, like everyone else, they'd had difficulties in their relationship, but the lack of children had never driven a wedge between them.

Patrick would be as devastated as she was about the news. And it wasn't like she was getting any younger. Even if she could get pregnant again in the future, the risks would only increase further with each attempt they made.

Kim let out a long, pained shout. Not a scream, but an angry, fearsome roar. She was angry with herself more than anything. How fucking selfish could you get? There she was, full of devastation and self-pity that the child she was carrying was less than perfect, but it was still a living child. It was still *her* child. She would love it unconditionally.

The tears stopped. A hard-edged resolve broke onto Kim's face as she battled against the turmoil in her mind.

It was five p.m. when she wound the car along the long driveway and rolled to a stop outside the grand double doors of her home. Patrick's car, his beloved Maserati, wasn't there. She had no idea what time he'd be back from work. She'd left a voicemail asking him to call. She hadn't given the details but had hoped from her tone of voice – and given he knew where she was going that afternoon – that he'd have understood what the problem might be.

She'd had nothing in response from him. She loved him dearly but he really could be a self-centred prick sometimes. A lot of the time actually.

Kim stepped out of her car and walked to the entrance, first unlocking the metal security grate and then the left of the double doors. She swung the door open and stepped into the marble-floored atrium, feeling a waft of pleasantly cool air on her face. She let out a long sigh, pleased to be back in her own space where she could shut herself off from the outside world once more.

She turned to push the door closed. Caught sight of the dark figure, off to her right, a split second too late.

Her old instincts were still there, but they weren't as sharp as they used to be. And she was pre-occupied. Maybe if it had been any other day, maybe if the news she'd just received had been positive, she'd have been more alert and it would have made the difference. A fraction of a second extra was probably all she needed to turn the tables on her would-be attacker.

And yet it was by such small margins that people regularly lived and died in all sorts of circumstances; accidents, close shaves.

But this was no accident, Kim knew. Far from it. And she realised as soon as the almond-scented rag was forced over her face that there was nothing she could do.

Seconds later, her body went limp.

And during the grave violence that soon followed, her unconsciousness was one thing Kim Walker would surely have been thankful for.

Chapter 3

James Ryker thanked the shop assistant and picked up the bag of groceries. He'd been going to the same store every other day for nearly twelve months but the assistant – always the same young man, barely out of his teens with an acne-scarred face – never once acknowledged Ryker for the local he was trying to be. Even in this far-flung place, thousands of miles of land and ocean between him and his old life, and where he'd never once caused any trouble, there was still something about Ryker that led others to be wary. At six feet three and with a beefy frame, he could to some extent understand why.

Or perhaps it was all in his mind.

Ryker headed on foot back toward his home, his senses high – as always. He doubted he would ever allow himself to feel truly safe. The one time he dropped his guard would be the one time he was caught out.

As he strode along the road, Ryker's slate-green eyes swept from left to right and back again, taking in everything and everybody around him. There was no pavement, not in this town, just a single strip of tarmac that ran through the main street, filled with mopeds, cars and pedestrians alike.

The tarmac was a recent addition. It was only present for a couple of miles either side of the town. Beyond that was a simple dirt track that snaked around the coastline and surrounding farmers' fields. The track was dry most months of the year and would send up plumes of blood-red dust every time a vehicle passed.

The place Ryker now called home was certainly remote, but it wasn't cut off. The area had running water, gas, and electricity, even a sporadic mobile phone signal. It was about as isolated as Ryker could bare – heading off into the wilds to live a life of solitude would probably drive him insane.

As he walked along the dirt, an open-topped four-by-four slowed as it passed. Ryker instinctively tensed, priming himself for action, even though his immediate thought was that the driver was about to stop to offer a lift. It had happened before. As a general rule of thumb, he'd found the locals to be extremely kind to each other, and on occasion to him and Lisa, the outsiders. He'd never once accepted such an offer of help.

A second later, the four-by-four sped up again and headed off into the distance, a dust cloud billowing out from its rear. Ryker held his breath until the dirt had settled. Perhaps the kindly offer had been hastily withdrawn when the driver spotted who the pedestrian was. That was fine. Ryker was well prepared to give a please and thank you when required but was otherwise happy to be left alone.

A few minutes later, Ryker's house came into view in the near distance – a simple and secluded beachfront property made of timber and glass. To some it would be a ramshackle hut, but to others, a bohemian rustic retreat.

Set atop a small rocky outcrop, a good two acres of land came with the house. Not that Ryker had any intention of turning it into a real garden of any sort. The beach was right there, a short clamber down the rocks, should he ever need outside space. Instead he left the land to grow freely, providing an extra element of seclusion for the property.

It was tranquil, not extravagant. The house wasn't a billionaire's exotic escape but suited its purpose and was in an enviable location overlooking clear waters. Considering where Ryker had come from, the depths he'd plunged to in his previous life, what more could he ask for?

The problem, he knew, was that no matter what mask he put on for the world, no matter how hard he tried to fit in, he could never truly let go of his past – of who he really was. He and Lisa were determined to fashion a life for themselves, but Ryker simply couldn't ignore the sense of suspense he felt. Not fear exactly, but not far from it. It dominated his mind, nearly every waking minute. Wondering not *if* they would come for him, but *when*. No matter how far he ran, no matter what he did to hide, that would be the case for as long as he was still alive.

But whoever came for him, whatever they threw at him, Ryker would take them on.

He would fight. He would survive.

After all, it was what he had always done best.

Some would call it paranoia. But Ryker wasn't paranoid. He was a realist. And as his gaze passed from the unkempt grounds and up the road, he felt a sudden jolt of vindication.

The twisting road in front of him weaved off towards a metal bridge, about a hundred yards long, spanning the mouth of a small river. On the far side of the bridge, Ryker spotted the same four-by-four that had passed him minutes earlier. It was facing him. Although he couldn't make out anything of the vehicles occupants, he could tell from the wispy smoke trailing up from the back end that its engine was idling.

At that moment, Ryker was sure of one thing:

Someone had found him.

Chapter 4

Exactly who *they* were, Ryker didn't know. Really it didn't matter. No one but he and Lisa knew of their new identities and their location. If someone – anyone – had found them, it was a problem.

A man like Ryker, who had lived in the shadows for so much of his life, always on the move, always looking over his shoulder, had become well used to forever analysing his environment for potential threats. It had formed such an integral part of his training all those years earlier – not to mention the many years subsequent – that it had become second nature. And that was why he didn't panic now. He simply put into motion a well-laid plan.

Keeping his eyes on the four-by-four in the distance, Ryker picked up his pace as he headed to his home. His brain was whirring. His first aim was clear: get to the house and find out whether Lisa was there. He had to make sure she was okay.

When he reached the front door, Ryker carried on going, snaking around to the back. Regardless of whether or not a threat was already on the inside, he wasn't going in the front.

He came up against a small frosted window on the side of the house. The window was locked shut, as it had been when Ryker had left earlier. Beyond the window lay the en-suite shower room to the house's only bedroom. In a small hideaway beneath the panel on the base of the shower tray lay a fully loaded FN Five-seven handgun containing twenty armour-piercing 5.7mm cartridges.

Ryker certainly wasn't ill prepared. He'd primed several entrance and exit routes to the house should he ever need to move with stealth. Although the bathroom window was locked, he'd fitted it himself to allow the simple yet secure structure to be prised open – should you know how.

Ryker checked around him and found the small slat of wood that he'd hidden beneath foliage. He used the slat to edge the corner of the window open at its weakest spot, then tugged sharply to snap the thin clasps which sat along the inner edges of the frame. The window opened two inches, enough to allow Ryker to release the handle. He pulled the window further open then slunk through the small space, slithering silently like a snake passing over rocks.

He crept forward to the shower, removed the weapon, and gave it a once-over. No problems. Moving with caution, he headed to the partially open door.

Ryker stole a glance before moving out into the bedroom, creeping in silence. His breathing was deep and calm, not even a murmur escaping his lips as he slowly inhaled and exhaled.

When he reached the bedroom doorway, he stood and waited. Listened. Nothing. No sound of movement from within his home. No sounds at all. He cautiously peered out over the open-plan space in front of him, index finger on the gun's trigger.

Ryker spotted the solitary figure, casually sitting in an armchair. And he relaxed. A little.

Gun still held out, but the feeling of threat somewhat diminished, Ryker moved out from behind the door and toward the man. 'You,' he said.

The man looked up. Certainly he wasn't the last person Ryker expected to see. In fact, of all the people who might have come looking for Ryker, this man – Peter Winter – was one of the most welcome. And least threatening.

'Ah, you're back.' Winter got to his feet, a knowing smile on his face.

In his late thirties, Winter was similar in age to Ryker, and a similar height too at over six feet, but he was fresh-faced and scrawny and he had a knowing confidence that had often riled Ryker in the past.

'How did you get in here?' Ryker quizzed, the tone of his voice making it clear the visit wasn't welcome. He continued to hold the gun out, pointed at the visitor. He didn't believe Winter was an immediate threat, but he'd been through enough to know he couldn't trust anyone one hundred percent.

Winter nodded over to the front door. 'Not the same way you did, clearly. Good to see you're still on your toes though.'

'You've got no right coming into my home like this.'

Winter hesitated for a second. Ryker's forthright tone and the fact he was still pointing a fully-loaded gun at Winter's face had, Ryker could see, drained some of the confidence and ease from his former boss – a Commander at the secretive Joint Intelligence Agency where, in another life, Ryker had worked for nearly twenty years.

'I'm not a threat,' Winter assured him.

'No. You're not. If you were you'd have a bullet between your eyes already. How did you find me?'

'By doing my job. Though I have to say, it wasn't easy. You've covered your tracks well. Ryker? That's your name now, right?'

'That's what my passport says.'

'German?'

'British.'

'No, I mean the name, not your passport. It's of German origin, isn't it? From the German word for rich.'

'If you say so,' Ryker said, not hiding his disinterest in the analysis.

'Almost seems ironic given what you left behind to come here.'

'I figured I didn't really need your money.'

'You could have just told me that instead of disappearing.'

'If I recall correctly, Ryker was also the name of a commander on Star Trek. So maybe the irony's aimed at you, *Commander.*'

Winter huffed sarcastically. 'That wouldn't be irony, more of a taunt.'

Winter may have once been Ryker's boss, but Ryker had never looked upon him as a superior. For starters, Winter had only assumed the role through default when the incumbent – Ryker's long-time mentor – had been murdered outside a cafe in Omsk, Russia.

'We set up a nice life for you,' Winter said. 'I'm not sure why you didn't take it.' He looked around the space he was standing in, turning his nose up at what he saw. 'You certainly could have afforded a nicer place than this.'

'There's nothing wrong with this place. And I don't need your money. Or you forever watching me.'

'We gave you a new identity. A fresh start. We were helping you. Protecting you.'

'Your idea was to keep me on a short leash should you ever need me. I'm sorry, but my idea of freedom is something different.'

Winter smiled. 'So that's what this is? Freedom?'

'It's the closest I've ever come.'

'You're partially right. I did always wonder whether I'd need you again. A man of your... skills is hard to come by.'

Ryker finally lowered his gun and stuffed it into his trousers' waistband. 'The answer's no.'

Winter sat and looked pensively at Ryker for a few seconds. Ryker didn't move, just waited for Winter to say what he'd come to say.

'Look, Logan... Abbott, Ryker, whatever the hell your name is this week, I know you don't want me here. I know you think you've earned your freedom. The right to live a life away from what you once were. But I never promised that. And I know deep down you never believed it. Part of me wonders whether you even want it.'

'You know nothing about what I want or what I am.'

'But I do. I've known you a long time. And you can't just run away from who you are.'

'It's not me I'm running from.'

'You sure about that? *This* isn't a life. Hiding away like this, forever looking over your shoulder. And it's not you. But I'm not going to sit here and try to convince you of that.'

'Good. So I guess you'll be leaving then.'

Winter got to his feet, and Ryker stepped to one side, giving his ex-boss a clear path to the front door.

'But let me say this one thing,' Winter added. 'I found you. And you know I'm not the only person looking. I know you think you can deal with whatever or whoever is out there gunning for you, and I can guarantee you'll give anyone who threatens you a damn good run for their money.'

'Very flattering, Winter.'

'Okay, look. This is beside the point. My real point is that I *do* still need you, Ryker.'

'I won't do it.'

'Hear me out, please.' Winter reached inside his jacket and Ryker couldn't help but tense as he waited. The last thing he was expecting was for Winter to draw a weapon, but he could never rule it out. In the end, Winter's hand emerged clutching some papers.

'You know,' Winter said. 'You're not the only person in the deep, dark world who wanted to get away from it all, who wanted to leave their past behind.'

Ryker raised an eyebrow.

'I need your help, Ryker. It's as simple as that.'

'My help to do what?'

'It's about the Red Cobra.'

Winter stopped speaking and stared at Ryker. Ryker opened and closed his mouth, searching for the right words to describe the confusion that suddenly enveloped his mind.

The Red Cobra. A name from the past. A name forever burned into his memory. A rival, of sorts. A lover, more than once.

In the end, Ryker said nothing.

'You remember her?'

'Of course.'

'We've found her.'

Ryker tried to betray no emotion, but Winter had him. Of all the possible bombshells, this had to be one of the biggest.

'Where?' Ryker asked.

'In Spain.'

'Then what do you need me for? You want me to kill her?'

Even as he said the words, Ryker questioned whether that was something he'd be able to do. At one time, certainly. But now?

'I'd say it's a little late for that,' Winter responded. 'We already found the Red Cobra. Dead. She's been murdered.'

Chapter 5

Ryker needed a few moments to compose himself. Both men took a seat. Winter didn't push Ryker. He'd laid down the bait. Now he seemed content to wait and let Ryker sweat over it.

The Red Cobra. A blast from the past. Her real name was Anna Abayev, though even Ryker – who'd come closer to her than most – had never known her by that moniker. She was an assassin. Born and bred. Highly trained but with a lethal hard edge that was simply part of her nature, her DNA.

Much of Ryker's skill had been taught and nurtured by the JIA, a clandestine agency operated jointly by the UK and US governments. A long and gruelling schooling period with the JIA had turned Ryker into a robotic operative. Ryker had Charles McCabe to thank for that. Mackie. His old boss who'd taken a bullet to the head when his secretive life had finally caught up with him.

That was all in Ryker's past, though. He wasn't that man anymore, even though he still had a deadly set of skills that few others possessed, as Winter said. The Red Cobra on the other hand... she really was something else.

'The car outside–'

'Backup. In case you decided to run,' Winter confirmed. 'Or turned on us.'

'What were you going to do? Mow me down? Shoot me?'

Winter shrugged. 'I wouldn't have wanted to. But I wasn't sure how you'd react to me finding you.'

'So you covered all bases. Just in case.'

'What more would you expect?'

Both men's attention was grabbed by the sound of the front door opening. Ryker stood, turned, and stared as Lisa walked in. Her long brown hair was wet and clung to her shoulders. She had a large and colourful beach towel wrapped around her glistening and tanned body, her toned physique clear. Ryker felt a sense of betrayal slice through him. Because of Winter or because he'd been reminiscing about Anna Abayev?

Lisa was half a step inside when she spotted Ryker. She smiled. But when she saw Winter, her face went pale.

'Angela,' Winter said. 'Or should I call you Lisa now?'

'You shouldn't call me anything,' she grunted, before turning to Ryker. 'What is he doing here?'

'We were getting onto that,' Ryker said.

'Please, Lisa, come and sit down.'

'I'd rather not.' She moved over to the fridge, took a bottle of water then padded across the floor to the bedroom. 'James, get rid of him.' She slammed the bedroom door shut.

Winter looked at Ryker for a few seconds. Neither man said a word. Lisa's demand reverberated in Ryker's mind. She was right. He shouldn't even have been contemplating helping Winter. He should have thrown him out of there the second he'd laid eyes on him.

But then what? Run away as far and as fast as they could once more? Another new location? Two more new identities?

Maybe that was what Lisa wanted. But it wasn't what Ryker wanted. Not really.

Despite his protestation, even before Winter had mentioned the Red Cobra, Ryker had already been undecided as to whether he would agree to Winter's request for help. Together, Ryker and Lisa had set about making a life for themselves, just the two of them. Away from the chaos that had clouded their lives, their relationship, for so long. It wasn't them against the world anymore. It was just... them. Yet deep down, he wasn't satisfied. Not completely. There was something missing.

Isn't that basic human nature, though? Hasn't every single one of the many billions of humans who have walked the earth felt the same way? Always clamouring for the perfect life but never quite reaching it, always wanting more. The grass is always greener. At least that was Ryker's way of justifying how he felt.

And hearing the name Red Cobra... How could he not at least hear Winter out now?

'How do you know it's her?' Ryker asked.

'Purely by accident.' Winter was still clutching the papers he'd taken from his pocket as though waiting to deal his full hand – should he need to. 'She was killed three days ago. At her home in southern Spain.'

'Who killed her?'

'That was one thing I was hoping you might help with.'

'I'm not sure what's in it for me.'

'What do you want? Money?'

'To be left alone.'

'I can't figure out if you've actually managed to convince yourself of that or not.'

'Would it make a difference to you either way?'

'No. Because I need you. It's as simple as that. You got close to her. Closer than anyone else I know.'

'I tried to kill her. And it's not much of a surprise that she's dead now. Only that it took so long for someone to find her.'

'Longer than it's taken to find you, that's for sure. Though keeping your tracks clean when there's two of you is always going to be harder.'

Ryker couldn't help but be offended by the statement, yet he knew it was true. The Red Cobra had disappeared nearly eight years earlier after jumping off a cliff in the middle of the night in northern Germany with three bullets in her.

Eight years. Not a sniff of her since then.

He and Lisa had been on the run for less than one year.

'Maybe her death isn't really a surprise,' Winter continued. 'And if *we'd* found her first then perhaps the outcome would have been the same. And therein lies the problem.'

'How so?'

'This wasn't a random attack. Someone found her. They butchered her. This was a statement. Revenge.'

Winter threw down the papers he'd been holding onto the coffee table. Ryker leaned forward and glanced at them – photographs. He used his hand to sift through them. His heart pounded as he scanned the gory images. Butchered. Winter hadn't been wrong. There was little left of the poor woman to identify what was what.

Although he didn't outwardly react, Ryker was shocked by what he saw. He wasn't unaccustomed to seeing dead bodies, or even to killing people, but such viciousness would never fail to trouble him. It brought closer to the surface his own painful memories.

'We don't know who did this,' Winter said. 'But we need to find out. And soon. There's very possibly a leak within our own intelligence services.'

'What makes you think that?'

'The Red Cobra had a lot of enemies. Not just agencies like the JIA but all sorts of criminal gangs across the world who'd fallen foul of her... services.'

'But why do you think this was a leak?'

'We had a profile of the Red Cobra.'

Ryker raised an eyebrow. 'And?'

'For years, she carried out her work without leaving so much as a hint of tangible evidence. But we had a set of fingerprints linked to that profile – from way back, before she was an operative.'

'And the dead woman matches those fingerprints.'

'Exactly. She was going under an alias – Kim Walker. British, supposedly. When the local police in Spain brought the murder to the attention of the British authorities, there was no record of this woman in any databases. She had a passport, a driver's licence, both fakes, but nothing else. No birth records, no employment records, or anything else that matched the identity. The Spanish police took her fingerprints, passed them over to the Met to help the police identify her.'

'And when Scotland Yard ran those fingerprints in the system it alerted the JIA.'

'Exactly.'

'Do the police know that?'

'No. The profile is heavily restricted. The police search would simply have shown no match. But the Met have assigned one of their detectives to help find out who this woman really was. He's in Spain already, working with the police there.'

'You still haven't explained how you think there's been a leak.'

'When the alert came in, we did some checks in the metadata of our systems. There's a record of her profile being accessed a little over a week ago. It wasn't highlighted at the time because the access was from a legitimate user account on a terminal at MI5 headquarters. Or so it seemed.'

'But the user had no idea what you were talking about when you *questioned* them.' Ryker made speech marks with his fingers as he emphasised the word that significantly played down the lengths to which the JIA would go to get answers. He wondered what had happened to the poor sod whose ID had been compromised.

'It's not an inside job,' Winter said. 'At least not by that user. He's clean. But someone somewhere found a way into the system.'

'Sounds professional.'

'Professional, yes. Official? We don't know. It's possible the hack was the work of another agency but the nature of the death suggests otherwise. Like I said, this was a revenge attack. Personal. Regardless, someone accessed our system to find information on the Red Cobra. And now she's dead.'

Ryker looked down at the photographs again. At what was left of the poor woman's face. 'Except she's not.'

Winter raised an eyebrow. 'Not what?'

'The Red Cobra isn't dead.'

Winter glanced down at the bloody images then back at Ryker, confusion on his face.

'I know her,' Ryker said. 'I know her better than almost anyone else who's alive. You had a profile on the Red Cobra? Your profile was wrong.' Ryker tapped the pictures in front of him. The blood-stained face of a dead woman he'd never seen before. 'I don't know who that poor woman is, but I can tell you with certainty that she isn't the Red Cobra.'

Chapter 6

When Winter left, Ryker locked the front door then double-checked the remaining doors and windows. Satisfied everything was secure, he walked over to the closed bedroom door. He let out a deep sigh and turned the handle.

Lisa was lying on the bed, facing away from him. Her hair was still wet but her bronzed skin was now dry and matte, and she was dressed – a pair of shorts and a loose fitting cotton top. Ryker guessed she'd showered following her saltwater swim – an almost-daily routine. He could see from the reflection in the mirror on the far side of the room that she was awake. Ryker moved over and lay down on the bed next to her. His body aligned with her curves, fitting into her naturally as it always did, and he couldn't help but feel a fleeting moment of arousal before she spoke.

'You agreed to help him.' She wasn't angry, more disappointed. But was it disappointment in him or just in the way that life works out?

'I have to.'

'No, you don't. You could have said no.'

'And then what?'

'And then nothing. Winter would go away. He's not going to have you killed, or give up your new identity, just because you refused to help him.'

'Probably not,' Ryker said, though he knew he could never rule out such a thing.

'Then why did you say yes?'

'Because this one really is my problem.'

Lisa shuffled, half-turning so that she was facing him.

'You wanted this, didn't you?'

Ryker took a couple of seconds too long to reply. His silence gave away his answer. 'I need to do this. You can change my name, you can give me money, you can send me to any corner of the world to live as a free man. But a small part of who I once was will always remain inside of me. That's the man you fell in love with.'

'I know. It's not that I don't love him. It's just that I'm... scared. Scared that if you go out there – even if it's for the right reasons – you may not come back to me.'

'I'll always come back.'

'Not if you're in a coffin, you won't.'

'That's not going to happen.'

'Don't you think we've been through enough troubles?'

He considered her words, which significantly downplayed the deadly situations they'd fought together. Through it all, he'd always felt an unwavering loyalty to her and a desire to keep her from harm – even though at times it seemed like his loyalty was misplaced.

Ryker remained silent and Lisa looked away from him again. In many ways he was surprised that she was being this amenable. There he was, on the brink of destroying the ever-so-frail life they had been building and her protest was mild to say the least. Either she was keeping her anger bottled up or she'd seen this moment coming. Was his going back to the JIA just an inevitable outcome?

'What's the job?' she asked.

'I can't say.'

'If you want me to support you on this maybe you should.'

'I need to find someone. Someone else who doesn't want to be found.'

'How apt.'

'Indeed.'

'A woman?'

The question was double-edged but he wasn't about to wait. 'Yes.'

'You know her?'

'From a long time ago.'

'Huh.'

Ryker knew what she was thinking but he didn't try to defend himself. He saw no point. What had happened between him and the Red Cobra was in a different life. 'You could come with me.'

Lisa smiled. 'No. This, here, this is my life now. With you. Angela Grainger, FBI agent, is dead. She was killed in a shootout in a car park in Beijing. Remember?'

'I remember. Carl Logan, English spy, was killed out there too.'

'The fugitive lovers.'

'That's what the papers said. A real life Bonnie and Clyde.'

'And when are the press ever wrong?' Lisa smiled again.

'But you're *not* dead,' Ryker assured. 'I still see Angela inside you every day. And I like her.'

'You *like* her?' Lisa teased.

'I *love* her.'

'Then come home to her.'

'I will. I promise.'

Chapter 7

Before he'd left, Winter had passed to Ryker the profile, put together by MI5, MI6, and the JIA, on Anna Abayev, also known as the Red Cobra, plus some papers outlining the investigation so far into Kim Walker's murder. Ryker perused the files as he sat in the back of a taxi on the way to the airport. He'd destroyed them and discarded the remnants by the time he boarded the plane that would take him to the mainland before he headed onward across the ocean to Barcelona and then Malaga.

The details Ryker had read were still flowing through his mind as he walked up the steps to enter the turboprop plane. The profile on the Red Cobra was sparse to say the least. Anna Abayev's fingerprints had been on record from a double-murder that had taken place in Georgia in the mid-1990s. The young Anna – just sixteen at the time – had vanished from the scene and details of her movements and whereabouts in the following years were flimsy at best. In fact, Ryker reckoned he held more detailed knowledge of the Red Cobra's methods and movements in his brain than the UK's intelligence services had managed to gather on her in almost two decades. But then there weren't many people who had come as close to her as Ryker.

He took his seat by the window and watched the other passengers clambering on board. Headspace and leg-space was limited in the cramped cabin and Ryker, with his height and bulk, willed the seat next to him to remain empty. The last passenger to board the plane however – a bearded and bespectacled man in his forties, Ryker guessed – bumped and squeezed into the seat next to Ryker, apologising as he did so.

Ryker murmured in acknowledgment before his busy mind took him back to the task at hand, and the conversation with Winter the previous day.

'Who will I be working for?' Ryker had asked.

'You'll be working for me,' Winter said.

'The JIA?'

'Not exactly.'

'Who knows about this then? Me being involved, I mean.'

'Only me and those who need to know.' Winter paused.

Ryker remained tight-lipped, waiting for the Commander to add to his vague responses.

'We've set up a full cover identity for you,' Winter said eventually. 'If that's what you're worried about. Birth records, university, electoral, taxes, it's all there.'

Ryker raised an eyebrow as the words sunk in. Winter had gone to a lot of trouble already in setting up Ryker for the job. Which meant he'd always expected Ryker would agree to help. Ryker felt a little foolish about that.

'What's the story?'

'You're a freelance investigator. Appointed by the Home Office to assist the Metropolitan Police. You don't have any legal jurisdiction in Spain, but then neither does the Met, and I'm not sending you out there to make an arrest. I need to know what's happening. Who killed Kim Walker and why. And why that dead woman is linked to the Red Cobra's profile.'

'Name?'

'James Ryker,' Winter said with a wry smile.

Ryker glared at his ex-boss, bit his tongue.

'It was easier that way. I've had to pull a lot of strings to get this far. Using an identity you'd already created made more sense.'

Ryker still said nothing, but he was angry. Winter had chosen to use Ryker's now-real identity for an undercover operation. It felt like a kick in the teeth. As though Ryker's new existence, his identity, was of no importance to Winter or the JIA. He still belonged to them.

'James Ryker has been brought in because he has real-life experience of hunting the Red Cobra,' Winter said. 'So feel free to use details of your own experiences with her.'

'I thought you said the Met doesn't know about the Red Cobra? That they're trying to figure out who Kim Walker really was?'

'They don't, yet. But it's the easiest angle to get you – and keep you – in there. We're not going to publicise it to the world, but we'll make sure the right people know.'

'The detective who's out there, who is he?'

'His name is Paul Green. Work with him as much or as little as you like. I've never met him, haven't got a clue how good he is. I'll leave that to you to figure out.'

'And what about you?'

'What about me?'

'What's your involvement going to be?'

'You're my involvement. I thought this was something you'd be able to handle on your own.'

'Yeah. It is.'

'But don't for a second think that means this isn't a big deal. Because it is. We don't know how far this problem stretches. Our system contains details of thousands of highly confidential operations; names of agents, informants.

Someone has breached that system. If that information gets into the wrong hands, then the lives of hundreds of people at MI5, MI6, the JIA could be on the line.'

'Mine included?'

'No. You're already dead, remember?'

Winter smiled again. Ryker didn't. The play seemed simple enough. A big deal? Ryker had seen bigger. The computer system had been hacked once, but according to Winter all that had been accessed was a limited profile of a wanted assassin. Gaining access to details of agents, informants and operations was surely another matter altogether.

Was the JIA really worried that could happen? Maybe they were. Either way, Ryker got the impression Winter hadn't yet declared his full hand. If the threat were as big and as real as Winter was suggesting then something else must have tipped off the JIA. Another hacking attempt. Knowledge of other profiles being accessed. Agents already compromised. It was possible. But there was another, more worrying, possibility that Ryker saw.

Why was the JIA so concerned about the Red Cobra all of a sudden? Particularly if they'd thought she was the dead woman right up until Ryker had set the record straight. She was a wanted criminal, not an agent. So what was it about her that the JIA wanted to keep under wraps? It wouldn't be the first time in his life that Ryker had been used as a pawn to hide the dirty secrets of the governments he worked for.

Ryker was brought out of his thoughts when the man sitting next to him knocked a bundle of papers into his lap. The man apologised profusely as he frantically collected up his belongings.

'It's not a problem,' Ryker said as he handed the last of the papers back to the man.

Ryker looked over and saw he had a laptop computer laid out on his fold-down tray. The papers he'd dropped were full of printed type. Ryker, having glanced for a couple of seconds, deduced their context. 'You're a writer.'

'Yes,' the man said, looking surprised. 'How did you know?'

Ryker nodded at the papers.

'A nature writer,' the man said, sounding enthused. 'I've been out here for three months, keeping a diary. I'm hoping to turn it into a book. Did you know some of the rarest snakes in the world are found right here on this island? It's a real hotbed. I've been searching for them, recording them.'

'No. I didn't know that.' Ryker turned away from the man, hoping he could avoid entering into a lengthy discussion about searching for rare snakes. He'd never trusted writers. Never trusted anyone who took pleasure in writing everything down, recording it. Making it permanent. He wanted to leave as little evidence of his existence as he could.

'So what do you do?' the man asked.

'Whatever it takes,' Ryker said, staring straight ahead.

Then he shut his eyes, memories of the Red Cobra still sloshing in his mind as he drifted off to sleep.

Chapter 8

Nineteen years earlier

Anna Abayev was nearly fourteen the day she was introduced to Colonel Kankava, a beast of a man who changed her forever. She'd been living in Georgia for five years, a period of real stability for her family, if not for the country in which she was living.

Contrary to popular belief of those who knew of her, Anna wasn't Russian by birth but was actually Serbian. Her Russian father had met a young local woman while working in the former Yugoslavia in the early eighties, a number of years before the country had torn itself apart in civil war. Anna had never known her mother, she'd died during childbirth. Anna had always felt guilt over that, even though her father never made any suggestion that he blamed his daughter for her mother's passing.

Anna's father had long despised his home country's then communist regime. His dismissal of his own people was a move which had seen him gather many enemies in the country he called home. They'd spent time in countless countries during her early childhood, always on the move to stay safe and to allow her father to take on jobs to keep providing. It was to Georgia that Anna had the strongest affiliation.

The country, newly independent following the collapse of the Soviet Union in 1991, had been going through a period of immense turmoil. The economy was in free-fall and rival factions vied for control of the country leading to various bloody coups and internal conflicts. Hardly the perfect environment for bringing up a young family.

Despite this, Georgia was the place – perhaps due to familiarity as much as anything else – that Anna thought of as home.

Although her father had amassed sufficient money for them to live securely during the preceding years, without his needing to work and travel as he had done during Anna's earlier childhood, resources were running thin and it was becoming more and more difficult for him to turn down the offers for his specialist work. Plus, having been in one place for so long, he was becoming increasingly paranoid that the wolves from his past were closing in.

Anna had sensed for a number of weeks that something would have to give.

'But I could come with you?' she protested as her father led her by the hand up the tree-lined driveway on a snowy winter's morning. The crooked branches on the leafless trees silhouetted against the moody sky made the entire scene sinister. With each step they took, Anna grew increasingly terrified of what lay beyond the walls of the crumbling blue-and-white-painted mansion, where her father was sending her to work as a domestic maid.

'No, Anna,' her father said, sternly but with warmth. 'You need to stay here and go to school. You're getting big now. Your education is important. And you can earn good money here while I'm gone. The Colonel will pay you to help the soldiers.'

Her father had explained that Kankava was a former colonel in the Soviet Army. A native Georgian who, following independence, had aligned himself with the Mkhedrioni paramilitary group who were vying for control of the country. Despite the Mkhedrioni succeeding in overthrowing the government in a violent and bloody coup d'état in 1992, further in-fighting led to their eventual outlawing in 1995. Kankava had taken that as his opportunity to retire and set up a small charitable foundation for wounded war veterans. He bought a once-grand eighteenth-century mansion, renovated it, and opened the doors to some forty veterans who shared the same sympathetic nationalist views as Kankava.

Anna had no interest in the veterans or their politics. She just wanted to be with her father. 'But why can't you stay too?' Anna stopped walking. 'You said you'd always look after me. Protect me.'

A tear escaped Anna's eye. It began to roll down her cheek but stopped after a couple of seconds.

'I can't, Anna. It's become too... dangerous.'

Her father didn't elaborate and Anna didn't probe. She knew her father's business put him in a dangerous position, that he had many enemies, but he never talked about it in any detail. They had come to an unspoken understanding that she'd never ask and he'd never tell. See no evil, speak no evil, hear no evil. Or something like that.

'When will you be back?' she asked.

'As soon as I can.'

'But what does that mean? Days? Weeks? Months? Years?'

'It means as soon as I can.'

Anna didn't push him. It really didn't matter what she said in protest. He'd already made his decision. And it was final. She knew that.

They continued walking. Anna tried her best to hold back the tears that were welling.

When they reached the over-sized doors to the house – bare oak that was crumbling at the corners – her father reached out and rang the bell.

After a few seconds, the door creaked open. Beyond the fatigue-clad man who stood in the entrance, Anna caught sight of the wood-panelled walls and military paraphernalia that adorned the interior. The smell of the home that wafted out of the open door made her nose tingle and she cringed: furniture polish, boiled vegetables. Bleach to overpower urine and faeces, and whatever else. It smelled of... oldness.

Death and decay. That was all that lay within the walls of that house, Anna decided.

Anna looked at the man who had opened the door. One arm of his military fatigues hung clumsily by his side. An amputee. He was grey-haired. Young Anna had no idea how old he was. He could have been anything from fifty to ninety. To her he was simply old, that was all she knew. A thick beard covered his face reaching up close to his eyes, which were steel-grey. He stared down at Anna and the sides of his mouth turned upward as if in a knowing smile.

'This must be Anna,' he said, after shaking her father's hand.

'Yes. My precious Anna,' her father said, ruffling her hair like she was still five years old. 'You take good care of her for me.'

'Oh, I will.'

'Anna, this is Colonel Kankava. He's in charge here. Anything you ever need, you ask him.'

'Come on, Anna, let me show you around.'

The Colonel extended his hand. Anna looked at her father then back at the face of Kankava whom she already detested. But she did her best to bury her true feelings and took his hand. He led her inside. She turned to her father who was still standing on the step outside.

'Angel, I've got to go now,' he said.

'No!' Anna shook the Colonel off her, and moved back to her father but he held up his hand. 'Please. I'll be back soon. I promise.'

'No. Don't leave me here! You can't!'

Her father said nothing. He hung his head. Tears cascaded down Anna's face. She continued to protest but it made no difference. Kankava edged past her and gently shut the door.

Thus bringing to a close the life of Anna Abayev, the girl.

Chapter 9

Some three months passed at the mansion known as Winter's Retreat. Anna had celebrated her fourteenth birthday with Kankava, two other young maids in their early twenties, and a small birthday cake with a single candle that Anna made. She'd not once heard from her father. Kankava said he hadn't either. In fact, he didn't even know which country her father had since travelled to.

Three months. To Anna it felt like a lifetime. She'd already begun to wonder whether she would ever see him again.

Kankava allowed Anna to go to a local school three days a week. The other four days and every evening, she provided assistance in Winter's Retreat; cleaning, cooking and tending to the veterans. That was the worst part. The men's ages ranged from early twenties to well into their sixties. Some were amputees, some suffered various forms of paralysis, others were mere vegetables who barely resembled living and breathing beings.

Most of the men looked upon Anna with a sickly glint in their eyes, as they did upon the other maids: Viktoria and Maria. Anna would cringe and hold her nose, somehow keeping back the tears as she wiped the men's arses, changed their catheters, bathed them.

Anna hated every minute of it, but she also hated herself for feeling so disgusted by her role. These men needed help. They were war heroes. They had fought for Georgia and for the lives of others. Yet she felt revulsion at having to assist them in a time of need. Shame on her.

Kankava had reminded Anna of the same on more than one occasion. Reminded her that it was her father's wish that she perform these duties. And she didn't want to disappoint her father, did she?

It wasn't all bad, though. There was one patient whose company she had warmed to. Alex. In many ways, he reminded Anna of her father. He was in his early forties. He had a hard face, battle worn and scarred, but his eyes and his manner were kind. To Anna he looked like a movie star from a Hollywood action film: all brute and brawn.

Alex was paralysed from the neck down. His mind, on the other hand, was fully cognisant and he was truly engaging. And he was one of few men at Winter's Retreat who didn't look upon Anna like *that*.

'It was your birthday?' Alex asked after swallowing a mouthful of food.

Anna was sitting next to his bed, a plate of boiled potatoes, carrots, and stewed beef on her lap.

'Yes,' Anna said.

'How old?

Anna looked down at the food, feeling embarrassed. 'Fourteen.'

'I thought you were older.'

'I guess I look older.'

'Not a good thing for a fourteen-year-old girl.'

'I'm not a girl anymore.'

'Yes you are. And don't let anyone in here tell you otherwise.'

Anna gave Alex another mouthful. He chewed the meat as he stared into space.

'You like it here?'

'Yes,' she lied.

Alex laughed. 'You don't have to pretend with me.'

'I like to help.'

'You like the idea of helping.'

'That's not how it is,' Anna retorted.

Alex smiled. 'That's fine. We do need you here. I just find it strange that a girl of your age is not out in the world having fun.'

'I've never been like other girls.'

'I'm sure. Your father is Vlad Abayev?'

'Yes,' Anna said, surprised. 'You know my father?'

'I know who he is, yes. I'm surprised he let you come to this place.'

'What's that supposed to mean?' Anna responded. Usually Alex was kind and accommodating but she got the feeling he was trying to test her.

'Nothing. Forget it.'

She glanced at the tattoos on Alex's arms and neck, as she often did. She knew from bathing him that he had many more on his torso and back. Prison tattoos, she assumed – there to tell his life story, brag about the crimes he had committed, show his ranking amongst his peers. Though precisely what they indicated she had no idea.

Even though Alex wasn't that old, the tattoos had become misshapen and crinkled as a result of the vast amount of bodyweight, muscle in particular, that he'd lost. She imagined what he must have looked like in his prime when he was full of life and bulked up. Alex the warrior, rather than Alex the bed-ridden cripple. She would liked to have seen that.

'You like the tattoos?' Alex said, catching her eye.

'I don't know.' Anna shrugged. 'Some are nice. But they must have hurt.'

'Not as much as earning them.' Alex paused. 'Can I ask you a question?'

Anna hesitated, feeding Alex another lump of meat. 'Yes.'

'Do you like the Mkhedrioni?'

Anna shrugged again.

'That's what most of the men here were,' Alex said.

'I never thought about it much.'

'That's a lie. You tend to us every day. You must have thought about who we are and what brought us here.'

'It's not a lie. I'm helping because you need it and because I don't have anywhere else to go.'

'You could run away if you don't like it here.'

'There's nowhere for me to run to. And why would I run when I have a safe place to live, and money.'

'You're a bright girl, Anna. I see it in you. You've got character. You're different to the others.'

'Thanks. I think. But I meant what I said. I don't know much about the Mkhedrioni. I was only nine when we won independence. I'd not heard of the Mkhedrioni before then.'

'No, but you heard of us since?'

'Of course. You were everywhere. Every other street in Tiblisi had roadblocks manned by Mkhedrioni. All the boys at school wanted to be just like them. Like you.'

Alex smiled as though fondly reminiscing those deadly days. For a time, the Mkhedrioni had ruled the streets of Georgia – the government too. But in essence they weren't far removed from the criminal underworld – the Georgian mafia. In fact, many of its highest-ranking members were exactly that.

'I thought it was terrifying,' Anna added. 'You couldn't go anywhere without having a gun pointed at you.'

'We were keeping you safe,' Alex said. 'We fought for you and for every other Georgian.'

'Before the Mkhedrioni, were you a soldier?' Anna asked. 'In the army?'

'No. Some here were. Not me. I'm a Vor. But we fought together. Put our differences aside to fight for this country.'

That explained the tattoos. Anna felt herself blush at her naive question, hoping she hadn't offended Alex. She knew well of the Vory – a subculture adopted through Georgia's long established links to Russia. Many of the Mkhedrioni's leaders were Vors. Thieves in law. Men who gave their lives to the criminal code. Not soldiers at all. In fact it was part of the criminal code that a Vor could never be seen to bow down to officialdom of any sort. To serve in the army would have been treachery.

But not all the Mkhedrioni were Vors. Many were ex-Soviet soldiers – like Kankava. Many others were simply bored young men who liked the idea of holding a gun, and had watched too many gangster movies.

The Vors, on the other hand, were men of power and corruption and violence. Men to be feared.

But Alex wasn't fearsome to Anna. Not anymore.

'Are you scared of me?' Alex asked, looking pleased with himself for the revelation of his past life.

'There's nothing to be scared of.'

'No. That's right.' Alex nodded as though impressed with the answer. 'And you should always believe that. People can try to frighten you, they can tell you things and do things to you against your will, but it's your choice whether or not to be *scared.* And if you can't help but be scared, don't show it. Never show your weaknesses.'

Alex stopped talking and looked at Anna intently. She wondered whether he was expecting her to speak.

'I see something in you, Anna,' he said eventually. 'I see strength.'

'Thank you.'

'Do you know how I came to be in here?'

'No.'

'I was a good fighter. Good with guns, good with knives. I was perfect for the Mkhedrioni. But you know what my downfall was?'

'What?'

'I was a show-off. You know the type of man. The top dog. I had to be best at everything. I had to prove myself to my men constantly. Ten of us were swimming in the Black Sea. We took turns finding higher and higher cliffs to jump from. I went higher than any of the others dared. But... look at me now.'

Alex trailed off, his usual upbeat manner dissipating.

'We all make mistakes,' he said more solemnly after a few moments of silence. 'You're fourteen. You've got your whole life ahead of you. But it only takes one mistake to change your life forever.'

Alex became distracted. He stared past Anna. She turned and saw Kankava standing in the doorway. Kankava studied Anna for a few seconds and she began to feel uncomfortable.

'Anna, when you're finished, I need your help,' Kankava said.

'It's okay.' She got to her feet. 'I can come now.'

Kankava turned and walked out. Anna was moving toward the doorway when Alex spoke. His words sent a chill through her.

'Remember what I said, Anna. Don't ever show them you're scared.'

Chapter 10

Anna followed Kankava down the corridor towards his living quarters. Anna, Maria, and Viktoria shared a single bedroom on the mansion's top floor, but Kankava had his own private space on the ground floor that included a bedroom, bathroom, lounge, and dining room. His quarters were strictly off limits and Anna had only previously been in there one time when Kankava had sent her in to fetch a jacket for him. As she kept pace behind him, she felt increasingly uneasy at the prospect of leaving the relative safety of the communal areas.

Kankava unlocked the door that led into his space and stood aside to wave Anna through. He shut the door behind her. Anna flicked her gaze across the lounge. Numerous pictures of battle scenes hung on the walls, together with a gigantic centrepiece above an ornate fireplace that showed a gallant St George – a truly nationalist symbol – defeating a gruesome-looking dragon. Below the picture were two ornamental swords, criss-crossed over each other.

'You shouldn't listen to everything that Alex tells you,' Kankava said. 'The Vory are not men to be trusted. Their whole lives are about lying and thieving.'

Anna frowned. 'But he was a Mkhedrioni. Like you.'

'I'm nothing like him,' Kankava said with disdain. 'The only thing we have in common is that we both fought for Georgia. But we fought in very different ways.'

'But you're helping him. By having him here.'

'Wanting to help someone is different than wanting to like or respect them.'

Anna said nothing but in many ways she realised she agreed with the Colonel's words.

'Please, this way. I need your assistance.'

Kankava walked past Anna and into the adjoining bathroom. Anna followed, silently impressed with the exquisite porcelain fittings that looked like they may have been original to the house. But when she looked over to Kankava, she was suddenly filled with dread.

'My arthritis is getting too bad,' Kankava explained, holding up his one useful hand. It had an awkward tremor she'd not noticed before. Whether or not the tremor was genuine she wasn't sure. 'Maria and Viktoria usually have to do this for me but they were too busy. Please, could you help?'

Kankava looked down at the toilet and Anna tried her best not to show any reaction. *Don't ever show them you're scared.* Words Alex had said to her moments earlier and which were similar to what her father had drummed into her for many years.

'Of course,' Anna said, moving forward and reaching out with one hand.

She took hold of the zip on Kankava's trousers with the tip of two fingers, trying to make as little contact as possible. She clumsily pulled the zip down then shut her eyes as she reached inside, holding back the urge to retch when the stale smell from Kankava's groin filled her nose. She fumbled for a few seconds before managing to pull out his flaccid penis which she held above the toilet bowl.

Kankava urinated, and Anna cringed and looked away. But when she did so she caught sight of Kankava in the mirror above the sink. He was giving her a lurid smile. She whipped her eyes away.

'You have very delicate hands,' he said. 'I could get used to this.'

Anna said nothing.

'Do I disgust you?'

Anna again held her tongue, even though the truth was yes, he really did. Kankava stopped pissing and Anna went to push him back into his trousers but he threw her hand away.

'Do I disgust you?' he repeated, his tone more brash this time.

'No.'

'Liar!'

Kankava swiped at Anna with the back of his hand, catching the side of her mouth. Her bottom lip split and throbbed. She held her hand up to her face as Kankava angrily zipped himself up.

'I'm the same as all the other men in here,' Kankava blasted. 'You help them each and every day. But you never look at them with the same contempt with which you look at me.'

Anna turned and moved to the sink and washed her hands in scolding hot water, trying to remove the remnants of Kankava from her skin. His words filled her head. He was right, she did think of him differently. She'd never liked him – a natural instinct. Perhaps that was unfair. Most likely, she mused, it wasn't. He was sinister and creepy.

'I'm sorry,' she said. 'I didn't realise you needed my help. I guess I thought you were more able.'

Kankava smiled, calmed. 'I try to be, dear Anna. Nobody likes their independence to be taken away from them. But I'm not getting any younger. I've often wondered how long it will be before I'm just another patient here rather than the man in charge.'

Anna finished washing her hands then dried them on a small towel by the side of the sink. 'Is that all?' she asked, wanting more than anything to get the hell out of there.

'Yes. For now. But I'd like you to come back and help me again tonight,' Kankava said. 'Before I go to bed. Maria and Viktoria can't always be expected to do everything for me. And you're not a little girl anymore.'

'Of course,' Anna said, though she felt sick at the thought.

'Good. When you've finished your rounds at nine, you come straight here.'

'I will.'

'I look forward to it,' Kankava purred. 'Go back now. Don't let me keep you from your work.'

Anna spun round, and walked as quickly as she could out of there, a mixture of anger, embarrassment and fear gripping her.

Don't ever show them you're scared.

She would try her damnedest. She always had. But if Kankava was thinking what she thought he was thinking, then she wasn't sure how long she'd be able to hold out.

Chapter 11

It was nearly eleven p.m. when Anna crept back to her bedroom that night. The pain she felt in her groin was nothing compared to the anger in her mind. She was furious at her own naivety. She'd been staying in the house for three months. How could she not have seen the signs earlier? She shared a bedroom with Maria and Viktoria every night yet she'd never deduced what happened when the others were sent to help Kankava. She'd never questioned the unlikely stories of how they'd come to have the bruises and marks on their skin. It had seemed plausible that perhaps they had fallen or one of the patients had lashed out at them. After all, some of the more able-bodied men were known for their violent outbursts.

Or maybe she had known all along but had simply been in denial.

Regardless, Anna was also furious at Maria and Viktoria. How could they not have warned her? She was only fourteen. Why had they not tried to protect her?

Anna was glad to see the lights were off as she opened the bedroom door. At least that way Maria and Viktoria, if they were even awake, wouldn't see the tears which covered Anna's face. But no sooner had she closed the door than

Maria's bedside light came on. Anna saw that both women were awake.

'Are you okay?' Maria asked, sitting up. She looked genuinely concerned but Anna felt only anger.

'How could you let that happen to me!' Anna screamed before beginning to sob. 'Why didn't you warn me?'

Maria jumped from the bed and rushed over to put an arm round Anna. But comfort was the last thing Anna wanted from these two.

'Don't touch me!' she boomed, her face contorting with rage as she shoved Maria hard in the chest.

Maria stumbled backwards and fell to the floor, a dumbstruck look on her face. She turned to Viktoria as if questioning what to say or do. Viktoria got to her feet and went to help Maria.

'We didn't know,' Viktoria said. 'We didn't know he would do that to you. We would have told you. We really would.'

Viktoria's heartfelt tone did little to calm Anna. She was raging. Yet these two, Anna realised, were likely as much victims as she was. Perhaps they had thought they were doing the right thing in not telling the truth sooner. Protecting Anna from the evils of life like a parent would.

But they should have known, Anna firmly believed. They should have known what Kankava would do to her, even if they couldn't bring themselves to admit it.

'What happened?' Viktoria asked, a look of disgust on her face.

'I'm not going to talk to you about it,' Anna spat. 'I don't ever want to think about it.'

'It's okay,' Viktoria said. 'We're here for each other. We have to stick together.'

'Stick together?' Anna said. 'What are you talking about? You two waltz around here *allowing* this to happen. What the hell is wrong with you?'

'There's no other way,' Maria said, bowing her head.

'There's always another way,' Anna countered.

'Please, Anna,' Viktoria said. 'You're angry. And you have every right to be. But don't go getting silly thoughts. I know what you're thinking. Kankava is one man, right? Just one old man. But it's not like that. Not here.'

Anna wasn't sure how to take those words. If anything they only made her position even more disturbing.

'How can you stand to be here?' Anna said.

'They'd kill us if we tried to leave,' Maria said.

'Who?'

'Who do you think?' Maria said.

'Anna, we don't know why your father brought you here,' Viktoria said. 'Perhaps he really didn't know. But this place, what happens here, it isn't just Kankava.'

'The Mkhedrioni?' Anna said.

'Where do you think the money comes from to run this place?'

'But they don't even exist anymore.'

'Of course they do. Making something illegal doesn't make it go away. The Mkhedrioni still exist. And this place... it's theirs. We're theirs.'

'We'll try to protect you,' Maria said. 'We'll try everything we can. You're young. Too young for this. But please, don't try to run. And don't try to fight it. It never works out well if you do.'

'Listen to her,' Viktoria said. 'If you want any kind of life, you have to listen.'

'You're weak,' Anna said. 'Both of you. I can never be like you.'

Viktoria shook her head. 'Maybe we are. But we're alive and we're safe. You can hate us if you want. We won't think any less of you. But whatever you choose to do, don't ever say we didn't warn you.'

Anna said nothing more to the two women as she moved over to her bed, pulled back the covers, and climbed in fully dressed. She'd never seen Maria and Viktoria as friends. They were colleagues, acquaintances. They were ten years older than her, such a big difference to a teenage girl. She'd trusted them, respected them, but she'd never opened up to them about who she was. And she resolved at that point she never would.

She *wasn't* like them. She couldn't stand for what Kankava and the Mkhedrioni were doing. She just couldn't. Yet the more she thought about her position, the more her will seemed to break down.

Anna wondered whether maybe Maria and Viktoria had once been like her. In ten years' time would Anna be the one to break the sordid news to the next young thing that walked through those doors? She shivered at the thought. She couldn't allow that to happen. She would do anything to stop herself becoming like them.

Anna barely slept that night, only drifting off in the small hours. When the alarm went off at seven a.m., she was finally in a deep sleep and awoke a groggy, confused mess.

After forcing herself out of bed she began her daily chores, first helping to cook breakfast before moving around the veterans – feeding those who needed feeding and cleaning up after those who could manage by themselves.

When she came to Alex, she felt a strange unease as soon as he laid eyes on her. What did he know? She meekly sat in the chair next to his bed. He studied her.

'You look... different,' he eventually said.

'Just tired,' Anna said, thrusting a spoon of scrambled egg toward Alex's mouth.

He took it and swallowed quickly. 'You often cut your lip sleeping?'

She felt at the small scab on the bottom of her lip. 'Accident.'

'Yeah,' Alex said. 'I'm not going to ask you about it. Don't worry. But remember, it's only my body that doesn't work. My head, my brain, is as good as ever.'

Anna felt she knew what Alex meant by that. A Mkhedrioni himself, maybe he had always known about what Kankava was and what happened to the girls at Winter's Retreat. And it wasn't like he was in much of a position to stop it.

She remembered the conversation she'd had with Alex the night before.

'You said you knew of my father. That you didn't know why he would send me to this place. What did you mean by that?'

Alex sighed. 'I know of him, yes. Not your father as you know him, though. But his reputation.'

Anna frowned. 'Why do *you* think he'd send me here.'

'People can be very complex. I don't know him so I can't answer that. I'm sure he had your best interests at heart.'

Anna scoffed. As much as she loved her father, she couldn't comprehend how her being at Winter's Retreat was in any way good for her.

'I heard a lot of stories about your father,' Alex said. 'Much of it was probably fable but there must have been some truth there too. There's truth in all legends, one way or another.'

'You think my father is a legend?'

'To some yes.'

'I haven't heard from him for months. Do you think–?'

'He's still alive. You'd have heard if he wasn't. No news is good news.'

Alex took a break from talking as he wolfed down several mouthfuls of food.

'Anna, do you know who your father is?' he asked after finishing the last of his eggs. '*What* your father is?'

'Yes,' was her immediate response but realised it wasn't true. 'No, actually. I know him as my father, but... I don't know.'

'Will you let me tell you a little about him then? Perhaps that will give you some of the answers you need, as to who you are and why he brought you here.'

Anna shifted in her seat, intrigued but also uneasy about what Alex had to say. Did she want to know? Would it change the way she felt about the man who had single-handedly brought her up? Perhaps it was best to leave him on the pedestal that he'd always been on, to close her mind off to who her father really was.

But he'd sent her to this place. Perhaps if she knew more about him, she'd know why he'd do something like that.

'Tell me,' Anna said, before she could talk herself out of it. 'I want to know.'

'Okay, I'll tell you,' Alex said. 'Your father, Anna, is an assassin. He kills people. For money. But he's not just any assassin. He's probably the best, the most infamous, this country has ever seen.'

Chapter 12

Anna spent the day mulling over Alex's revelation. She wanted to know more about her father, but the conversation with Alex had been cut short when Maria showed up to help move Alex to change the bedclothes.

Anna finally got her chance to speak to Alex alone again later that day. 'Do you know where my father is?'

She reached down and pushed the sponge into the soapy water then gently rubbed it along Alex's legs. Even though she knew he could feel nothing as she bathed him, she got the impression that he found the process soothing nonetheless. Perhaps it was the memories of bathing, from back when he was able-bodied. Memories that were hard-wired in his brain, that still triggered relaxation, even though he could no longer feel the warm water against his skin. It wasn't too dissimilar to what she saw in some of the amputees who believed they could sometimes sense the presence of their lost limbs.

'No,' Alex said. 'I don't know where your father is. How could I? I don't get out much these days.'

Anna smiled. 'But you said you knew of him. Perhaps you could help me find him?'

'I only really knew of him by reputation.'

'You said that before. So tell me what you know.'

Alex sighed before he spoke. 'What I'm about to tell you... no one else in this place knows. And I wouldn't dare tell them. Vlad Abayev might be a father to you, but that's not who he really is. The name people know him by is a name to be feared. Like an infamous warrior from times gone by. People would talk about him, share stories about what they'd seen and heard. Some would only whisper his name for fear of being struck down. That was the power of his legend. Others, of course, believed he was a myth.'

'But not you?'

'No, not me. I *saw* what he could do.'

'You said you only knew him by reputation?'

'I never spoke to him. In fact, that night, I never even saw his face. All I saw was his shadow. Everyone knows of him, but few people have seen his face and survived to tell the tale.'

'But he came here. He walked me right up to the front door. He was standing there in plain sight.'

'I know. But did anyone else see your father that day?'

'Kankava did.'

'Kankava knows your father. Apparently. I don't know the story.'

'No,' Anna said. 'And neither do I.'

'But even if someone else had seen your father out here, they wouldn't have realised who he really was. His legend is well known. His real identity, what he looks like, isn't.'

'I'm confused. How do you know him if you've never seen his face? How do you know my father is this legendary assassin?'

'I just know,' was all Alex said, not looking Anna in the eye.

She couldn't quite read his mood. He seemed so hesitant about the story he was telling. Was he playing her, overdramatising the story? Or was he genuinely rattled by the prospect of revealing what he knew?

'And you haven't talked to anyone else here about this?' Anna asked.

'No. This must all sound strange to you. He's your father, and you love him. But he's a very dangerous man.'

Anna squeezed the water out of the sponge and laid it down on the side of the white porcelain bath. Like Kankava's private quarters, the fixtures in the main bathroom were old and ornate. But here they were also worn, the porcelain lined, the cracks looking like a snaking network of blue veins. And the decor was cold. White tiled floors, white-painted walls. There was nothing homely about the room. 'You said you saw what he could do?'

'Yes.' Alex stared into space.

Anna's father had always been so loving to her, so doting, but she'd long sensed there was another, darker, side to him. It wasn't lost on Anna that most fourteen-year-old girls would be shocked to find out their father was a hired killer. But not Anna. The more she heard from Alex, the more intrigued she was about who her father really was. What he was.

And what *she* was.

'And?' Anna asked.

'I saw him murder two of my comrades. In cold blood. Just like that. One second they were standing there, a few yards in front of me, and the next they were dead.'

'How?'

'There were four of us. We were manning the two entrances to a building where the Mkhedrioni were meeting. Nobody heard him coming. Nobody suspected a thing. I barely blinked, and all of a sudden this... shadow.'

Anna said nothing, didn't move, as she waited for Alex to carry on. She now firmly believed that telling the story had shaken him.

'The other guard and I ran over to help our friends,' Alex eventually continued. 'They were dead before anyone knew what was happening – their throats sliced, stab wounds to their kidneys, their hearts. Multiple blows that had taken just a second or two to inflict. I'd seen violence before, people being killed, I'm a Vor, but that? It was something else. It was so surreal, like a dream.'

'Why did he kill them?'

'To get to his target. Your father slipped past us into the building while we were still trying to figure out what was happening. He took out the target before anyone had even raised the alarm. And then he vanished into the night.'

'Who was the target?'

'It's not important,' Alex said, though Anna knew there was more to the story than Alex was letting on. There was silence for a few seconds before Alex spoke again. 'Your father was once a spy. Did you know that?'

'No. I didn't.'

'For the Russians. He travelled across Eastern Europe, infiltrating rebel groups, passing information back to Moscow.'

'My father hated the regime.'

'Not always. He wasn't an idealist. He didn't care for politics. He just cared about protecting his own interests. And money. That's not a bad thing. Deep down, it's what drives most of us; self-preservation.'

'So what happened?'

'I don't know the details of why, but someone in Moscow betrayed him. Your father found out and–'

'He killed them?'

'Yes. But not just one man, an entire family. The man's wife, his brothers, sisters – six people in total. He made a statement. After that he went into the shadows, loyal to no one but himself. And his family.'

Anna didn't outwardly react to Alex's words. Was she shocked to hear of what her father had done? A little. But she also felt a longing for him, and a burning sense of pride that her father had always done what was necessary to protect his own family.

Right up to the point where he'd sent his young daughter to Winter's Retreat, that is.

'Do you know what people call him?' Alex said.

'No.'

'After that day, when he'd butchered that family, that's when the legend started. The Silent Blade. That's what people called him. And it wasn't hard to see why.'

Anna opened her mouth then closed it quickly before any words escaped.

Alex raised an eyebrow. 'You've heard that name?'

'I heard people talk about it yes. But I never–'

'Believed that Silent Blade was your father?'

'No. Not that. I never believed Silent Blade was real.'

'He is, Anna. He's very real. Maybe not everything you heard really happened, but, like I said, most legends have truth to them.'

'I need to find him. I can't stay here.'

'He'll only be found if he wants to be found. You should stay here, where you're safe.'

'Safe?' Anna said, her tone harsh.

Alex stared at her for a few seconds, and Anna knew he was still holding onto something.

'You're young, Anna. It's a big and nasty world out there. Your father put you in here for a reason. And knowing the man he is, my advice to you is to stay here until you know that reason.'

Anna said nothing for a good while, hoping Alex had more to offer. She reached forward, took out the bath plug and listened as the water gurgled out, then set about getting the rusted pulley ready to hoist Alex out of the bath.

'I have to find him,' she said.

Alex let out a long sigh. 'I really don't think you should do that. *But,* if you do decide to, I know a man who might be able to help.'

'Who?'

'A Vor. Like me. Your father worked for him one time.'

'One time?'

'Let's just say that job didn't go quite to plan for either party.'

Anna gave Alex a questioning look but didn't push for more. It wasn't important and she didn't think Alex would tell her what he knew even if she asked. 'What's his name?'

'Come closer.'

Anna leaned toward Alex and he whispered the name into her ear.

She moved back again. 'They were friends?'

'No, Anna. Your father had no friends. Not then. Not now. And if you decide to go out into that dark world to look for him, remember this: Don't. Trust. Anyone.'

Chapter 13

Present day

Ryker's journey across the Atlantic and onwards to Southern Spain was gruelling, taking well over twenty-four hours. Having rested in a simple hotel on the outskirts of the Andalusian city of Malaga, Ryker headed to a car rental shop early the next morning and took the second cheapest option he could find – a two-door Ford that he just about managed to squeeze into.

At nine a.m. the temperature was already stifling, with the midsummer sun blazing in the blue sky above. Ryker was dressed in a light cotton shirt but his jeans felt heavy and cumbersome even in the morning heat, and he put the air-conditioning in the car as cold as it would go.

It was a Thursday morning, rush hour, though once out of the city, the newly constructed and remarkably smooth motorway was nearly empty as Ryker travelled the short distance west to the house where Kim Walker had been murdered.

To his left was the cool blue of the Mediterranean. The coastline was dotted with several enclaves crammed with high-rise concrete apartment blocks and hotels that seemed to cling to the water's edge. They had first sprung from the ground in the seventies when British tourists began descending on the Costa in their droves, and the many half-built shells Ryker could see suggested construction was still ongoing. It was a stark contrast to the historic city of Malaga that he'd flown into, and to the white-washed villages that were visible here and there up in the mountains to his right.

As Ryker turned off the main carriageway, he realised it was to the latter that he was headed. He dropped the gearbox of the underpowered car down to third, then second, and eventually first in order to make it up the ever-increasing incline of the Sierra de Mijas mountain range that rose prominently above the glistening coast behind him.

White painted villas and small complexes were scattered along the twisting road. The further Ryker went, the more lavish the properties became.

Soon there was little view of the houses – manicured front hedges and high walls secluded the expensive properties from the road.

Ryker eventually came to a stop outside the house he was looking for; Casa de las Rosas. A set of green metal gates, ten feet high, sat at the entrance to the property. Either side of the gates lay a six-foot white wall with terracotta tiles on top. A swathe of rose bushes in full bloom burst out over the top of the wall; whites, pinks, reds.

Ryker looked at the entrance. An intercom system was fitted onto the left-hand wall. But the left gate was already wide open. Ryker only hesitated for a second before driving through.

As the car crunched slowly along the gravelled drive, a panel van came by in the opposite direction, likely explaining the open gate. Ryker managed to pick out only one of the Spanish words on the side of the van; mueble. Furniture. A removal van? Ryker wondered. Or delivery?

Ryker kept going and parked his car in a grand turning circle that came complete with a fifteen-foot high water feature in its centre. He had no idea how much property cost in this part of the Costa del Sol but it didn't take a genius to figure that an extravagant property like this was worth millions.

Winter had only relayed the basics but Ryker knew Walker had made his money from property – buying, selling, renting, renovating. The property market on the Costa del Sol had boomed for years as more and more British and other Europeans bought second homes there. Many developers had made millions before the market had crashed dramatically following the mass global recession of the late 2000s. It appeared Walker had managed to keep hold of a lot of his money one way or another.

Kim Walker – whoever she really was – had married the rich Brit and gained everything she could ever need. Money-wise at least.

But just who was she? And why were her fingerprints on a file linking her to the Red Cobra – one of the most proficient assassins Ryker had ever come across?

Ryker stepped from the car and approached the house's large oak double-doors. He rang the bell then knocked loudly and waited.

A few seconds later, the left door inched open and Ryker looked down at an olive-skinned lady – fifties with a wrinkled face, wearing plain blue linen trousers and a blouse.

'*Si*,' the lady said, looking suspiciously first at Ryker, then past him to his car.

'*Habla Inglés?*' Ryker asked.

'Yes, of course,' the lady said in a heavy accent. 'How did you get in here?'

'The gate was open,' Ryker said, looking over his shoulder, back down the driveway. 'Because of the van. New furniture?'

'What? Yes. Some of it. What do you want?'

'I'm here to see Patrick Walker.'

'He's not here.'

'Will he be long?'

'I don't know.'

'Can I come in to wait?'

'Who are you?'

'I'm James Ryker. From London. I'm here about–'

The lady put her hand up to stop Ryker and he did.

'Please, I don't like to talk about that. I've already said what I know more than enough times.'

'Okay. But I do need to speak to Mr Walker.'

'He's up in the village. It's a ten-minute drive. He had a meeting. At Casa Colon I think. It's a restaurant there. One of his.'

'Thank you,' Ryker said, a split second before the front door was slammed shut in his face.

The maid wasn't far wrong. Nine minutes later, Ryker was driving into Mijas, a quaint white-washed village high up in the Sierra with spectacular views down to the coast. After driving along cobbled streets he parked his car and made it on foot towards a small square in the town where the map on his phone – a pay-as-you-go he'd bought for cash at the airport – had shown him Casa Colon was located.

The village was awash with colourful bunting and as Ryker neared the square the throngs of people – tourists and locals alike – grew exponentially, as did the sound of lively music and rhythmic clapping. The picturesque square was lined with various small restaurants, cafes and shops. Along the buildings on each side were hanging baskets overspilling with a variety of colourful flowers. Ryker squeezed his way through bodies, and soon spotted the reason for the large gathering; a banner hanging across the street proudly announced it was the village's annual fair.

He saw too where the noise was coming from. In the centre of the square stood a small wooden stage where two young women in traditional Flamenco dresses – black and red – were dancing to guitar music being blasted from portable speakers. The synchronised tapping of their feet on the wooden platform echoed around the enclosed space, and the crowds of people let out a series of well-timed *Olés* as the dance progressed.

Ryker stopped and stared through the crowd, who were enthralled by the music and the sightly dancers. The elegance of their poise, the intensity in their expressions. The way their skirts lifted each time they spun or kicked – high enough to reveal several inches of flesh above the knee, but not so high as to cause offence at a family viewing.

Both dancers were attractive, with dresses cut-low to reveal their cleavages and fitted tight to highlight their curves. They both had dark hair, held in tight buns that pulled their hairlines back and opened up their unblemished faces. Ryker could well understand why the crowd was so engrossed in the performance.

But after a few seconds, Ryker was distracted. Off to his left, he spotted the pavement terrace of Casa Colon. Along one side a passageway ran between the buildings to a lookout point that gave a glimpse of the sea beyond.

Another dancer – taking a break perhaps – was there. Dressed similarly to the other two, but she was... different.

She was with a man. They were too far away for Ryker to hear a word of the conversation but it was clearly heated. Both were gesticulating, glaring at the other, their mouths moving wildly as they spoke. She went to walk away but the man grabbed her by the wrist. She spun round and slapped him hard in the face before storming along the passageway back to the square, where she moved through the crowd toward the stage.

Ryker's gaze fixed back on the man. At first he looked shocked, holding a hand to his cheek where the woman had belted him. His look quickly turned to anger and he glowered at her walking away from him.

The man was smartly dressed in a pair of khaki trousers, shiny brown loafers, and a white cotton shirt that had several buttons undone. He had neat black hair and designer aviator sunglasses that obscured much of his face.

But even with the sunglasses on, Ryker had no doubt who the man was. He'd seen his picture in the papers Winter had given him.

He was exactly the man Ryker was looking for: Patrick Walker.

Chapter 14

Ryker stared on at Walker; hands now on his hips, the anger on his face unmistakeable. His left cheek was burning red from the slap. After a few moments, Walker walked forward, through the passageway to the edge of the crowd. He stopped. Ryker turned his attention back to the stage where Walker's steely glare was now fixed.

The music had stopped and the woman Walker had been talking to joined the other two dancers just as the next song began. She was similar in age and size to the other two, her dress was cut the same, her hair styled the same. Yet she stood out. Her lipstick was darker – not far off black and a stark contrast to the bright red of the others. She had a black rose tied into her hair, where the other two had red. She was definitely attractive. Not the most beautiful woman Ryker had ever seen, but there was something about her. She was mesmerising.

As the dance began, Ryker couldn't take his eyes off the black-flowered woman. The way she moved, her body gliding, hips swaying, it was almost hypnotic. She was doing the exact same dance as the other two yet her performance was so much more powerful, dramatic. Angry.

For the next five minutes, Ryker didn't once look away. He wondered whether her striking performance was part of the show, the story of the dance. Good versus evil. Whoever this woman was, she certainly had a dark side.

And Ryker was drawn to it.

When the music stopped, the crowd erupted in rapturous applause. The two red-flowered dancers looked at each other and smiled, then began thanking the crowd profusely. The black-flowered woman turned and stormed off the stage. She grabbed a small holdall and edged her way through the crowd who clapped and cheered her as she passed – the undoubted star of the show.

She headed for a narrow street at the far end of the square that led upward to where the town's small bullring was visible. Ryker looked over and spotted Walker. He was barging through the audience, heading after her.

A second later, Ryker was doing the same.

Ryker was twenty yards behind Walker by the time he'd squeezed his way through the crowd. He picked up his pace, passed the bullring then walked around the edge of an ancient brick church whose bell tower looked as though it was actually part of an old Moorish castle. The church sat prominently at the top of a rocky outcrop and was surrounded by trees, fountains, and flowered gardens.

Walker caught up with the woman, who was stomping away as best she could in her high-heeled shoes. Walker grabbed her by one wrist, swung her round and grabbed the other too. He shouted at her. She shouted back, no fear in her face or voice. Only anger.

Ryker bounded up to them. His movement caught the woman's attention, which in turn distracted Walker, who let go of one of her wrists and began to turn round. Ryker didn't give him a chance to say or do a thing. He grabbed hold of Walker's arm and twisted it into a hammerlock. Walker squirmed and cried out.

'Let her go,' Ryker said.

Walker turned his head. His face was creased with rage. Ryker, on the other hand, was calm. Walker began to spin, trying to move out of the hold. He balled his fist, swinging it around.

Ryker saw it coming.

He let go of Walker's arm, caught the flying fist mid-air and sent a head-butt onto the crown of Walker's nose. Ryker didn't put his all into it. Just enough to set the scene. Send a message.

Walker fell to his knees and clutched at his nose which poured with thick red blood. 'What the hell!' he screamed. 'My nose! You've broken my nose!'

'It's not broken,' Ryker said. 'I barely touched you.'

Ryker looked up. The woman was stood in front of him, staring. He gazed into her dark eyes. She looked away, down at Walker, then back up at Ryker. She flicked a devilish smile then picked up her bag, turned, and walked away.

Ryker watched, unable to take his eyes off her swaying hips. At least not until Walker brought him back down.

'Who the fuck *are* you?' Walker said.

'You know what?' Ryker said. 'I'm still trying to find the answer to that.'

Chapter 15

An hour later, Ryker was sitting on an opulent cream leather sofa in Patrick Walker's lounge. The housemaid, Valeria, had made them a large pot of filter coffee, which was sitting, half-empty, on the glass coffee table that separated the two men. Walker's nose had stopped bleeding, though a layer of dried blood was visible on the edges of his nostrils. His manner toward his guest was nothing but hostile.

Not surprising really, given their introduction to each other. Walker had only invited Ryker to his home after the intervention of Detective Green, the police officer from London who'd been sent to Spain to help figure out who Kim Walker really was, and who had killed her. Walker had called Green at Ryker's insistence – it was the only way Ryker could see to stop the situation in the village escalating out of control. Green was now on his way to Walker's. There were no pleasantries between Ryker and the host as they waited.

'What did you say your name was again?' Walker said, eying up Ryker not just with suspicion but with outright disdain. Walker had a Southern English accent. Not Queen's English but certainly he seemed to come from money, or at least had had an expensive education, Ryker decided.

'James Ryker.'

'But you're not with the police.'

'I'm not a policeman. I'm working with them.'

'You'd better hope you have some high friends because you can be sure I'm reporting you for this.'

'Go ahead. And that way you can properly explain what you were doing with that woman up in the village.'

Walker humphed but said nothing to that.

'If you're not police, then why are you here?' Walker asked.

'Because I'm good.'

'Good at what? Beating up grieving spouses?'

Ryker paused for a second. He had to expect the continued digs from Walker. Ryker's strong-armed manner was hardly the right way to get on someone's good side. But he wasn't about to apologise for butting Walker in the face. As far as Ryker was concerned it was Walker's fault for having been so heavy-handed with the woman.

'I'm good at finding the truth,' Ryker said.

Walker humphed again, looking uncertain. He took a sip of his milky coffee before setting it down.

'Who was she?' Ryker asked. 'The woman.'

'None of your goddamn business.'

'You don't have to like me, but there really isn't any benefit in you holding back. Like I told you already, I'm here to help catch your wife's murderer.'

'Good. I hope you do. But that doesn't mean you have the right to pry into all of my personal affairs.'

'Affairs?' Ryker said. 'Perhaps you should choose your words more carefully.'

Walker blushed crimson. Ryker knew he was right.

'She's got nothing to do with what happened to Kim.'

'Says you.'

'Okay, if you're going to be a dick about this then you get out of my house. Right now!'

Ryker didn't move. 'I saw a van coming out of here when I arrived earlier. Delivering furniture. Or taking some away. You moving out?'

'Does it look like I am?'

'I'm not sure. That's why I'm asking.'

'No, I'm not moving out. I was just... clearing some of Kim's things.'

Ryker didn't outwardly react to the explanation. He wasn't one to question someone's response to their spouse being murdered. But Kim Walker had been dead less than a week, and clearing out her things so soon seemed odd. It could be nothing.

Walker looked at his watch. It was the fourth time he'd done so since the two men had sat with their coffee. The man was clearly nervous, on edge in Ryker's presence, and they hadn't yet had any sort of meaningful conversation.

A loud buzzing noise came from out in the hallway. Ryker heard the pitter-patter of light feet across the marble floor and then Valeria's soft voice as she answered the intercom. Walker took one more sip of his coffee then got to his feet.

'Looks like he's here. About bloody time too.'

Walker couldn't wait to get out of the room. He shot past Ryker who casually stood and followed Walker to the front door. Walker was already out on the driveway when the blue saloon car pulled to a stop.

The man who stepped out of the car looked to be in his late fifties, possibly early sixties. He had a goatee beard that was almost grey, the salt and pepper effect matching the short, thin hair on his head. He was at least a couple of stones overweight with a round belly that protruded over the rim of his creased trousers. His cheeks were flushed red and his forehead was wet with sweat.

'Detective,' Walker said as he walked up to the man and shook his hand.

Walker turned round and faced Ryker, as did the man.

'This is him?' the man asked.

He moved toward Ryker, stretched out his hand.

'DS Green. Metropolitan Police. I've been expecting you. Though not quite like this.'

Ryker shook Green's hand. 'James Ryker.'

A Detective Sergeant. Not a very senior rank for a man pushing retirement age, Ryker mused. However unfair it might have been, he drew a conclusion from Green's rank and his appearance as to the type of policeman he was. A stalwart. A man who did things his way and no other. An old school detective who hadn't moved with the times and hated to be told what to do by those younger than him. Perhaps he was a decent enough policeman in the field – on his own. But Ryker would bet his boots that Green lacked any kind of leadership qualities and people skills.

'I think we should probably have a bit of a chat, don't you?' Green said.

'Yeah. Why not.' Ryker turned to head back inside.

'Not here. I think Mr Walker has probably had enough of you for one day. Come on, let's go and get something to eat.'

Ryker shrugged. He noticed the smug look on Walker's face but Ryker couldn't care less. He wasn't there to get one over on anyone.

Without another word, they jumped into Green's car and headed back up the hill toward the village.

'Quite an entrance you made,' Green said.

'Self-defence.'

'You're lucky you're not working for me or you'd be on the first plane back home. You realise he could sue you, sue us, for what you did?'

'He could try.'

'And he might well win, regardless of whether you think you were in the right. He's got the clout to do it. Walker is a rich and powerful man around here. And the last thing you want is the local police on your case. They're unhelpful at the best of times.'

'I'll admit it was a mistake,' Ryker said. 'But he didn't give me much of an option. He needs to be more careful who he picks fights with.'

'Perhaps the same could be said of you.'

They reached the village, and Green found a parking space on the side of the road next to a row of cafes and restaurants. The two men got out of the car and headed to the nearest open place. They took a shady table on the pavement terrace, out of the fierce midday sun. The waiter came and Ryker ordered a steak and chips and a bottle of sparkling water. Green nodded in appreciation of Ryker's choice then asked for the same, adding a half bottle of red wine to his order.

'A private investigator, huh?' Green said, referring to the fake identity that Winter had set up for Ryker.

'That's what they say,' Ryker said, wanting to embellish as little as he could. He'd become well used to being undercover over the years he'd worked for the JIA, and had learned it was best to give little away about a fake identity. The less he gave, the less chance for slip-ups.

'You work on your own?' Green asked.

'When I can.'

'Ex-police?'

'No.'

'How'd you get into it then?'

'It's a long story.'

'It's early in the day. I'm sure you could tell it if you wanted.'

'If I wanted to, yeah.'

The waiter brought the drinks over, and both men took a large swig of their waters. Ryker was parched from the heat and Green too seemed to be struggling – his face was even redder and sweatier now than when he'd first stepped out of his car at Walker's house.

'I could never get used to this heat,' Green said, as if picking up on Ryker's train of thought.

'That's why the locals have siestas,' Ryker said. 'No one likes being out in this kind of heat.'

'Except mad dogs and Englishmen.'

Ryker smiled.

'How long have you been investigating?' Green asked.

'Long enough.'

Green shook his head. 'I'm sensing you're a man of few words.'

'I use the ones that are needed.'

'You've investigated murders before?'

'Are you interviewing me for a job here?'

'No, I'm just trying to figure out what kind of a man you are. I mean, here we are in a foreign country where we have no legal jurisdiction, assisting the local police in the murder of a British national, and after five minutes on the case you go and punch the victim's husband in the face.'

'I didn't punch him.'

'What? Punch, head-butt, that's beside the point.'

'Then what's the point?'

'The point is I haven't a clue why they'd send someone like you here.'

'Someone like me?'

'I'm not quite sure yet what you're bringing to the table.'

'What, because you have all the answers?'

'No. I don't. Not yet.'

'So do you or do not know who killed Kim Walker?'

'No, I–'

'That's why I'm here,' Ryker said. 'And that's all you need to know.'

Chapter 16

The food came and Ryker blasted through his steak and chips in less than five minutes. He'd not had a full meal since boarding the first pond-hopping plane almost two days earlier. He wished he'd had some red wine to wash the food down with but he knew that with the combination of the heat, the early hour, and his groggy state, alcohol was the last thing he needed.

Green ate his food at a much more leisurely pace. 'How much do you know so far?' He took a swig of his wine.

'Not a lot. I'd intended to talk to Walker about that, find the lay of the land. But we didn't exactly get off on the right foot.'

'No. You didn't. And if you'd come to me beforehand, like I expected you to, then I'd have warned you against speaking to him anyway. He's given official statements to me and the Spanish police on numerous occasions already. He's grieving. This is a tough time for him – it's only been a few days. We need to keep out of his hair if possible.'

'If possible.'

'He's also got a prominent and rather noisy lawyer. Things will get messy for you very quickly if you're not careful.'

'Why is his lawyer involved?'

'I'm not that bothered what your history is, but think about what you're dealing with here. A man has lost his wife. You need to show some tact.'

'Have you ruled him out?'

Green chewed on a bit of meat before answering. 'Not officially. But I don't think it was him.'

'So what's your theory then?'

'You're asking me? From what I gather it's *theories* being spouted by the boffins back home that have caused *you* to be here.'

'And which theories would those be?'

'That Kim Walker wasn't who she said she was. She was using a bogus identity. And she may have been killed as some sort of revenge attack because of her past.'

Ryker was a little surprised at how much of the true picture Green had figured out. Whether that was through his own work, official channels or simply the inevitable chin-wagging within police forces he couldn't be sure. But he'd be careful not to give Green any tangible details of what he knew about the Red Cobra. Not unless he needed to.

'And does that fit what you know?' Ryker asked.

'It could do. But at the moment we've got a lot of loose ends and no one knows what direction this investigation will go in. Kim Walker was pregnant, did you know that?'

'Yes,' Ryker said with a sickening feeling. Whoever Kim Walker really was, her murder was one of the most gruesome and heart-wrenching he'd ever seen.

'Four months,' Green said, a hint of anger in his voice. 'The forensics team believe the baby died before she did, though how they can be so sure of that, I really don't know. A blunt-force blow to Kim's stomach was the most likely cause of the baby's death.' Green reached down into his briefcase and took some papers which he passed over to Ryker. 'Kim was attacked as she walked into her house. The intruder was already inside, we think.'

'No signs of forced entry.'

'No, none. The husband, the maid, the gardener, the pool cleaner, anyone who knows that house, who had any kind of access, they all have solid alibis.'

'No cameras?'

'CCTV? No. The Walkers had decent enough security but they weren't paranoid. Just good old locks and bolts.'

Ryker looked down at the papers. They included the same bloody photographs that Winter had already shown him. Ryker didn't need to see those again. He handed them back to Green, averting his eyes from the gory images.

'It was horrific,' Green said. 'The maid found her like that. Lucky, I guess, that it wasn't the husband.'

'Yeah.'

'Kim was knocked unconscious with chloroform. She was raped. Her stomach was cut open while she was still alive. It's not clear why. The baby wasn't taken out. There were numerous other stab wounds, slashes, all non-fatal. She was partly suffocated, a plastic bag put over her head and tied around her neck, but it was a blunt-force blow that killed her. One of several that she received to her face and head.'

'And the scene?' Ryker asked.

Green paused as a young couple – both with bright-white skin, Northern European tourists, no doubt – walked arm in arm along the street in front of the restaurant terrace. The grisly conversation was hardly something they'd be keen to overhear on their sunny Spanish getaway.

'Kim was found in the entrance hall,' Green carried on when the couple were out of earshot. 'Attacked, beaten and killed in the same spot, it looks like, though the ordeal certainly wasn't quick. We've found zero trace evidence of a third party. The house was clean. I mean, the maid seems to scrub that place from top to bottom every day from what I've seen anyway, but the area around Kim's body was heavily bleached. The door and frame of the front entrance were thoroughly scrubbed down too, no prints on them. Not even Kim's or Patrick's.'

'And no other trace evidence? Clothing fibres? Blood? DNA?' Ryker asked.

'Nothing. Maybe the killer was wearing a plastic suit. Gloves. Shoe covers. But nothing's been recovered to confirm that.'

'All in all very professional then.'

'Very,' Green said. 'But also an absolute statement. A killer with that kind of forethought and knowledge of evidence transfer... I mean he could have taken the body and disposed of it, and we'd have no clue where Kim went or what happened.'

'He?'

'What?'

'You said he. The killer.'

'A figure of speech. An assumption.'

'Those are two different things,' Ryker said.

'An assumption then. And she was raped. Yeah, perhaps with an object rather than a dick, but I've never seen a woman do a thing like that.'

'You haven't. I have.'

'You don't think the killer's a he?' Green said, perturbed. 'You know something I don't?'

'I know lots of things you don't.'

'About this case?'

'I'm just saying. Don't assume it's a he.'

'Thanks for the lesson,' Green said, his irritation evident. It looked like Ryker's initial assessment of Green had been spot on. Here was a man who really didn't like to be questioned.

'My point was about the body,' Green said. 'Left on display like that, in the hallway of her home. The killer – he or she or it or whatever you want to say – wanted her to be found that way.'

Ryker didn't say a word for a minute or two. Slowly he could see Green calming again. Ryker wasn't going to set out to rile the detective, but he also wasn't the type to sit back and keep schtum when the obvious needed stating.

'Where was Walker?' Ryker asked.

'Playing golf,' Green said. 'Three of his friends confirm they were with him. And four members of staff at the golf club say they saw him there that day.'

'And was he home on time?'

'Actually he was later than planned. By about two hours.'

'Why?'

'Just was. Drinking. Eating. Socialising. Business. Whatever rich men do after golf.'

Green said the last words with a hint of contempt. Or was it jealousy?

'He was supposed to find the body,' Ryker said.

Green shrugged. 'Maybe.'

'And you say you have no theories?'

'I didn't say that exactly.'

'No, not exactly. But you've not been very open about what you think happened, either.'

'I've told you everything I know,' Green protested.

'No, you've told me all the facts. You haven't told me what you think.'

'What I think?'

'Why do you think Kim Walker was killed?'

'I haven't a clue.'

'It's pretty damn obvious to me.'

'Obvious?' Green said, offended. 'Go on then, tell me.'

'One way or another, Kim Walker was killed because of Patrick Walker. Her husband. I'm certain of it.'

Chapter 17

'Jesus fucking Christ,' Green said.

Ryker raised an eyebrow.

'And there's you warning me about making assumptions,' Green added, a look of incredulity on his sweat-drenched face.

'It's not an assumption,' Ryker said. 'It's a deduction. Or call it a hypothesis if you like.'

'I don't think Patrick Walker killed his wife.'

'No. He didn't. I didn't say that.'

'And I don't think he paid to have her killed either.'

'Because?'

'Because there's no motive for him to do so.'

'How about because he was screwing someone else behind her back.'

Green said nothing. He took another sip of his wine but his gaze never once left Ryker.

'You knew about that, right?' Ryker asked.

'Yes.'

'And do you think it's connected?'

'No.'

'Who is she?'

'Her name's Eva.'

'Where can I find her?'

'I already spoke to her. The Spanish police too. I'm not sure what you expect her to tell you. She's a kid. Twenty-three.'

'You said I can't speak to Walker either. So who exactly would you like me to speak to?'

'I didn't say that. Just that I don't think you should go around harassing everyone. There's plenty of material, statements, that the locals and I have put together that you can read.'

'Yeah. Because all of those statements have gotten you so far already.'

'Oh, so you think everyone's going to all of a sudden give a different story, tell us exactly what happened, just because you're on the scene now?'

'I can but try,' Ryker said, smiling. Green didn't reciprocate. 'You already told me you don't know why Kim Walker was killed or who did it. So I'm not sure why I'd waste my time reading your reports. You can help me here or I can do this on my own. But one way or another, I'll get to the bottom of what's happened.'

Green sighed and poured himself another glass of wine. 'Do you *want* to work with me? Because I get the sense you're not really looking to do that. That you're a lone wolf who'd rather tread on everyone's toes.'

'I'll do whatever's needed.'

'I was like you once,' Green said after taking a long drag of wine from his glass.

'I don't think you were.'

Green shook his head. 'It's true. I was headstrong like you, never trusted anyone, always thought I'd do a better job than anyone else would.'

'You're using the past tense. You don't think that way anymore?'

'Of course I do. But I'm not as naive as I used to be. I see now that such an approach doesn't always work in my favour. And when I see those same faults in other people, it's always so damn obvious.'

Ryker stopped for a few seconds as Green's words sunk in. There was a lot of truth to them. That was the way Ryker had always been. As an agent for the JIA, he was supposed to have done nothing but follow orders. Never question, just do. But whatever training they'd put Ryker through, however much they'd tried to control his mind, make him nothing more than a killing machine, he had always fought back. He'd always questioned and looked for answers. It was simply part of his nature, something that could never be taken away from him.

In the end, it was one of the main reasons why Ryker's career with the JIA had come to such a spectacular close.

'Where can I find Eva?' Ryker asked.

Green sighed then reached for his mobile phone. He tapped away before reading off an address to Ryker, who made a mental note.

'It's her father's place,' Green said. 'Like I said, she's a kid.'

'A kid who was screwing Patrick Walker.'

'I don't pretend to understand the whys and wherefores, I'm just saying.'

'Thanks for lunch,' Ryker said as he wiped his mouth with his napkin. 'I'll pay next time.'

'You're not going over there like that, are you?'

'What, would you rather drink some more wine first?'

'Okay, Ryker. I know you're eager to figure this out,' Green said, glaring. 'And that's good. But if you bite off more than you can chew, if you go rubbing up the wrong people the wrong way, it's not going to end well for you.'

'Noted.'

'Be careful out there.'

Ryker walked away from the table, Green's words swimming in his head. His first impression of Green had been right, that was for sure. But he sensed there was even more to Green's awkwardness than him being an over-the-hill middle-ranked detective with a beef against the world. Ryker got the impression he was scared. But of what?

Ryker caught a taxi back to Walker's house to pick up his car. He took the opportunity to call Lisa. He'd sent her a text message the previous evening shortly after landing, but hadn't spoken to her since leaving her at home almost three days earlier.

In the nearly twelve months they'd been living together, he hadn't been away from Lisa for more than a few hours, and he was missing her. But the fact was, he was still getting used to being in a meaningful relationship. He loved Lisa, he really did. Hell, look at how he'd fought for her, the things he'd done, the people who'd been hurt and killed while he saved her from the clutches of the FSB, the CIA, and the JIA who were all gunning for her. In doing so, he'd salvaged a life for them both. But still, the nuances and expectations of being in an adult relationship were alien to Ryker.

He felt bad for not having called her sooner, but he'd quickly become engrossed in the job. His work had been his life for so many years and it was a hard habit to break – even though he was no longer an official JIA agent, and never would be again.

It was more than that, though. He'd been distracted by the resurgence of old memories of the Red Cobra. And as he dialled he felt a pang of guilt over that.

As it was, the call went unanswered – the large time difference not helping, she was probably sleeping.

Ryker left a brief voicemail before putting the phone away and getting his mind back on track.

When he arrived at Casa de las Rosas, the maid opened the front gates to let Ryker in. He hopped into his car without seeing or speaking to Walker and drove the short distance back down to the coastal road, then headed west and on to Marbella – one of the wealthiest and most fashionable areas of Andalusia.

Marbella – largely overrun by non-Spanish – was a town awash with fast cars, luxury boats and expensive playboy pads. Walker's wealth was one thing, but what Ryker saw in Marbella was on another level. At least Walker seemed to have some taste to go with his money. His house was glorious and sympathetic to the surroundings. Or maybe that had been Kim's doing. Much of what Ryker saw in Marbella, though, was simply money without sense.

Ryker headed toward the address Green had given him, using his mobile phone's GPS map to guide him. The exclusive housing complex was located on a small stretch of coastline where several huge mansions stood directly in front of the beach. The gated entrance to the estate was manned by two security guards. Ryker didn't want to go in that way. He could only assume that the whole area beyond the gates was covered by CCTV cameras too.

Ryker drove on for a couple of minutes and parked his car on the road next to a half-built run of apartments that looked as though it had been mothballed. Huge signs proudly displayed the site as being one of the finest luxury spots on the sunlit coast. The grey breeze-block shells of the reality were a far cry from the artist's colourful impressions. Ryker had noticed several similarly abandoned developments already on his short stay in Andalusia – clear evidence of the recent bust that had followed the boom.

Ryker headed on foot to the beach, then traipsed across the soft sand back towards the millionaires' row. Or was it billionaires'?

The beach was secluded, quiet. Other than two joggers and a dog-walker there wasn't a soul in sight. The Costa del Sol was vast and although numerous pockets of it were heavily built-up and the beaches routinely crammed, it wasn't difficult to find quieter stretches like this one.

Ryker held out his phone, using its precise GPS tracking to locate the house he was looking for. It was monstrous with a stone-effect finish, and ten sets of windows stretched across each of the home's three floors. Large columns gave the building an old-world colonial appearance, though it seemed from the immaculate condition of the stonework, and the finish of neighbouring properties, that the house was almost brand new.

Satisfied that he wasn't being observed from the beach, Ryker moved toward the house and scaled the small wall that separated the landscaped gardens from the sand.

Keeping low as he moved between bushes and trees, Ryker approached the back of the property, looking for any signs of life as he went. He saw none: no pool cleaner or gardener or anyone else around. All the doors and windows were shut tight. The glare from the sun made it difficult to see what lay beyond the many panes of glass, and it was possible that someone was sitting a few yards inside the house, watching Ryker's every move, but the thought didn't deter him.

Ryker continued moving, as stealthily as he could. He came up against the back corner of the house, then he slid along the wall. He approached the first set of windows, beyond which he could make out a large home office. Neat bookshelves were crammed with old tomes. In contrast, the large desk that sat in the middle of the room was scattered with loose papers. Ryker kept on moving.

Next he came upon a grand sitting room, then an open-plan kitchen diner that looked to be about the size of Ryker's entire house. As well as a large window in the kitchen, the dining area had a set of bi-fold doors leading out into the back garden. Ryker tried the handle. Locked. Not a problem: the type of lock was one of the simplest to pick.

Ryker was reaching into his trouser pocket for the small torsion wrench and picks that he'd brought with him when he suddenly spotted movement inside the house.

A figure walked into the kitchen, initially none-the-wiser to Ryker's presence. Eva. She was red-faced, dressed in a skin-tight running top and shorts, and bright green trainers. Ryker was about to scuttle away, out of sight of the window, when she looked up.

She saw Ryker immediately. For a split second, a look of panic swept across her face. Then came a knowing smile. Ryker relaxed and Eva moved toward him, released the lock and opened the door. A waft of pleasantly cool air escaped.

'You again,' she said in English. Her foreign accent was barely recognisable.

'I was hoping you were home.'

'You were? The easiest way to find out would have been to knock on the front door.'

'I prefer to catch people off guard.'

'Yes, I get that impression about you. Why are you here?'

'We need to talk.'

'About what?'

'About the man you're sleeping with. And why someone would murder his wife.'

Chapter 18

'Come in,' Eva said. She stepped to the side and Ryker walked into the house, scanning the opulent expanse in front of him.

He'd rarely seen such an overt display of wealth. Marble covered both the floor and the seemingly never-ending worktops in the kitchen. Sleek chrome appliances glistened. A large chandelier dangled overhead in the dining area above a grand table that would probably seat a couple of dozen people. Large artworks hung on the walls and expensive-looking ornaments did their best to further fill the extensive space.

'Nice place,' Ryker said, not entirely convincingly.

'Who are you?' Eva said.

Ryker turned to face her. She was breathing heavily and her face and top were wet with sweat.

'Good workout?'

'A run. Yes it was good. But hot.'

'You ran out in that heat?'

'You get used to it. I'll ask you again, who are you?'

'The name's James Ryker.'

'And why are you here?'

'I'm working with the police.'

'You don't look like a policeman. You're too... I don't know.'

'I'm not a policeman.'

'So what are you then?'

'A helping hand.'

'Helping with what?'

'I'm investigating the murder of Kim Walker.'

Eva looked away from Ryker. She was a cool character, full of sass and self-confidence. But clearly she wasn't beyond being rattled. And Ryker could tell that Kim Walker was not a comfortable subject for her.

'I've already given a statement to the police about that.'

Ryker raised an eyebrow. 'And why would you be required to do that?'

Eva turned back to face him. Above her already rosy cheeks, Ryker was sure he saw her blush. 'Because of me and Patrick.'

'How long have you been sleeping with him?'

'Is this an official visit?' Eva glared at Ryker, the first sign of anger evident.

Ryker shrugged. 'Maybe.'

'I'd rather have my lawyer here before speaking to you any more.'

'You have a lawyer? Why do you need a lawyer?'

'He's my father's lawyer.'

'And where's your father?'

'At work.'

Ryker paused. The talk of lawyers made him wary – as it had when Green had mentioned Walker's lawyer. Whatever these people had to tell, whatever they knew of Kim Walker, with high-profile lawyers on the scene no one would be willing to open up. Perhaps that was why Green and the local police had made so little headway.

'This is just a little chat,' Ryker said. 'A getting to know you. Can we do that? There's no need for you to call a lawyer.'

Eva stared at Ryker again and he held her gaze. He saw the same raw intensity in her eyes as when he'd first seen her in the village. Ryker had to admit he was drawn to it, even though he sensed that Eva was not someone to be trusted.

'Thanks for helping me earlier,' she said.

'It was nothing. I was just there to speak to Walker. Had to get his attention somehow.'

Eva laughed. 'You must really have a way with people.'

'Why were you two arguing?'

'It's a long story.'

'A story you're going to tell me, right?'

Eva hesitated for a few seconds. 'Okay. But look at me. I'm covered in sweat. I really need to take a shower. Fix yourself a drink and I'll be back down in five minutes. Yeah?'

'Okay.' Ryker raised an eyebrow and looked around the huge kitchen.

'There's coffee. Tea. Beer. Liquor. Whatever. Help yourself.'

Eva spun round and sauntered off. As she reached the doorway, she glanced over her shoulder and smiled to see Ryker still had his eyes on her. She left the room and Ryker heard her padding up the stairs.

After a few moments, he moved over to the kitchen area, found a glass and poured himself some water from a bottle in the fridge.

Despite her allure, Eva gave Ryker an eerie feeling. He was drawn to her, there was no doubt about that. She had a seductive air that even in her early twenties she already seemed an expert at exploiting. But Ryker also knew Eva was a trouble-maker. She'd spotted him roaming in the back garden, had almost without question invited him into her father's home, despite knowing little about who Ryker was, and within minutes had left him on his own.

Was she setting him up for a fall?

Maybe. It didn't matter. The window of opportunity was there nonetheless. Ryker headed straight out of the kitchen and through an expansive entrance lobby to the office he'd seen when he was outside. The door was locked. Not a problem. Ryker set down his glass on the floor, took out his picks, and in less than a minute, was inside.

He casually moved over to the desk and rummaged through the clutter, taking in as much as he could in the few minutes he expected he had. He remained vigilant for the sound of Eva coming back down the stairs, or for anyone else in the house. But he wasn't that worried about being caught out. His job was to find answers, not to abide by the rules that constrained the police.

Among the papers, Ryker found piles of invoices, statements and correspondence with two different banks discussing loan facilities. A company called Empire Holdings cropped up more than once. He also noticed several references to a development with the name Blue Dolphin Villas. Much of the correspondence was marked as being to or from an Andrei Kozlov – with the address of the house that Ryker was currently standing in.

Ryker tried the desk drawers. The top two were locked. He didn't attempt to pick them, just kept going. The third wasn't locked. Ryker opened it.

The only objects inside were a pair of reading glasses and a small leather-bound book. The front cover was bare except for a gold-embossed cross and Cyrillic writing that Ryker knew was the Russian word for 'bible'.

As Ryker pushed the drawer shut, he caught a glimpse of a shadow. He looked up to see Eva standing in the doorway. He was surprised he hadn't heard her coming. Her entrance had obviously been intended to startle him. It hadn't worked.

'Find what you were looking for?' she asked without any hint of shock or anxiety in her tone.

Eva was casually leaning against the doorway, dressed in a light summer dress that fell a few inches short of her knees. Her wet hair hung over her shoulders. Even though her face was now cleared of the thick make-up that had covered it for her dance routine earlier in the day, she was still a picture to look at. In fact Ryker thought the natural look suited her, even if it did make her features less intense.

'Was trying to find the toilet,' Ryker said. 'The door was open.'

'You're not a very good liar.'

Ryker shrugged.

'Come on,' she said. 'Let's go and sit somewhere more comfortable.'

She turned round and Ryker followed her through to a sitting room, where two large cream leather sofas were arranged opposite each other adjacent to an ornate stone fireplace.

'Your father's Russian,' Ryker said. 'Andrei Kozlov.'

'Yes.' Eva turned to face him. 'You didn't know?'

'I thought you were local. You look Spanish.'

'Eva Kozlov. Hardly a Spanish name.'

'I didn't know your last name.'

'You're really not a very good detective, are you?'

'I'm not any kind of detective.'

'I was born in Russia.' Eva sat on one of the sofas and crossed her legs in a manner which exposed as much skin as possible. Ryker remained standing, trying his hardest to keep his wandering gaze on her face. 'But my mother is half-Spanish. I guess that's where my looks come from. We moved here when I was nine. So I've been in Spain more than half my life.'

'Where's your mother?'

'Dead.'

Ryker had noticed various happy pictures of the family as he'd walked through the house. Mother, father and daughter. 'I'm sorry,' Ryker said, feeling somewhat lame for his bland response.

'It's fine. It was years ago. Cancer.'

'Why did you move here? To Spain, I mean.'

'For my father's work. He's a–'

'Property developer.'

'Yes.'

'And that's how he knows Patrick Walker. And how the two of you came to know each other.'

Eva said nothing, but Ryker could see a sliver of vulnerability in her eyes. Walker was obviously not a happy subject for her.

'Why do you want to speak to me?' Eva said, more cagey than before. 'I told you, I already gave my statement.'

'Tell me what you know about Kim Walker.'

'I'm not sure I'm the best person to ask that. I barely knew her.'

'Okay. Then how long have you known Patrick Walker?'

Eva paused for a few seconds as though trying to figure out the correct answer. Or perhaps whether or not to tell the truth. 'Eight years. A bit more maybe. But I was a girl then, I didn't really know him. Just that he was a colleague of my father's. They've worked on projects together for years now.'

'And he hadn't met Kim Walker at that point, when he started working with your father?'

'No, I don't think so.'

'So how did Patrick meet Kim?'

'I don't know.'

'You don't know? She turned up one day by his side and you never asked or heard why?'

'I told you, I was a girl. I can't really remember the first time I met her. Perhaps you should be asking Patrick these questions, not me.'

'Did Kim know about the affair?'

'I don't think so,' Eva said after a moment of silence. She was now looking anywhere but at Ryker. 'I certainly never told her. And I don't think Patrick did. What we were doing, it wasn't serious. I didn't ever expect him to leave her, and he never said he wanted to. It was just fun.'

Ryker huffed at Eva's heartless statement. She really was a piece of work. 'So when did you start sleeping with him?'

Eva gave Ryker a cold glare. Gone now was any nicety. 'Maybe you should read my statement.'

'Come on, it's not a hard question. And I'm not trying to trick you.'

She sighed. 'Fine. It was recent. About six months ago.'

'And how long have you *wanted* to sleep with him?' Ryker asked with a wry smile.

'Why the hell are you asking me these questions?'

'I'm just interested. I mean how exactly does a twenty-three-year-old girl end up in bed with a married man in his forties?'

'I'm sure you can use your imagination. Even someone like you must have had sex before.'

Someone like you. Ryker didn't seek to clarify what she meant by that even though the choice of words intrigued him. 'But who was the seducer. You or him?'

'If all you're interested in is petty gossip then I think it's about time you left.'

'And so do I,' came an angry male voice from behind Ryker.

Ryker turned to see a pint-sized man standing behind him. He was a good eight or nine inches shorter than Ryker. Scrawny too. But he had a confident and arrogant look on his well-tanned face, together with piercing dark eyes. He was late forties, maybe early fifties, and dressed smartly in blue pressed trousers and a cotton shirt with a thick-knotted tie.

'Andrei Kozlov, I'm guessing,' Ryker said, not in the least bit surprised or put off by Kozlov's entrance. In fact, the second Eva had left him alone to go and shower he'd wondered how long it would be before company turned up. He'd been in two minds as to whether it would be her lawyer or Daddy that she called about the unexpected visitor. Clearly the latter was still her main comfort blanket.

'Yes,' Kozlov said. 'And you are?'

'James Ryker.'

'What are you doing in my house?' His voice was raspy – too much smoking or too much shouting. Maybe both.

'He says he's with the police,' Eva said, getting to her feet and looking her confident self again.

'*With* the police?' Kozlov questioned. 'So are you a policeman or are you not?'

'Not,' Ryker said. 'Just helping with their enquiries. Into the murder of Kim Walker.'

'He was asking me about Patrick and Kim,' Eva said.

'She doesn't know anything,' Kozlov said with distaste. 'And if you want to talk to anyone in my family again you do it with my lawyer present. I already made that point clear to your colleague.'

'Certainly,' Ryker said. 'You can call your lawyer now if you like?'

'No, I would not like that. Who exactly are you?'

'I already said. I'm James Ryker.'

'Yes, I know that, but who do you work for?'

'The British Home Office.'

'You can be sure that you haven't heard the last about this intrusion. Now get out of my house.'

Ryker shrugged. He couldn't care less about Kozlov's little power trip. He moved toward Kozlov in the doorway. Kozlov, looking slightly less confident with the figure of Ryker bearing down on him, moved to one side. Ryker stepped past and walked down the hall, sensing that both Kozlov and Eva had followed him out of the room. Ryker stopped and turned.

'One more thing.' He looked over at Eva, who was standing behind her father. 'You never did tell me what you and Patrick were arguing about this morning. Why he grabbed you like that. Quite a temper on that man. I was sure he was going to hit you.'

'Go!' Kozlov said, his face creasing with anger.

Eva smiled, the same wicked smile she'd given Ryker earlier in the day. Then she stuck out her tongue. Ryker couldn't help but smirk at the deliberately childish gesture. Kozlov spun round to look at his daughter but she'd already resumed her passive look.

Yes, she was a trouble-maker, no doubt about it. Ryker didn't trust her. But he was certainly intrigued.

Ryker began moving again, into the kitchen.

'Where are you going?' Kozlov shouted, rushing up behind Ryker. 'I told you to leave.'

Ryker stopped and turned to face down Kozlov. 'Heading out the same way I came in.'

Kozlov didn't blink as he stared at Ryker. 'There's an old saying my grandmother told me many years ago; when you can't be sure of the ground beneath your feet, the best course is to turn back. And my advice to you, Mr Ryker, is to turn back now. Before it's too late for you.'

Ryker held his tongue at the thinly-veiled threat. Or perhaps it was merely a friendly warning. Either way, it took Ryker back to the conversation with Green at the restaurant. It seemed everyone in Andalusia was concerned for Ryker's wellbeing.

'Thank you for the hospitality,' Ryker said looking at Eva. 'And Andrei?' Ryker stomped his shoe on the shiny marble tile underfoot. 'The ground I'm standing on is as solid as can be. But thank you for the advice. I'm sure we'll be seeing each other again.'

'Be careful what you wish for, Mr Ryker.'

Chapter 19

Ryker had learned little of substance from his escapade to the Kozlov residence. What he did know was that everyone knew more than they were telling. Kozlov and Walker were in bed together, in a manner of speaking. Both were rich men, developers. Eva was quite literally in bed with Walker, sleeping with her father's business partner. And Walker's wife had been murdered.

Ryker was barely scratching the surface but there was already a lot about the situation, the relationship between those four people, that Ryker didn't like. So far no one had welcomed Ryker's presence. Nor did they seem genuinely enthused at the prospect of getting to the bottom of Kim Walker's murder.

If they had something to hide, neither Walker nor Kozlov appeared particularly afraid or even perturbed by Ryker's sudden appearance on the scene. Both were arrogant and cool men, certainly, and both had the weight of an expensive legal team behind them – apparently – but still their actions suggested something else to Ryker: that they thought they were above the law. And in Ryker's experience, there were only a few reasons why people would come to believe that.

Ryker headed back to his car. The few minutes inside the air-conditioned Kozlov mansion had cooled him nicely, but by the time he neared his vehicle, with the heat of the afternoon sun on his back, he was a sweaty sodden mess again. Together with his tiredness from the long haul travel and lack of a good night's sleep, he felt rotten and made his mind up to call the day short and head back to his hotel.

He was five yards from his car when he felt his phone vibrating in his pocket. Ryker took it out and saw he had a missed call and a text message from Lisa, apologising for not answering his earlier call. Ryker was about to hit the button to ring her back when movement ahead caught his eye. He looked up and spotted two men ahead of him. His instincts screamed: the men didn't belong there.

Both men were tall, broad-shouldered. One was wearing a tight-fitting t-shirt that bulged from the muscles underneath. He was olive skinned with jet black locks of hair that fell around his face. The other man – older, fairer skinned with a heavily lined face and an army style buzz-cut – wore a jacket. A crazy choice of clothing given the heat. Perhaps that was normal for some of the hardened locals, but this guy didn't look much of a local. And Ryker could think of only one good reason someone would choose such clothing: concealment.

The men walked toward Ryker with purpose, their lips moving as they murmured instructions to each other. Ryker held his ground, waiting to see what would happen. His initial suspicion was confirmed a couple of seconds later when the man on the left – Buzzcut – reached into his jacket and brought out a foot-long monkey wrench. These two were hardly out for a quiet afternoon stroll.

The men were more than ten yards from Ryker. He could rush for his car and hope he had the speed to get inside, fire up the engine and race off into the distance before they accosted him. Unlikely.

Then there was the other option. The one Ryker chose. It'd been a long time since he'd been out in the field. Nearly a year had passed by since he and Lisa had ended their previous lives and headed off into the sunset. Ryker was rusty. Perhaps these two lumps would provide some much-needed practice.

Ryker caught the eye of the black-haired man – Rambo. The look on his face told Ryker he was the leader. It wasn't clear whether he was armed. He could have been carrying a knife or a gun stuffed behind his back. Ryker was sure he'd soon find out the answer.

He looked up and down the street. It was quiet, but still this was no place for what was to come. It would only take one random passerby to scupper Ryker's plans. He needed space. He needed time. He had to find out who these men were, why they'd been sent there, and by whom. Kozlov was Ryker's immediate guess but he wasn't ruling out other possibilities.

Ryker moved purposefully off to his right, towards the derelict construction site. He spotted the two men stop – obviously contemplating their next move. Ryker didn't hesitate to see what they chose . He strode up to the rickety metal fence that ran around the site and hauled himself up and over, then moved off toward the not-so-glorious holiday homes.

The row of apartments were in various states of build. At the near end the concrete and brick shells were almost complete, just awaiting a render finish, interior stud walls, plastering, doors, windows. At the far side they were in a much earlier stage of construction with nothing more than concrete pads, out of which hundreds of rusted steel rods protruded haphazardly into the air.

Ryker moved with purpose to the near side, where the more complete buildings gave better cover. He glanced behind, confirming that the men had followed him inside the complex, then moved around the back of the buildings and in through the front doorway of one. He pulled up on the inside wall and readied himself.

From there he had a good view through the apartment to a small window at the back which gave a glimpse of where Ryker had come from. And if the men chose to come at him from the opposite side, snaking around the far side of the buildings, he'd spot them coming a mile off: in front of him was a clear view to the front along the whole run of apartments – at least a hundred yards.

Ryker spotted Rambo first. He was alone, edging around the same way Ryker had gone. And Ryker had been right about his choice of weapon. A handgun. Black. Looked to be a Glock. Ryker was pleased about that. He didn't like not being armed on the job and was grateful for the opportunity Rambo was about to present him.

Ryker ducked down and held tight, waiting for Rambo to approach. Ryker strained his hearing for any indication of the man's movement. He heard nothing. Ryker wondered whether Rambo had stopped moving, or even gone back on himself.

But then, with Ryker staring out into the open, he spotted the slightest shadow appear in the doorway in front of him. Just an inch.

It was gone again a split second later. This guy wasn't dumb, he'd at least spotted his error. But it was too late to take it back. Ryker now knew exactly where he was.

As stealthily as he could, Ryker moved across the room to the bare concrete staircase and ascended to the first floor, hoping Rambo was quietly waiting for his friend to catch up before springing an attack.

On the first floor, there was a gaping hole in the breeze-block construction. Ryker assumed an impressive floor-to-ceiling window had been planned, to take advantage of the stunning sea views. It was exactly what Ryker needed. He crept to the edge and carefully peered down below. Sure enough, Rambo was right there, pressed up against the wall, waiting for his moment of attack.

But still no sign of Buzzcut. Where was he?

Ryker didn't dwell on the thought. He stepped over the edge...

The man had no clue what was coming. Ryker landed on Rambo's shoulders with a thud and a crack, and both men tumbled to the ground in a heap. Rambo was dazed and confused from the sudden attack. Ryker was alert, ready, one thing on his mind: he wanted that gun.

Without hesitation, Ryker swivelled his body round and put Rambo into an arm bar, hyperextending the elbow joint to the point of bursting. Rambo squirmed, grunted, and moaned – maybe he knew what was coming. Ryker pushed against the resistance and there was a crack and a pop as the man's arm dislocated. Rambo screamed out in pain. Ryker reached down and pulled the handgun from Rambo's limp grip. Then he sprang to his feet, gun in hand, pointed at the man's face.

Ryker smiled. Yeah, he was rusty, out of practice for sure, but it felt good to be back.

Ryker spotted movement. He spun and saw the glint of metal as Buzzcut's wrench arced toward his face. He ducked. The wrench hurtled through the air but missed. Ryker saw his target, a yard away. He sprang up, fist-balled, and sent a crushing uppercut onto Buzzcut's chin. His head snapped back. He wobbled, stumbled. Ryker smacked him in the side of the head with the grip of the gun. Buzzcut collapsed to the ground and landed in a heap next to his buddy.

Ryker shook himself down and looked over the two lumps. Both were out of the fight. But Ryker wasn't finished. He wanted answers.

He was about to begin his interrogation when something unexpected happened: a gunshot rang out. A blast of concrete powder burst in Ryker's face from the nearby ricochet. Ryker darted back toward the buildings, trying to find cover from the unseen shooter. He pulled up against a wall.

In front of him, the two men lay on the ground. Buzzcut's eyes were closed. He was out cold. The movement in his chest told Ryker he was at least breathing. Rambo was awake. He was still writhing on the ground in agony, clutching at his stricken limb and staring aghast at the misshapen mass.

Neither man was an immediate threat.

Ryker looked up and searched the area outside. He had clear sight down the row of apartments and across the nearby coastline. There was no shooter in that direction. There simply wasn't anywhere for them to hide. Ryker dashed across the building and pulled up against the adjacent wall. From there he had a better view back to the road.

No sign of a shooter, or even a potential hiding place. Ryker crept along the wall, heading further into the apartment shell. He moved through a doorway, his eyes focused on the bright glare coming through the open window space in front of him, through which he had an almost unobstructed view of the street.

Still no sign of anyone with a gun.

Ryker felt pressure against the back of his head so he stopped.

A male voice spoke to him in Spanish. Ryker could understand the language quite well, enough to know what the man had just said – who he worked for. In fact, one of the words he'd used, above all the others, was understandable in countless languages. *Policia.*

That was a fight Ryker didn't want.

Ryker dropped his gun and put his hands above his head.

A second before something hard was smashed against the back of his skull.

Chapter 20

The throbbing in Ryker's head was still there the next morning, making it an effort to move even an inch. He'd been pistol-whipped, knocked unconscious, by an officer from the Policia Local – the municipal police in Marbella and the surrounding area. From what Ryker had gathered, the officer was responding to an anonymous call claiming an armed man was wandering the streets.

After falling unconscious, Ryker had woken up in the back of the patrol car and then been frog-marched into a cell at a police station in Marbella where he'd been left for a number of hours before anyone had come to speak to him.

Then, when he'd finally been moved from the cell to an interview room the previous evening, events had got really interesting. Despite Ryker's protestations, the arresting officers claimed there were no other people on the construction site. That Ryker had been alone.

Ryker certainly didn't believe that Rambo and Buzzcut had suddenly jumped up and vanished. And then there was the supposed call from a worried citizen that the police were responding to. Ryker didn't buy it.

The only explanation was that at least one bent policeman was on the payroll in Marbella, and they were likely working for the person who'd sent those two goons after Ryker. Kozlov was the obvious culprit, but Ryker was keeping an open mind.

When Ryker had finally been allowed to make a phone call in the small hours of the morning, he'd managed to briefly speak to Green. Less than impressed – not just about being woken, but by the trouble Ryker was causing *him* – Green had soon been onto Walker's lawyer, Graham Munroe, and then his contact at the Policia Nacional, an inspector named Miguel Cardo.

Ryker wasn't in tune with the many nuances of the Spanish police but from what he knew the Policia Local took on everyday policing in urban areas. Then there was the Guardia Civil, a more military-orientated force that had responsibility outside urban areas, including policing highways and borders. Finally there was the Policia Nacional, responsible for major criminal investigation.

It was the Policia Nacional who was leading the investigation into the murder of Kim Walker. Unfortunately for Ryker, that meant he was at something of a loss with the Policia Local who'd arrested him. Because not only did they have no clue who Ryker was, they also knew nothing about Kim Walker's murder. They were a different police force in fact from the equivalent Policia Local who patrolled the Mijas area where the murder had taken place.

Which meant Ryker had no chance of a quick release once he'd been arrested for possessing an illegal firearm.

Nonetheless, Green, Munroe, and Cardo had together somehow set in motion a chain of events that ultimately led to Ryker being released without charge that morning, and Cardo was the man who arrived with this welcome news. By that point, Ryker had been at the station for the best part of twenty-four hours.

The inspector could have been a cartoon character. Every inch of him screamed policeman. He wore a navy-blue suit and light-blue shirt, and had slicked-back black hair, a pointed nose, and a thick black caterpillar moustache.

'It seems you have some friends in high places,' Cardo said to Ryker. His English was good, though came with a thick Spanish accent.

The two men walked out of the police station into the bright light and heat of another sunny morning in Andalusia, which only seemed to make Ryker's headache worse. He badly needed some aspirin.

'Friends isn't really the right word,' Ryker said.

Cardo frowned. 'My English was not right?'

'No, your English was fine. I'm just not sure the people you've been speaking to are really my friends.'

'No? But they have certainly helped you.'

'Yes. As have you. And I'm grateful.'

Cardo stopped walking. 'But I'm not.'

'Not what?' Ryker said, raising an eyebrow and looking over at Cardo.

'Not grateful. For you being here. In Spain. Sending your detective, Mr Green, okay, but you? I don't know why they would send you.'

Cardo walked again. Ryker followed.

'Yeah well, I'm here.'

'I know. Like I said, you have some big friends. Bigger than me. They want you here, and there's nothing I can do about that.'

'The sooner I get some answers about what happened to Kim Walker, the sooner I'll be gone.'

'You don't think I've tried?'

'I've only just met you. I don't know the answer to that yet.'

'And Kim Walker was only just murdered. Six days ago.'

'Seven.'

'Okay, seven days ago. Still, it's early. And we're working hard. I've been doing this job for thirty years. I get results. But it can take weeks, months, to solve a case like this.'

'I'm sure you're very good.'

'I am. That's why I don't like you being sent to tell me how to do my job.'

'I've got no interest in doing that.'

'I hope not.'

'But likewise, you don't tell me how to do mine.'

'I absolutely won't,' Cardo said. 'Because to be quite honest, I have no idea what your job here actually is.'

'To find answers. I thought I said that already.'

They reached a black Seat hatchback. Cardo stopped and took out a remote clicker which he used to unlock the doors. 'I'll take you to your car. Then you should go and see your colleague, Mr Green. You work for him, not me.'

'I don't work for him.'

Cardo looked at Ryker questioningly but didn't say anything. Ryker and Cardo got into the car, and the inspector started the engine and pulled away from the kerb.

'What do you know about Andrei Kozlov?' Ryker asked.

'Not much,' was Cardo's vague response.

'Does *he* have friends in high places?'

Cardo glanced over at Ryker. 'I didn't know of Kozlov until this investigation. I've looked into him. He's worked with Patrick Walker for a number of years. Kozlov is a property developer. He's rich. That's it. He's not some criminal kingpin, if that's what you're thinking.'

'You know that for sure?'

'As sure as I can be. I've worked in the criminal investigation department for many years. Kozlov has never been of interest to us.'

'I'm not sure that proves anything.'

'Why? Because you think we're all incompetent idiots out here?'

'I never said that.'

'But that's what you think?'

'No. It's not. What I think is someone, somewhere, is not playing ball. Those two goons were sent after me by someone.'

'Goons?'

'Two men. On the construction site.'

'You were found there alone.'

'The police were lying.'

'Why would they do that?'

'Exactly.'

Cardo and Ryker went silent for a few seconds. The traffic eased as they moved out of the town centre toward the construction site and the gated complex where Eva Kozlov lived with her father.

'Would you like some advice, Mr Ryker?' Cardo said as he pulled up alongside Ryker's car.

Ryker laughed. 'You're going to tell me to be careful, right?'

Cardo frowned and glared at Ryker but said nothing.

'You know what,' Ryker said, opening his door to get out. 'I'm done with getting advice around here. If I wanted to be careful, I'd have gotten a different job.'

Chapter 21

The four aspirins sloshing around in Ryker's stomach kicked in within minutes. He was driving back up the steep incline into the Sierra when his phone vibrated in his pocket. He fumbled around, trying to remove it, expecting – hoping – that the call was from Lisa.

His lack of attention on the twisting road nearly got the better of him. A sharp bend came up unexpectedly and Ryker jerked on the steering wheel, jolting the car to the right. He put his foot to the brake then heard a honking horn as the car behind came within inches of shunting him.

Ryker ignored the angry driver who promptly overtook him on the blind corner. He grabbed his phone before slamming on the accelerator. The engine whined as the revs peaked, trying to pull the car up the steep bank. Ryker looked at his phone. The call hadn't been from Lisa but from Green, and Ryker felt himself deflate slightly. He wanted to talk to her, feeling increasingly anxious that they'd not spoken since he'd left home. The last thing he wanted was for her to be unnecessarily worried – or even angry – with him. She was already giving him the benefit of the doubt in having allowed him to travel to Spain to reassume a role with the JIA. He wanted to keep her on side. He was about to call her when the phone buzzed again. Green.

'Yeah.'

'Ryker. Are you out?' Green sounded angry. Rushed.

'I'm out.'

'You need to get over here right now.'

'Where?'

'Walker's house. He's been attacked.'

Green ended the call.

With the thoughts of Lisa fading, and feeling a renewed sense of purpose and clarity, Ryker put his foot down as far as it would go.

Four minutes later, he pulled up outside the gates to Casa de las Rosas. The gates were locked shut. Ryker opened his window and pressed the call button on the intercom.

After a few seconds, the left gate slowly swung open. Ryker closed his window and drove through.

The front door to the villa was open when Ryker parked up. Green was standing there, waiting.

'What's happened?' Ryker asked, walking up to the detective.

'He's not hurt. But he's pretty shaken.'

'Where is he?'

'Inside.'

Ryker went to walk into the house but Green pushed his hand out onto Ryker's chest to stop him.

'First how about you tell me what happened yesterday?'

Green's air of superiority riled Ryker. 'I'm sure you've heard the details already.'

'But I want to hear them from you.'

'I don't answer to you.'

'You think? Then who bailed you out?'

'Yeah. Thanks for that. But that doesn't mean I work for you now.'

'You can chalk that one down to professional courtesy,' Green said. 'But I won't be bailing you out again. You understand me?'

'I understand.'

'Already you've head-butted Walker, broken into Kozlov's house, and been arrested for carrying an unlicensed weapon.'

'I didn't break into Kozlov's house.'

'What? That's hardly–'

Ryker barged past Green into the house, then strode through to the sitting room where he and Walker had sat the previous day. Walker was there on one of the sofas, pale, staring down at the floor in front of him.

'What happened?' Ryker asked.

Walker said nothing.

'An intruder got into the house,' Green said coming up behind. 'A couple of hours ago. In broad daylight. Walker was still asleep upstairs at the time.'

'And?'

'Walker woke up with a figure on top of him in the bed.'

'A figure?'

'A man, he thinks. Dressed in black.'

'Did you see his face?' Ryker asked Walker.

'No,' Green said. 'He wore a mask.'

'What kind of mask?'

'Over there.' Green pointed to a sideboard on top of which was a plastic evidence bag. 'I found it outside the front door.'

Ryker moved over to the sideboard and picked up the bag. Inside was a rubber mask in the mould of a giant snake's head, jaws open wide to display oversized fangs and a forked tongue.

'Did he hurt you?' Ryker asked Walker.

'No,' Green said.

'Cut out his tongue perhaps?' Ryker said, unable to hide a cynical smile.

'You think this is funny?' Green said.

'Not at all. I'm just not sure why Walker has lost his voice.'

'Because he's traumatised.'

Ryker didn't bother to argue the pros and cons of that one. He certainly knew how it felt to be traumatised. But he could hardly comprehend why Walker had become a muted idiot all of a sudden.

'No. He didn't hurt me,' Walker confirmed.

'Walker was knocked unconscious,' Green added. 'Chloroform we think. The attacker left a note.'

'He showed it to me before he knocked me out,' Walker said. 'That's why he came. To show me.'

'When Walker woke up, the guy was gone,' Green said.

'How did he get in?' Ryker asked.

'Don't know. The security system wasn't set. Walker doesn't use it when he's home. There's no sign of forced entry.'

'You've had forensics here?'

'They're still upstairs. Found nothing so far – no prints or anything else obvious anyway. Walker said the guy was wearing gloves. The mask will need to be looked at properly but my guess is there'll be nothing to see there either.'

'What about the note?'

'Over here,' Walker said.

Ryker moved forward. He saw a plastic bag on the floor by Walker's feet. Walker's eyes hadn't left that spot since

Ryker had entered the room. Ryker moved over and picked up the bag.

'Please don't take it out,' Green said. 'Not unless you put gloves on first.'

Ryker didn't respond. He didn't need to take the paper out. He could already read the short note just fine. Only five letters were scrawled onto the white paper. Two words: 'I know'. Written by hand in thick red ink. At least Ryker hoped it was ink.

Underneath the writing was a hand-drawn picture, a couple of inches in size. It was crude, but unmistakable. The head of a snake. A red cobra. The drawing was positioned where others would have signed their name.

Green must have noticed the look on Ryker's face.

'You know who left this?' Green asked.

'Yes,' Ryker said. 'And it wasn't a man. It's a woman.'

'And you know what the note means?'

'Yes. I know what it means.'

'Well?' Green asked when Ryker failed to volunteer any more answers.

Ryker looked down at the forlorn figure before him. 'Walker, I think you'd better start praying.'

Chapter 22

Seventeen years earlier

Two more long and pain-filled years passed by at Winter's Retreat. Another two girls joined the small band of workers, both teenagers. Older than Anna in years, though so much younger in maturity and world experience.

Viktoria was still there. Maria had disappeared the previous winter. One day she'd been in the house, everything as normal, the next she'd gone. Viktoria mused that Maria had finally built up the courage to run, that she had long planned to do so and was probably already safely away in a different country.

Anna doubted that. Maria was too weak in mind to have ever tried such a thing. Most likely she was dead, killed by an over-zealous Mkhedrioni or, for once in her life, for trying to fight back. Either way, Anna saw Viktoria's ramblings of heroism as nothing more than a means to help keep up morale among the girls.

But Anna didn't need any false encouragement.

She'd had a single letter from her father in the whole time she'd been at the house. It had arrived three days before her sixteenth birthday. It was post-marked as coming from

Bosnia but Anna wasn't sure she believed he was there. The letter was brief, assuring Anna he was fine and that he would come for her soon. She took comfort in knowing he was alive but felt betrayal at the words he had hastily scrawled. More than anything bitterness was what she'd come to feel when she thought about her father.

On the evening of her sixteenth birthday, Anna was awarded with the now commonplace token treat of a shitty little cake with a shitty little candle. Kankava and the women shared the cake in the kitchen before the Colonel dispatched the other women for their final duties of the day, building up to whatever sordid horrors lay in store that evening.

'The other girls will be busy tonight,' Kankava said to Anna when they were alone. 'We have some special visitors coming. But it's your birthday, you take the night off. You come and see me instead. Eleven p.m. I'll be back in my room by then.'

Kankava got up from his seat and walked out. Anna sat, barely moving, her breaths so slow and shallow that anyone passing might have thought her dead.

For more than three hours, she remained seated in the kitchen, alone. Contemplating. Planning. When the hands on the clock above the kitchen doorway edged towards eleven, Anna's heart thudded with expectation.

Moments later, she heard the faint chimes from the grandfather clock in the main lobby, and she rose and walked casually through the dark and eerily quiet house to Kankava's quarters.

She knocked on the door lightly.

Barely a second later, Kankava – dressed in a red silk robe – pulled open the door. He smiled seductively at Anna, who brushed past him.

Kankava shut the door then moved past Anna.

'Get changed here,' he said, indicating the black ball gown that was spread over a sofa. 'Then come through.'

Kankava left her and Anna threw off her day clothes, underwear too, then squeezed herself into the two-sizes-too-small dress. The routine, one of many, was becoming habitual.

Anna stood and looked at herself in the mirror for a good while then cursed under her breath. She picked up her clothes and rummaged for the two syringes. She grabbed them and stared at them for a few seconds.

When she was ready, Anna held her left hand behind her back as she sauntered over to the bedroom door. She pushed the door open. Kankava lay on top of the bed clothes. His gown was still on but he'd let it slip open exposing his chest and giving a glimpse of his groin that sent a shudder through Anna. But she had her mask on and he would never have suspected.

With a pouting face and provocative prowl that made Kankava murmur with excitement, Anna glided over to the bed. Her hand, still held behind her back, gripped the syringes so tightly that she worried they might shatter.

'Sixteen,' Kankava whispered in delight as Anna crouched by his side. 'Look at you. I must be the luckiest man alive.'

'No. No you're not. Not tonight, baby.'

Anna thrust her hand forward and plunged the nibs of both syringes into Kankava's thigh. He let out a startled gasp. She pressed the plungers down as far as they would go, sending the huge dose of morphine into his bloodstream.

Before he had the chance to struggle, Anna jumped up onto the bed, straddling Kankava. She pinned his arm down with her knee and clasped a hand over his mouth to muffle his shouts and cries. He fought against her for barely thirty seconds before the morphine began working its magic, taking away any remaining strength in Kankava's tired body.

It was a shame she'd had to give such a big dose, she thought. With it he'd be dulled to the pain he was about to experience. But he was at least pliable that way.

Anna jumped off, moving with conviction. She slid the cord out of Kankava's gown and stuffed one end into his mouth to muffle his weary shouts. He clumsily swiped at her as she wound the remaining cord around his head twice before knotting it to secure it in place.

When she was finished, Anna looked down at Kankava and smiled.

'A birthday treat,' she said. 'From me to you.'

She strode over to the fireplace and stood on tiptoe to remove one of the two ceremonial swords displayed there. She pushed her finger onto the blade. It was far from razor sharp. Maybe it had never been used for the purpose it was about to see. But it would surely be good enough.

Anna turned and slid two steps to Kankava. With a fervent smile on her face, she swept the sword forward in a huge arc and brought the weapon down onto Kankava's wrist. The dull blade dug deep into his flesh, but it took three more hits before the arm was severed and Kankava's hand tumbled to the ground. The colonel bucked and wailed as much as he could with the drug crashing through his bloodstream.

'Oh dear,' Anna taunted. 'Looks like you'll be needing even more of my help now. Here let me give you a hand.'

She picked up the severed hand by the fingers and dropped it close to Kankava's face. He cried out pathetically.

'Maybe this is what you want?' Anna said as she sat back down next to Kankava on the bed.

She seductively brushed her hand up the inside of his bare leg, right up to his crotch. She grabbed his scrotum then violently tugged and squeezed with all the strength she could muster. Her face creased over, turning bright red. She felt a pop. Then another. Kankava's eyes rolled. She released his crushed testicles. Blood was gushing from his arm stump. He was fast losing consciousness, she realised, from a mixture of blood loss, pain and the morphine.

'I hope you've enjoyed our time together,' Anna whispered into Kankava's ear. 'I hope you think it was all worth it.'

She wanted to finish this while he was still with it and knew what was happening to him. And before any remaining doubts in her mind – however small they were – took hold.

Anna stood, picked up the sword once more, then without a second's thought, thrust it down onto Kankava's neck. But she got the angle of the blade all wrong. Kankava's eyes bulged, but the sword barely broke the skin. He gasped for breath, and Anna wondered whether the blunt-force blow had crushed his windpipe. She didn't contemplate for long. She slashed the sword down twice more and a spray of blood erupted from the now-gaping wound, some of it splashing onto Anna's arm, causing her to reel in disgust.

Backing further away, she dropped the sword, which clattered to the ground and sent droplets of thick blood spattering across the floor.

Part of Anna looked at Kankava with great wonderment and curiosity. Part of her was disgusted at what she saw. Anna felt a wave of nausea rise up from within. She turned and dashed out of the room.

Anna stripped off the dress, using it to wipe the blood off herself as best she could. She threw back on her work clothes then dashed through the house to her bedroom to collect the meagre belongings she'd be taking with her: a winter coat, a single photograph, a locket that her father had bought for her tenth birthday, and the paltry money she had collected and occasionally stolen from the Mkhedrioni who'd abused her during her years of service at Winter's Retreat.

As Anna descended the stairs from her bedroom, she pushed the growing feeling of disgust at what she'd done to one side. There was no doubt she was shaken, more so than she had imagined, but she needed her mask back for this final task.

She moved through the darkened rooms then came to a stop looking at the man asleep in the bed in front of her. She took two steps forward, reached out, and turned on the bedside lamp which glowed softly. He stirred and opened his eyes. He looked at her with confusion, then with fondness. Then with knowing.

'Anna,' Alex said before taking a few seconds to further compose himself. 'You finally did it, didn't you?'

Anna smiled. 'Yes.'

'Good for you. I always thought you had it in you.'

'You did.'

'What will you do now? Where will you go? I can help you.'

'No. You can't. I only came to say goodbye.'

'I'll miss you around here.'

'No. You won't. You won't be able to.'

Alex looked at her quizzically. Did he already know?

'I liked you, Alex,' Anna said. 'I've enjoyed talking to you. You remind me of my father. I never told you that.'

'I'm flattered. I truly am.'

'But I know the truth,' Anna sneered. 'You're no different to the rest of them. No different to Kankava.'

Alex looked confused. Anna was almost disappointed in his lacklustre response. She'd never really seen the man who was inside him – the warrior, the Vor. She'd only ever seen the cripple who liked to chat to a young teenage girl. In a way, she wished he could fight back, show how strong he really was. At the least, she had expected that when this moment came he would fight back with his tongue. But it appeared he no longer had any fight in him.

'I know what the other girls have to do for you,' Anna continued. 'You may not touch them, you may not rape them, but only because you can't. I see it in you. I know what you are. Goodbye, Alex.'

'No, Anna!'

She reached out and placed her hand firmly over his mouth. He moaned and tried to shout but he was helpless.

As Alex's brain was starved of oxygen and shut down for good, Anna stared into his pleading eyes. What she saw – fear – only proved what she already knew, and saddened her further. Alex wasn't the Vor he claimed to be. Not anymore. He was weak. He was pathetic.

He was nothing.

'Shhh,' Anna whispered. 'Remember what you told me, Alex. Don't ever let them see that you're scared.'

Soon after, Anna removed her hand. Alex was still, his lifeless eyes staring up at her.

Anna got to her feet and silently headed back through the house. She unbolted the main doors, stepped out into the bitter cold night, and walked away from Winter's Retreat, never once looking back at that disgusting place.

Chapter 23

It took Anna over two weeks to track her father to a ramshackle town ten miles north of Bucharest, Romania. Not Bosnia where he had claimed to be. Sixteen-year-old Anna had lied, begged, stolen and killed her way through countries and across borders to get there. Skills that came naturally to her, it seemed.

At first, Anna was surprised at how easily she could manipulate adults more than twice her age. The men in particular would drop to their knees and do whatever she asked at the merest suggestion that they might get a piece of the teenage beauty. Not that she'd ever actually stoop to that level. Not after what had happened to her at Winter's Retreat. Anna was prepared to do almost anything to track her father down, to survive. But not *that.* Her looks were undoubtedly a powerful weapon in her arsenal nonetheless.

After her initial surprise at her apparently inbred skills, had come regret. Because after what had happened at Winter's Retreat, and now that she knew who her father really was, she would never get to live a normal life like all the other girls she'd known at her school back in Georgia. They would go on to get jobs, husbands, have children. But then, had she ever really seen herself as their peer?

Once the regret had subsided, she felt disgust – at herself for what she'd done, and for what she saw as the life that lay ahead.

Finally, after she banished those negative thoughts and emotions from her mind, she'd been left with determination. Anna knew now what she was. And no one on earth could stop the inevitable from happening.

Anna walked down the dirt road, passing various mish-mashed breeze-block messes that barely resembled houses. Large tarpaulins were propped in place here and there adjacent to a number of the homes to create additional covered space for the meagre properties. A heavy rain storm had not long passed and the ground underneath was sodden and soft. Anna cringed with every squelch that her knee-high leather boots made.

Had her father fallen so low that this was a place he would call home?

Back in Georgia, before Winter's Retreat, they'd lived in a penthouse apartment overlooking beautiful manicured gardens. Her father had sent her to Winter's Retreat so he could travel, earn even more money. Doing what he did best – killing people. With his lucrative work they should surely have been moving up in the world.

Yet he'd somehow wound up living in a shit-hole town in the middle of Romania that didn't even appear to have electricity. Anna had never before been to the country, though she knew from the books and newspapers she'd read at Winter's Retreat that, like Georgia, it had a troubled recent past following the fall of communism. Yet the level of poverty she saw as she traipsed along the muddy road was eye-opening.

When she reached the property she was searching for, Anna stopped and looked around her. The area was deserted, no sign of anyone. The dirt road gave way to a haphazard run of broken paving slabs that led up to her father's house. At least the house where she expected to find him.

Anna moved slowly across the blocks, her senses high. She believed the information she'd been given – about her father's whereabouts – to be genuine, but there was no way she could be one hundred percent sure. Not without seeing for herself.

And there was always a chance she was being set up.

In fact, given the troubles she'd gone through in locating him, and the hard time she was having in understanding how her father had ended up in this place, her sense of paranoia was growing by the second.

With each step Anna took, the advice she'd once been given by Alex reverberated in her mind: Don't trust anyone. The ethos was quickly becoming second nature to her. She realised, though, that even if her father really was living in this downtrodden place, he also lived and breathed by that ethos.

And her father, the deadly assassin, certainly wouldn't be one to welcome unexpected guests to his home.

Anna placed her foot down onto a slab. The edge of it gave way, sinking into the uneven ground. The back of the slab lifted, just an inch, sending a small pebble scuttling across the stony surface. The noise wasn't much louder than a whisper but Anna's brain was whirring.

Feeling her heart quicken, Anna slowed her pace further, eyes darting back and forth as she scoured her surroundings for any signs of traps or tripwires or other pitfalls. She took two more steps before she stopped moving again. By that point, her heart was thudding almost uncontrollably as adrenaline coursed through her, and her breathing was heavy and fast.

She daren't risk another step. She simply didn't know what she might be walking into if she were to surprise the deadly Silent Blade.

There was only one option left.

'Pappa!' Anna shouted. 'It's me.'

She waited. Nothing.

'Pappa!'

A few more seconds of silence. Anna spotted movement. She turned her head slightly and saw an elderly man on the street, walking along hand-in-hand with a small boy. The man stared at her intently – suspiciously – for a few seconds as he carried on his way.

Then the front door of the rickety house creaked open, just a few inches. Anna whipped her head back round. She could see nothing but blackness inside the house but she moved forward again, senses still primed.

'Pappa?'

Anna was two steps from the open front door when movement off to her right – much closer this time – caught her attention. She stepped sideways to her left, her stare fixed in the direction the movement had come from.

Nothing there.

A second later, she was grabbed from behind. An arm wrapped around her chest, pinning her arms to her sides. She felt cold metal against the skin on her neck. She was bundled forward in through the open front doorway. She heard the door slam shut behind her.

The attacker released her, shoved her forward, further into the darkness. Anna spun and looked at the black space ahead. Nothing. Where the hell was he? She started to panic. Her body, her head jerked in all directions. She was about to bolt towards the door when...

'Anna?' came a man's voice.

Anna stopped. She held her breath as she stared into the darkness, where she was sure the voice had come from.

A few seconds passed. She saw nothing. Heard nothing.

'Anna, it really is you.' His voice came from the other side of the room.

Then out of the shadows a figure emerged. A figure she'd longed to see. Her father. Vlad Abayev.

The Silent Blade assassin.

Chapter 24

Anna sat in an armchair in the sparse living area that was crammed with worn furniture and lit by a single overhead bulb. Vlad came back into the room from the tiny kitchen carrying two mugs of steaming coffee.

Despite the surroundings, Anna felt a sense of ease and relaxation that she hadn't known for too long. It had been nearly three years since Anna had last seen her father. Time hadn't been kind to him; he looked fifteen years older. The picture in her head was of a man in his prime. Handsome, full of strength and life. Now he looked... damaged. Weak and old. He was still handsome, but his eyes were darker and tense, his forehead was creased, his hair was scruffy, and he had thick stubble with messy splashes of grey.

How much of the look was real and how much of it was a persona he'd adopted for his job, Anna couldn't be sure. She hoped it was the latter. The thought that her father, the person she'd looked up to most in the world, had fallen so far in such a short time was hard to take.

Vlad set the cups down on a wobbly coffee table, and Anna got to her feet. She flung herself at her father, taking him by surprise as she wrapped her arms around him then sunk her head into his chest. He reciprocated, hugging his daughter tightly.

The feel of him, his distinctive smell that Anna wouldn't even know where to start describing, fired so many pleasant memories in her mind. Anna had grown at least two inches in the years she'd been at Winter's Retreat but she still fitted snuggly into her father's chest. She would have stayed in the warm embrace for much longer, but Vlad took his arms away, stepped back, and gazed down at his daughter.

'You look... beautiful.'

Anna felt her cheeks blush.

'I can't believe it's really you. You're so grown up.' He reached out and brushed a lock of hair away from her face.

'It's really me.' Anna smiled.

Vlad reached out toward Anna's neck. She didn't flinch. He gently took hold of the locket that was dangling there.

'You still have it,' he said, glowing.

'Of course.'

She took the locket from his hand and looked down as she opened it up to reveal two pictures, tiny head shots. One was of Vlad as a young man in his twenties, the other of Anna as a nine-year-old girl. Vlad stared at the pictures then turned and with a pained face sat in an armchair. Anna closed the locket and took a seat in the chair opposite.

'What's wrong?'

'Nothing,' Vlad said. 'I've not been well. But I'm getting better.'

An injury or illness? Anna wondered. She decided against asking.

'How long have you been here?' Anna asked, unable to hide her dissatisfaction as she looked around the decaying room.

'Just a couple of months.'

Anna's eyes moved from her father over to the mess on a set of drawers in the corner of the room. An ashtray, overflowing with cigarette butts, was surrounded by at least a dozen bottles of spirits, most of them empty or not far from it.

'It's not me, Anna,' Vlad said. 'This isn't me.'

Anna said nothing for a few moments. 'Then why are you here? Why is it like this?'

'It's hard to talk about it.'

'A job?'

'Not exactly.'

'You're hiding?'

'Hiding. Running. Surviving.'

Anna humphed at his words. 'So what is that?' she asked, looking over at the empty bottles again.

'It's who I need to be right now.'

'You sure about that?'

'Yes. I'm still the same man I always was. The same man you knew.'

'But I never did know the real you, did I,' Anna said, her words tinged with bitterness.

'Of course you did, Anna. You knew the man I wanted to be. The man I had to be for you.'

'I'm not sure that's the same thing.'

Anna leaned forward and picked up her coffee from the table. She pulled the mug toward her face. The vapour from the liquid caught her nose. It smelled stale and bitter. She took a sip. It tasted even worse.

'Hard to find good coffee around here,' Vlad said, smiling – in embarrassment, Anna sensed.

'Hard to get good anything around here, I'm guessing.'

'The Tuica isn't too bad.' Her father looked over at the spirit bottles.

Anna didn't respond to the quip. Her mind was too occupied with her next question. 'Why did you leave me in that place?'

Her blunt words caught her father off guard and he stared at Anna for a good while before answering.

'I had no choice,' he said. 'It was becoming too dangerous for you. For me too.'

'You think that place was safe for a teenage girl.'

'Safe? You're still alive, aren't you?'

Anna said nothing in response, and the same old question reverberated in her mind: Did he know?

It was the only question she wanted to ask. Yet she knew she never could. Because she wasn't sure she wanted to know the answer. 'Were you ever coming back for me?'

'Yes. I said I would.'

'But you didn't.'

'I said I'd come for you as soon as I could. As soon as it was safe. It never was.'

'So you would leave me there forever? Never once wondering what had happened to me?'

'I'm sorry. It was the only way I could see. But don't ever believe I didn't think of you. I thought about you every day. You're one of the few things that has kept me going.'

They both took a break from the increasingly awkward conversation. Anna tried again to drink her mug of coffee, hoping that, despite the taste, at least the warm liquid would soothe her. She took a small sip but it made her gag and she set the nearly full cup back down for good.

'Is that milk off?' Anna asked.

'There isn't any milk in it. Hard to get good fresh milk around here.'

'Then why is it that colour?'

Her father shrugged. 'Best not to think about it.' The look on his face hardened. 'How did you find me?'

'It wasn't that difficult.'

Vlad smiled again. 'You're a lot more like me than you realise.'

Anna agreed with that. Though she wasn't sure it was a good thing. 'There was a man in Winter's Retreat. Alex Meskhi.'

Vlad pursed his lips and shook his head, his way of showing the name meant nothing to him.

'He was a Vor.' Anna saw the twinkle in her father's eye.

'Never trust a Vor, my dear Anna.'

'That's not far off what he said.'

'He knew me? This Alex?'

'No. Not really. But he gave me the name of someone he said could help me find you.'

'Who?' Vlad asked, eyebrow raised.

'Levan Chichua.'

The look on her father's face changed to one of anger.

'Chichua,' he said, practically spitting the name.

'He's looking for you too, apparently.'

'He has been for years. Like I said, you shouldn't trust the Vory. So Alex Meskhi was trying to set me up?'

'Maybe. Or maybe he really did think Chichua could help find you.'

'And did he?'

'I'm here aren't I?'

'You are. And they're not.'

'That's because they're both dead,' Anna said, calmly.

Her father stared at her coldly and she saw a look in his eyes that she'd not seen before. It was the look of a dangerous man. A man to be feared. A killer. Silent Blade.

Anna smiled and got to her feet. 'Come here. Take a look at this.'

Anna once again saw the man she knew – her father. It was as though there were two different people inside him and it took a split second for one to overcome the other.

But which man was real? Which persona was in control of the other?

Anna took the photo from her jeans pocket and held it out. Vlad came over and put an arm around her shoulder as he stared down at the picture. He beamed.

'Do you remember?' Anna asked.

'Yes.' He took the photo from her hand and brought it closer to his face.

'It was my eleventh birthday. I don't remember it ever snowing on my birthday before.'

'No. Me neither.'

'We had fun that day.'

'Yes. We did.'

'I've always loved that picture.'

'I didn't know you had it.'

'It's the only picture I have of us together'

'I don't have any,' Vlad said, his smile vanishing.

'That picture has kept me going for so long.' Anna looked up and stared into her father's eyes, feeling her own eyes welling up. He gazed back, and she could see the love and devotion that he was feeling. 'But that man,' Anna said. 'He's not you. Not really. Not anymore.'

Before Vlad could say another word, Anna whipped her hand behind her. She unsheathed the small hunting blade that was strapped to her lower back. She thrust the knife forward and plunged it into her father's side. Four inches of metal sliced through skin and flesh, and penetrated his right kidney, severing the renal artery at the same time.

The simple blow was a fatal one. Anna knew that for sure. She'd placed the blade there with precision and knowing. Vlad would bleed out within a minute, two at most. But she wasn't finished.

She withdrew the knife. Her father stepped back. His eyes were wide open in shock, his skin white. Anna cried out as she thrust the knife forward again, into her father's stomach. He let out a painful gasp. Anna pulled the knife away, and he sunk to his knees.

Vlad held one hand over the gushing wound on his belly. A large patch of red spread across his shirt. With his other hand he reached up to Anna.

Tears rolling down her cheek, she grabbed his hand. Held it. Felt the strength in his grip weakening by the second.

As he faded away, the pool of thick red blood beneath his body growing outwards exponentially, Vlad's gaze never once left his daughter's.

'I'm so sorry,' he said.

Anna felt her bottom lip quivering, and fought to keep her composure. She had to stay strong. But soon there was nothing she could do to stop herself sobbing uncontrollably.

'I'm so proud,' her father spluttered, blood pouring from his mouth. He managed what Anna took to be a smile. 'You really are my daughter.'

They were his final words. Anna let go of his hand. It flopped down. His head slumped forward.

After that Anna's father – Vlad Abayev, the legendary Silent Blade assassin – was no more.

Chapter 25

Present day

'And you're telling me that this Anna Abayev is the person who left the note?' Green asked.

'Yes, I think so,' Ryker said.

The two men were sitting at a polished stone dining table on one of two patios at the back of Casa de las Rosas. Walker was inside with his lawyer, Graham Munroe, who'd arrived a half hour earlier. Munroe was claiming Walker was too traumatised to be interviewed by Ryker. There was only so long Ryker would go along with the silly legal shenanigans. Green might have been happy to sit around and play by the book but that had never been Ryker.

'After killing her father, Anna went on to become one of the most infamous assassins of a generation. The Red Cobra.'

Green scoffed at Ryker's words. Ryker flicked him a glare. There was nothing humorous or flippant about what he'd said.

'It all sounds a bit, you know...'

'What?'

'Hocus-pocus. Assassins. Silly names.'

'It's real. As real as it gets.'

'If this kind of thing – paid assassins – even exists then why the daft name? I mean, wouldn't the whole point be that she was so good no one ever knew which murders she was even responsible for.'

'To a large extent, you're right. She was brilliant at what she did. Her crime scenes were among the most meticulous I've ever seen. For most of the killings she's been linked to there was zero trace evidence. But the intelligence services are so called for a very good reason: they gather intelligence, through whatever means they can.'

'Like through coercion and extraordinary rendition to black sites? Yes, I'm familiar with some of the concepts. I watch the news.'

Familiar with the concepts? Clearly Ryker was a bit more intimate with the lengths the intelligence services would go to in order to gain information than Green, but he held his tongue.

'Like that, yes,' Ryker said. 'But a reputation like the Red Cobra's can't be built solely through squeaky-clean assassinations and dubious accidents. She's a freelancer. People, the kind of people who would need her services, need to know of her work. She has to have some identity.'

'So where did the name come from?'

'I don't know when it started. The red cobra is a type of spitting cobra, and she's been known to use pepper spray to incapacitate her victims. Plus she supposedly wears bright-red lipstick. But I say that's bullshit – embellishment. A large part of the power of her identity as the Red Cobra is that she's a beautiful woman – hardly common in her line of work. I guess linking the name to a feature of her looks is a natural end result.'

'So the calling card – the note she left for Walker – is that her usual MO?'

'Not usual, no. But not unusual either. Think of it like this; when one ruthless gang or mafia family are waging war against another, they want their enemy to know they've been hit. Using a shadowy figure like the Red Cobra to attack your enemies adds power to the acts she carries out. It creates fear.'

'How do you know all this anyway?' Green asked, still sounding sceptical.

Ryker didn't answer the question, just stared at Green until the older man finally seemed to get it.

'Fine. So say I do buy the story. What has this Red Cobra, a deadly assassin according to you, got to do with Kim Walker's murder? And Patrick Walker?'

'It was thought that Kim Walker was Anna Abayev,' Ryker said. 'Kim's fingerprints matched those of a profile that MI6 hold on the Red Cobra.'

'That's who you really work for? MI6?' Green said, and his eyes lit up as though it was a moment of great excitement for him.

'No,' Ryker said. 'I don't.'

Green frowned. 'What exactly are you saying then?'

'I don't know who Kim was, who she *really* was, I mean. Or how her fingerprints wound up on that file. But she certainly wasn't the Red Cobra.'

'How can you be so sure?'

'Because I knew Anna. The Red Cobra. She's not Kim.'

'She could have had plastic surgery, changed her face.'

'Could have. But I don't think so. The Red Cobra is still out there.'

'The note? You think the note is legitimate then? That it's really from her and not someone playing games?'

'I can't be a hundred percent sure, but I'd be a fool not to take it seriously. And if she wants Walker dead, then whatever the reason, he's in big trouble.'

Green went silent, and Ryker could practically see the cogs slowly turning in the detective's mind.

'Who *are* you?' Green asked, sounding somewhat in awe, but also slightly angry.

'I'm James Ryker.'

'I knew there was something fishy about you. Coming here like you did. No one had ever heard of you. I checked you out. Got some colleagues to do the same. Yeah we found your history – jobs, school, blah blah blah. But so what? A thirteen-year-old computer whizz could build a profile like that in minutes.'

'If you say so.'

'I knew there was more to you than that. Why would the Home Office have sent some private eye out here when we have the best investigators already working for the Met?'

Ryker shrugged. 'You *think* you're the best. But only because you don't see everything that's really happening. Closet mentality.'

Green clearly took offence at Ryker's words. 'I've seen and done my fair share.'

'I'm sure you have. But the Red Cobra is another level.'

'If *you* say so. Yeah I'm sure you've seen some crazy shit. Whoever you really work for maybe you've killed far more people than me in your time. You know why? Because I've never killed a single person. But so what? It's not something to brag about. I'm guessing you're not used to carrying out murder investigations, to dealing with witnesses and victims, and analysing the most incomprehensible bits of evidence to find the tiniest of clues that lead you to the crooks.'

'No. And I never said any different. I'm not sure what your point is.'

'My point is don't take me for a fool, Ryker. I may not know what it's like to be a government sponsored assassin or whatever it is you think you used to be, but if you want to get to the bottom of Kim Walker's murder, I can help you.'

'And I wouldn't have told you what I did about the Red Cobra otherwise. But I'm telling you this in confidence. What you now know–'

'What? If I tell anyone, you'll slit my throat while I sleep?'

Ryker smiled. Green didn't. 'Let's say it's in all of our interests that you keep quiet.'

'We need to get Walker into protective custody.'

'Why?'

'Why? Because from what you've told me there's a legitimate threat against his life.'

'Maybe he's got it coming. I'm increasingly getting the feeling that Walker isn't the vanilla businessman everyone thinks he is.'

'Maybe not,' Green said. 'But in the real world the police are there to protect people. We're not killers no matter how much some of the scumbags we deal with deserve it.'

'So you do think Walker is a scumbag?'

'Actually not. I think he's a grieving husband who's got himself into a hell of a mess.'

Damn right, Ryker thought. Though he didn't bother to probe Green on exactly what kind of mess he was talking about. Ryker already had his own thoughts on that. 'You can try to protect Walker. Do whatever you want. But I'd put money on the Red Cobra still finding him if she wants to.'

'But *why* does she want to?'

'And that's the question. Whatever Walker got himself caught up in, it got his wife killed. And pretty soon it's going to get him killed too.'

'And what do you think he got himself caught up in exactly?'

'You tell me.'

'I have no idea,' Green said. And Ryker sensed that Green fully believed his words. But then some people are great actors, Ryker knew. 'You think the Red Cobra killed Kim?' Green asked.

Ryker thought about the question before answering. 'No. But I think her death and the Red Cobra's presence are connected. Particularly given the link to Kim Walker and Anna Abayev's profile.'

'Then what do you suggest we do now?'

'Go and speak to Walker.'

'Munroe isn't going to let you do that. The only way we'll get the chance is if we have Walker arrested. But we have nothing to arrest him for. And no jurisdiction out here anyway.'

'Cardo has jurisdiction.'

'Cardo isn't here.'

'How about withholding evidence in a murder investigation?' Ryker said. 'Surely that's a crime?'

'I mean, it is and it isn't. I'm no lawyer, but no one is compelled to testify against themselves. Innocent until proven guilty. Right to silence, and all that?'

Ryker turned and looked up at the mansion behind him. He spotted Walker through the windows of the sitting room. He was sat on his own, his face sullen, still staring down at his feet. Walker looked a sorry state. Ryker had interrogated some hard nuts in his time but Walker wasn't one of them. Getting what he needed from him would be simple. If only he was given the chance.

Ryker got up from the table.

'Ryker?' Green said, sounding suspicious.

'I guess we'll have to do this the old fashioned way.'

Chapter 26

Ryker strode back into the house, Green scuttling behind him. Graham Munroe was in the hallway, talking on his mobile phone. Munroe was slick and slimy, and oozed superiority, and Ryker hated everything about him.

Ryker bounded up to the closed double-doors that led to the sitting room where Walker was still sulking. Munroe must have seen the look of determination on Ryker's face. He suddenly burst into action and darted over to intersect Ryker.

'What are you doing?' Munroe asked, barging in front of Ryker.

Ryker ignored him and brushed past. He grabbed the door handle. Munroe grabbed his arm. Ryker spun round and the look in his eyes sent Munroe squirming back two steps.

'You have no right,' Munroe said, his voice wavering as he tried to regain his composure.

But Munroe could do nothing physically to stop Ryker, and all three men in the hall knew it. Ryker was about to turn to head into the living room when there was a buzz on the intercom by the front door. He, Green and Munroe each turned their attention to the small box on the wall. Ryker and Green didn't move as Munroe back-stepped away from Ryker. He pressed the button on the intercom and looked at the small screen as he listened to the crackled response.

'It's the police,' Munroe said.

Ryker rolled his eyes. That was all he needed.

Not a minute later, two uniformed officers from the Policia National walked in through the front doorway. Ryker's attention was drawn to the holstered guns around their waists. He still wasn't armed but was increasingly coming to the conclusion that he needed to change that.

Munroe spoke to the policemen briefly while Green and Ryker looked on with intent. The conversation was in Spanish, but they were speaking so quietly, Ryker could make out few of the words.

When they'd finished the chat Munroe and the two officers looked over at Green, then at Ryker. Ryker couldn't be sure what Munroe had said to the two men about him but they certainly looked wary.

'Inspector Cardo has sent these officers to protect my client,' Munroe said. 'He'll have a twenty-four-hour watch until we know what is happening here.'

'Good for him,' Ryker said.

They weren't leaving him many options. He moved forward toward the officers. They looked at him quizzically, then at each other questioningly, as though unsure what was about to unfold. Munroe side-stepped away, obviously expecting some sort of ruckus.

'Where are you going?' asked Green, the only man in the hall who'd understood Ryker's innocent intention.

The two officers eventually got it too and moved out of the way to allow Ryker past and to the front door.

'We're not exactly making much progress standing around here,' Ryker said, stopping in the doorway and looking over at Munroe. 'Not while your client has his heart set on withholding evidence.'

'I'm not so sure you want to be making accusations like that, Mr Ryker.' Munroe said.

Ryker glared at Munroe; the look was enough to make the lawyer back down. Ryker turned and carried on out. He had his phone to his ear as he moved toward his car. The call connected after a few seconds and was answered on the third ring.

'Ryker,' Winter said. 'I was thinking about you actually.'

'Oh, Winter, I know you've always been fond of me...'

'Very funny. I heard about your little escapade to the local nick. Old habits die hard with you, it seems.'

Winter's tone was forthright and Ryker got the impression the commander was trying to exert his authority, something at which his old boss, Mackie, had been an expert. But Winter just didn't have the same gravitas, and Ryker certainly wasn't about to start bowing down to Winter's seniority now.

'I presume my thanks need to go to you for helping to get me out.' Ryker sat in the driver's seat of his Ford, fired up the engine, then headed past the policemen's car and toward the exit.

'Actually, that lawyer of Walker's did a pretty good job on his own,' Winter said, 'but yeah, we gave it a little push from this side too.'

Ryker was a little surprised by Winter's words. Had he misjudged Munroe? But then if Munroe really wanted to help, all he had to do was give Ryker access to Walker.

'The Red Cobra is here,' Ryker said.

For a few moments, Winter said nothing. Ryker could hear the JIA Commander's steady breathing coming down the line so he knew the call was still running.

Ryker turned right, back onto the main road that headed down to the coast. The car was stifling from having been sat in the sun all day, and Ryker pushed the air-con as cold as it would go and the power right up. The dashboard vibrated from the force.

'You think the Red Cobra killed Kim Walker?' Winter said.

'No. Not at all. But I think she *will* kill Patrick Walker. Unless I can stop her.'

'Why would she want to do that?'

'I'm still trying to figure that out,' Ryker said as he gazed into the distance at the tranquil Mediterranean. Such a picturesque setting. But what dirty secrets lay hidden? 'I still know nothing about Kim Walker. About who she really was.'

'No. And neither do we.'

'What do you know about Andrei Kozlov?'

'I'll be honest with you, Ryker. I know hardly anything about this investigation. That's what *you're* there for. So you tell me.'

'Kozlov is a Russian developer. Walker's partner. I get the sense Kozlov's not what he seems.'

'How so?'

'For starters, five minutes after leaving his house yesterday I was attacked by two goons.'

'Yeah, and apparently the policeman who brought you in knew nothing about those two.'

'And what does that tell you?'

'That you may be opening a can of worms out there. That you need to be careful and watch your back.'

'You'd be amazed at how many people have said that to me recently. But you're right. This place isn't what it seems.'

'You mean it's not all sun, sex, and sangria?'

'No, I'm sure there's plenty of that. But you can probably add in scandal, scumbags and sanctimonious pricks to the mix too.'

Winter laughed. 'I can look into Kozlov and let you know what we find.'

'Thanks,' Ryker said. 'I need a gun.'

Ryker's blunt statement was met with silence on the other end.

'Can you do that for me?' Ryker added.

He knew the JIA would have assets in the area who could provide a weapon. That was the way his job had always worked. Virtually no one, even those in positions of power, knew of the JIA's existence, and Ryker's role as a black ops agent for the JIA had come with zero official acknowledgment. He couldn't carry guns through airports or across borders like some law enforcement agents were able to. He'd always been supplied with firearms on the ground, in-country, through officially unofficial sources.

Winter would be able to organise for Ryker to be armed without any problem. So his silence wasn't because he couldn't.

Winter let out a long sigh.

'There's more going on out here than I think you realise,' Ryker said. 'And the Red Cobra is here. I know it: I need a gun. And if you won't get it for me, I'll find another way.'

'Okay, okay. I'll find a source.'

Ryker smiled, pleased that Winter had come to the same conclusion he had: that it was preferable for the JIA to supply a weapon than for Ryker to bring further heat on himself by stealing one or finding one directly on the black market, which he'd been well prepared to do.

'It'll take a few hours but I'll arrange a drop for you.'

'Thanks.'

'Anything else?'

'What about the leak?'

'The cyber attack you mean?'

'Yeah. Have you found anything else?'

'We're getting there.' Winter sounded less than satisfied. 'Whoever carried it out really knows what they're doing. The way they've covered their tracks is as complex as we've seen. But in time we'll crack it, I'm sure. If I find out anything, you'll be the first to know.'

'Same,' Ryker said.

'And if you see the Red Cobra, you kill her on sight. You get that? We can't risk her escaping again. Not after what happened last time.'

Ryker said nothing, just squeezed his hands around the steering wheel. His mind took him back to the last time he'd seen her. Up on that cliff top when she'd had a gun pointed to his head. She could have killed him. She'd hesitated. Her hesitation had saved his life, and nearly cost the Red Cobra hers.

'Ryker? You still there?'

'Yes.'

'Have I made myself clear?' Winter said, once again wielding the position of command. 'You see her, you kill her. Don't even think about it.'

'Understood,' Ryker said.

And it was true, he understood the instruction just fine.

Whether he would actually follow it, he really couldn't be sure.

Chapter 27

Moments after putting the phone down, it buzzed again. Ryker looked at the screen. It was Lisa. For a fleeting moment, he debated whether or not to answer. As much as he missed her and wanted to talk to her, his mind was becoming consumed with the investigation at hand. That was his nature. His work for the JIA hadn't just been a job, it had been his *life* – something he lived and breathed twenty-four hours a day. And he could feel himself being drawn back into that mind-set, that way of living.

But as comfortable and normal as that felt for Ryker on many levels, he knew he had to resist going back to being like that. What was right was that he and Lisa stick together and be there for each other no matter what. He was all Lisa had in the world. She had no job, no friends, no family. Ryker on the other hand *did* have something else in his life. He had an ally in Peter Winter. And because of that, Ryker had a job. Maybe not the same job he used to have, but the JIA still needed him and apparently had no qualms about using Ryker for their shadowy operations. Winter had come knocking and Ryker had agreed to his request for help. Ryker couldn't let that decision drive a wedge between him and Lisa.

He answered the phone. 'Hi.'

'Hey.'

In an instant, Ryker felt more relaxed at the familiar sound of her voice. 'What time is it there?'

'Early. Are you okay?'

'Yeah. I'm fine. Sorry, we should have spoken sooner. I tried calling.'

'I was worried about you.'

'No need to worry. Are you okay?'

'Yeah.'

'You been for a swim?'

'Not today. Not yet.'

There was a moment of silence, and Ryker felt awkwardness seeping back in. Was she being deliberately cagey with him or was he imagining it?

'Have you found her yet?' she asked.

'No. Not yet.'

'How long will it take?'

'I don't know. Days. Maybe longer.'

'I miss you. I miss you so much.'

'Yeah. I miss you too... I'll be back soon.'

'Not soon enough.'

Another silence followed. He could hear her slow and steady breathing, He wanted to tell her more, about what he was doing, where he was going, but he knew he couldn't. And he really didn't know what else to say to her. What did they even have to talk about? Their lives out on the run were quite unremarkable.

'I've got to go,' he said. 'I'm just about to arrive somewhere. I'll call you again later, yeah? We can talk properly then.'

'Of course.' She sounded dejected. 'Speak later.'

'I love you.'

'Love you too.'

Ryker ended the call and put his phone down on his lap, feeling agitated – with himself more than anything – by the stilted conversation. How could talking to the woman he loved make him feel so uncomfortable?

As Ryker neared Marbella, he did his best to push the thoughts of tension in his home life to the back of his mind. He passed by the construction site where the day before he'd been knocked unconscious by a bent policeman. And what of the two heavies who'd been sent after him? They'd vanished it seemed.

Moments later, Ryker pulled up outside the tall metal gates of the complex where Eva Kozlov lived with her father. Ryker was hoping Andrei wasn't home. If he was, Ryker was certain he'd not get very far. Kozlov, like Walker, would hide behind his well-paid lawyer as long as he was able to. Eva on the other hand... she was hardly going to betray her father just like that, but Ryker knew she liked to play games. She had to be his best bet for getting the investigation moving.

A solitary uniformed guard sat in the wood-panelled security hut outside the gates. He came out to greet Ryker with a look of mistrust on his face. Maybe he was like that with everyone. Or maybe he was like that only with people who drove cars worth less than a hundred thousand euros.

'I'm here to see Eva Kozlov,' Ryker said to the guard in English. It was an assumption that the security detail on an estate where there likely wasn't a Spanish-born resident would have at least passable English. Ryker's assumption was confirmed when the guard spoke.

'And you are?'

'James Ryker.'

'Okay, but what is your business here?'

'I'm working with the Policia National.'

That seemed to knock the guard back a step, though the cynical look remained. 'ID?'

Ryker reached into his jeans pocket for his passport. He showed it to the guard who looked at it sceptically.

'I didn't say I was a policeman,' Ryker said, guessing that the guard was wondering why he was showing a basic passport rather than an official ID card. 'Just that I'm working with them.'

'Okay. Let me call through and see if there's anyone home.'

The guard wandered back to his box-hut, sat on his swivel chair, and picked up a phone. Ryker could see the man's lips moving as he spoke to someone on the other end but could hear none of the words.

Less than a minute later, the guard was back at Ryker's window.

'She's home,' the guard said, his voice stern. 'And says you can come in.'

Ryker held back a wry smile. It looked like he'd been right about Eva.

'Third house on the left,' the guard said.

He went back to his hut and seconds later, the double metal gates silently swung open.

Ryker drove through, feeling as though he were entering another world. Everything about the estate screamed wealth. The perfectly trimmed grass verges. The spotless tarmac and pavements, with not even a hint of scuffs or scratches or chips. Trees and flowers that didn't seem to have a leaf or a twig or a petal out of place. It was like a fantasy. And then there were the houses. And the cars. The whole estate and what it stood for seemed so far detached from the reality of life that lay beyond the gated walls.

Ryker saw no one other than the occasional uniformed worker tending the estate as he drove along the road to the Kozlov's residence. He parked his car next to two shining SUVs in the driveway then got out and headed to the front entrance complete with Romanesque pillars.

Ryker knocked loudly on the thick door and it was opened a few seconds later by an unfamiliar man. He was a similar age to Ryker. Not as tall, not as wide – physically he didn't look much. But he had a hard face with a scar that ran across his left cheek up to and over his eye, and a steely glint in his stare that told Ryker he wasn't someone to mess with. Ryker knew the type. He'd seen it before: every time he looked in a mirror.

This guy was dangerous.

The man said nothing. He stepped aside so Ryker could get past and waved his arm to indicate for Ryker to carry on through. Ryker cautiously walked into the house, and continued down the hallway and into the marbled kitchen. He glanced behind him every couple of steps to see the man slowly following, his hard gaze fixed on Ryker, his hands hanging by his sides, at the ready. The man nodded, indicating for Ryker to keep going, and he continued through to the open back doors then stepped out into the garden.

Ryker spotted Eva immediately, sitting in a lounger next to the pool. She wore nothing but a skimpy bikini that left little to the imagination and a pair of tinted sunglasses that covered much of her face, and was holding an iced drink in one hand. She smiled when she saw Ryker and got to her feet.

'Hello, James,' she purred.

'Eva,' Ryker said, sounding as cool as he felt.

He had to admit, Eva looked stunning, with her toned body and sun-drenched skin. But Ryker was not about to be side-tracked by a beautiful woman, particularly one he mistrusted. He wasn't sure Eva quite realised that yet. In the meantime, Ryker was happy to play along and let her think she had the power. It may yet work in his favour.

Ryker moved toward her. He looked behind and saw the man stood at the back door with his arms folded across his chest. He was staring at Ryker.

'You've met Sergei.' Eva looked over Ryker's shoulder.

'Yeah. You're a bit old for a babysitter, aren't you?'

Eva laughed. 'I love the bravado. He may not look much, but he's no pushover.'

'Why's he here? Daddy getting paranoid?'

'Daddy's always paranoid.'

'About what?'

'Why don't you ask him?'

'Because I want a truthful answer.'

'You don't like him, do you?'

'Your dad?'

'Yeah.'

'I'm not sure it matters either way.'

'To you, maybe not.' Eva stooped her head down and lifted her glasses to reveal her eyes. 'I'm up here, James.'

'Why don't you put on some clothes. Then we can talk.'

'I'm sorry that me looking like this is such a distraction for you.' Eva finished her drink, sucking at the straw until it slurped in the bottom of the glass. She fixed her sultry gaze squarely on Ryker. 'You thirsty?'

'What you drinking?'

'Lemonade. But I'm feeling it's about time for something stronger.'

Ryker looked at his watch. Nearly five p.m. 'Why not.'

'But not here,' Eva said, moving back over to the lounger. She quickly dressed in a short denim skirt that showed off every inch of her toned legs and a strappy-top that did little to cover her ample cleavage.

'Won't your babysitter mind?'

'I'm not a prisoner here.'

'Of course you're not,' Ryker scoffed. Prison? He would certainly trade some of the cells he'd been holed up in for being cooped up in the Kozlov's mansion.

'But he is coming with us.' Eva walked past Ryker and up to Sergei who didn't move as Eva reached out and playfully squeezed his cheek, smirking as she did so.

Ryker smiled. Sergei simply stared through him.

'Come on boys,' Eva called. 'Let's get out of here.'

Chapter 28

Sergei the henchman drove. Eva and Ryker sat in the back of the luxury SUV, where everything was so shiny and clean it looked like it had never been used. Every few minutes, Sergei would glare into the rear-view mirror, his suspicious eyes on Ryker.

'Does he ever talk?' Ryker asked Eva as he glared back at Sergei.

'Of course he does.'

'Does he speak English?'

'Not a word.'

'Really?'

'Really.' Eva leaned forward in her seat and tapped Sergei on the shoulder. 'Hey, do you speak any English, you stupid ugly monkey?' Sergei said nothing. No reaction on his face. 'Would you like to see my knickers?' Eva said. 'White cotton. Like your little sister. Your favourite. Perhaps you'd like to take them off with your teeth.'

Not a twitch from Sergei.

'Okay, I think you've proved your point,' Ryker said. Either that or Sergei was one cool character. Actually no, Ryker was sure Sergei was a cool character regardless.

'He's quite playful really,' Eva said. 'If you get him in the right mood.'

'I'm sure he is.'

'I like you, James,' she said, giving him a beaming smile.

'Thanks.'

'You're not married.'

'What makes you say that?'

'No ring.'

'Ah. No, I'm not married.'

'But there is a special someone?'

'Yes. There is,' Ryker said, feeling slightly awkward.

'She's a lucky lady.'

'You could say that.'

'What's her name?'

'Where are we going?' Ryker said, looking out of the window and seeing the familiar road that led up to Mijas village.

'For a drink.'

'Long way to come for a drink.'

'I like it up here.'

'Me too. Just didn't think it would be your... style.'

'What's that supposed to mean?'

'It wasn't an insult. Just this place, the village, doesn't seem very trendy for–'

'A rich man's daughter? What, you thought I'd take you over to Puerto Banus so we could ogle at the billionaires' yachts and sip cocktails while watching Ferraris and Lamborghinis crawl by.'

Ryker shrugged. Actually she was spot on with her deduction.

'I'm not materialistic like that.'

'No. You just sunbathe at your mansion all day and have your chauffeur drive you out for half an hour when you fancy a drink.'

Ryker smiled. He was playing with her, not trying to rile her. But he thought he saw a little hurt in her eyes.

'It's not all fun and games, you know, being brought up with all the money in the world.'

'I'm sure it's a real hardship.'

'Don't be such an arsehole,' she said, more on edge. 'I didn't choose to be born into money. And it doesn't define who I am.'

'Okay, I'm sorry. I wasn't trying to upset you. I like it up here. The village is nice. Picturesque. It's a good choice. I thought someone your age would go somewhere more hip.'

'Oh, so now it's my age that's a problem? You think I'm a dumb kid who goes out binge drinking and eating kebabs at two a.m.?'

Ryker laughed. The twinkle in her eye told him Eva was playing him a little. 'Sounds like a decent night out to me.'

'Sorry to disappoint but I thought we'd go for something a bit more laid back.'

'I can do laid back.'

Moments later, Sergei pulled the car over to the side of a narrow road that ran through the village.

'We're here,' Eva said. 'Let's go.'

Ryker and Eva got out of the car. The stench of piss caught Ryker's nose as a diminutive man led a drove of donkeys along the cobbled street. Eva saw Ryker's face.

'For the tourists,' she said, shrugging. 'A donkey ride through a traditional Andalusian white-washed village.'

'Do you get a peg for your nose?'

'Very funny.'

'He's not coming with us?' Ryker indicated Sergei who remained in the driver's seat.

'He'll wait down the road. We don't want him spoiling our fun, do we?'

'Definitely not.'

Eva took the lead and headed across the street to a quaint tapas bar that had several blue-painted hanging baskets in full bloom across its front. The couple walked inside and the smell of freshly cooked food caught Ryker's attention.

The bar looked like it had been recently refurbished, carrying on the blue colour scheme of the outside, but the style was old-school; wood-panelling, meats hanging from the bar, bottles of wine stashed in racks along one wall. A chalkboard displayed the day's tapas. Ryker's belly growled thinking about it.

They took a seat by the window, away from the only other couple in the bar, and ordered two glasses of red wine from the waiter.

The wine came and Ryker gave in to temptation and ordered a plate of chorizos. Some cheese too.

Half an hour later, Ryker had finished off the food and was working through a second of glass of wine and a third basket of bread. The alcohol and food was making him feel contented, but still focused.

The chat was banal and a little flirty. What more would he expect from Eva? It hadn't escaped his attention that every so often she'd shuffle a little closer to him. Her shoulder, arm, leg was within an inch of Ryker and more than once she'd accidentally brushed him.

Accidentally? Ryker thought. No, bad choice of wording. 'It's quiet.'

'It's early. It'll get busy later on.'

'You're a regular here?' Ryker asked, having noticed the warm smile and overtly friendly manner of the waiter.

'I own it.'

Ryker couldn't help but smirk at that.

'Oh get over yourself,' Eva said. 'It's not what you think. I used my own money to buy this place.'

'Your own money?'

'My. Own. Money. I bought it, a derelict shell. I put together the plans, oversaw the refurbishment, found the staff. My father had nothing to do with any of it.'

'It's nice. You've done a good job.'

'I know I have.' Eva glared at him. 'Perhaps you need to rethink who I am.'

'Perhaps I do.'

'I love this place. This village. This is who I am. Not what you see in Marbella. Not the money.'

'Not the mansion or the pool or the cars.'

'No. I don't just own this bar, I have a restaurant too. I'm making a life for myself. I'm working, doing things I love to do. I help out with local activities too. Charities, foundations.'

'The dancing?'

'Yes. There you go. Every other day we – the others at least – perform in one of the local towns. They get a small payment for each performance. I don't. The whole group is funded by donations, mostly from me. I pay to be a part of that. For the other dancers to be a part of it.'

Ryker nodded, impressed with her passion.

'And I may live in a mansion in Marbella, but my grandma has lived in this village for nearly ninety years. It's her home. It feels like my home too. My real home.'

'But *you* don't live here.'

'No.' She looked down at her drink. 'My father won't let me. He wants me with him.'

'Why?'

'Because... it's dangerous.'

'And why would that be?'

Eva paused before answering. 'Who do you think my father is exactly?'

'That's what I'm trying to find out.'

'So ask me? What do you want to know?'

'Why did your father come to Spain?'

'To make a living.'

'Why couldn't he do that in Russia?'

'Have you seen what's happened since the collapse of the Soviet Union? Lots of us have left, seeking a new life.'

'Away from the watchful eyes of the Kremlin.'

'That's not what I meant.'

'So is he pro-Moscow or anti-Moscow?'

Eva gave Ryker a cold stare before answering. 'Anti.'

'So they hounded him out. He ran off to Spain.'

'Do you hate all Russians, Mr Ryker, or is it only rich Russians?'

'I don't hate all Russians, or even all rich Russians. But I do mistrust a lot of people.'

'Why do you mistrust my father?'

'Because he's very rich. And I'm sorry to say that a lot of men that rich don't get there through playing by the rules.'

'A bit far-fetched, don't you think?'

'No. I don't. Plus there's an ongoing murder investigation that he's trying everything he can to distance himself from. And because yesterday minutes after leaving your house I was attacked by two men.'

Eva looked unsure. 'I didn't know about that.'

'I'd be upset if you did.'

'Why do you think it was my father?'

'A hunch.'

'Is that it?'

'No. After being attacked yesterday, I'm pretty sure at least one policeman in Marbella, where you live, is bent. And now all of a sudden you have your own personal bodyguard to take you out for drinks. A bodyguard who

I'm certain has a dark past. I see it in his eyes. It's a look only certain people have. People who have seen things. People who have done things.'

'Do you have it?' Eva asked with a devilish stare. 'The look?'

'Yes, Eva. I do.'

Eva held Ryker's gaze as she sipped on her glass of wine. Despite her battle to keep in control, Ryker could feel the mood of the conversation shifting. He could sit there all evening drinking and flirting – clearly that had been Eva's intention – but it wasn't going to get him anywhere. Ryker wasn't in Spain to hook up. He wanted answers from Eva.

'You're quite the conspiracist, aren't you?' Eva said.

'No. I just say what I see.'

'He's not what you think. My father.'

'You have no idea what I think.'

'Actually I reckon I do.'

'Then let me ask you this. One simple question. And I want a truthful answer. Can you do that?'

Eva looked doubtful, her normal confidence escaping her. 'Yes.'

'How long has your father been working for the Russian mafia?'

Chapter 29

Eva looked scared. 'That's quite a thing to say to someone,' she said, trying her best to regain her composure.

'I say what I see.'

'And can you explain why you would think that?'

She sounded truly outraged. Offended. But it didn't deter Ryker one bit. He was quite certain of his deduction.

Ryker sat back as the waiter came over to remove their empty wine glasses. Eva ordered another. Ryker asked for a coffee. Two wines were plenty. He didn't want his judgment clouded by alcohol. Not now.

'Let's start simply then,' Ryker said. 'How long have you known Sergei?'

'I don't know,' Eva said, frowning. 'Two, maybe three years.'

'He came over from Russia?'

'Georgia, I think.'

For a moment, the unexpected answer sent Ryker's brain whirring. Georgia. Ex-Soviet state. A lot of its culture, including that of its mafia, shared many similarities with Russia. More than that, though, Georgia was where Anna Abayev, just a teenage girl, had first killed. The pieces of the jigsaw hadn't yet fully fitted, but they were coming closer together.

Ryker brought himself back on track. 'You've noticed Sergei's tattoos?'

'On his hands? Yeah, I guess.' Eva shrugged.

'And on the rest of him?'

'I've never seen the rest of him.' Eva scowled. 'Why? Have you?'

'No. And I don't need to. Have you heard of the Vory? Thieves in law?'

'Of course I have.'

'And what do you know?'

'That they're mostly make-believe. People create scare stories that make the Vory out to be these all-powerful beings who rule the world. Most of the real Vory are in prison. That's where the Vor culture started and that's where they'll stay the rest of their lives. They're a bunch of lowlifes. A prison gang. The ones on the outside are mostly petty criminals who *want* to be like the Vory they read about in the papers and see on TV shows.'

Ryker agreed with every word she'd said. The organised criminal underworld, rising in prominence in Russia in the early twentieth century, had been virtually exterminated following the 1917 Russian revolution. The secret police of Stalin's government shunted criminals and political opposition alike into the many forced labour camps. The Vory and their anti-authority culture was born in the gulags and crept into the outside world as the years went by.

Following the break-up of the Soviet Union, organised crime, led by the Vory, was once again able to infiltrate every aspect of society. Including the government. But many Vory were still fiercely opposed to all elements of government authority. They were the ones who fled Russia, taking their money and their criminal culture with them.

Ryker would have betted his life that Sergei was one such Vor. And if he was there in Andalusia, working as a babysitter for Kozlov, it meant Kozlov was somehow connected to that world too. But Kozlov didn't strike Ryker as a leader of the mafia. Probably just a money spinner. There would be others in the mix somewhere. The big fish.

'You think Sergei is a Vor?' Eva said with what Ryker determined to be fake incredulity.

'I don't think it, Eva. I know it.'

'What, because of a couple of tattoos on his hands?'

'No, not just that.'

The drinks came, and Eva took a large swig of her wine. Ryker picked up his cup and inhaled. The scent of the thick, treacly black coffee sent a wave of clarity through his brain.

'And what about my father?' Eva said. 'You're saying you think *he's* a Vor?'

'Not at all. In fact I'm certain he's not. But I do believe he's got himself mixed up with them, one way or another.' Ryker sipped the coffee. 'I'm right, aren't I?'

'Let me put it like this. If what you're saying, these accusations, if they're true, shouldn't you stay away rather than pry? The Vory are very dangerous people, are they not?'

Ryker scoffed. 'Seriously? That's your answer. Some lame threat. What, is Sergei going to take me out the back for a beating? Perhaps you've misunderstood exactly who I am, Eva.'

Her cheeks blushed red. This wasn't the cock-sure woman he'd seen before, which only further confirmed his growing suspicions.

'You didn't answer my first question,' Ryker said, to keep the pressure on. He wanted to see her reaction when cornered. 'How long has your father worked for them?'

'I'm not saying another thing about it,' Eva snapped. 'This is crazy. *You're* crazy.'

Eva downed the remainder of her glass of wine and got to her feet. Ryker smiled at having rattled her.

'Sit down,' he said. 'Come on. I'm sorry. Why don't we talk about something else. Your grandma? This village? Your charity work. How you live in a billionaire's mansion and drive hundred-grand cars but hate material things.'

For a second it looked as though Eva was about to explode. He could see she wanted to take charge of the situation, to be the one to hold the power. But virtually all of her power came from her looks and her charm, and her ability to use those traits against unwitting men. Ryker wasn't going to fall for that, no matter how strong her allure. She was lost in the situation she now found herself in and it was clear she knew it.

'I think I'm done here. Bye, James.'

'My car's at your house,' Ryker said, not moving from his seat.

'Then you can find your own way back there to collect it.'

'Daddy wouldn't be pleased if he came home to find it there, would he? To know that you'd gone out with me.'

'Fine. Come with us. Get your car then go.'

Ryker smiled. 'Thanks.'

They walked the short distance back to the SUV. Sergei was leaning against the driver's door and smoking a cigarette, his face passive as ever. He looked up when he spotted Eva and Ryker heading over.

'Come on,' Eva said to him in Spanish. 'It's time to go.'

Sergei looked surprised at them being back so soon but still didn't say a word.

The sun was setting as they headed back down to the coast. Despite the silence in the car, Eva seemed to warm up again as the awkwardness from the conversation in the bar dissipated. She tapped away on her phone for a few minutes then finally looked up at Ryker and smiled. It came across as warm and pleasant. But Ryker didn't buy it. She was planning something.

'Sergei,' Eva said. 'My friend here told me he thinks you're a Vor. Can you believe that?'

She spoke in Russian. Perhaps she thought she was being cute. Or clever. Or snide. Or all three. Clearly she'd not reckoned on Ryker speaking Russian fluently. He'd worked in Russia and the ex-Soviet states countless times in his long JIA career, and it was by far his most comfortable foreign language.

Sergei said nothing, just glanced at Ryker in the rear-view mirror then back to the road.

'He says he's going to have you arrested. Sent to the gulag,' Eva continued, smiling. 'What do you think you should do to a man like that?'

'If you believe a word that comes out of her mouth,' Ryker said, in Russian, 'then you're even dumber than you look.' Sergei again made eye contact with Ryker and held it for a few seconds. Ryker didn't care that he'd insulted him. The last thing he wanted was to show a man like Sergei any hint of weakness. 'And I've been to a gulag. I've been held there, more than once. I'm not a threat to you. Not unless you make me one.'

When Sergei finally looked away, Ryker gazed over at Eva. He could see the anger in her eyes. But it was him that should have been angry. Her words to Sergei had been one hell of a stab in the back for Ryker. It wasn't that he'd thought he could trust Eva, but to have her try to lay a trap for him while he was sat next to her? That was cold. Heartless.

Ryker knew he wasn't off the hook though. He could only hope that his words would ward Sergei off. For now. But Ryker wondered what Eva had been doing on her phone – what message she might have sent. Ryker's brain filled with thoughts of what might come next. Last time he'd been to the Kozlov house, Rambo and Buzzcut had come after him. Who or what would it be this time?

He contemplated reaching out and choking Sergei as he drove. It would take away any immediate threat.

But was that a step too far?

Yes. All Ryker had was the suspicion that Sergei was a Vor, probably a low-ranking one, and that alone wasn't reason enough to take a man's life. Even if he was about to drive Ryker straight into an ambush.

Instead, Ryker prepared himself for the worst. It was the sensible thing to do. In the end, he was surprised when Sergei simply kept going along the same roads back to the Kozlov's house. Ryker had been expecting to be driven to some secluded spot where they'd try to take him out.

Still, the estate where the Kozlov's lived was such a secure and private location that it wasn't unthinkable that the trap for Ryker lay within the gated sanctum. It was dark out now – much easier to attack with stealth under the cover of night.

Yet when they arrived at the house, there wasn't a person in sight on the property, nor any additional cars. Ryker looked over at Eva suspiciously as the car came to a stop. Eva smiled at Ryker as she reached for her door handle. Was it all in his mind?

Ryker opened his door and stepped out, did a quick scan of the grounds around him. Saw no one. But it was difficult to tell with the faint glow of the streetlights. Sergei got out of the car. Ryker didn't take his eyes off him. He was ready, waiting for the move.

It didn't come.

'Next time you want to come over for a little chat,' Eva said, sourly. 'Don't bother. Come on, Sergei.'

Eva walked away from Ryker toward the house. Sergei followed. Ryker didn't hesitate. He turned round and walked with purpose back to his car. He just wanted to get out of there.

He had his hand on the door handle when he stopped. He glanced along the side of the car. It was difficult to see clearly in the dark, even with the glow from nearby streetlights, but the metalwork was covered in a thin layer of dust from the dry, sandy air. Ryker stepped back and inspected the body of the car, paying particular attention to the handles, the door frames, the panels that ran along the underside. He was looking for finger marks. Scuffs in the dust. Anything that would indicate someone had been snooping around the car. Or underneath it.

Ryker dropped down onto the ground, lay flat and looked under the car, using the light on his mobile phone to help him see more clearly. He saw nothing unusual. He moved around each of the four sides, inspecting the chassis as closely as he could. No. There was nothing there.

Maybe he was being overly suspicious. But he had to be sure.

When he was done, Ryker went back to the driver's side and opened the door. He sat on the seat and sunk the key into the ignition. As he turned the key, he held his breath. The engine rattled to life and Ryker exhaled.

He looked up at the mansion and spotted Eva standing in one of the ground floor windows. She was staring over at him with a wicked smile plastered over her pretty face.

Okay, that's plenty of excitement for one day, Ryker thought without even the faintest hint of amusement. It was about time he got some much-needed sleep.

Chapter 30

Early the following morning, Ryker was rudely awakened by the incessant buzzing of his mobile phone. He groggily opened his eyes and waited a couple of seconds as his brain re-calibrated where he was: his hotel room in Malaga. Ryker answered the vibrating phone. It was Green.

'Ryker, where the hell are you?' The policeman sounded harried.

'In bed,' Ryker said, pulling himself upright, suddenly alert.

'Get the hell up and get yourself over here, right now.'

'What is it?'

'It's Inspector Cardo. He's dead.'

From Malaga, it took Ryker a little under an hour driving along a twisting mountain road up the Sierra de Mijas to reach the hotel where Inspector Cardo's body had been found. On the outskirts of the Moorish town of Alhaurin el Grande, the hotel was on a modern road junction that connected the town directly to both Marbella and Malaga.

As Ryker approached, it was clear to him that the building out-dated the recently tarmacked roads by a considerable number of years. Large wine barrels were scattered around the outside of the hotel – makeshift tables for drinking and eating at. Built from a hotchpotch of stones and timber, the hotel looked like a rest stop for ranchers and their horses from years gone by. It wouldn't have looked out of place in the Wild West. All that was missing was a paddock to tie up your horse and some swinging saloon doors.

High up in the Sierra, the location was a remote and unusual position, and Ryker couldn't fathom why Inspector Cardo had chosen to stay there.

It was ten a.m. when Ryker arrived and already the temperature was steadily rising towards thirty degrees with another unblemished blue sky above. There were three marked police cars in the hotel's car park. Ryker also spotted Green's car. He parked next to it. As Ryker stepped from his Ford, he saw the detective approaching.

'Ah, sleeping beauty,' Green said. 'Glad you could join us.'

Ryker said nothing.

'This is not good, Ryker,' Green said. 'Not good at all.'

'What is this place?'

Green stopped walking. 'What do you mean?'

'Why was Cardo staying up here?' Ryker looked out over the landscape down to the coast. The morning sun cast a warm orange glow over the hills and valleys that were dotted with white villas and small villages, and swathes of pine, orange and lemon trees. 'I mean it's picturesque, but it's the middle of nowhere.'

'I'm not sure what you're getting at,' Green said. 'It's hardly the most relevant detail to be concerned about right now.'

'So you don't know the answer is what you're saying.'

'No, I don't know the answer.'

'So it might yet be relevant.'

'Could be. Probably isn't. This way,' Green said, turning.

Ryker followed Green through the car park and past the hotel building. The smell of freshly cooked meat and vegetables came and went as they walked by the kitchen for the hotel's bar and restaurant. Whatever was on the day's menu, it smelled amazing. Perhaps that was why Cardo had chosen the place.

They walked by Cardo's car. A police officer was standing next to it. The driver's door was open. Ryker glanced inside as he and Green headed to where a low metal barrier separated the car park from a wilderness of rock and pine trees that dropped into the valley below.

As Ryker approached the edge, he saw a gaggle of uniformed policemen plus a team of forensics – dressed head to toe in white coveralls – gathering around a small white tent about thirty feet below. Ryker looked down at the scene, then around at the car park. At Cardo's car.

'He was pushed over the edge?' Ryker asked.

'I don't think he was going for an early morning hike,' Green replied.

Ryker noticed the blood spatters on the tarmac, leading from the car to the barrier. 'He was attacked up here.'

'Well done, Einstein. Let's go and take a look. Before you burn out your little detective brain.'

Ryker didn't react to Green's taunt. He was too busy thinking. Green stepped over the barrier and then cautiously scrambled down the rocks to the tent. Ryker followed, noticing that a few of the policemen had turned their suspicious eyes onto him.

When they reached the scene, Green introduced Ryker to the policemen, but Ryker took little notice. He moved over to the tent and lifted the flap to peer inside. He didn't flinch as he stared down at the twisted and bloody form of Inspector Cardo.

The body was pressed up against the stump of a tree. From the outside, Ryker had seen that beyond was an almost sheer drop at least another fifty feet. One of Cardo's legs was bent awkwardly underneath him, clearly snapped. An arm too looked like it was dislocated. The fall down the rocks had caused quite some damage.

But it hadn't killed him. No, it was a knife that killed him.

Cardo's lifeless body was fully clothed but each of the three stab wounds he'd suffered were noticeable from the small rips in his shirt and the patches of thick blood around them. Two wounds were in his chest. One in his side.

'I don't know if he was alive or dead when he was pushed over the edge,' Green said, from behind Ryker, 'but those wounds would have killed him either way.'

'Yeah,' Ryker said without turning to face Green. 'That was the intention. Anything of interest found on him?'

'His phone. Wallet. ID. Car keys were on his driver's seat.'

'Anything else in the car?'

'Nothing that stands out.'

'His room?'

'We haven't got there yet. An officer is outside making sure it's not touched.'

'Let's go then,' Ryker said, turning around.

'That's it? You're done down here?'

'What else can we do here? He's dead. And we just said how it happened.'

'Did we? Perhaps take a step back for my benefit then. What exactly happened here?'

Ryker stopped and turned to face Green. 'Cardo was going to his car. The killer grabbed him before he got in, probably taking him by surprise from behind. The three stab wounds were delivered in quick succession. The two to the chest first, each intended to puncture a lung. Two attempts to make doubly sure. There's a lot of bone around there. Two lungs, two attempts. The third in the side was a kidney strike. Enough on its own to be fatal.'

Green nodded, apparently impressed with Ryker's words. Or maybe just his confidence.

'Why in that order?' Green asked.

'The knife was left in the third time. To limit blood loss. You catch the renal artery and blood leaks everywhere. Leaving the knife in helped to counter that. But it also made Cardo easier to move.'

'You think he was still conscious at that point?'

'Doesn't matter. Either way, the knife in the side gave the killer some leverage to pull him along. The stab wounds were chosen deliberately, fatal blows that wouldn't draw much blood immediately. The killer could have slit his throat and let him bleed out by the car.'

'But there *is* still blood on the ground. That's how he was found.'

'I know. Unavoidable when you're stabbing someone. The wounds were intended to be fatal but also *relatively* clean, to prevent mess on the killer's clothes. The attack was out in the open, in daylight, in a hotel car park. It needed to be quick, clean. A few blood spots is fine. Blood spraying here there and everywhere, not so much.'

'So what was the point in throwing Cardo over the edge then?'

'Simply to make our job more difficult. Through bad luck or judgment, the body got stuck on that tree stump. Otherwise he'd have been nearly a hundred feet down that ravine. We'd have had a hell of a time getting down to him, if the body had been spotted at all. Good for us. Bad for the killer.'

'Yet the blood trail was there and the door to his car was wide open. Pretty obvious he was around here somewhere.'

'The body catching on the tree stump was a mistake. It sent her off track. Once she'd killed him and dumped the body, she chose to get the hell away rather than attempt to clean anything up. She's good. And ballsy too, attacking someone – a policeman – in the open like that. But clearly she's a bit out of practice.'

Green raised an eyebrow. 'She? So you know who did this?'

'I'm pretty sure, yeah.'

'That old friend of yours? The Red Cobra.'

'I think so.'

'Why Cardo?'

'Good question. Let's go to his room.'

Ryker and Green hauled themselves back up the rocks to the car park.

By the time they reached the top, Ryker's hands were scraped and aching, covered in thick dust, as were his clothes. Green had fared similarly and looked less than impressed.

They each dusted themselves down as best they could then headed over to the hotel.

They entered through the main entrance. Ryker turned round to Green who indicated he should keep going. They reached a staircase and walked up to the first floor where the hotel's few rooms were located.

'Room five,' Green said.

Ryker had already guessed that. There was after all only one room with a uniformed police officer idling outside. The officer stood straight and held his ground when he saw Ryker and Green approaching. Green pushed in front of Ryker and did the talking necessary to get the two men inside. The policeman glared at Ryker as he stepped into the room. It seemed everyone could sense he was the outsider. Not one of them.

Cardo's room was basic. The floor was covered in red terracotta tiles. There was a rickety old wardrobe and a mismatched set of drawers with an old portable TV on top. On the opposite side was a single bed and accompanying table and lamp. The room was clean, the bed made up. No sign of Cardo's belongings anywhere.

'He was already staying here?' Ryker asked.

'Yeah.'

'And he hadn't checked out?'

'No. Put these on.' Green handed Ryker some blue plastic gloves.

Ryker pulled on the gloves, then explored. 'Was this guy anal or did he just not own anything?'

'Anal,' was Green's response as he walked into the bathroom.

Ryker opened the wardrobe door to reveal two suits and two shirts, pressed and hung. Underneath was a spare pair of shiny black leather shoes. Ryker left the doors open and went to the drawers, pulled each of them open. All he found were neatly folded black boxer shorts and socks. He moved back to the wardrobe and searched inside the small case that was next to the shoes. Empty. Next he went through the pockets of the suit jackets and trousers. He found a mobile phone.

'You said Cardo had a phone on him?' Ryker said as he took the phone out of the pocket and looked it over.

'Yeah,' Green said, coming out of the bathroom. 'Why?'

Ryker held the phone up for Green to see.

'Don't open it,' Green said. 'That needs to be bagged up. Searched properly.'

'Yeah. I know.' Ryker tossed the phone over to Green, who caught it, then Ryker carried on his search. This time he found what he was looking for. He took out the folded piece of paper from Cardo's suit pocket. 'Come here.'

'What is it?' Green asked.

Ryker unfolded the paper and stared at the red-inked words and the symbol underneath. The message was simple; I'm coming. He held the paper out for Green to see.

'Shit. So it really was her.'

'Yes.'

'And Cardo knew she was after him?'

'Maybe he didn't know what it meant. Or didn't believe it was real. Either way, he never said a word. More fool him.'

'What the hell is going on here?'

'I'm not sure. But I know a man who might.'

'Walker.'

'We need to speak to him.'

'But Munroe–'

'Screw Munroe,' Ryker said. 'This time I'm not taking no for an answer.'

Green opened his mouth to speak then stopped when Ryker's phone vibrated. Ryker took it out of his pocket and looked at the screen. He didn't recognise the number. The country code was Spain.

'Hello,' Ryker answered with suspicion in his tone.

'It's Eva. Eva Kozlov,' came the smooth voice down the crackly line.

'This is a surprise.'

'I need to see you.'

'And why's that?'

'There's something you need to know. About Inspector Cardo.'

Ryker only thought about the proposition for a couple of seconds. 'Tell me where.'

Chapter 31

Eight years earlier

The Red Cobra walked up the steel stairs of the apartment block, her backpack tight on her shoulders. Her footfalls were barely audible, even in the thick black boots she was wearing, and despite the rickety stairs she was treading on. Moving with caution and stealth was second nature. Her breathing quickened as she assuredly ascended, though it was well within control. She was taking it easy. Always better to take your time, leave something in reserve. Just in case.

When she reached the top floor, the Red Cobra pushed open the thick metal door and exited the stairwell into the hallway. The apartments of the building – a post-war block that was in some need of modernisation – were largely occupied. Its central location in the heart of Berlin meant it remained a popular building despite its current state, particularly for early twenty-somethings with little money.

The Red Cobra approached the door to apartment 1515. With her gloved hand, she reached into a pocket and drew out a key, turned it in the lock, then pushed open the door. She would leave the tight-fitting leather gloves on as long as she was inside the apartment. No point leaving evidence.

It was dark inside. She didn't turn on the lights, just carefully closed the door behind her. The studio had two windows to the outside world. Through them, the Red Cobra could see the glittering orange lights of the Berlin skyline, broken up by large patches of black from the nearby Tiergarten – Berlin's largest inner city park.

The Red Cobra slid the backpack off her shoulders and moved through the bare space to the right-hand window. She kneeled onto the floor and unzipped the main pouch of the backpack. She took out a granola bar. She'd not had breakfast and she didn't plan to eat again for a number of hours and felt like she needed the energy. Gently, she tore off the end and pulled the bar out of the packet, being careful not to break off any crumbs. Then she stuffed the empty packet in her jeans pocket before pushing the whole bar in her mouth. Cheeks bulging, she chewed.

When she was finished, she rummaged in the backpack, pulled out a water bottle, and took a swig before setting it down on the floor. Next she took out a tripod and her spotting scope. She propped the tripod in place, attached the scope, then got her sights aligned and focused on the building rising tall into the sky two hundred yards away – the Waldorf Astoria hotel.

She found the windows of the suite she was looking for and took a few seconds to make sure she was happy with the focus. The curtains in the hotel room were closed, and the lights were off. It was six a.m. and the target was still in bed. This was the third morning the Red Cobra had been here and she was beginning to notice a routine in the target's movements.

The Red Cobra reached into the backpack to retrieve the digital camera and the coupler that enabled her to attach the camera lens to the eyepiece of the scope.

When the device was set up and ready to go, she sat and waited.

Sunrise came an hour later. The Red Cobra was awake and alert. Another hour had passed when she noticed the faintest twitch of a curtain. She turned on the camera and hit the red record button. The target's wife opened the bedroom curtains first, then a minute later in the large lounge area.

During her two previous visits to the studio, the Red Cobra had gathered more than thirty hours of recordings that she'd transmitted over the internet to her employer. So far there had been nothing notable in the recordings she'd taken, but this was what she'd been asked to do. She knew little of whom the target was, she didn't much care. She was certain that before long her orders would change. After all, operating a digital camera and scope was hardly her main skill-set.

Three more hours passed. The target and his wife showered and dressed – he in a smart grey business suit, her in tight-fitting jeans and a blouse. Then they ate a belated breakfast in the room.

Not long after that the target's assistant arrived together with the usual small entourage. Then the target and his crew left, leaving the wife to her own devices. She too eventually left, on her own. Perhaps another shopping trip to the nearby designer stores, the same as yesterday.

About twenty minutes after that, the door to the suite opened again and in walked the assistant. He wasn't alone. Two men were with him. The Red Cobra didn't recognise either. Her attention was grabbed. The two men, one dressed smartly, the other casually, roamed through the room.

Searching, checking. The Red Cobra knew what they were looking for. Threats. Bugs.

The men spent the best part of half an hour scouring the suite. Then the casually dressed man came up to the window and peered outside across the Berlin cityscape. At first he looked down, then across to the left, past where the Red Cobra was stationed.

Then he turned his gaze straight ahead. He stared across at the Red Cobra.

She pulled away from the camera and looked straight out of the window. Two hundred yards. She could make out the windows of the target's suite at that distance but no detail of what lay beyond. She could barely even make out the figure of the man, even though she knew he was there.

He couldn't have spotted her, surely?

She focused back on the small screen on the camera. 'Shit.'

The man had a pair of binoculars up to his face.

The Red Cobra threw herself to the floor and pulled the tripod on top of her. It crashed down and the camera went scuttling across the floor, the little red recording light still on. She lay there, still, for five minutes, thinking.

When she finally moved, she stayed low. She crawled across the floor, pulling one of the legs of the tripod with her. She grabbed the camera along the way and continued moving until she was up against the door of the apartment, as far from the window as she could get – some twenty feet. She could only hope there was enough shadow in the apartment and glare on the windows to keep her presence obscured, if the watcher was even still there and had eyes on her windows.

Either way, she had to know.

As low to the ground as she could get, she lifted the scope and peered into the eyepiece. She adjusted the focus slightly. It had been knocked out of position when she'd pulled over the tripod. When it was properly adjusted she stared over to the Waldorf hotel and the suite of the target once more. The assistant was still there. Sat in an armchair.

The other two men were gone.

The Red Cobra only took a few seconds to decide what to do. The risk was simply too big. She needed to get in touch with her employer, ask what was happening. And what they wanted her to do next. First, though, she had to get out of there.

Chapter 32

Less than a minute later, the Red Cobra was descending the stairs, her bulging backpack over her slender shoulders once more, a baseball cap pulled down firmly on her head.

She reached the bottom of the stairs and moved out into the main foyer of the apartment block, heading left toward a fire exit rather than out through the main entrance. She pushed down on the release bar to swing open the double doors and walked into a dingy and dank back alley. It was raining heavily. The Red Cobra huddled down into her leather jacket and sunk her hands into its pockets.

She kept her head down as she walked along, scanning the area as best she could. She turned left at the end of the alley onto the main street. The pavement was intermittently busy with both locals and the occasional tourist – likely heading toward the nearby Kurfürstendamm, one of Berlin's busiest shopping streets – though the heavy rain seemed to have deterred most folks from venturing out on foot.

Up ahead, two suited men approached, each carrying ridiculously big umbrellas. The Red Cobra had to stoop to her right to get past unimpeded and without breaking her pace. She stumbled off the pavement into a puddle in the gutter.

The men carried on oblivious. She cursed at them under her breath. Then was caught by surprise when she stepped back onto the pavement only for an unseen figure to barge into her. She spun round, her eyes fixed on the man who'd knocked into her.

'*Es tut mir sehr leid*,' he said.

The Red Cobra understood his German: *I'm very sorry.* She said nothing in return, just stared at him. He wore blue jeans and brown boots, and he had on a rain jacket. The hood partially covered his face, but she saw enough to recognise him.

The man from the hotel.

She felt her body tighten, priming herself for attack. Inside her jacket pocket, her left hand wrapped around the handle of the eight-inch blade she was concealing, her grip so tight it felt like the handle would burst.

The knife, a long-time companion, was sheathed in a specially stitched compartment that ran from the inside of the left pocket across her midriff. She rarely ventured outside without a weapon of some description. The blade, although large, was easily hidden if you knew how, and so much more practical than lugging a gun around. They were cumbersome and noisy, and they needed re-loading. They simply didn't suit her needs. The knife on the other hand...

A second passed. Then another. The Red Cobra stared at the man. The street was quiet, but not empty. She was in two minds as to whether to gut him right there. She was certain she could do it before he could defend himself.

Before a third second passed, the man stepped back, apologised again, then turned and walked away.

The Red Cobra stood for another beat before she too turned and walked off in the opposite direction. She was calm on the outside, but inside her brain was on fire.

She walked for nearly two hours, taking a circuitous route through the city. She remained wary the whole time, employing every counter-surveillance technique she knew to spot any lurkers, but she saw no indication that the man or anyone else was following her.

Eventually, the Red Cobra headed across the border that had once separated east from west. She'd never known the city as it had been back then; she was only a child in the late eighties when the wall came down. Yet moving into the east of the city, she could still feel the presence of the old regime. Of communism and the Soviet Union. Was it the people, or the architecture? Perhaps it was just the tourist sights, from Checkpoint Charlie to crumbling sections of graffiti-covered wall to the myriad rusting Trabi cars available for hire.

Whatever it was, as the Red Cobra headed through Alexanderplatz back to where she was staying – a nondescript three-star business hotel – she felt more at home in her surroundings in the east than she had in the west.

Under the canopy of the hotel entrance, the Red Cobra shook herself down, removing the excess water that was dripping from her head to her toes. She walked in through the main doors and, head down to avoid her face being caught on the CCTV cameras, moved directly over to the staircase.

With her eyes still busily scanning her surroundings, but not so much as to make her look on edge, the Red Cobra walked along the corridor on the second floor. She was just about at her door when a man stepped out of his room four doors down.

It took a split second to determine he wasn't a threat. Still the Red Cobra kept on going, past her room and past the man. She took a series of left turns, working around the square layout of the floor until she emerged back at her bedroom door again. This time, the corridor was empty. She took out her keycard, unlocked the door and stepped in.

Once safely inside, the Red Cobra threw off her backpack, her cap, her jacket, and her boots, then she sat on the end of the bed. Her head was swimming with thoughts of her next step.

After a few minutes, she grabbed her laptop and sat on the bed while it fired up. She located the secretive chat portal she had been using to communicate with her employer. She left a coded private message to tell her employer the spotting position was compromised, that she'd need time to find another if they wanted more surveillance, and that there was a potential threat to eliminate.

She sent the message then stared at the computer screen, hoping for an immediate response. The employer wasn't online, but would have received a notification of her message.

After fifteen minutes, there was still nothing.

The Red Cobra got up and headed to the bathroom. She turned on the light and stared at herself in the mirror. Then she pulled off her shoulder-length blonde wig and released the pins to allow her long dark brown hair to fall over her shoulders. Next she took out the blue contact lenses to reveal her naturally hazel irises. She undressed and took a soothing shower.

As soon as she was dry, she once again checked the laptop for any messages. There were none. Then she lay down, shut her eyes, and nodded off to sleep.

The Red Cobra awoke over two hours later when the ding from her computer told her a message had arrived.

She felt groggy as she woke up from the deep sleep. The past few days she'd been filled with adrenaline as she'd staked out the hotel suite in the Waldorf. She welcomed the chance for a brief rest even if she was now feeling unusually anxious.

She opened up the message and grunted. The note was simple. Hold tight. Await further instructions.

She swore at the screen and angrily closed the laptop lid. A second later though she'd calmed. She hated not knowing, not being in control, but this was the job she was being paid for. And handsomely too. There was little point in second guessing the orders. Best to ride over the frustration, and wait and see what happened next.

The Red Cobra dressed in jeans, high heels, and a sparkling blouse then put on some make-up before heading out of her room and downstairs to the hotel bar. It was nearly six p.m. and the bar would soon be full of post-work drinkers. She may have been working, but the Red Cobra still needed her downtime, and despite her secretive and dangerous job, she wasn't averse to striking up a conversation with strangers – hiding in plain sight, she knew, was often a good tactic. And her striking good looks meant she could count on attention, when she wanted it, wherever she went.

The Red Cobra sauntered into the bar and was pleased to see a number of eyes caught by her presence. She moved over and sat on a tall stool by the bar, then ordered a dry gin martini from the young bartender who by now recognised her face but didn't know her name.

The drink arrived and the Red Cobra sipped it then spun round in her chair to look out across the room. One or two men quickly looked away from her., eyes down at their drinks. That was fine. It was early, and she knew she already had their attention. Sooner or later one of them would come over. They always did.

She turned back round to the bar.

In the end it was sooner, rather than later.

'Do you mind if I sit here?' the husky male voice said after a few moments. He spoke in German, not the Red Cobra's native tongue, but she knew his words had been perfect.

She turned to look up at the man standing next to her, a warm and ever so slightly sultry smile on her face in greeting.

It was a hard task – a very hard task – but somehow she managed to maintain that smile even when she saw the already irritatingly familiar face staring down at her. It was the casually dressed man from the suite at the Waldorf.

Chapter 33

'*Ich spreche nur ein bisschen Deutsch*,' the Red Cobra lied. *I only speak a little German*. She emphasised the words in all the wrong places.

'But you do speak English, don't you?' the man said. 'I heard you order your drink.'

The Red Cobra was thinking on her feet. In fact she could speak several languages fluently, including both English and German. She regularly used English when working on jobs. It was the easiest choice. Most people understood her in the many countries she travelled to. Plus there was something nondescript and unmemorable about a English woman travelling on business rather than a Georgian or a Russian or a Slovakian or a Serbian who no one could understand.

'Yes, I speak English,' the Red Cobra said, realising there was little point in playing dumb.

'But you're not English,' the man said, obviously picking up on her accent. 'So where are you from?'

'Here and there.'

The man laughed. 'Yeah, me too.'

The Red Cobra smiled, resigned to going along with whatever game this man had in mind. It wasn't like she could leap up and choke him to death in the middle of a packed hotel bar, whoever the hell he was.

'What are you drinking?' the man asked.

The Red Cobra shook her glass. 'Martini.'

'Bit strong for me, this time of night.' He ordered himself a half-litre beer from the barman, downed a third of it, and finally took a seat next to her.

'So what's your name?' he asked.

'You can call me whatever you like.'

'How about Anna?'

The Red Cobra did her best to hide her reaction. But she was feeling anything but her usual confident self. Anna surely wasn't a random name he'd plucked from nowhere.

What did he know?

'Sure. If you like,' she said, smiling. 'And what should I call you?'

'You can call me Carl. Carl Logan.' He extended his hand and she didn't hesitate for even a second before reaching out and giving it a gentle shake.

'So are we going to play games all night, Carl?'

'All night? That's quite a proposition. I only met you five minutes ago.'

'You're very confident, aren't you?'

'I like your hair that way. More natural.'

'Wow, charming too. How about you get to the point.'

Logan smiled and took another big gulp of his beer. 'What are you doing here?'

'I was trying to have a quiet drink.'

'I mean in Berlin.'

'Working.'

'Spying?'

'That's not me.'

'But that was you in the apartment.'

'Which apartment?'

'It's a bit late for that.'

She thought for a moment. Curiosity got the better of her. She had to find out what was happening. 'Surveillance.'

'It's a good location,' he said. 'Unobstructed view to the hotel. Not a great exit route though. One stairwell. One lift shaft. One street entrance. One exit at the back. Easy to run into problems.'

'It was the best I could find.'

'Yeah. I thought the same. I guess that's how I found you so easily.'

The Red Cobra hid her anger at his scathing comment. She sipped her martini, doing her best to remain cool and calm. 'How *did* you find me? Here I mean.'

Logan said nothing, just stared at her. She shook her head. How could she have been so stupid? She'd been so focused on him when he'd bumped into her in the street, on whether to kill him or let him go, that she'd fallen for a cheap trick.

'Where?' she asked, referring to the tracking device that she knew he must have placed on her.

Logan shrugged, keeping quiet. It only angered the Red Cobra further to see him thinking he was in control.

'You know who he is?' Logan asked. 'The man you've been spying on?'

'No,' she lied. Though it wasn't an outright lie. She knew his name, a few details about him. Just what she needed. She didn't care for any more. 'I do only what I'm told. I don't ask questions.'

Logan paused and gave her a cold, hard stare. She could tell he knew her answer was bullshit. But what did he expect? For her to blurt out everything she knew?

'Igor Gazinsky,' Logan said. 'You heard of him?'

'No.'

'Oh, come on. He's a pretty big deal. Worth billions. Made his money stealing state assets from the Russian people during privatisation. You know the type.'

'I've heard of the type, yes. Oligarchs. You don't like them?'

'Them? Oligarchs. I've not met many. The ones I have met probably wished I hadn't. And what do you think of men like that?'

The Red Cobra shrugged. 'I'm not into politics.'

'You're not? Then I'll ask you again, why are you spying on Igor Gazinsky?'

'Because I'm being paid to.'

'Do you want to kill him?'

'Why would I want to do that?'

'Because he's a horrible human being.'

'Do *you* want to kill him?'

'I haven't been asked to yet.'

'And neither have I. Yet.'

'So how about we help each other out here?'

'What do you think I am, exactly?' the Red Cobra asked with genuine curiosity.

'I think you're dangerous. Lethal. I think you're someone I should never trust in a million years.'

Perversely, the Red Cobra was pleased with his comments. 'And yet you want me to help you?'

'I'm used to working under such conditions.'

'And who exactly is it that you work for?'

'You tell me, I'll tell you.'

'I work for myself,' she said. 'It's better that way.'

'But you said you don't know Gazinsky? So there must be someone else paying you. Someone with a beef against him, I'm presuming. So who is it?'

'I'm not going to tell you that.'

'Okay. Then how about I start first. I work for the British government.'

'That's hardly a bombshell, given the conversation so far.'

'That doesn't make you nervous? To know the intelligence services are on to you?'

'On to me for what? And no, why should it?' Though really her brain was moving at a thousand miles an hour trying to figure out how she could recover this mess. Of course she already knew the intelligence services of many countries had her on their radars. After all, she'd been paid by some of them, one way or another. But no one had ever been close to apprehending her, or even to conclusively linking her to any of her jobs. Her reputation was built largely on hearsay and fable. So to be sat in a bar like this with a spook... it wasn't exactly good news.

'Would you like to know what I'm doing here, in Berlin?' Logan asked.

'Oh, I'm dying to know. Look at me. Can't you tell how excited I am to find out?'

Logan smirked, and despite herself, the Red Cobra reciprocated.

'I don't know what you've been told about Gazinsky. I'm guessing your orders are to surveil him. Then assassinate him.'

The Red Cobra shrugged.

'And to be honest, that's fine with me,' Logan said. 'But not yet. I won't allow you to kill him yet.'

'You won't *allow* me.'

'No. You see, that's why *I'm* here. To protect him. To make sure no harm comes to him in Berlin.'

'You said he was a horrible person?'

'He is. But this is my job. Gazinsky is scum. He's corrupt as hell. But such is life. He could also make a good asset for my employers. Which, I'm guessing, might link in to why you're here. To stop that from happening.'

'I'm not working with Moscow, if that's what you're thinking.'

'No. I'd have known if you were. And we probably wouldn't be having this conversation.'

'You think you know a lot, don't you?'

'Yes. About some things I do.'

'Why do you want me to help?'

'You've got certain... talents. Talents that are hard to find. Someone like you could be useful to someone like me. And I know you don't have real loyalty to anyone. That's fine. You do this for the money. That's fine too. You tell me who sent you here, or I'll find out the hard way. You tell me, I'll pay you twice as much to walk away.'

'You think I do this for money?'

'You don't? Great. So you'll help me for free?' Logan smiled.

'Why are you protecting Gazinsky? What's the play?'

'Isn't it obvious? You're staking-out that hotel suite. I was there checking it's safe. You didn't wonder why that might be happening? What might be planned?'

'A meeting,' the Red Cobra said. 'There's going to be a meeting.'

And she got it, even before Logan confirmed it. That was why she hadn't yet been given the green light. Her target wasn't just Gazinsky. It was whoever he was due to meet with.

'My boss is meeting with Gazinsky,' Logan said. 'Tomorrow. Gazinsky is a spy. He works for us now. And that's why I can't let you kill him. At least not until we find out what he knows.'

Chapter 34

The Red Cobra looked away from Logan and finished the rest of her martini. Then she ordered another. Logan signalled the barman to make him one too.

'May as well give it a go,' he said.

Logan and the Red Cobra sat silently as the barman made the drinks. She looked over at Logan. He turned to her and smiled. She had to admit, he wasn't at all bad looking. His green eyes shimmered under the lighting of the bar. His face was strong, hardened. He was confident, certainly – it was an attractive trait – but the Red Cobra got a strange feeling when she stared into his eyes. Because she saw nothing. No emotion. No feeling.

He was lethal, dangerous. Two words he'd moments earlier used to describe her and she saw the same in him. But that didn't worry her, not one bit.

One way or another, this was going to be an exciting game.

'So your boss meets with Gazinsky, and then what?' she asked when the barman had brought them their drinks and moved off to attend to some new arrivals.

'I'll know that after the meeting.'

'Will you still be protecting Gazinsky?'

'I don't know. But until the situation changes, I'm not going to let you get to him.'

'Which you've assumed is what I want to do.'

'That's my assumption, yes. But you haven't been asked to do that yet, right?'

'Right.'

'So are you going to tell me who's paying you?'

'No.'

'What happened to I tell you, you tell me?'

'I never said you should trust me.'

Logan smiled again. A more flirtatious smile than last time. 'No. You didn't. I'll have to find out another way.'

'You can try.'

They both took a sip of their drinks.

'Anything else to add?' Logan said.

'How do you mean?'

'About this job? About you being in Berlin?'

'Nothing.'

'Great. Looks like we've got the night off then.'

'A night off?'

'I'm all done revealing my hand. So unless you've got anything to add.'

'No. I don't.'

Logan held up his martini glass and the Red Cobra picked up hers and chinked it against his.

'Cheers,' he said.

'*Zum wohl.*'

Five martinis later, they were giddily walking along the corridor on the second floor toward her room. The Red Cobra glanced up at Logan as they idled along. He was a few inches taller than her, even with her heels. She could tell underneath his shirt he was lean – not bulked up, just fit and strong. She guessed given his height and frame that he weighed over two hundred pounds, almost twice as much as she did. Physically he was exactly the type of man she would have picked up that night anyway. The fact he claimed to be an intelligence agent, that he was a potential enemy of hers, only made the prospect of what was to come more thrilling.

She hadn't yet decided what to do with him. She certainly couldn't have killed him out in the open, in the bar. But in the bedroom, behind closed doors?

The Red Cobra opened the door to her room and stepped in, Logan a pace behind her. He gently pushed the door closed. She was still facing away from him as he reached out and grabbed her arm then swung her round. He pulled her towards him – not a hostile move. He had something else on his mind.

But as she was moving, the Red Cobra lifted her knee up, reached down and grabbed the handle of the pocket knife from her ankle strap. As Logan brought her close to him she pushed the blade upwards onto his neck.

They both froze, staring into each other's eyes with intent. She was panting. Excited. And a little nervous, she had to admit. He was calm, a knowing look on his face.

'I was wondering how long it would take,' he said.

She said nothing. Did she really want to kill him?

Five seconds passed. The Red Cobra could feel her heart thudding. She was so close to Logan she could feel his heart too as it slowly and steadily beat against her.

After a few more seconds, her own heartbeat seemed to relax, falling in line with his.

The knife was still on his neck, pressing against his stubbly skin. He leaned forward an inch, pushing against the blade. She didn't move. He pushed further forward. The knife nicked him. A dribble of blood ran down his neck, under the collar of his shirt. She moved the blade back, just a little. He followed it. Pursed his lips. Before she could stop herself, she did the same.

And then it happened. She didn't even know how he did it. The move was too fast. The pain in her arm shot through her shoulder, into her neck. Her hand opened. It was a reflexive reaction. No matter how hard she'd been gripping the knife's handle she wouldn't have been able to hold on. He'd caught a pressure point on a nerve and there was nothing she could do.

With the knife still falling to the floor, Logan twisted her round. One of her arms was behind her back, a hammerlock. He wrapped his thick left arm around her body, pinning down her other hand and arm.

His size and strength meant she couldn't move. At least not unless she wanted her arm broken.

Perhaps that was what it would take.

His face was pressed up against the back of her neck. She could hear him breathing, feel his warm breaths against her skin.

He whispered into her ear, 'Try anything like that again, and I'll kill you.'

Then after a few seconds passed, he lightly kissed her neck. It made the hairs on her neck and shoulders stand on end and sent a pleasant shiver down her spine.

She smiled. 'Is that a promise?'

He relaxed his grip and she turned round to face him. She stared into his glowing eyes for just a moment. Then she reached up and pressed her soft lips onto his.

Chapter 35

The Red Cobra awoke the following morning to the sound of a phone vibrating. She opened her eyes and spotted the phone on the bedside table. She reached out, flipped the lid and pulled the device to her ear.

'Check your inbox,' the voice said. Then the call went dead.

She closed the phone and looked over at the other side of the bed. Empty.

Shit.

Feeling suddenly alert, the Red Cobra jumped up out of the bed. She was naked. She grimaced. Her head was pounding. She looked over at the clock by the TV. Nine a.m.

What the hell had happened? She could remember being in the room with Logan. Kissing him. Stripping off. Having sex with him on the floor. Then on the bed. Then... no, after that, she didn't know. Her mind was a blank. She couldn't remember if they'd lain in each other's arms. She couldn't remember him making a quick exit either. Had he stayed the night? She had no clue.

That was odd. She didn't think she'd had that much alcohol, but maybe the combination of gin and exhaustion had taken its toll.

But she also wondered whether Carl Logan had drugged her.

Ignoring the daggers in her head, she raced over to the laptop. The almost invisible seal she'd put across the lid was still there. She opened the laptop, booted it up, and went straight into the computer's metadata. There was no record of the machine having been used since the previous afternoon. So Logan hadn't been snooping there. That was a relief.

Her phone. She went back to the bed and grabbed it. She was always so careful about using a mobile. She deleted call histories, messages, as soon as she could. This time she had a slight moment of panic that perhaps she'd left something on there. It only took her a few seconds to realise that wasn't the case.

She breathed a sigh of relief then went to her backpack and searched through that, then the rest of her meagre belongings. Nothing was missing. Nothing seemed to have been moved or tampered with.

So what the hell was going on? Why had Logan upped and scarpered?

For once in her life, the Red Cobra felt embarrassed. Or was it ashamed? She felt like she'd been used. Even with the martinis sloshing around inside her, she'd felt like she'd been in control of the situation with Logan. Like she was the one playing him.

But was it really the other way round?

The more she thought about it, the more it worried her. And he had called her Anna at the bar. It had struck her at the time but she'd not dwelled on the point for long. Now it came back to the forefront of her mind.

How much about her and her past did Carl Logan already know?

The chat portal finally loaded up and the Red Cobra checked her inbox. Again the message was brief, coded too. But it was clear what it meant. She was to carry on the surveillance of Gazinsky and wait for the meeting that was planned, with a man called Charles McCabe. British Intelligence, like Logan had said. And then she was to kill them all. Which she could only assume meant Logan too, if he happened to be there.

It was a welcome message. She didn't like being made a fool of.

The Red Cobra sent a return message to confirm her intentions, then deleted both that and the message she'd received. Then she shut down the laptop. She moved over to her backpack and checked over the material on the outside. It was the obvious place for Logan to have bugged her the previous day.

She found the small tracking chip within minutes. It was tiny, the size of a freckle. One side was sticky allowing it to be pressed easily into place. She found it stuck onto the underside of one of the pocket flaps – an innocuous position. She admired the move that Logan had made to put the chip there, even if it did make her look stupid.

She would get her own back.

After showering and dressing, the Red Cobra put on a flame-coloured wig and some emerald contact lenses then made her way across Berlin on foot. She had her backpack though she wasn't planning on heading back to the apartment to spend the day looking through a camera lens. What was the point? Logan already knew about that location. Most likely he'd have a man stationed there from now until the meeting between Gazinsky and McCabe had taken place. If she was to continue to surveil, she needed to find a new location.

That was easier said than done. The apartment had taken her days to find and properly arrange, putting in place all the correct documents and contracts to keep her trail clean. She simply didn't have time to do that all over again.

She required a more direct approach.

A little over an hour later, the Red Cobra walked through the luxurious lobby of the Waldorf Astoria. She headed straight past the many eager staff members and into an open lift behind another guest. She realised as the guest – a man in his fifties – pressed his room card onto a small pad that the lift only worked with an active card. He pressed the button for the fifth floor. She looked at the man, catching his attention, then gave him a seductive smile.

'Fifteen, please,' she said, assuming he'd understand her English.

He smiled back, then placed his card up against the pad a second time before pressing the button for the fifteenth. The button lit up and she thanked the man as they reached the fifth floor. He gave her another look before he exited. What, was he thinking she was about to head off to his room with him because he pressed a damn lift button for her? The Red Cobra ignored him. Seconds later, she was on her way up again.

The plan? She had to get into Gazinsky's suite. She would kill them all, as she'd been asked to do. But she didn't need to sit and wait for the meeting with Charles McCabe to conclude. She'd kill whoever was in that suite already, then take out whoever else arrived after.

When she came out of the lift, the Red Cobra smiled when she spotted her opportunity. A maid's trolley, two doors down from where she was.

The Red Cobra walked over, scanning in front and behind her to make sure no one was watching. She spotted a CCTV camera at the far end of the corridor but with her cap low and her head down the camera would never get a good capture of her face. And she doubted there was anyone sat watching live feeds covering such an extensive building so there was little chance of her tripping an alert with what she was about to do.

When the Red Cobra reached the doorway to the substantial room that the maid was cleaning, she did one more scan up and down the corridor. Satisfied, she stepped in through the open doorway and quickly shut it behind her.

The noise caught the maid's attention. She was in the process of dusting the coffee table in the middle of the lounge area. The look on her face… she knew she was in trouble.

The Red Cobra sprang towards the petrified woman.

Three minutes later, in the maid's blue and white dress, the master keycard dangling from her waist, the Red Cobra stepped back out into the hotel corridor. She placed her backpack – now filled with her clothes – into the maid's trolley, out of sight under blankets, then casually pushed the trolley down the corridor to Gazinsky's suite.

She pulled the keycard up and placed it into the slot on the suite's door. The red light flicked to green and she heard the lock release. She put one hand to the handle. The other she balled and knocked gently on the door three times.

'*Hauswirtschafts*,' she said, pushing the handle down and the door open.

The Red Cobra took two steps into the room. The door closed behind her. She stopped. She didn't need to go any further. She'd surveilled this room for over thirty hours over the last few days. She knew the layout. She knew the location of sofas and drawers, wardrobes, the bed. Where Gazinsky and his wife had placed all their belongings. And it was clear to the Red Cobra that this room was now empty.

Gazinsky was gone.

Chapter 36

The Red Cobra didn't panic. Doing so wouldn't help her. Instead she backtracked out of the suite and up the corridor with the trolley, from which she grabbed her backpack. She then opened the door to the room she'd been in moments earlier, entered, and closed the door. The maid was on the floor, writhing around, frantically trying to undo the dressing gown belt that was tied around her wrists. She murmured, trying to cry out, but the fabric stuffed in her mouth was muffling her cries. She was going nowhere.

The Red Cobra stripped off the maid's dress, opened the backpack and as quickly as she could, put her own clothes back on.

'I'm sorry,' she said to the maid, a second before opening the door and heading to the lift, which she activated using the maid's key card.

When she exited the lift on the ground floor, the Red Cobra set her sights on the main exit. She dropped the maid's card into a bin then strode toward the doors, wanting nothing more than to get out into the fresh air and determine her next step.

Her plan was halted only seconds later though when she heard the all-too-familiar voice.

'Good morning,' Carl Logan said.

The Red Cobra was riled by what sounded like a jovial, taunting tone, but she ignored him and carried on walking out into the street.

'You're quite the chameleon, aren't you?,' he said. He must have only been a step or two behind her. She didn't let up. 'Blonde, brunette, red. How do you remember who you really are?'

'I'm sure you're used to pretending too.'

'You're right, I am. Part of the job, eh?'

'A necessary evil.'

'I had a good time last night.'

The Red Cobra stopped. She turned round, expertly keeping the anger that was bubbling inside off her face. Logan stopped too and stared at her.

'You didn't say goodbye,' she said.

'You were sleeping. You looked peaceful.'

'Sleeping? I was unconscious. That's pretty lame, you know. Having to drug women to get them to have sex with you.'

'I didn't drug you. You were pissed. Maybe you should stay off those martinis next time.'

'Next time?'

'Figure of speech.'

'Oh, for a moment I thought maybe you were a decent human being and wanted to get to know me.'

'I hadn't ruled it out. I had a good time.'

'Yeah. Sure you did.'

'So what now?'

'I'm not sure what you want me to say.'

'We had to move Gazinsky. It wasn't deemed safe for him here anymore.'

The Red Cobra strode away down the street again. She walked through a crossing that was on red without once looking. A car screeched to a halt and the angry driver blasted on his horn. The Red Cobra didn't react.

With Logan keeping pace next to her, she headed along the wide pavement alongside the ruins of the Kaiser Wilhelm Memorial Church, which stood as a permanent reminder of Berlin's war-torn past, the scarred shell of its bell tower jutting into the sky like a jagged tooth.

'You got the better of me,' she said. 'You win. Let's all go home.'

'I know that's not what you really think.'

'Why are you even bothering with this charade?'

'Because I like you.'

'*Like* me. That's coming from you? I don't think you're capable of such a feeling.'

Though she realised, she was hardly one to talk. Perhaps she shared more with Logan than she wanted to believe at that moment.

'Depends how you define like,' he said. 'And exactly what it is about you that I like.'

'My breasts?'

'They're not bad. Nice actually. But I was talking more on a professional level.'

'I'm flattered.'

'This way.' Logan pointed to his left to one of the entrances to the sprawling Tiergarten.

'Why?' the Red Cobra asked, her suspicious mind questioning what he was up to.

Logan stopped and held his hands up. 'It's not a trap. Just thought it'd be better to talk somewhere quiet rather than roam the streets.'

'No.' She carried on walking. 'I prefer the streets. Easier to get lost in.'

'Fair enough.' He picked up his pace again. 'You're being set up with this job. You must know that?'

'Being set up for what?'

'The man you think you're working for. He's with the Russians. SVR. They're setting you up. You take out Gazinsky, then they're going to kill you. Hang you out to dry publicly too.'

She took a few moments longer than she probably should have to digest his words. She had to admit part of her was sucked in. It wasn't like she fully trusted her current employer. In her line of work that simply wasn't possible. Her father had instilled that in her for years.

So perhaps it would come down to whom she trusted the most. But who was that? The man who was offering her two million dollars to kill Gazinsky? Or Carl Logan?

'If that's true,' she said. 'If they're setting me up, I'll handle it.'

'It is true. What I said yesterday, I meant it.'

'Which bit.'

'That we can work together. You'll be paid. But you need to stop what you're doing here. Leave Gazinsky to us.'

'They'll kill me.'

'They're going to try to do that whatever you choose.'

'How do you know they set me up?'

'I know a lot about you, Anna.'

'Why do you think that's my name?'

'Would you prefer me to call you something else? Red Cobra perhaps?'

Her face remained passive even though inside Logan's words sent a shiver right through her.

'You can call me whatever you want,' she said. 'It doesn't mean you know me.'

'Think what you like. I've told you this already: I won't let you kill Gazinsky. Or McCabe. If you come after either of them, or me, I will kill you. I won't hesitate even for a second.'

'And if you try to stop me, I'll kill you. We can both talk macho bullshit, you know.'

The Red Cobra stopped walking and took a seat on a metal bench. They were near to a busy crossroads filled with cars and bikes. Throngs of people were scurrying around just yards away. If she needed to make a quick exit from the conversation, she felt she could easily lose herself in the crowds – it was certainly a far safer place than the middle of an expansive park.

Logan sat next to her. 'Fair enough. But do you really want to risk everything for a lowlife like Gazinsky?'

'You are?'

'No. There's more at stake than just him. The man we're after is the man you're working for. Potanin.'

The Red Cobra remained silent. Logan certainly knew far more about her than she knew of him. She had to admit that worried her. Her choices of next step were becoming fewer by the second. One of those options was killing Logan there, in the street. Not a bad option in many respects, she mused. At least it would give her a chance to get away and regroup.

But what then? She'd only create more problems for herself, add unneeded enemies to the list. And she was intrigued as to why Logan was speaking to her like this. Did he really not see her as a threat?

'Potanin? Never heard the name,' she said.

'That's a lie. You've heard the name. Whether or not you actually knew that was who you were working for is a different question. I'm not an idiot. I know how these things work. Clients, brokers, middlemen, drop boxes.'

'I said I've never heard of him before.'

'So it's a him now?'

'An assumption.'

'No. A lie. Let me ask you this. Do you trust Potanin?'

'I don't trust anyone.'

'A good mantra to live by. But you can stop pretending now. I found your messages to him.'

She looked over at Logan and caught the glimmer of a smile. It pissed her off.

'Last night,' he said. 'You were asleep. I was bored.'

'My computer?' she said, thoughts crashing through her mind. 'I don't think so. I checked it this morning.'

'Checked what? Did you know you can download an entire hard drive without even having to turn a computer on? It's called imaging. You make a replica. Easy if you know how.'

'I'm not dumb. I know how it works.'

'Good. Then you'll also know we can piece together deleted data, as long as it's not already been overwritten on the drive.'

'Depends if you have the right drive.'

Logan laughed. 'Well, yes. So when you use messaging that's routed through a server in the middle of the Pacific Ocean, it does cause a slight problem. But then again, there's a solution to every problem. And we had the resources to crack this one. The data on your hard drive told us where you'd been at least – the web addresses you'd visited. A deleted internet cache isn't too difficult to piece together. Then it took a bit more work to find the server those messages were sent through, and retrieve them.'

She let the words sink in. She knew what he was saying was true. Plausible in theory at least. But had he and whoever he worked for really managed to do all that in just a few hours? For starters he would have needed equipment to do the initial imaging, and he certainly hadn't been lugging anything with him at the bar. Then she felt her cheeks flush at the thought that a third person might have been in the room stealing her data while she lay naked in the bed.

But even if that was the answer, surely they couldn't have reviewed and pieced together everything on her computer in such a short space of time? And how would they have identified the host server, accessed it and retrieved the encrypted messages so quickly, never mind deciphered them and linked the user account to Potanin?

She didn't buy it. Logan knew about Potanin from another source. It was the only answer. His words were aimed at belittling her and making her feel like she'd made mistakes.

Not that his bullshit made her position any less precarious. He still knew far more about her and her job than she was comfortable with.

'Did you know Potanin's with the SVR?' Logan asked.

'No.'

'Does that bother you?'

'No,' she lied. In reality she hated anyone who was loyal to Moscow. After what they'd done to her father, that would never change. 'He's paying me. That's what matters.'

'Last night you said something different.'

'Maybe I did.'

'Okay, let me lay my cards on the table. I don't want to hurt you, Anna. I don't know why, but I don't think you deserve it. You've got yourself caught up in a situation that's much bigger than you imagined. This isn't one rich man killing off a rival. This is governments waging dirty wars against each other. And every person in that war is nothing more than a pawn. We're all expendable. Especially you.'

'And you?'

'Yes. Me too.'

'Then why don't you run too?'

'I'm not asking you to run.'

'If I turn my back on this job, on Potanin, that would be my only choice.'

'No it wouldn't. You could stand and fight.'

'Stand with you?'

'Yes. Forget about Gazinsky. He's just a gateway to take us onto bigger things. We'll go after Potanin together.'

'And then?'

'And then you've got nothing to worry about. I'd say it's the only way for you to come out of this without a pack hunting you down.'

When he put it like that, she could see the path she had to take: the path of least resistance. Neither Gazinsky nor Potanin meant anything to her. Self-preservation was more important.

'Okay,' she said. 'I'll help you.'

Chapter 37

Present day

Ryker made his way along twisting country roads towards the location Eva had given him. She said she had information on Cardo. Ryker had to find out what that was.

The inspector's death was a shock, no doubt about it, not just because of how he had been killed but why. Ryker was increasingly coming to the conclusion that Kozlov was involved with the Russian mafia. Or was it the Georgian mafia? And Walker, too, had perhaps become embroiled in the criminal underworld, whether wittingly or through coercion. Was Cardo part of it too? If so, that was potentially a big worry for Ryker. If the mob's reach stretched that far into the police then he wasn't sure exactly whom he could trust.

And that certainly included Eva, whom he was about to meet. He could only prepare himself for the worst, expect that she was about to set him up.

The biggest question still was: how did everything link back to the Red Cobra? Why had she killed Cardo? Why did she want to kill Walker?

Ryker called Winter as he drove.

'Inspector Cardo was murdered,' Ryker said when the commander answered the call.

'I heard.'

'I thought you didn't know what was happening out here?'

'I don't. But the murder of a policeman connected to your investigation is the sort of thing that gets tongues wagging.'

'What did you find on Kozlov?'

'Not much. Clean record. He's not on any watch lists.'

'I find that hard to believe.'

'Why?'

'I've seen too much out here already for Kozlov to be squeaky clean. You've got the wife of his business partner murdered. The henchmen sent after me at that construction site. His daughter's babysitter is a Vor from Georgia–'

'Georgia? You don't think–'

'Maybe. Somehow this all links to the Red Cobra. One way or another, everything's leading me to think the mafia are involved in this mess.'

'Are you serious?'

'Absolutely. Russian, Georgian, both, I'm not sure. But if they have the ear of not just the local but national police too, then it's not a big stretch to figure why Kozlov has never been under suspicion.'

'Okay. I'll keep digging into him, see if I can find a connection to any known criminal gangs operating in Andalusia. Russian, Georgian, the rest.'

'I'm off to meet his daughter now.'

'His daughter?' Winter asked, a hint of knowing in his voice.

'It's not like that.'

'Of course not. You're shacked up these days, right?'

'Right.' Ryker couldn't help but feel a pang of guilt toward Lisa who he'd again missed a call from earlier.

'Did you get the package?'

'Yes. Thanks.' Ryker moved his hand down to the bulge on his waistband where the Colt M1911 semi-automatic pistol was stashed. Winter had come up trumps organising the drop so quickly – Ryker had only had to make a short detour to pick up the weapon, together with three magazines of ammunition. The gun was an old model, probably as old as Ryker, but in good condition nonetheless.

'Just go easy with that. I'm not giving you carte blanche to go all Rambo out there. That weapon is for life and death situations. Nothing else. You get yourself in trouble with the locals because you couldn't keep your pistol in your pants, then it's up to me and no one else as to whether or not we get you out of jail again.'

Ryker understood Winter's warning. Even if he'd still been an official JIA agent, the situation would have been much the same. One of the main purposes of the JIA's set-up being secretive was so they could easily disavow all knowledge of an agent's operation should it go pear-shaped and should they feel the need.

'Have I made myself clear, Ryker?'

Ryker gritted his teeth at Winter's forthright tone. 'Yeah. I get it.'

'Good. I'll let you know if I find anything on Kozlov.'

'Thanks.'

Ryker ended the call. He made a point of calling Lisa but she didn't answer. He left a brief voice message assuring her he was okay.

An hour later, he turned his car off the road into a small park on the outskirts of the town of Ronda. He continued along the yellow-gravelled path and parked his car under the canopy of the many carob trees.

Even though he'd had the air conditioning on full blast the whole way, the shade from the fierce sun was still a welcome relief. Ryker had travelled inland to reach Ronda and the temperature had risen every few miles as he left behind the cooling sea breeze. The thermometer on the car dashboard was reading thirty-nine Celsius. When Ryker opened his door and felt the blast of super-heated air against his skin it took him a couple of seconds to adjust.

But thoughts of the debilitating conditions were soon at the back of his mind when he spotted Eva just ten yards away, hanging off the rear-end of a black SUV that was no longer shining but covered in yellow dust from its journey from Marbella.

She wore a tight-fitting summer dress, the same designer sunglasses as the previous day, and a large sunhat that shaded her head and shoulders. She strode up to Ryker, her hips swaying seductively. Ryker remained unimpressed with what he saw. Eva was a trickster, her look designed to tempt and deceive. Ryker wouldn't fall for it, no matter how hard she kept trying.

'You alone?' Ryker asked. 'No chaperone today.'

'I'm alone right now.'

Ryker noted the ambiguity in the answer. There was no sign of Sergei or anyone else. But he wouldn't trust that she'd really come out here by herself.

'What's this about?'

Eva smiled. 'This way. I want to show you something.'

They walked side by side across the park. Coming out of the treeline, Ryker squinted as the sun hit his skin. Soon they came upon a black metal railing beyond which was a sheer drop down a cliff-face to the valley below.

'It's incredible isn't it,' Eva said. 'You can see why this place was settled, with views like that.'

'Yep,' Ryker said, without feeling.

Privately, he admitted that the vista across the valley and beyond was spectacular. From their prominent perch, they had an unobstructed view over miles of farms and olive groves that trailed into the distance, enclosed by sweeping hills and mountains. The whole landscape was scorched yellow and orange from the unrelenting sun.

'It was Celts who first put a town here,' Eva said as they began walking again. 'Maybe your ancestors.'

'Maybe.'

'They didn't last long though. The Romans soon took over. Then the Suebi, then Visigoths. Finally the Arabs conquered it. This town has incredible history. Such a clash of cultures over the centuries.'

Ryker was finding it hard to read Eva. He was sure she wasn't simply all about seducing men – she was too intelligent and complex for that. But quite what her true agenda was with him, he didn't know. She seemed to flip so suddenly from sultry to sweet, from chatty to withheld.

'Why are we here?' Ryker said, starting to sound as irritated as he felt.

'You'll see.'

They walked on in silence, passing through streets, until they came to an old stone bridge spanning a deep gorge that cut the town in half. The two sides of the town were perched dramatically on the edges of the canyon, and it looked as though the buildings could crumble into the abyss at any second.

Ryker peered over the side of the bridge as they crossed, down into the depths below. The spiked rocks lining the canyons walls – which stretched down at least a hundred yards – made it feel like he was staring into the wide open mouth of a gigantic monster.

'The El Tajo canyon,' Eva said.

'Impressive,' Ryker couldn't help but say.

'Ernest Hemingway wrote about this town.' When Eva got no response from Ryker she added, 'You've heard of him, yeah?'

'I've heard of him.'

'There's a scene in one of his books where the town's people throw fascist sympathisers off a cliff to their deaths. Many believe it relates to actual events he saw in Ronda at the time.'

Ryker knew the book well. *For Whom the Bell Tolls.* As he looked downwards he could well imagine the horror of the people who had been so ruthlessly hauled over the side.

'Did you bring me here for a history lesson?' Ryker asked.

'No. But I thought you might be interested. I told you before: I'm passionate about this region. I like to share my passion.'

'Okay. Let's stop the games now. You said you wanted to talk about Inspector Cardo. He's dead, you know.'

Eva tutted. 'Yes. I heard.' Eva appeared to be finding it hard to keep eye contact with Ryker.

'So let me ask you this. Do you know *why* he was killed?'

Without any word of response, the glint Ryker saw in Eva's eyes told him the answer.

Chapter 38

Eva remained tight-lipped as they carried on their walk. Ryker was becoming more suspicious of her intentions by the second, but he was also intrigued to see what would unfold. Was she really about to reach out to him about what she knew of Inspector Cardo's murder? Ryker hoped so. It wasn't unthinkable that Eva was caught up in a murky and dangerous world simply because of who her father was, and that she was looking for a way out.

But it was equally likely that Eva was simply leading Ryker straight into an ambush.

One thing he knew for sure: he was glad he was now armed.

They came to a stop outside a back entrance to the town's bullring.

'Bullfighting?' Ryker asked. 'Let me guess, you want me to experience some more culture.'

'There's no bullfighting at this time of day. It's too hot. But I do want to show you around. Maybe you could stop being such an arsehole?'

She really was a piece of work. Here he was in the midst of a murder investigation that was very likely in some way linked to her family, and she wanted to chat about the history of Andalusia.

'Whatever you think my father is involved in, that's not me,' Eva said, her tone harder. 'It's really not. I didn't ask for any of it.'

'Maybe not. But if you really want to help, you can stop playing games and tell me what you know.'

'It's not that easy.'

'Why not.'

'Don't you think there are consequences?'

'You mean like Cardo?'

Eva stared at Ryker for a few seconds and he saw a sliver of vulnerability in her eyes. Perhaps this escapade really was a cry for help.

The look was gone a moment later when her features quickly softened again. 'Come on, let me show you around.'

The security guard on the door smiled for Eva then moved to the side to let her and Ryker through. They walked along narrow corridors before coming out into the stands of the theatre itself. Despite Ryker's scepticism, he felt slightly awestruck as he looked out across the arena. It was every bit what he would expect to see of a gladiator's amphitheatre from ancient Rome: bright yellow dust bowl in the middle, steep, sweeping terraces all around, with a strutted and tiled roof overhead.

'See,' Eva said with a warm smile. 'I told you it was worth seeing.'

Ryker looked out into the middle of the bullring. Several boys – teenagers – were there, dressed up as matadors in tight-fitting and sequinned outfits. There were also two men. One was barking instructions. The other was standing by what looked like an oversized wooden wheelbarrow with bulls' horns attached to the end.

'They're from the local bullfighting school,' Eva said, answering Ryker's unspoken question. He and Eva moved away from the stairwell and took a seat in the shade on the stone bleachers. 'Usually they train in the school, on the farms. As a special treat every now and then I organise for them to come here and experience what it's like to be inside the bullring.'

'You organise it?'

Eva shrugged. 'My father's friend owns the bullring now. And more than one of the ranches in the region where the fighting bulls are reared.'

Ryker huffed but didn't say anything in response.

'I like to help people,' Eva said.

It was as though the more times she said it, the more she truly convinced herself of those words.

'And what about your father? And his *friends?* They like to help people too?'

'They do good things. They make a lot of money for this region.'

'Yeah. In the end it always comes down to money.'

Ryker watched as one of the young matadors moved away from the group. He was taking deep breaths, readying himself for action. The man with the cart moved to one side, giving himself some space from the young man who let down his red cloth that was attached to a long stick. In his other hand was a mock spear.

Seconds later, the man with the cart charged. Dust billowed upwards from behind. The boy stood, his spine straight like a dancer in pose, not a hint of movement in his legs, his arms, his torso. It looked like the cart was about to mow him down. Ryker found himself holding his breath.

At the last moment, the boy swept to the side, drew back the spear and went to stab it onto the top of the fast-moving cart. But he moved too late. The wheel of the cart caught his leg and sent him spinning into the air. There was an explosion of dust as the boy landed in a crumpled heap on the ground. One of his friends raced up to him to see if he was all right. The teacher simply bellowed at the young matador's mistake.

'Tough schooling,' Ryker said.

'Of course. A matador has to be prepared to risk his life.'

'They don't train with animals?'

'They do. But not with fighting bulls. Every fighting bull only fights once. In the arena.'

Ryker raised an eyebrow.

'The bulls are sent for *tienta,* testing, when they are about two years old, to test their aggression. Some are selected to fight. Others for breeding. Others are simply slaughtered for meat. But the ones selected for fighting, they never meet a man on foot until the day they fight. The mothers on the other hand, they are regularly tested with men to determine which will give the most aggressive bulls. It's always said a bull's fighting instinct comes from its mother.'

'Not much fun for the bulls, though, right?' Ryker said. 'And the best ones, the ones selected for fighting, suffer the most.'

'The bulls are treated very well their whole lives. Some people don't like bullfighting. They say it's cruel. But I think there's far worse cruelty in the world than bullfighting. I admire the tradition. I admire the training the matadors go through, the way they put their lives on the line to entertain others. And if you'd ever seen a live fight, I'm sure you'd admire it too. It's not just a sport, it's an art form.'

As she spoke, the next boy in line had his turn against the cart. He fared much better, pirouetting on the spot as the cart sped past and landing a solid blow with his spear as he turned. Ryker had to admit the confidence and poise in the boy's movements impressed him. The other students erupted in applause.

'Do you want to see them?' Eva said.

'See what?'

'The bulls. They're here already. There's a fight later today.'

'I'd rather we got to the point. Cardo.'

Eva ignored him and got to her feet. Ryker followed, his irritation building. He was also feeling increasingly edgy, and stayed focused and wary as he followed Eva, keeping on the lookout for any hint that he was being set up.

They walked back to the stairwell and took a left, away from where they'd earlier entered. More corridors took them into a holding area. A narrow raised walkway ran along the middle, below which were various gated pens. The stench of piss and faeces filled the air, and the noise of several aggressive bulls – snorting, rustling, banging – echoed against the stone walls.

Ryker stepped to the edge and looked down at the sorry beast below him. It was massive, far bigger than he'd imagined. He certainly wouldn't fancy standing nose to nose in the ring with that thing. Even worse would be to fall into the enclosed pen...

Ryker's suspicion grew. He straightened up and instinctively brushed his hand against the Colt in his waistband.

'Quite something, aren't they?' Eva said. 'Before the fight, men will stand up here, shouting at them, poking them with sticks, making them angry.'

'One last humiliation before it's time to die.'

'You're still not convinced about this?'

'No. I'm not. I think I've had enough of the tour now. You said you needed to talk.'

'Your snooping is putting you in danger,' Eva said, her sudden, blunt statement surprising Ryker.

'In danger of who?'

'I'm not the problem here. Nor is my father. We're a good family.'

'Eva, I've been in this game long enough to tell the good guys from the bad. You're young, you're impressionable, I'm sure you've got a good heart. But you do know more than you're letting on – about whom your father is working for and why Kim Walker was killed. And why Inspector Cardo was killed.'

'That's the thing, though. Cardo really was a shock.'

'How so?'

'I'm telling you what I heard. This isn't my world. I wish I didn't know anything.'

'You keep saying that. I don't care. Just tell me what you know.'

'Cardo was dirty.'

'I guessed that.'

'He had been for years.'

'And I'm sure there are many more like him.'

'Maybe. But his death was a shock. It wasn't... you know–'

'He wasn't killed by the mob,' Ryker said. 'I think that's what you're getting at.'

'The mob. I hate that word. But you're right. Cardo was loyal. He was important, and my father's friends are in a panic now. Not just about who killed Cardo and why, but what the killer knows. And who could be next.'

'Let me ask you a simple question, Eva.'

'Okay.'

'Do you know why Kim Walker was killed?'

'Yes.' Eva looked down at her feet. 'No. I mean, I don't know exactly. But I heard something.'

'Tell me.'

Before she could answer, Ryker's attention was grabbed by two figures emerging along the corridor twenty yards ahead. Two men. One was tall, with short dark hair, and a weathered and hardened face. With his Slavic features, he didn't look dissimilar to Sergei except he was noticeably bigger in the frame. The other man was Buzzcut, the guy Ryker had knocked out at the construction site two days earlier.

Without any words spoken, Ryker knew why the men were there.

He'd been expecting the trap sooner or later.

'It wasn't me,' Eva said. Her surprise looked genuine.

It didn't matter one way or the other. The men were there either because of Eva or someone connected to her. Ryker stared over at the two men. They were approaching with caution, edging along the raised gangway. Ryker stole a glance behind him. The coast was still clear that way.

Ryker looked down at the men's hands. As he did so, both men brought shiny black handguns into view.

Peter Winter had made himself clear: Ryker's Colt was only to be used in life-or-death situations. As far as Ryker was concerned, this fitted the bill.

Chapter 39

Ryker was an easy target for the two men. As quick as he was with a gun, he was unlikely to have the time to pull off two shots before he was fired upon. Eva, though, she wasn't a target, surely? And given the exposed position Ryker was in, that meant Eva was his only choice for cover.

With the Slav raising his gun upward, Ryker stooped behind Eva, grabbed her, and thrust her forward toward Buzzcut. Her hat went flying, down into the pit below. The sight of Eva hurtling toward Buzzcut was enough to momentarily distract him. That was all the time Ryker needed. Crouching and darting forward, he whipped out the Colt and fired off two shots, deliberately aiming low (he would never take a life when there was another option available). The bullets caught the Slav in his leg; one in his thigh, the other bang centre of his knee joint. He screamed as he collapsed to the floor.

Ryker burst toward Buzzcut, letting off two more hurried shots as he moved. He didn't hit with either, but the melee attack was enough to get the better of his foe. As Ryker barged into Buzzcut, there was a cascade of gunfire, but all the goons shots were wayward. Ryker sent the man tumbling over the edge of the walkway and the shooting stopped.

Down below, an angry bull leaped towards the fallen man, grunting and growling. Buzzcut screamed out and the beast hammered him against the metal door, the vibration rattling along the walkway and up through Ryker.

Ryker looked up from the pen, glanced quickly to his left then his right, weighing up his next move. His decision was made easier when another gunshot rang out. A bullet ricocheted off the metal gangway inches from Ryker's feet, sending up a spray of sparks. Reflexively, Ryker ducked and scanned the area for the shooter – the shot certainly wasn't from either of the goons, they were out of the game, and Eva was huddled on the floor.

The only possible place that the shot could have come from was in the direction Ryker and Eva had approached. Without another moment's thought, Ryker moved quickly in the opposite direction – where Buzzcut and the Slav had come from.

Ryker soon found himself hurtling out onto the terraces of the bullring. Two more shots rang out as he raced through the stands towards another exit, the bullets thudding into the stone bleachers. The noise of gunfire in the enclosed theatre was booming and the sound bounced around the bowl for what seemed like seconds.

The cluster of teenagers and their teachers had stopped their lesson and were cowering down, panicked looks on their faces as Ryker darted along the stands. Ryker didn't dare look back, but he knew the shooter must have come out into the open when he heard gasps from the onlookers.

Another gunshot blasted. Ryker was already throwing himself down the next stairwell. The bullet struck the wall by his face and dust and stone fragments burst into the air. Ryker quickly wiped the grit from his eyes and headed along the inner corridor of the cavernous interior.

In the maze of corridors, pens and anterooms, he was quite sure he could use his skills to fight back and win against whoever was shooting at him. The problem was the onlookers in the arena. Not only could they get caught in the crossfire but they'd also likely be straight on to the police. The safest option was for Ryker to get out of there while he had the chance.

Ryker used his instincts as he weaved through the labyrinth of corridors until he eventually came to an exit door. It was shut, but had a security barrier across its centre. A fire exit. Ryker pushed down on the bar, then cautiously stepped out into the blazing sunshine.

He heaved a sigh of relief as he stuffed his gun into his jeans, underneath his shirt. Then he began a steady march away from the bullring – running would only draw further attention to himself now that he was out in the streets again.

Ryker checked behind every few yards. Not long after, he saw two men emerge from the still open exit. It was too far to make them out in much detail, but they headed in the same direction as Ryker. They didn't seem to be carrying guns, but then they wouldn't be so foolish as to brandish their weapons out in the streets.

Ryker passed over the Puento Nuevo, glancing down at the canyon below. It gave Ryker one final thought. As he approached the end of the bridge, he noticed a stone staircase that wound down the side of the bridge to a lookout point. A narrow trail then led along the side of the cliff.

If he could lure the men down there...

Ryker descended the stairs. He stood and waited at the bottom, pulling himself up against the thick stone wall of the bridge. He had to be quick. The area was quiet, but the town was busy. He didn't want a random passerby happening upon him as he shoved a man over the edge.

He heard footsteps on the stairs. Two sets. Ryker tensed, bracing himself to attack.

Then he quickly wound himself back down when a man and a woman came into view. Arm in arm, they sauntered off along the path.

Ryker stood for a few moments longer. No sign of the men. Then he heard an eruption of sound above. A police siren suddenly cut through the air. If the two attackers hadn't already scarpered, they certainly would now.

And that was exactly what Ryker chose to do too.

Less than two minutes later, Ryker was sat back in his car, air-conditioning on full blast as he headed away from Ronda, back towards the coast.

Chapter 40

Ryker kept his senses on alert as he drove along the mountainous roads toward the Costa del Sol. Eva's car had still been parked opposite Ryker's when he'd left Ronda. He'd seen nothing more of either her or the two men. And there was no sign now in his rear-view mirror of Eva's car or any others on the quiet roads. No police chasing him either, which could only be a good thing.

He'd gotten away. He was unscathed. But he was left feeling frustrated and bitter. Frustrated that his trip had taught him little about what was happening in Andalusia, except for some useless details about bullfighting. And bitter because people out there were trying to hurt him. Eva, Kozlov, Walker; one or a combination of them had conspired to hurt Ryker, possibly kill him. That was something Ryker wouldn't stand for.

Ryker made another call to Winter.

'You find anything?' the JIA commander asked.

'I'll tell you this: that's twice now that my liaisons with the Kozlov family have led to armed men chasing me down.'

'Please don't tell me you've got yourself locked up again?'

'No. This time I got away.'

'And the armed men.'

'I didn't kill any of them.'

'That doesn't exactly fill me with much confidence. So what did you find on your little excursion?'

Ryker filled Winter in. On the meeting with Eva, the men with the guns, how Ryker had shot at Buzzcut and the Slav before escaping from the other men. Winter took it all in without saying a word.

'The Russian mafia are somehow linked to Kim Walker's murder,' Ryker added.

'Why?'

'I still don't know. But they're in a panic now that one of their most trusted bent cops has been taken out.'

'Cardo?'

'Yeah.'

'Does the mafia know about the Red Cobra?'

'I don't know. What about at your end?'

'The hack attack. We traced it. You're not going to believe this but the attack was masterminded by one Miguel Ramos.'

'Spanish? Not what I was expecting.'

'No. I guessed you wouldn't be, but that's not all. He's only fifteen. A school kid who lives with his mother and grandma in central Malaga.'

Ryker raised an eyebrow.

'You said the hacker was a pro, that the trail was as complex as you'd seen?'

'It's true. These kids... that's what it's like these days.'

'Who knows about this?'

'Just us.'

'Good. Can you keep it that way? Cardo was bent. I don't know who else out here is.'

'I've no reason to pass the intel to anyone else. You're my eyes and ears on the ground.'

'Thanks. If you send me an address, I'll pay him a visit.'

'Go easy on him, Ryker. He's just a teenager. Part of a hacker group. He's not a criminal kingpin. Someone's using him.'

'I'll go easy on him. I promise. But you'd better prepare yourself for some more hassle at your end.'

'What are you talking about?'

'It's time to stop playing nice. The gloves are coming off.'

Ryker ended the call before Winter could ask any more questions or raise any protests.

It was nearly dark by the time Ryker pulled up outside the gates to Casa de las Rosas. A police car was stationed outside. Two officers stood guard, guns on hips, torches in their hands. One came over to Ryker's window, and Ryker wound it down.

'James Ryker. I'm with Detective Green.'

The policeman said nothing, just moved to the intercom on the wall where he began talking while his friend stood watch.

Moments later, the gates swung open and the officers stood to the side. Ryker drove through and parked up next to Green's car. Another officer stood outside the house. The door opened as Ryker approached. Green was on the other side. The officer moved out of the way.

'You get pretty good protection when you're mega rich,' Ryker said to Green.

'Money really can buy you anything.'

'Not quite anything. Where are they?'

'Sitting room.'

A further two officers stood guard by the closed doors to the sitting room.

'Open the door,' Ryker said to the policemen. They looked at each other quizzically.

'It's locked,' Green said. He moved forward, past Ryker, creating another barrier. 'Cool it a bit, yeah? There're six armed policemen here. Don't go making any rash moves.'

'I'm cool.'

'Good.'

'Get us into that room.'

Green hesitated then turned round. One of the officers moved out of the way and Green went up to the sitting room door and knocked loudly.

'Munroe. It's Green. Ryker too. We need to come in.'

A few moments later, Ryker heard the lock being released on the inside and the door swung open. On the other side was a policeman. Green had said six, so this was the final one. And he couldn't have been better placed.

Green walked into the room. Ryker followed. As soon as he stepped through the doorway, he calmly closed and locked the door behind him and took a second to fully scope out the space ahead.

Then he sprang into action before anyone even had an inkling of what was to come.

Ryker reached out and grabbed the holstered gun from the policeman's waist. He slammed the edge of his other hand onto the back of the officer's neck, hitting a pressure point of nerves that sent the officer keeling down onto the floor. Ryker then leaped forward, past Green and Munroe who had barely reacted, and rushed up behind Walker, grabbing him around his neck. Ryker kicked out Walker's legs and eased him down onto his knees before pulling the policeman's gun up and pushing the barrel into the back of Walker's head.

'What the hell are you doing?' Munroe screamed.

'Ryker, think about this,' Green said, trying his best to sound calm.

Walker said nothing, just whimpered.

'Get out of the room,' Ryker said. 'I need to speak to him. I won't hurt him unless you make me.'

'You're going to fry for this,' Munroe said.

'No, I'm not. Green, take Munroe out. Explain it to him. Do what you need to do. I have to speak to Walker.'

The policeman was stirring. He opened his eyes and lifted his head, his gaze fixed on Ryker.

'There're six armed policemen in this house,' Munroe said. 'You can't get away with this.'

'You want to end up like Cardo?' Ryker said. 'Because that's what's going to happen. I'm trying to save you. Save these policemen too. But I need to speak to Walker. Now.'

'Okay.' Green held out his hands, trying to show he was calm in the charged room. 'Come on, Graham. Trust me on this.'

Green looked over at Munroe. For a few seconds, Munroe did nothing, just stared at Ryker. Then he looked back at Green.

'I won't hurt him,' Ryker said. 'I won't hurt any of you. Not if I don't have to.'

Silence. Ryker moved the gun down, away from Walker's head.

'You're finished, Ryker,' Munroe said after a few seconds. 'You hear me?'

But Munroe's final protest was half-hearted. Green took hold of the lawyer's arm and shepherded him out. The policeman groggily got to his feet. Munroe spouted some words to him in Spanish – Ryker didn't catch them. The policeman nursed his neck then stepped through the doorway, followed by Munroe and then Green.

'I hope you know what you're doing,' Green said as he reached out to close the door behind him.

'I wouldn't be here if I didn't,' Ryker said, a second before the door was pulled shut.

Chapter 41

'Get up,' Ryker said.

He moved around Walker, who got to his feet and then stepped away, cowering – none of the arrogance he'd displayed when Ryker had first met him remained.

'What do you want?' Walker asked.

'The truth.' Ryker put the handgun down on a coffee table. He didn't need the policeman's gun. He still had his Colt in his waistband if Walker were stupid enough to make any kind of move.

'You don't have to do this, Patrick!' Munroe shouted from the other side of the door.

'Yes, he does,' Ryker said, his voice raised. 'Go and relax. Make yourself a pot of coffee. If Walker is a helpful as I think he's going to be then I won't be long.'

Silence from the other side of the door. That was good enough for Ryker. Walker slumped down onto a sofa. Ryker stood over him.

'I don't want to hurt you, Patrick,' Ryker said, sounding more genuine than he really felt. 'But I need answers. And if you don't leave me a choice...'

Walker hung his head. Ryker took that as a sign of compliance.

'The note you received,' Ryker said. 'Tell me what it means.'

'I haven't a clue!' Walker looked back up.

'I don't believe you.'

'It was *you* who said you knew who sent it! Not me.'

'I didn't ask you who sent it. Do you want to die, Patrick?'

'What? Of course not.'

'Then talk to me. Because you've pissed off the wrong person.'

'Who?' Walker said, his confusion sounding real.

'Tell me about Kim.'

'What about her?'

'Your wife's identity was a sham. You knew that, right?' The startled look in Walker's eyes suggested that he didn't. 'Andrews was her maiden name?'

'Y... yes. It was.'

'But there was no Kim Andrews. The identity was fake. I want to know why, and who she really was.'

'I've no idea!' Walker protested. 'I mean, what the hell are you even talking about?'

Ryker glared at Walker for a few seconds. His surprise and confusion certainly appeared genuine enough.

'How did you meet her?'

'How did we meet? It was here. In a bar. We dated. We married. We've been together for years.'

'What about her family. Her parents.'

'Her dad died when she was a teenager. She never knew her mum.'

'You never suspected she wasn't who she said she was?'

'No. Why would I?'

'Never even the smallest inkling? Lack of friends? Awkwardness talking about her past?'

'She talked about her past all the time. About school. Her jobs.'

'What jobs?'

'I don't know. She worked in a shop, then a bar I think. She ended up as a nursery school teacher. She's loved kids her whole life. It was the perfect job for her.'

Ryker could tell that Walker was having a hard time holding his emotions together. Talking about Kim was pushing him to the edge.

'She worked here in Spain?'

'No, before we met. I talked to her about going back to work but she didn't need to. It's not like we needed the money.'

'Why'd she come here?'

'A boyfriend. Her ex. They moved out here together. He was an English teacher.'

'Name?'

'Jack.'

'Jack what?

'I've no idea what his second name was. We never met.'

'You ever travel to England with her?'

'No,' Walker said. 'Why would we? Neither of us have family there now. Are you saying... none of it's true?' Walker asked, sounding genuinely saddened at the thought. 'That none of what she told me was true?'

Ryker paused. He got the sense Walker really didn't know about Kim's past. Walker hadn't just made up what he'd said on the spot. There'd been no hesitation, no tell-tale signs of deceit, and Ryker was pretty good at spotting the signs. A big part of his previous life had been interrogation. He'd also been interrogated countless times himself. In training, and in real life. He knew the difference between a lie and the truth, and the difference between the truth and a well-orchestrated story. Walker's surprise about his dead wife's secret life was real.

'I can't tell you how much is true,' Ryker said. 'Because I simply don't know.'

Walker's eyes welled up, but he held the tears in and fought to keep his composure. 'Why would she *do* that?'

Ryker looked away from Walker over to the stone fireplace. A row of pictures sat on top in a variety of crystal, wood, and metal frames. Each was of Walker and Kim, the happy couple, all smiles and love. They looked so... normal.

Ryker didn't like Walker and didn't trust him. But at the same time, the man's wife had been murdered. Even though Ryker believed Walker was in some way responsible, he could also see the man was grieving. Still, Ryker was determined to get to the truth. He had to find out what Walker knew.

'I loved her.' Walker got up from his seat and went over to the fireplace. He picked up a large glass frame and stared down at it. 'I really loved her.'

'I'm sure you did.'

'This picture... We were on our first holiday together. Thailand. She loved it there – the ambience, the culture. We went back twice.'

'Never been,' Ryker said, trying to sound interested.

'We were so happy. We were always happy together. Kim was such an easy person to get along with, and when we found out she was pregnant... I've never felt so fulfilled in my whole life. Mainly because I knew how much it meant to Kim. A baby was the one big thing missing in her life.'

'But you *were* sleeping with Eva Kozlov,' Ryker said, bringing Walker back down to earth.

'Fuck you.' Walker returned the picture, averting his eyes from the stare of his dead wife. 'You don't know what

Eva's like. She's evil. She lures people in. She plays with them then spits them out. She never wanted to be with me – not really. She just wanted to wreak havoc with my marriage.'

Ryker said nothing. Walker's description of Eva sounded spot on. But it was all well and good thinking that about her with hindsight. Walker had still fallen into bed with Eva, more than once. He wasn't exactly an innocent party.

'And what about Andrei Kozlov?' Ryker asked.

'We're good friends,' Walker said, sounding unsure.

'I went to visit him yesterday. Not long after I did, two heavies came after me.'

'I heard.'

'Who sent them?'

'I don't know.'

'You?'

'Of course not!'

'Kozlov then?'

'I said I don't know.' Walker's tone was now hard and defiant – a stark contrast to the emotion he'd shown moments before. Walker sat back down in his chair.

'You're lying.'

Both men went silent. Ryker's mind was whirring. 'How did you and Kozlov meet?'

'Playing golf. Years ago.'

'Before you met Kim?'

'Yes.'

'And?'

'And he was a developer, like me. We saw an opportunity to work together, and pool our resources to take on jobs we'd never have been able to do alone. We've worked together numerous times over the years.'

'And when did you first find out that he was bent?'

'Bent?'

'Don't be an idiot, Patrick. Kozlov is a crook. I can smell it a mile off.'

Walker shook his head. 'You have no idea what you're getting yourself into here, do you?'

'You think?'

'I didn't want this.'

'Didn't want what? The nice house? The nice cars? The designer wife?'

'I loved her.'

'So you keep saying. To be honest, I don't care whether you did or didn't. I just want to know what you've got yourself mixed up in. Somebody wants you dead. Somebody who I know won't stop. What I can't figure out is why.'

'You may think you know who sent that note, but I really don't,' Walker said. 'So you're going to have to help me out here.'

Ryker sighed. 'You know the saying; the elephant in the room. This elephant is so fucking big it's about to burst through the roof.'

'What are you talking about?'

'That note. I know who it's from.'

'You said that already.'

'I did. But you haven't once suggested that the note is from the same person who killed Kim. I mean, an outsider looking in might think that's at least a possibility, if not an obvious conclusion. Wife murdered. Husband threatened.'

Walker didn't say anything.

Ryker knew his instinct was right. 'The thing is, you *know* the note isn't from the person who killed Kim. Which leads me to only one conclusion.'

'Which is what?'

'That you do know who killed your wife. And you also know why.'

Chapter 42

Walker held Ryker's eye contact but didn't say a word. His response, or rather lack of it, only further cemented Ryker's belief.

'I'll ask you again,' Ryker said. 'What is Kozlov up to?'

'You have no idea what you're getting yourself into.'

'You said that already. Kozlov's got a henchman. Name's Sergei. You met him?'

'Sergei? A henchman? What are you on? He's a dogsbody. A chaperone. He hasn't got more than two brain cells in his ugly head.'

Ryker had to laugh at that. 'I'm sure he's no genius. But he is dangerous. He's a Vor. You heard of them?'

'No, I haven't.' It was an obvious lie. Even Walker didn't seem to believe it.

'Try again. I'm not new to this, Walker. I'm not like the policemen out there. I've lived and breathed organised crime for years. I spotted the set-up here almost immediately. Two rich property developers. One is a weed who'd crap his pants at the first sign of trouble, the other is a smug Russian who thinks he's way more powerful than he really is. So you need to start talking now.'

Walker took an age to reply. Ryker gave him the chance to build up to whatever he was going to say. No point in pushing. He had a good reading of Walker and knew he was trying to think of further ways to bullshit, debating whether it was really worth it. The long, dejected sigh he let out before he spoke suggested the false answer he'd been contemplating was too obvious and too difficult to hold for long.

'It's not Kozlov.'

'What's not Kozlov?'

'I thought he was legit. To start with he was. I went into business with him with my eyes wide open. I never expected it to go this way.'

'And which way is that?'

Walker put his head in his hands. 'I... I can't say.'

'Call it what it is, Walker. The Russian Mafia. The Bratva. That's who Kozlov is mixed up with, who you've got mixed up with.'

Walker looked up and closed his eyes for a couple of seconds. When he opened them again, they were glazed over as though no life lay behind them. 'Not Russian. Georgian.'

'Not much difference in my eyes.'

'You don't sound surprised.'

'I'm not.'

'I was. I still am. Just saying words like that – mafia, Vory – they sound so surreal, like this can't be happening to me. I'm a good person. I really am.'

'You think the Georgians had Kim killed?'

Walker sobbed. The answer to the question was clear enough.

'Why?' Ryker asked.

'Money,' was Walker's simple response.

'How much?'

'Ten million euros.'

'How?

'It was bullshit,' Walker said, for the first time sounding angry. Perhaps he did have some balls, Ryker mused. 'They saw me as an easy target. Tried to milk me.'

'When did it start?'

'About three years ago. I'd been working with Kozlov for years before that. Everything was fine. We were making money. We were friends. Then all of a sudden a silent partner comes on the scene.'

'Name?'

'It's not a person. Just a sham company.'

'Empire Holdings.' Ryker recalled the documents he'd seen at Kozlov's home. There'd been invoices. Correspondence.

'You know about it?' Walker asked, confused.

'Just putting the pieces together.'

'It's a bogus company. It's only there to drain money from the developments.'

'You didn't question it?'

'Of course I did! But Kozlov warned me off, said we had no choice, that we'd still make money.'

'That's okay then, as long as you're still raking in millions.'

'That's not it at all,' Walker spat. 'I was scared. I didn't know what else to do. To start with, it was small. I thought it might stay like that, I hoped it would, but pretty soon they were skimming so much off there was nothing left.'

'Hardly a profitable way to run a business.'

'And therein lies the problem. The projects struggled. There was no profit left for me and Andrei. Soon we were having to put more and more of our own money in to keep projects ticking over.'

'Let me guess; then *they* helped you out more and more.'

It was a classic scheme, Ryker knew, making Walker indebted to the mob so he had nowhere to go. Walker looked down at his feet, clearly ashamed – of exactly which part of the mess Ryker wasn't sure.

'They became... less silent,' Walker said. 'All of a sudden it was Empire Holdings that spotted the opportunities. They would identify and acquire the land, obtain the permissions, set up the contractors. Everything was done in their name. Essentially I became a manager, a glorified employee.'

'And you never asked what was happening? Who was pulling the strings?'

'No. I know I should have, but I didn't. Kozlov told me the people behind Empire were dangerous. That we had to keep going and we'd make money as long as we kept quiet.'

'Empire was buying the land cheap,' Ryker said, thinking out loud, 'so the developments could start making profits again. Probably extorting land owners and local government officials to make it work.'

'I can only assume.'

'And no doubt giving kickbacks to whoever they needed to.'

'Their hands reach everywhere.'

'The police too,' Ryker said, thinking back to recent events.

The conclusion he'd rightly come to after the fight on the construction site was that the arresting officer, possibly others, were bent. How far did the corruption spread, though? Ryker wondered again about Cardo. The Red Cobra had killed him. Now the reason was becoming more clear. She wanted Walker, but he wasn't the only target. Maybe Walker wasn't even the big target, just a pawn. It was the Georgians, the mafia, that the Red Cobra was after.

And anyone who'd become mixed up with them, bent policemen included.

What about Green? Ryker suddenly thought. His standoffish manner with Ryker when he'd first arrived. Not just his caginess about Ryker digging, but the fear that Ryker had sensed. Had the mafia already silenced him too? 'Does Green know?'

'About what we just talked about?'

'Yes.'

Walker shook his head, confused. 'Certainly not from me. And if so, he's never let on.'

'Munroe?'

'Not everything. But he's my lawyer. Of course he knows about Empire, and what was happening with the developments.'

Ryker believed Walker, which only made him dislike Munroe all the more. Ryker was sure Munroe was only looking to save his client's backside but the delaying tactics he'd been playing had only served to put Walker in a perilous position.

As for Green, Ryker would have to keep his eye on the detective. But then, if Green had fallen foul of the Georgians, perhaps even received a note from the Red Cobra like Cardo and Walker had, wouldn't he have said something? 'You said you owed them ten million. Why didn't you pay them?'

'I couldn't!' Walker protested. 'I don't have that kind of cash. I mean, I would've had to sell everything to get it.'

'Did you offer to do that? Seems a better course than what's happened.'

'You're saying it's my fault they killed Kim?'

Ryker didn't answer, but what did Walker expect him to say? Of course it was his fault.

'I didn't know they were capable of... that,' Walker said.

'Capable of killing your wife, you mean?'

'Yes.'

'But you knew they were dangerous.'

'Knew they were dangerous? I've seen movies, I watch TV. My knowledge of the mafia comes from fantasy, not real life. Kozlov *told* me they were dangerous. But...'

'But they never threatened you. You never saw what they were capable of.'

'No.' Walker looked down at his feet.

'But you do think that's why she was killed? There's no other reason?'

'Are you saying there's another reason?'

Ryker didn't answer. If Walker was telling the truth – that he owed money but the Georgians had never threatened such violence – then Kim's sudden and horrific murder did seem extreme and unusual, particularly when the mafia had such a hold over Walker. If they wanted money they could have carried on milking him for years; he would never have let on to anyone. So why kill his wife like that? Ryker was certain it was Walker's connection to Kozlov and the people behind Empire that had led to Kim's murder, but Ryker didn't believe she was killed over ten million euros.

The only conclusion Ryker could come to was that Kim Walker was murdered because of who she really was. At least, who the Georgians thought she was.

The Red Cobra.

'I think we're done,' Ryker said.

'But... what happens now?

'It's getting late. Now we eat. Then we sleep. Life goes on, Patrick. I suggest you enjoy it while you still can.'

Chapter 43

Ryker spent the next half hour getting Munroe to climb down off the wall. With the help of Green, the lawyer eventually calmed as the reality of the situation sank in. Ryker sensed Munroe's heated response to the exposure of the truth about his client's business partners was partly fuelled by embarrassment. Still, despite the deadly situation they found themselves in, Munroe was threatening to end Ryker's career. Ryker didn't fight that. It wasn't as though he had a career, and nor did he want one. But Munroe liked to think he held the power and that was fine with Ryker.

Eventually good sense won out, and the three men debated their next steps. Walker's maid cooked up a pasta meal for the many houseguests, giving the men further time to ponder.

Once they were finished and the policemen had been despatched to their watch posts, Ryker, Munroe, and Green started up their conversation once more.

The lawyer's instinct was that they should go to the Spanish authorities with the information they had. Ryker quickly played down the suggestion. For starters they didn't know how far the corruption spread. If Munroe wanted to protect his client – physically rather than legally – then did he really want to run the risk of tipping off a corrupt officer? And secondly, doing so wouldn't take away the immediate threats: the Red Cobra and Georgians. The Red Cobra was out there somewhere and, for whatever reason, she wanted Walker's blood. And the Georgians? They'd had Kim Walker killed. Since then, Ryker's snooping had twice put him in danger of the mob's enforcers. If Ryker didn't hold off, then the Georgians wouldn't stand for him much longer.

With the night ticking by, the men ultimately decided they would batten down the hatches until morning. There were six armed policemen on site at Casa de las Rosas. None of them were told the truth about Walker, the Georgians, and the Red Cobra. They didn't need to be. The policemen were there for protection duty, and that was all Ryker needed them to be.

Taking charge of the situation, Ryker outlined a plan for the ten men that would allow each of them time to rest that night and made sure all the house and grounds were covered by surveillance. To help them, they locked down half of Walker's mansion. They didn't need to try to cover the whole expansive interior.

At midnight, Ryker took the opportunity to get some rest in the downstairs library where they'd earlier dragged some mattresses from the many guest bedrooms. He was alone in the room – a twenty-foot square that had two walls of floor-to-ceiling bookcases crammed with books and ornaments of various shapes and sizes.

The other men in the house were all on edge, clearly not used to being in such a dangerous situation. Ryker, on the other hand, was calm. He tried calling Lisa, but like earlier in the day, he got no answer. He left her another voicemail, a slight feeling of anxiety seeping into him as he questioned why it was becoming so hard to reach her. Was she really safe out there on her own? Winter had already found them. What if someone else had come looking too.

Barely two minutes later, Lisa called back and Ryker answered immediately. 'Where are you? Are you okay?'

'Yeah, of course. Why?'

'I don't know, I just thought... nothing.'

'What's wrong?'

'Nothing. I thought maybe you'd gone sightseeing or something.'

He knew she'd understand his words: *Sightseeing Or Something:* SOS. Given their lives on the run, they'd long before decided on numerous SOS word combinations to allow them to alert the other discreetly should they ever be in danger.

Lisa laughed. 'No. I was taking a shower. Is everything okay?'

'Yeah. It's fine. It's nice to hear your voice.'

'I miss you. It's so quiet here.'

'I know. I miss you too.' There was an awkward silence. 'It's late here. I need to get some sleep.'

'Maybe next time we can chat properly.'

'Maybe next time I'll be home already.'

'I hope so.'

They said their goodbyes and within seconds of lying down on the bare mattress, Ryker was asleep. He dreamt of Lisa. In the dream, they were having sex – bizarrely, in Andrei Kozlov's sumptuous bedroom. Ryker was lying on the giant bed, with Lisa's naked, supple body riding on top of him. It was one of those dreams from which Ryker didn't want to wake up. So when he felt something cold press onto his neck, when his eyes suddenly shot open, for a split second he felt abject disappointment.

But only for a split second. Because that's all it took for Ryker to figure out what was happening.

The room was dark. Not black. The curtains were drawn and the lights were off, but the spotlights from the garden outside – usually tripped only by movement – had been set to stay on through the night and the glow from them seeped into the room through the thin curtains. It was enough light for Ryker to make out the black-clad figure that was sat on top of him on the mattress. And with the vivid and colourful images of Lisa's naked body quickly fading, there was no mistaking the feeling of the object that was on Ryker's neck.

Cold metal. A knife.

The figure wore a mask. Ryker couldn't see the face, but he knew who it was.

The Red Cobra held a finger up to her lips. Ryker remained still, though he was fuming.

'Don't call for help,' she whispered.

Her smooth voice sent a shock of memories through Ryker's mind. Where moments earlier he'd been dreaming of Lisa on top of him, he now had a flash of the Red Cobra, Anna Abayev, in Lisa's place, back in the hotel in Berlin where they'd shared a bed.

'It's good to see you, Carl.'

'What do you want?'

'I don't want to hurt you.'

'Then take the knife away from my throat.'

She did so, pulling the blade down by her side.

'What do you want?' Ryker asked again.

'You can live. Or you can die. Time to make your choice.'

'I'm not dying tonight.'

'Then help me.'

'Help you to do what?'

She leaned forward, moving to a few inches from Ryker's face. When she spoke, he could feel her breath on his cheek. It made him shiver.

'Kill them all.' Her whisper was barely audible, somehow adding to the power of her words.

The Red Cobra moved back upright. She took off her mask. If there had been even a sliver of doubt in Ryker's mind about whether it really was her, it disappeared in that instant. He could never forget that face.

Years had passed since Ryker had last seen the Red Cobra. He'd often wondered what had become of her, about how differently their meeting each other could have ended, and whether he could have helped her. Mostly, he wondered why she hadn't killed him when she'd had the chance.

Strangely, it was good to see her face. Reassuring. The Red Cobra gave Ryker a knowing smile. She opened her mouth to speak. She never got the chance.

The Red Cobra's appearance hadn't changed. She was still pretty, and it was clear her body was still lithe and toned. And lightweight. Ryker grabbed hold of her wrist and thrust an arm around her back, pinning her to him, then sprang up from the mattress, the Red Cobra wrapped around him still. He drove forward, carrying her with him, and slammed her into the bookshelves.

The crushing impact knocked the wind out of her. Her body was suspended in the air, held in place against the shelves by Ryker's weight. He crashed her hand onto the wooden shelves behind. On the third impact, the knife fell from her grasp and clattered to the floor.

Ryker looked into her eyes. For a second, he had a moment of doubt as she stared back at him. He imagined himself kissing her. Her kissing him back. How she tasted.

Then Winter's words burrowed into his mind: *You see her, you kill her. Don't even think about it.*

Ryker brought up his forearm, then pushed it into the Red Cobra's neck and began choking her.

It only took a few seconds for panic to sweep across her face. She clawed at Ryker's arm and flailed at him with her fists, then tried to punch him in the side. For all her mastery in the art of killing, she was simply no match for Ryker's strength.

But Ryker was too angry at the situation he'd found himself in. With Walker. With Eva. With the Red Cobra – not just in Spain but in Germany all those years earlier.

Anger clouded his judgment. The man who'd first met the Red Cobra wouldn't have made such a mistake. Long before, Ryker – Carl Logan – had been taught not to fight with anger. He'd learned to control it. Anger wasn't needed for the mechanic operative he'd become for the JIA.

But he wasn't that man now. He was James Ryker.

With Ryker distracted by his own determination to choke the life from the Red Cobra, she swept her arm up and sprayed him in the face. He knew immediately what she'd used: pepper spray.

The pressurised liquid burst onto Ryker's skin and into his eyes. In an instant, it felt like his face was on fire, like his skin was melting, his eyelids bubbling and boiling. He couldn't see a thing.

Ryker couldn't hold on. He let go, stepped back, and heard the Red Cobra thud to the ground. He shouted out as the pain in his face consumed him. He still couldn't see, but he poised for the attack he knew was to come.

He wasn't up against an amateur, though. This was the Red Cobra. Only luck would have seen him block the unseen attack. It seemed he was all out. The blow from the

Red Cobra to the back of his head caught Ryker unaware. He hadn't heard a sound from her as she'd moved behind him.

Unable to muster a response, Ryker collapsed to the floor.

Chapter 44

Eight years earlier

Whether she'd chosen to help Carl Logan or not, the Red Cobra knew she was playing a dangerous game. She was used to that. That was her life. But whatever the many and varied reasons for the choice she'd made, she couldn't ignore the strong pull she felt toward Carl Logan. Was it his supreme confidence? Or how he seemed so emotionally detached from what was a deadly situation?

Was he detached, or simply in control?

Carl Logan reminded the Red Cobra of her father. He too had been charming and kind when he wanted to be, particularly when he was playing Dad. But she'd come to know that beneath the surface, he was quite a different beast. He'd worn so many faces in his life it was impossible to know who he really was. The same could be said for her, of course.

She cursed herself for comparing anyone to her father, whom she still loved dearly and sorely missed. But, she figured, the similarities she saw between Logan and her father were a big reason she felt so drawn to Logan. And why she'd agreed to help him.

Not that it meant she wouldn't slice him open if the time came. She had to be prepared for that, no matter what.

'How long's the drive?' the Red Cobra asked.

'About an hour,' Logan said, staring out of his window.

They were travelling in a high-powered black Audi saloon. Logan was sitting in the back, behind the driver. The Red Cobra was next to Logan. The driver was the man she'd seen with Logan in Gazinsky's hotel suite. He was again smartly dressed in a black suit. She couldn't determine whether he looked more like a young businessman or a clichéd well-groomed secret agent from a Hollywood movie. Whichever it was, he was a mile away in looks and persona to the mysterious Logan. The driver had been introduced as Martin. She wasn't sure whether that was his first or last name and hadn't sought to clarify.

'Where are we going?' the Red Cobra asked Logan.

'East.'

She knew there wasn't much left of Germany heading east from Berlin. Soon they'd be into Poland. That made her nervous.

'I don't have my passport,' she joked.

'Sure you do.' Logan turned to face her. He looked down at her rucksack, sitting between her legs. 'You're carrying everything you had with you in Berlin. Aren't you?'

He was right. She was. She'd packed her things that morning before setting off to the Waldorf to track down Gazinsky. She'd never intended to stay in Berlin another night. She looked away from Logan, out of her own window, and watched the city buildings blur past.

'We're not leaving Germany,' Logan said, 'if you were worried about that.'

The Red Cobra turned back to face him. 'I'm not worried. Just curious.'

'Good.'

'Why out of the city?'

'It's a safe place.'

'Safe for what?'

'Safe for you to meet someone.'

'Gazinsky?' she asked with optimism.

'Maybe. You'll see.'

This time it was Logan's turn to look away. And that signalled the end of the conversation for the rest of the journey.

They were soon out of the city and onto the Autobahn 11, heading east towards the town of Eberswalde. The Red Cobra wondered if that town was their destination. But they passed right by it, heading closer and closer to the Polish border.

The Red Cobra felt her nerves grow. In her line of work, she had to travel across borders with the utmost caution, because it invariably left a record of her movement. She had enough cover identities to allow her to move freely around most of the world but hopping from one country to another was still a potentially fraught move. She liked to leave as little trail as possible. Plus she had countless enemies in countless locations, and Poland was certainly one such location.

In the end, despite her wariness, she needn't have worried because Logan hadn't lied. They weren't leaving Germany. But just where were they going?

Not long after leaving the Autobahn they headed down a twisting road and into a thick forest that was filled with pine trees and oaks, the green canopy above them so condensed that it was like driving at night.

They passed isolated houses here and there, and the occasional small cluster. Eventually they turned onto an even narrower road that continued for a couple of miles, coming to a stop at a rustic stone and timber house that looked in some need of love and care. Martin parked the car next to a grey SUV directly in front of the house. The lights were on inside.

Somebody was home.

Not for the first time in the journey, the Red Cobra wondered whether Logan was laying a trap for her. Was he about to turn on her out here? Imprison her? Interrogate, torture? Or maybe the plan was simply to kill her straight off and bury her in the remote woodland.

But if Logan wanted to kill her, why bring her all the way out here alive? It simply wasn't necessary. He would have killed her already.

Or tried to at least. She still firmly believed she'd be able to get the better of him if he made a move.

She wondered again whether this was the place they had stashed Gazinsky. And if Charles McCabe was there too, that would mean all the targets Potanin had given her would be right there in front of her.

That would certainly put her in one hell of a dilemma.

'Come on.' Logan opened his door and stepped out.

The Red Cobra did the same. Martin got out of the driver's seat but then hung back, by the car, as she and Logan walked toward the house's large front door. They were a yard away when the door creaked open.

Inside, the Red Cobra spotted another suited man, dressed much like Martin, though this guy was older, forties probably, and also much thicker in the frame. His suit jacket was undone and he made no effort to conceal the holstered handgun that was strapped to his side. The

Red Cobra, hands in her jacket pocket, caressed the handle of her hunting blade. A comforter.

As she stepped in through the open doorway, two paces behind Logan, he suddenly stopped and turned to face her.

'Give me your backpack.' He held out his hand.

She gave it to him without hesitation.

'What weapons do you have on you?' he asked.

The Red Cobra thought before answering. She didn't want to give up her hunting blade, nor the pocket knife that was strapped to her ankle. But did she have a choice? There was always the choice of taking the hunting blade and using it to kill every man in sight.

Perhaps that was a step too far, though. For now.

'Two knives,' she said. 'One in my jacket. The other on my ankle.'

'Leave them here.'

The Red Cobra hesitated then relented. She took the small pocket knife out of the ankle strap first and handed it to the suited man. Then she drew out her hunting blade. Logan stared at her, as though impressed with her choice of weapon. She handed that over.

'Anything else?'

'No.'

'Okay. Butcher will pat you down.'

'I feel like I'm about to meet the president or something.'

'I guess you never know.'

The suited man, who Logan had called Butcher, searched across the Red Cobra's body. He took a little too long feeling around her groin and chest, his disgusting sausage-like fingers squeezing her flesh. She didn't react. Just made a mental note.

Butcher found nothing and the search was soon over.

'So is it Gazinsky that you've got holed up here?' the Red Cobra asked Logan again.

'No. Follow me.'

The Red Cobra glared at Butcher before following Logan down the wood-panelled corridor. It led into a sitting room, with walls of bare stone and an obscenely large fireplace but otherwise bereft of fittings. This place certainly wasn't a home, not anymore. There were no ornaments, knickknacks, or personal belongings of any kind.

On a large brown leather sofa – one of two – sat a middle aged man. He had thin hair, a goatee beard, and thick-rimmed glasses, and wore a pinstripe suit. The Red Cobra recognised his face immediately, from the information she'd received from her employer.

'This is Charles McCabe,' Logan said.

'Mackie,' the man said, getting to his feet, and offering the Red Cobra his hand. 'Please, call me Mackie. It's good to finally meet you, Anna.'

His voice was loud but smooth, his accent what she thought was English upper class. The Red Cobra shook Mackie's hand. Gazinsky wasn't here, but two of her targets were. Interesting.

Mackie took his seat again. The Red Cobra sat on the sofa opposite. Logan remained standing.

'Wow, you really are beautiful,' Mackie said. The Red Cobra held back her grimace at the old man's lame flattery. 'I heard you were, but seeing you for real... even prettier than I imagined.'

'Thanks,' she said without any feeling.

'I feel sorry for the poor sods you sucker in with that pout. I'm sure there've been many.'

The Red Cobra almost smiled. With that comment, she saw Mackie for what he actually was. Not a pervy man but a unique talent spotter.

'You should see her without the wig,' Logan said, smiling at her.

Mackie chuckled. 'I'm glad you came here.'

'Why *am* I here?' the Red Cobra asked.

'It was Logan's idea,' Mackie said. 'He likes you.'

'Yeah, he told me so.'

'Not like that, Anna. He thinks you've got potential.'

'Potential for what?'

'To work with us.'

'I work alone.'

'So does Logan.'

'Then why do you need me?'

'Because you're good. Very good.'

'I'm flattered.'

'I knew your father,' Mackie said, and that bombshell knocked the Red Cobra off course. The pleased look on Mackie's face showed that he knew it too.

'My father's dead,' she said, trying to hide that she was rattled by Mackie's revelation.

'Yes. I know that. I'm looking at the woman who killed him.'

The Red Cobra said nothing.

'I liked Vlad,' Mackie said. 'You could always count on him. In some ways it was a shame that... you know.'

'How did you know him?'

'How do you think? I hired him, more than once. He was excellent at his work. Discrete. Seamless. Not cheap, but you get what you pay for.'

'He wasn't good enough, though, was he?' the Red Cobra said.

'In the end, no, you're right. He wasn't. But everyone has their downfall eventually. It'll come to all of us whether we like it or not.'

'What do you want me to do for you exactly?'

'Help Logan get to Potanin.'

'Why?'

'Because that's what I need to happen.'

'That doesn't sound like a very good reason.'

'It doesn't? That's the only reason you'll ever get from me. I'm not here to debate the morality of what we do. I thought that would ring true with you.'

'Potanin wants me to kill you,' the Red Cobra said. 'Kill Gazinsky too. And Logan.'

She looked over at Logan. He was staring at her but his face was passive.

'Of course he does,' Mackie said. 'And did you question why he wants that?'

'No.'

'Good. Then you understand how this works already. So now we can stop talking about reasons and who deserves what. All we're doing here is changing your employer.'

'And what's in it for me?'

'You get to continue being alive. And you'll be paid, of course.'

'And if I refuse?'

'Then it'd be a shame to see your expertise go to waste. I'll be frank with you, Anna. It's luck that brought you here.'

'How so?'

Mackie shrugged. 'This isn't personal for you. You thought you were after Gazinsky. A battle of rivals – two corrupt billionaires. But that's such a small glimpse into what's happening here. Why do you think Potanin asked you to wait? Why did he have you surveilling Gazinsky? He could have sent you in there to kill Gazinsky days ago.'

'Because he wants me to kill you too.'

'Absolutely. Gazinsky is such a small cog here. Yes, he's important to me. He's prepared to turn his back on his home country and give us everything he knows. It'll be useful to hear that. But I don't care for him. He's never going to be one of us. Once we've got what we need we'll send him on his way again. Is that harsh? Maybe. But he's not important enough for us to waste time, money and effort protecting. He's expendable.'

'And me?'

'Everyone's expendable,' Mackie said. 'When they stop being useful. You see Logan here?'

The Red Cobra looked over at him. 'Yes.'

'He's not expendable. Not yet. Because he's reliable. He gets results. To be honest, I would have expected him to kill you two days ago when he first realised there was heat on Gazinsky.'

'He could have tried,' the Red Cobra scoffed.

'But he didn't,' Mackie said. 'If you'd been anyone else he would have taken you out before you even knew he was onto you. That's what he does. But this time he didn't.'

'Why?'

'Because he saw who was out there. The infamous Red Cobra. You've been on our radar for a long time.'

The Red Cobra let Mackie's words sink in.

A few seconds later, Butcher came into the room, a sour look on his hard face. He was carrying a radio receiver which crackled with static. He walked over to Logan and whispered into his ear. Logan took the radio then went to Mackie, bent down, and whispered to him. Mackie's expression turned from one of cordiality to outright hostility. It was an alarming transformation.

'Two cars approaching,' Mackie said, his eyes fixed on the Red Cobra. 'Eight men. You've got five seconds to tell me what's happening. If you don't, you're dead.'

Her heart drummed. This was it. The game was up. It was time to make her move.

Chapter 45

Four seconds passed without the Red Cobra or anyone else saying a word. She was trying to figure out what to do next. In the end, she only saw one option.

The Red Cobra leaped up and snaked around the back of Butcher who was standing just two yards from her. In an instant, she'd grabbed him round the neck with one arm. With her free hand, she took his gun from the holster and placed the barrel against his temple. Logan and Mackie didn't make a move. She was quick, but still, their lack of reaction confused her. Worried her a little too.

'And now what?' Mackie asked.

The Red Cobra said nothing.

'When did you do it?' Logan asked, with what seemed like genuine interest rather than surprise or anger. 'And how?'

'What did I say?' Mackie said to Logan, the hostility in his voice still clear. 'I was fifty-fifty.'

'I was sixty-forty,' Logan said. 'Maybe I shouldn't have been so confident.'

'We all make mistakes.'

'I let her go to the ladies. Before we went down to the car. That's when she did it, I'm guessing.'

'Yeah.' Mackie nodded. 'That's probably when she confirmed the hit. A simple text message most likely. But how did they find us here?'

'A tracking chip. Must be.' Logan turned to the Red Cobra. 'Where is it?'

Logan's carefree tone made her uneasy. Her finger was on the trigger of the handgun. She knew if she pulled it and blew out Butcher's brains that she'd probably have a second or two to dive for cover back into the hallway. Could she make it? Probably. But what then?

'I didn't set you up,' she said.

'Bullshit.'

'I didn't! If it's me they've followed I don't know how. It's the truth. I didn't make a call, or send a text or anything like that. I really didn't.'

'Then why are you holding a gun to my man's head,' Mackie said.

'Security,' she said.

'Really?' Mackie said. 'What the hell do you think you're going to do next? Potanin's men will kill you too when they arrive. Logan explained that to you already. Potanin was never going to let you live. Do you not get that?'

'I'll take my chances.'

'Then go ahead and pull the trigger. All these men are trained for this. You won't get past us all.'

'Maybe. Maybe not.'

'They're trained to give their lives for me. If I give the say-so,' Mackie clicked his fingers, 'Butcher will spin around and do his best to kill you.'

'He wouldn't stand a chance,' she said. Butcher remained still; she couldn't even sense or hear him breathing.

'No, probably not,' Mackie said. 'Butcher knows that. But he'd be prepared to try anyway, to sacrifice himself for me, and for the others. And his fight, whatever he can give, would be enough to allow Logan to take you down. You're a dead woman, Anna, unless you lower that gun.'

There was noise – footsteps – off to the left, down the hallway. Probably Martin, though the Red Cobra didn't dare take her eyes off Logan and Mackie to confirm. She heard his voice a second later.

'They're thirty seconds out,' Martin said, without a hint of angst.

'And now you've got a gun pointed at your head, Anna, by a target you can't even see,' Mackie said. 'It's your call.'

A few more seconds passed. They felt like a lifetime.

'Martin, Butcher, get Mackie out of here,' Logan said. 'You know the drill, where to go. Anna and I'll take care of the guests.' Nobody said a word. 'Right?'

'Right,' Martin and Butcher chorused.

The Red Cobra was left with no other choice. She didn't want to die. She dropped the gun to the ground, fully expecting Martin to either shoot her or knock her out right there.

But a second later, Martin came into view and passed by her. Then Butcher moved off too. Together with Mackie they headed out the back door of the sitting room, into the woods, without saying another word.

The Red Cobra looked over at Logan.

'Come on then,' he said. 'Show me what you've got.'

She turned round and headed to the front door where her backpack lay on the ground. She grabbed her pocket knife and put it back in her ankle holster. The hunting blade she grasped in her hand. She slowly opened the front door. No sign of anyone yet. She rushed back into the sitting room.

'You go out the rear,' she said to Logan. 'Work your way around the house to the front. I'll lure them into here.'

They heard a gunshot outside, then several more in quick succession. They sounded distant. The men were coming at them from all angles it seemed.

'That's good,' Logan said, as though noticing the unease the Red Cobra was feeling. 'Butcher and Martin will take care of anyone coming in their direction. Less for us to worry about.'

'Go,' she said to him. He turned and moved over to the door, then stepped out into the woods.

'Help!' the Red Cobra screamed at the top of her voice. 'Help. In here! I'm hurt.'

She had to assume Potanin's men had been given orders to kill her. But that didn't mean they knew that she knew. She would pretend to be with them for as long as necessary.

She moved up against the wall next to the doorway to the sitting room and listened. Nothing. She shouted again, trying to sound as desperate as she could. Still nothing.

A second later, a small object came clattering into the sitting room from the hallway. It came to a stop, by the sofa she'd been sitting on moments earlier. She knew what it was immediately – a smoke grenade. The thick white plume spread out rapidly and within seconds she couldn't see a thing.

But she could still hear.

Soft footsteps were audible, approaching down the hallway. Just one set, she thought. She let out one last shout for help. The footsteps stopped, then a second later, started up again.

Through the fog, she spotted an inch of a rifle barrel poking through the open doorway, within touching distance. The Red Cobra sprang into action. She leaped across the doorway and slashed twice with her blade, aiming for the torso and neck of the figure she couldn't fully see. She heard a pained gargle and there was a heavy thud when a figure, dressed from head to toe in black, fell through the smoke into a heap on the floor.

After a few seconds, the hissing of blood pulsing through the wound in the man's neck died down and all went silent again.

The Red Cobra took a peek down the hallway. It was filled with smoke; she couldn't see a thing. That was good. She rushed towards the front door, pulling up next to the doorframe. She heard another series of gunshots outside. Closer than before. Logan?

She shouted again, the same desperate call as before. An automatic rifle blasted a burst of gunfire into the house through the open doorway. It was almost deafening. Whoever it had come from was close, very close, firing blindly into the smoke hoping to catch her. At least she knew once and for all that these men weren't going to be helping her.

Doing her best to ignore the ringing in her ears and the disorientation from the point-blank gunshots, she dashed out of the open front doorway. Three yards into her sprint, she saw the outline of a black-clad figure through the wispy smoke. She feinted left. He opened fire. As she swept past, she slashed at his arm with the knife. The man screamed and began to turn to follow her move. But it was already too late for him.

The Red Cobra spun in an arc and slashed the knife viciously across his torso, leaving a gaping wound over a foot long in his chest and down his belly. The man collapsed to the ground.

Panting heavy breaths, her mind now focused and alert, The Red Cobra stopped and looked around. The smoke dissipated. At the corner of the house, another man appeared. He lifted his rifle and pointed it at her. She was about to dive desperately for cover when...

A gunshot rang out.

A spray of blood, bone, and brain erupted from the side of the man's head. His lifeless body fell down.

Logan stepped out from around the corner. He was now carrying a rifle. A handgun was sticking out from his jeans' waistband.

'How many?' he asked, still a picture of calm. He walked up to her.

'Two. You?'

'Three. And Butcher radioed to say two more at their end.'

'Leaves one,' the Red Cobra said.

And as the words passed her lips, she saw him, hiding behind a tree directly behind Logan, just ten yards away. His finger was already pulling on his rifle's trigger.

'Down!' she screamed as she bundled into Logan. She'd expected her momentum to send him flying but his heavy frame seemed to absorb her movement and the two of them fell to the ground clumsily in what felt like slow motion. Or maybe it was that the adrenaline coursing through her was giving her enhanced focus.

Either way, with bullets whizzing by them, the Red Cobra grabbed the handgun from Logan's waist as they fell. She turned the barrel and fired two shots before she landed on top of Logan.

She heard the man cry out. She'd hit him. She didn't know where, but she could hear him wailing. Before she had a chance to do anything, Logan brushed her off and got to his feet, then strode over to the man. Logan pulled up the rifle and put a bullet in the man's head.

The Red Cobra was on her feet and brushing herself down as Logan marched back over.

'Thank you,' he said, without any feeling in his words.

'You too,' she said. 'We did good.'

'Yeah. Eventually. But we need to figure out how they tracked you.'

'I think I know.'

'What the hell were you thinking, pulling the gun on Butcher like that?'

'I had to.'

'For someone with your skills, you really are quite dumb.'

'Fuck you, macho man.'

'If you insist,' Logan said with a mischievous smile.

Chapter 46

It was three a.m. when the Red Cobra awoke with a start. She wasn't sure what had roused her so aggressively. She hadn't been having a bad dream and the room was silent. Except for her own heavy breaths and the much slower breaths of the man laying next to her in the bed; Carl Logan.

She looked over at him, stared for a good while as she calmed her breathing. Then she got to her feet. She picked up the white hotel-branded robe from the floor and wrapped it around her naked body which was cold but damp with sweat. She moved over and sat in an armchair, facing the bed where Logan was still sleeping soundly.

Before leaving the house in the forests, they'd taken apart all the electronic items she had on her. They'd found bugging devices in both the camera and her phone. That worried her. Because she'd purchased both items when she was already in Berlin. Potanin had somehow managed to plant the bugs on her probably while she slept. He'd never trusted her from the start, had probably always planned to kill her, like Logan said.

After destroying all her electrical items, she and Logan had performed a thorough search of her clothing and her body for evidence of any other tracking equipment. There was none. Regardless, on leaving the house in the woods the two of them had headed straight to the nearest town where they'd purchased new clothes for her. She'd had to give up her leather jacket, but had spent a couple of hours once back in a hotel in central Berlin stitching a sheath for her hunting blade into a newly acquired one.

Following that, the Red Cobra and Logan had eaten room service, drank two bottles of wine and ended up in bed together. Again. This time he hadn't tried to sneak out.

Instead, at three a.m., it was she who was awake with thoughts cascading through her brain.

She couldn't take the suspense. She had to know. And with her laptop and phone gone, there was only one way she was going to find out.

She moved over to the bed and picked up Logan's mobile phone. She opened the web browser. The connection was far slower on his phone than it would have been on her laptop but after five minutes of mostly staring at blank screens, she finally managed to open up her inbox on the chat portal she used to communicate with Potanin.

Sure enough, there was a message waiting for her.

She wasn't sure what she'd expected. It wasn't like Potanin would have ranted and raged within the coded message he sent. Nonetheless, she could feel his animosity as she read the threatening words on the screen.

The Red Cobra closed her eyes and gritted her teeth.

What the hell had she done? This wasn't over. Not by a long stretch.

She deleted the message, closed the browser, then went into the phone's settings and cleared the internet cache too. Then she placed the phone back down.

She'd been given a simple choice by Potanin, much like the choice Mackie had given her: live or die. Potanin was giving her another chance to take out the targets. And while there wasn't a part of her that *wanted* to take the lifeline that Potanin was offering, she knew she had to.

Because it wasn't just her life on the line anymore. Potanin had made that very clear.

The Red Cobra bent down and rummaged through Logan's clothes, looking for the handgun she knew he had. She found it and lifted it up, turning it over in her hands. Then she pointed the barrel to Logan's head. He didn't stir, didn't move at all, not even a twitch. She pushed the gun closer to him, until the end of the barrel was an inch from his closed eyelid.

'I already took the bullets out,' Logan said, eyes still closed, his body unmoving.

The Red Cobra felt a flood of anger – embarrassment too – rush through her. She dropped the gun and it clattered to the floor.

Logan opened his eyes and stared at her. 'You can stay, or you can go. It's up to you.'

She thought for a moment, then let out a long and sorrowful sigh, got to her feet, and pulled on her clothes. Logan lay in bed, his hard gaze fixed on her.

Belongings? She had none. Just her knives, a few bank notes and the passports she'd brought with her to Berlin with photos that resembled her appearance but attached to identities that were nothing more than a lie. Everything about her life was a miserable damn lie.

She pushed her hunting blade into the freshly stitched pocket of her new jacket, then took one last look at Logan. A man she could have loved, perhaps? No, she wasn't capable of such a thing. And he certainly wasn't.

They would meet again, though. She was positive of that.

Logan was, after all, still a target. But he wasn't the only target. He could wait. Next time they met, though, one of them would likely die. But not tonight.

Without either of them saying another word, the Red Cobra turned and headed for the door.

Chapter 47

Present day

Ryker hadn't seen the Red Cobra for eight years. Two weeks after leaving their hotel room in Berlin in the middle of the night, she'd ambushed and murdered Gazinsky and his wife at a remote beach hut in northern Germany. Ryker and the JIA had been trying to smuggle the Gazinskys out of the country. They never did find out what they needed from the oligarch.

The Red Cobra had ended up in a fight on a cliff top with Ryker. Or Carl Logan as he had been back then. She'd had a gun to his head, but she hadn't taken the shot. She'd hesitated.

He hadn't.

The last Ryker saw of her was her body falling out of view over the edge of the cliff as the bullets from his gun tore into her. She'd been presumed dead by many. Ryker had always thought differently.

She certainly wasn't dead. Not yet.

The one saving grace when the Red Cobra attacked Ryker at Walker's house was that the noise from Ryker – first in slamming the assassin into the shelves, and secondly his screams as the pepper spray bore into his eyes – was enough to alert Green and the armed policemen. Their responsiveness and strength in numbers were probably the only things that night that saved Walker – whom Ryker could only assume the Red Cobra had come to the house to kill.

Thankfully, the brief training that Ryker had given to the others before he'd gone to sleep had paid off. Walker, locked in the sitting room with an armed officer and Munroe, had quickly been shielded as the others searched the house and grounds for the Red Cobra.

They found nothing.

The effects of the pepper spray diminished within minutes. After an hour, the swelling in Ryker's face had reduced enough to allow him to see again. By the time dawn came a few hours later, the pain had almost subsided.

Ryker sat on a stool at the breakfast bar in the kitchen, drinking strong coffee and eating a ham and cheese sandwich. Munroe was there too, nursing his umpteenth black coffee of the morning.

'I don't know what else you expect us to do now,' Munroe said. 'We have to get Walker moved.'

'Yeah,' Ryker said.

The previous night he'd been against the idea. He thought he could contain the problem, but the fact was he no longer wanted to sit around and wait for an attack. He wanted to be on the front foot. And the more he thought about it, the more he realised he didn't care for Walker. Ryker's job wasn't to protect him; plenty of others could do that. Ryker wanted to get to the bottom of why Kim Walker had been killed, and why the Red Cobra was on a mission of revenge in Andalusia.

'Who can we trust?' Munroe asked.

'I have no idea,' Ryker answered.

'There must be someone.'

Ryker thought. There was Winter of course. But did the JIA commander care enough about Walker to spend the time and effort in protecting him? Ryker decided no was the likely answer.

'It's not my call,' Ryker said. 'Green is the one you need to be speaking to about protection. He can work with the Spanish police, the English too if needed, to make sure Walker is okay.'

'But you said we can't trust the local police?'

'You can't. But I know one thing: the Red Cobra is on her own. That's how she works. She's not *with* the Georgians. I'm sure the mob has paid off everyone they can around here, policemen included, but they all need to band together now. The Red Cobra's a threat to them all.'

Green came into the room. He looked confused.

'News?' Ryker asked.

'We know how she left.' Green moved over to the breakfast bar and pouring himself a cup of coffee. 'There's no physical sign of her path but the CCTV we put up shows her exiting over the back.'

'It's just trees and rocks that direction?' Munroe asked.

'Yeah. Quite a scramble in the dark to get back to civilisation from there.'

'She used the distraction to escape,' Ryker said. 'When the alarm was raised, everyone's attention focused in the wrong place.'

Green shrugged. 'She knew what she was doing. That exit route was planned.'

Ryker felt foolish that it had been so easy for her.

'But how did she get in?' Munroe asked. 'Not just onto the grounds but into the house?'

'Good question,' Green said. 'We have no idea how she got past us. Between eyes and the cameras, we had every angle covered.

'No you didn't,' Ryker said.

'Yes we did. We went through it all together last night.'

'There was one angle we didn't think of.'

'What are you talking about?'

'She didn't sneak into the house in the middle of the night. She was already in here.' Ryker felt a chill run down his spine at his own words. He guessed from the shocked looks on the faces of Munroe and Green that they were feeling the same.

Ryker got to his feet. Munroe followed suit.

'The hallway was covered,' Ryker said. 'Green was there.'

'Yeah,' Green said. 'She didn't come past me to get into the library. No way.'

'And you were there the whole time?' Ryker asked.

'Yeah,' Green said. 'I mean, I went to the toilet for thirty seconds but that was it. I left the door open. I had my eyes on the hall the whole time.'

'And the stairs?'

Green didn't answer. Ryker fought hard not to roll his eyes. It was a mistake by Green but the policeman could hardly have expected the Red Cobra to be sneaking by in those few seconds when no one else on the grounds had once suggested there was a problem.

'She was already upstairs?' Munroe said, shocked. 'But for how long?'

Ryker turned and walked out of the room, heading back through the hall then up the twisting staircase to the first floor. Green sheepishly followed, Munroe a step behind and looking bewildered.

'We locked every room down,' Green said, apparently still not ready to believe Ryker's words. 'We placed seals over the doors. Nothing's been disturbed up here. I checked it all already.'

'Except she knew what you were doing,' Ryker said. 'She probably watched and listened to you doing it. And it's not too hard to replace a seal if you know it's there.'

'What? But–'

'How many accesses to the loft?' Ryker asked, standing on the landing and looking up at a hatch above his head.

'Three,' Green said. 'That's the main one. The only one with a direct access, a retractable ladder. No way she was up there, it would have been too noisy bringing that ladder down. Have you heard that thing?'

'And the other two?' Ryker asked.

'A hatch in the master bedroom. Inside the wardrobes. But it doesn't go into the full roof space. Just a cubbyhole for storage. Not big enough to fit a person.'

'And the third?'

'In here,' Green said, turning around and walking along the landing.

He opened a set of doors that led into a linen cupboard. He pointed upwards, and Ryker looked at the small hatch. It was no more than a foot square. Ryker seriously doubted he could fit through there. But the Red Cobra?

'I don't know why it's there,' Green said. 'Maybe access to pipes or electrics.'

'Didn't you check it? Last night?'

'Of course,' Green said. 'But it's sealed shut. I tried to open it but it's been glued or painted in place.'

Ryker pushed past Green and climbed onto the first shelf inside the cupboard so he could reach the ceiling. He pushed the hatch. It lifted up in his hand. Inside was an empty storage space, no bigger than a cubic yard. Electrical wires snaked along one of the walls. Ryker looked down at Green who gawped in disbelief. His cheeks turned red.

'It didn't move,' Green said, as though trying to convince himself as much as the others. 'I tried it myself.'

Ryker shook his head. 'She was already in there. Probably sat on the damn thing when she heard you moving around, so that it wouldn't open.'

'I can't... but–'

'And now we know why Cardo was pushed over the edge of that ravine,' Ryker said, climbing down.

'Time,' Green said, finally getting it.

'Yes. Which is what I suspected. I just didn't know why.'

'She didn't want the police swarming this place to protect Walker straight away.'

'She needed time to get from that hotel and over here into position first. By hiding Cardo's body, she knew she was buying time before his murder was called in. Enough time to get over here, sneak in and lay low before we secured the damn place.'

'She was here the whole time,' Green said again as though he still couldn't fathom it. 'She could have killed us. She could have killed us all.'

'She could have, but she didn't.'

Five minutes later, the men were sat back in the kitchen. Green and Munroe were clearly shocked that the Red Cobra had been so close to them and they'd known nothing of it. But they didn't need to be scared. Not unless they were hiding something. The Red Cobra was after Walker, not them.

Ryker kept coming back to the same point. Why hadn't she just taken the opportunity to kill Walker? Twice she'd been in the house. Twice she'd left without a scalp. Ryker could think of two reasons. First, Walker wasn't a target. Yes, she'd attacked Walker, she'd left that note. But was it simply a clue, a message as to her real intention? The note certainly wasn't a direct threat against Walker's life.

The second reason was that the Red Cobra needed Ryker's help. Whatever she had planned, she can't have been sure she could see it through alone.

Either way, Ryker wasn't scared, not like these two were. He was simply impressed at the tactical move she'd made, and slightly embarrassed not to have figured it out sooner. Hiding in plain sight. They'd never once suspected she was already in the house, lying in wait. More fool them.

Ryker downed the rest of his coffee which was by then only lukewarm. 'It's time I got going,' Ryker said, looking at his watch. It was nearly eight a.m.

'Going? Going where?' Green asked worriedly.

Ryker debated for a moment whether to let Green in on his plans. In the end, he decided against it.

'I'm going to try and save your skins,' Ryker winked at Green then headed for the door. 'You can thank me later.'

Chapter 48

The Sunday morning traffic was light on the motorway as Ryker made his way from Casa de las Rosas into central Malaga. The hotel he'd stayed at when arriving in Spain was his first stop. He wasn't staying long though. As much as he felt he could do with some more rest, given the rude awakening he'd had in the middle of the night, now was hardly the time for sleeping. But he did want to pick up his belongings. His money. His passports. He didn't know when he'd again be getting a restful night in the hotel so there was little point in leaving his few valuables there.

After checking out of the hotel, for which he paid in cash, Ryker made the short trip through the painful one-way system of the city towards the apartment block where Miguel Ramos lived. It was less than two miles from the hotel but took nearly thirty minutes, the irksome journey only adding to Ryker's fractious mood, which wasn't helped by the fact he'd barely slept the night before following the Red Cobra's attack.

Ryker left his car in the closest public car park he could find – the cramped city streets left little room for on-street parking – then headed on foot to the apartment block.

He didn't know the city well but from what he'd already seen, it had the distinctive enclaves of most large urban centres. The old town centre, packed with tapas bars and restaurants that spilled onto the streets, shops and charming buildings, churches and museums, was pleasant and extensive enough to draw in the locals and throngs of tourists. But the real life and soul of the city lay in the mainstay residential areas that sprawled out into the distance.

The area Ramos lived in was a far cry from the charming historic centre, despite its geographic proximity. It certainly wasn't poverty-stricken but the many apartment buildings were all block-like, nondescript. The buildings weren't in serious disrepair but the large cracks and blemishes in their rendered walls – some finished in white, some yellow, others red, blue – showed they were in need of better care. Quite a contrast to the ostentatious wealth Ryker had seen on display just a few miles west in Marbella.

The dirtied-yellow building that Ryker walked up to had an arched passageway that led into a central open-air foyer. There was no security of any kind, no guards or concierge. The inside was tidy and clean. Ryker headed to the tiled staircase.

An old woman approached. She carried a walking stick in her hand and wore a long skirt and woollen jumper that Ryker couldn't fathom given the heat that was already building. She made eye contact with Ryker as she passed. He smiled at her. She just glared at him warily then carried on her way.

Was he really so off putting?

Ryker moved up the stairs to the third floor then along the exposed corridor that ran along the inside of each of the four sides to the building. He stopped when he reached Ramos's door, knocked three times, then waited.

The door was opened by a short and plump woman with scruffy brown hair and baggy unflattering clothes.

Judging by the condition of her skin, she looked to be a similar age to Ryker, early forties at most, but her bedraggled appearance made her look older. She glowered at Ryker, no warmth in her eyes.

'*Habla Inglés*?' Ryker asked. He didn't wait for an answer. 'I need to speak to Miguel. Is he home?'

'No,' the woman said. But the fearful look in her eyes gave away the lie.

'I'm not here to hurt him,' Ryker said, placing his foot in the doorway to stop her from shutting the door. He knew the gesture was at odds with his words and that to this woman he was a threatening presence. But there was little he could do about that. He wanted to get inside.

The lady looked down at Ryker's foot.

'I'm not here to hurt him,' Ryker said again, trying to sound comforting. 'But Miguel is in a lot of trouble.'

'Policia?'

'No. I'm not.'

'I'm sorry. He's not here,' she said, her accent so thick it took Ryker a moment to decipher the simple words.

She tried to close the door, banging it against Ryker's foot. Ryker didn't budge. He heard a noise in the back of the apartment and stared into the lady's eyes. She gave him a pleading look. She needn't have bothered.

Ryker shoved open the door, knocking the shocked woman back. He moved into the apartment and closed then locked the door behind him. He saw the look of fear on the woman's face and knew what was coming. He reached out, grabbed her, and placed his hand over her mouth just as she screamed.

A door inched open at the far end of the apartment. Ryker already had a hand on his Colt before the face appeared.

Chapter 49

All Ryker could see in the dim light of the open doorway was the shadowed outline of a face and the bright whites of two eyes. Ryker assumed it was Miguel. But it wasn't until the door opened further and the boy stepped out that Ryker took his hand away from his gun.

'Miguel?' Ryker asked.

The boy nodded. Fifteen? If Ryker hadn't been told that he'd have said the kid was no more than twelve. He was five feet nothing, wore a pair of football shorts and a white vest that hung off his bony frame. His floppy black hair made his soft face look feminine.

'I'm here to help you,' Ryker said. 'You're in trouble. I think you know why. But please, you need to get your mother to calm down.'

Miguel shouted to his mother, rattling off words that Ryker didn't understand with speed and purpose. Eventually his mother's cries died down.

Ryker removed his hand from her mouth and stepped back. 'Okay?' he asked, giving her a conciliatory look. She nodded. 'Good. Right, Miguel, we need to talk.'

'In here,' the boy said.

Ryker looked at Miguel's mother again. She gave the slightest of nods. Ryker moved past her and followed Miguel into his bedroom. The room was small and dark. The black curtains were drawn, and the low glow of the overhead light struggled to illuminate the meagre space. The room was spotless, though – not an item of clothing out of place, not a dirty cup or a plate in sight. Not quite what Ryker expected for a teenage boy.

The walls were adorned with various pictures of footballers and movie stars. Ryker glanced at them then looked to Miguel who was hovering over a desk that was crammed with computer equipment and wires that seemed to snake in and out of hundreds of ports.

'You know why I'm here?' Ryker asked.

Miguel looked down at his feet. 'Yes. You're with the English police. You want to arrest me.'

His English was good, not perfect, the foreign accent was certainly clear, but for a teenager it was impressive. A lot better than Ryker's Spanish, that was for sure.

'No, Miguel,' Ryker said. The boy looked up again, frowning. 'I'm not going to arrest you. I'm not with the police. But that is why I'm here.'

'Then what do you want? How do you know?'

'Tell me what happened.'

'It was just a game.'

'A game?'

'We hack. We dare each other.'

'Who's we?'

'My group. Los Bandidos.'

'And?'

'I know it's wrong. But... I didn't mean for anyone to get hurt.'

The boy hung his head again and Ryker thought he could hear him sobbing.

'You already know she's dead?'

'Yes. I saw it in the paper.'

'Who asked you to do to the hack?'

'I don't know who – another user. I never met anyone. We live online. It was just a dare.'

'Name? Of the user?'

'I don't know his real name, or if it's really a he. We called him Anton.'

'Anton? That's it? No surname? Nothing else?'

'That's it. He came online a few weeks ago, then he disappeared again. We don't ask questions. We get on with it.'

'Did he pay you?'

'Pay me?' Miguel asked, sounding surprised. 'No. I don't get paid to do this. I told you, it's just a game. A hobby.' He shrugged.

Ryker couldn't help but think back to Winter's early report of the hack attack. One of the most sophisticated he'd ever seen, he'd said. But it was just a fifteen-year-old boy sitting in his bedroom hacking for a dare. He wasn't even getting paid.

'Okay. Let's step back again. What exactly were you asked to do?'

'Anton had a set of fingerprints. He said they belonged to a woman named Kim Walker. The game was to find her real name.'

'That isn't a game, Miguel.'

'I know that now! But this wasn't just me. We were all trying.'

'How many of you?'

'I don't know. Five. Ten. Some started but didn't get anywhere. Others broke into systems but didn't find matches.'

'But you did?'

'I got lucky. We weren't told where to look. But she sounded English. I thought to look in England. Why would I ever expect someone to kill her?'

The more Miguel talked, the more Ryker felt out of his depth. This wasn't a world he was used to. The hackers he'd dealt with before were highly trained agents working in the shadows, in bunkers in secret locations off the grid with cutting edge equipment. Here was a fifteen-year-old kid who'd managed to hack into MI5 from his bedroom in Malaga.

And to Miguel it was a bit of fun. One friend egging on another to see who was the best.

Except this time it wasn't a game. This time a person had lost their life. Someone had found out about Kim Walker, found that she wasn't who she said she was, and when Miguel connected the dots back to the profile of Anna Abayev – the Red Cobra – Kim Walker had been killed.

'I need you to do something for me,' Ryker said.

'What?' Miguel said, looking confused.

'Sit down,' Ryker said. Miguel did so. Ryker indicated over to the computer terminals. Miguel got the idea. He reached out and pushed a button, and there was a clunk and whir then a whooshing sound as the system booted up.

'You want me to show you?' Miguel asked. 'How I found her?'

'No. I wouldn't understand it anyway. I need you to do some digging for me. A company.'

'What sort of digging?'

'Anything you can. The company is called Empire Holdings.'

'Which country?'

'I don't know. Spain. Russia. England. Try all three. Georgia too. I need names of people. Addresses. I don't know where it's located but it's operating here. In Andalusia.'

'Okay,' Miguel said, looking and sounding confident all of a sudden. 'Shouldn't be hard.'

'How long will it take?'

'Minutes. Hours. Depends what I find.'

The system came online and Miguel's fingers moved at a speed that Ryker had never seen before. He couldn't even begin to imagine what was going through the boy's head or how a teenager could learn such skills. But one thing was clear, even to Ryker's uninitiated eye, this kid wasn't just talented, he was a master of his trade.

'You'll keep your trail clean?' Ryker asked.

'Of course. As best I can. But then...'

'Yeah. We found you. But it's taken nine days of looking and the efforts of one of the most powerful intelligence agencies in the world.'

Ryker thought he saw the glimpse of a proud smile on Miguel's young face but it was gone again.

After a few minutes, Miguel's mother poked her head around the door and spoke to her son in Spanish. Ryker caught a few of the quickly spoken words. She was checking he was okay. He said he was, told her not to worry, asked her to bring some drinks.

Not long later, she brought in two cups of coffee. Ryker took them and thanked her. Miguel didn't once take his eyes of his screens or his fingers off the keyboard.

After nearly half an hour, Miguel suddenly sat back in his chair and let out a long sigh. Ryker moved over to him.

'You found something?'

'Something?' Miguel said. 'I've found lots. This is a real minefield. It depends how far you want me to go. I'll show you.' Ryker fixed his eyes on the left hand screen. It was showing scans of corporate records of Empire Holdings from the company registry in the Cayman Islands. 'The actual company seems to be empty, no real operations.'

'A shell.'

'Yes. The names of the people behind it aren't available in open records, but through accessing the system of the Registry, I managed to find the name of the sole shareholder.'

'Who?'

'Andrei Kozlov.'

Ryker shook his head. 'You said the company is empty, but it does operate. I've seen correspondence here in Spain.'

'I don't know much about companies. There's not much there, though, just a name, no tax returns in Spain, no official financial records, no website or anything like that. But the name does appear in Spain, yes, in planning documents with various *ayuntamientos*–'

'Town halls? Councils?'

'Yes. And in construction contracts, things like that.'

'Any other people associated with Empire, other than Kozlov?'

'Lots. Mostly look like Russian names. Dzaria. Papava. Kazaishvili.'

'Addresses?'

'This one,' Miguel said, pointing to the second screen. 'Seems to be the main one for Empire.'

It was Kozlov's home in Marbella, a good link, but Ryker wanted more. He already knew Kozlov was involved in Empire, but Ryker needed to find who was at the top of the food chain. Kozlov certainly wasn't the ringleader of the Georgian mafia.

'Others?' Ryker asked.

'Not for Empire. But I cross-referenced those other people's names in the databases of the Government of Andalusia and I found lots of different company names associated with them, lots of addresses too. But these two come up a lot.'

Ryker looked. One of the addresses was labelled as Cadiz, which Ryker knew was the name of both a city and the province in which the city was located. The other was in Algeciras, a major port city in the Cadiz province that was just a few miles from the northern tip of Africa. A well-known crossing point connecting all manners of trade – both legal and illegal – between Europe and Africa.

Ryker made a mental note of the addresses. They had to be worth checking out. 'Good work, kid.'

'That's it?' Miguel asked, spinning around in his chair.

'For now, yeah. That's it. I've got work to do.'

'What will happen to me?' In an instant, the enthusiasm Miguel had been showing moments earlier as he hacked his way through cyberspace vanished. Back was the fear, the awkwardness, and uncertainty. The reality of the situation.

Ryker couldn't help but think that this child simply wasn't cut out for the real world. Everything happy and comfortable in his life was inside a computer terminal. Online he must have felt invincible. In the real world, he was puny and geeky, and insignificant and lost.

Ryker thought about the question, but he didn't answer it. It wasn't his place to answer. Even if it had been, he simply didn't get a chance, because before he could open his mouth to speak a noise caught his attention. A loud knock on the apartment's front door.

Ryker stared over at Miguel. The boy looked panicked. Ryker turned and moved over to the bedroom door.

He inched it open, much like Miguel had done minutes before, and peeked out.

Across the other side of the hallway, Miguel's mother was tentatively opening the front door. She'd moved it only a few inches when it burst into her face, knocking her backwards against the wall. Blood poured from her nose and she clutched at it with her hand.

Stood on the other side of the door were two men. One was big, almost as tall and wide as the doorframe he was standing in. Ryker recognised him as one of the men who'd followed him from the bullring in Ronda.

The other man was smaller, more unassuming, but with a sinister look in his beady eyes.

Sergei. The Vor.

Chapter 50

Ryker's eyes darted across the two men as he pulled his Colt from his jeans. Neither man had a weapon in his hands, though both were wearing jackets so could be concealing. With Miguel's mother already dazed, the giant stepped forward and threw a punch into her face. Her eyes went wide in shock, then she slowly crumpled to the ground. Ryker shot his head back into the bedroom.

The boy wasn't there.

Ryker looked over to the window. The curtains were now pulled apart a few inches and flapped in the gentle breeze. Ryker darted over and looked out. He saw Miguel below, sprinting barefooted down the street. The boy glanced behind him, up at Ryker. The panic in his eyes was unmistakable even at distance. Ryker lifted the window further and stuck his head out to peer down.

Three floors below was a set of industrial waste bins, lids closed. No drain pipes or any other means to climb down. Miguel had jumped. Probably not a problem on fifteen-year-old knees when you weighed as little as a feather pillow. But the mere thought of Ryker's two-hundred-pound frame smashing down on his joints made him wince.

Too late. With Ryker stuck in a moment of hesitation, the bedroom door crashed open. Ryker spun round, raised his gun, and fired a single shot as he ducked down into a defensive crouch. The Colt boomed, the sound echoing through the small apartment. The speeding bullet caught the giant under his chin. At such close proximity, there was little to stop the projectile's momentum as it pushed through bone and brain. It burst out the top of the guy's head leaving an orange-sized hole. His body collapsed, remnants of his skull and the inside of his head spread over the floor and wall behind him.

Ryker still had his gun held out, pointing toward the doorway. He'd expected an immediate onslaught from the Vor. The big guy was certainly armed – his lifeless hand was wrapped around the butt of a Glock handgun. Ryker could only assume Sergei was armed too.

So where was he?

Ryker remained still for a few seconds. He heard nothing. Then after a few beats, Miguel's mother – out of sight – groaned. Ryker slunk to the door and pulled up against the adjacent wall. He stole a glance out into the hallway.

Miguel's mother was stirring. Still sprawled on the floor, she was making slow, awkward movements. But there was no sign of Sergei.

Ryker didn't hesitate another second. He turned and grabbed the Glock from the dead guy's grip, then headed for the window. If he went out the door, he'd only be tracking down Sergei, and Ryker couldn't be sure whether the Vor was hiding, waiting to pounce. In any case, taking out Sergei wasn't the immediate aim. Saving a fifteen-year-old boy from the mob was.

Ryker clambered to the window and moved himself over the edge. He hung his body down, his legs reaching below, and cutting the distance to fall considerably. Then he let go.

As soon as his feet touched down on the lid of the bin below, Ryker bent his knees and moved his heavy body into a roll. The move saved his joints from a jarring contact, but the momentum of the roll took him over the edge of the bin. Ryker dropped to the pavement and landed painfully on his left shoulder.

Despite the thudding impact, Ryker was up and on his feet within a second, running on adrenaline. He sprinted down the road, heading in the same direction Miguel had gone in. Ryker's Colt was back in his waistband. He quickly checked over the Glock as he ran. The magazine was full.

Every few steps, Ryker glanced behind. There was no sign of Sergei or anyone else in that direction, and no sign of Miguel ahead.

Ryker came to a junction and looked in each direction. Still no sign of where Miguel had run to. Ryker thought about shouting out, was about to, then screeching tyres off to his left caught his attention. He turned and looked down the road.

Fifty yards ahead, where the road intersected another, a panel van came into view. Smoke flew up from the tyres as it came to a crunching halt. As the side door of the van opened, Ryker spotted Miguel. He'd been hiding on the other side of a parked car. When the van stopped, Miguel sprang out into the open, running back down the road toward Ryker.

Without thinking, Ryker sprinted toward the boy. He shouted for Miguel to move out of the way. To get down. But Miguel kept on running. Running for his life.

The side door of the van slid open. Sergei was there, an automatic rifle in his hand. Without hesitation, he lifted the weapon and fired.

Ryker raised the Glock and screamed out as the rifle blasted. A succession of bullets tore through Miguel's torso and he plummeted. Momentum sent his skinny body skidding along the road to a stop.

As he ran to the fallen boy, Ryker opened fire with the Glock. The first bullet hit the tarmac. The second hit the side of the van. Sergei was turning his rifle on Ryker before a bullet clanked into the weapon's barrel. The Vor reeled back and shouted as Ryker pulled on the trigger of the Glock again and again. The van sped forward, Sergei hanging out of the open door with an evil smile on his face.

A second later, the van was out of sight and Ryker realised he was pulling the trigger on a now-empty gun. Frustration and anger gripping him, Ryker hurled the weapon and looked down at the sorry form of Miguel. He rolled the boy onto his back. His eyes were ghostly. Ryker got down on his knees and felt for a pulse. Then he leaned down further and placed his ear close to Miguel's mouth, looking downwards across the boy's chest.

It only took Ryker a few seconds to confirm what he'd already feared.

Ryker rolled away, but stayed on the ground. He felt numb. A harrowing scream from behind Ryker sent a shock of emotion through him. Ryker didn't move as Miguel's mother, blood streaming from her nose, slid to a stop on the ground and clutched at the body of her dead son. Ryker stared into the distance, trying to bring his mind back into focus, trying to remove himself from the horror of the situation in front of him.

It was no good. He couldn't. He'd barely known Miguel Ramos, but he was just a kid. A kid who was lost. A kid who'd been used. He didn't deserve to die. Not like that. And the mother... Ryker couldn't even imagine her pain.

Miguel's mother let go of her son and she flung herself at Ryker, screaming hysterically. She bashed him in his chest with her fists. She slapped him in the face. Punched him. Shoved him. He barely registered her.

Forcing himself back to reality, Ryker brushed her off and got to his feet. He didn't say a word to her as he walked away. Just filled his head with thoughts of bloody revenge.

Chapter 51

Ryker made a cursory call to Green as he sped back along the motorway away from Malaga. He only wanted to make sure there had been no further incidents at Casa de las Rosas – no further sightings of the Red Cobra. Green said all was quiet. He'd been making progress in organising a safe location for Walker, but it would likely take hours, possibly days, more to finalise. Until then, Walker would remain at home with his armed guard.

Ryker ended the call without saying a word of what he'd been doing, what he'd found, or of the fight that ended with a young boy being gunned down. And he certainly hadn't breathed a word of what he was now planning.

As he drove, Ryker tried his best to calm the fire in his mind. He knew it wouldn't help for what was to come. Strong emotions seldom help in a time of crisis. The time alone in the car seemed to do the trick. The image in his mind of Miguel Ramos dropping to the ground, his body covered in bullet holes, was still fresh and vivid; it would be for a long time. But Ryker was back in control.

It was approaching midday when he arrived at the construction site on the outskirts of Marbella where three days previously he'd been attacked. His destination was once again the Kozlov mansion. He wasn't about to announce himself by offering himself to the security guards at the main gates. Not this time.

As Ryker stepped from the car, the blast of hot air caught him off guard. The air was thick not just with heat but moisture too, and Ryker's back and his brow was already covered in sweat by the time he'd moved a few yards.

The beach was again quiet, other than the occasional jogger and dog walker. Ryker approached the Kozlov house, and when he looked up at the mansion, he felt a wave of hatred for what the expensive pile of bricks, glass, and marble stood for. Ryker wasn't sure who would be home – Eva, Andrei, Sergei? It didn't matter, he'd soon find out. Ryker couldn't pass this place by. The addresses in Algeciras and Cadiz were Ryker's next stops. But Algeciras was fifty miles further west. One way or another, Kozlov was involved in the sorry mess that Ryker was uncovering, and Ryker wouldn't let that slide. If Kozlov was home, Ryker would get answers.

And if Sergei was there...

Ryker kept his head low and his senses high as he moved off the beach and onto the mansion's grounds. As with his previous trip from the beach, there wasn't sign of a single person in the grounds as he crept toward the back of the house. But then, when Ryker was a few yards from the building, he heard the sound of a door opening and he slunk down behind a bush.

Eva came dashing out of the house, shouting to someone behind her as she moved. Ryker watched as she headed to the elaborate wooden summer house on the far corner of the plot. She went inside, out of view.

Ryker took the chance to move closer to the open patio door at the back of the main building.

Eva came out of the summer house less than a minute later. Ryker was able to again take cover behind foliage. Eva moved with purpose – she was rushing. Under one arm she carried what looked like a laptop; in her other hand she held a pair of oversized headphones. She spoke again to someone that Ryker couldn't see. Her father perhaps? Ryker couldn't be sure. He'd seen and heard nothing from inside the house. But he was determined to find out who was there.

When Eva was ten yards away, Ryker sprang into action. He jumped into the open and pulled the Colt up, the barrel aimed at Eva's head.

'Eva!' Ryker shouted to her.

Eva stopped running, turned to face him and froze on the spot. Only then did Ryker notice her swollen right cheek. It was bright red, turning purple at the edges, and the inflamed flesh meant her eyelid was partially closed. A result of him shoving her to the ground in Ronda, he wondered. Or had someone beaten her?

Eva's venom toward Ryker was clear when she spoke. 'You're a dead man, Ryker! Do you hear me? Dead!' Eva turned her gaze back inside the house.

'Who's in there? Your dad?'

'Behind you!' Eva screamed to someone out of sight, her eyes springing wide in shock.

There was the sound of slicing – metal against flesh. Once, twice, three times. Eva jumped with each noise but didn't make any attempt to move. Petrified at what she saw.

A blood-curdling scream came from inside the house. There was a pained gargle as a man – Ryker didn't recognise him – stepped forward out of the open doorway. He held a gun in his hand but no shots had been fired. Blood gushed down from the gaping wound in his neck and intestines spilled from his gut. He collapsed to the ground. A large pool of blood spread out from his lifeless body.

Ryker sprang forward and pressed himself up against the wall of the house. Eva was still glued to the spot.

'Eva,' Ryker said.

She didn't respond. She was now trembling with fear.

'Eva,' Ryker repeated. 'What do you see?'

'They're dead. They're both dead!'

'Do you see her?'

'Yes!' Eva screamed, taking a step back, then another, a look of horror on her face.

Ryker dashed across the open doorway and took a split second to take in the scene inside before pulling up against the opposite wall. In the kitchen, another man was sprawled, a patch of thick red blood surrounding him on the white marble floor. Ryker hadn't seen the man's face clearly but he didn't think it was Kozlov or Sergei.

After a few seconds of silence, Ryker moved back into the doorway, gun held out. He caught sight of a shadow moving quickly across the space beyond the kitchen doorway, out in the mansion's grand hallway. The speed of movement of the shadowy figure in the interior darkness made it appear almost ghostlike, as though the air had suddenly taken shape and burst into life.

Ryker's finger twitched on the trigger, but he held his nerve and didn't fire. He wasn't about to waste bullets on a target he couldn't properly see. But the Red Cobra was there, no doubt about it. Ryker waited, watching and listening for any further sign of movement. Any sign of his enemy.

But there was nothing.

Then he heard a scream from outside. Ryker turned and saw Eva running toward him. He sprang to action again.

Eva met him head-on a yard outside the house and burrowed into him, crying and shaking.

Ryker quickly surveilled the area outside. 'Where?' He didn't move Eva away. She continued to nestle into him.

'Over there.' Eva pointed to the far corner of the house where a passageway led around to the front of the property.

Ryker stared over. There was no sign of anyone there. 'You're sure?'

His eyes darting, he stepped to the side, taking Eva with him, moving out of the line of fire from the open back door. Not that he expected the Red Cobra to shoot at him. Guns had never been her style.

Eva lifted her head from Ryker's chest and looked around, back in the direction she'd pointed. Then she straightened up. 'She's gone.'

Ryker wasn't sure if it was a question. 'I don't know. Are there any more men?'

Eva shook her head.

'You sure? Don't try to play me, Eva. If you lie to me I'm going to shoot you. Are there any more men?'

'No!'

'Okay. Where are the car keys?'

Eva pointed to the man on the ground. Ryker cautiously moved over, his eyes still twitching here, there, and everywhere. He felt around the man's body and pockets. Not just looking for keys but for anything of use. The guy's gun was swimming in blood. Ryker didn't bother taking it. He found a wallet. Ryker took a quick look at the picture driving licence inside. A Russian name. Not one he recognised from Miguel Ramos's digging. Then he found a remote clicker for a Mercedes.

Ryker held the key up.

'That's the one,' Eva said.

Ryker got to his feet. He turned and moved toward Eva.

'Keep your head down and your eyes peeled. You see anything you scream.'

Eva nodded.

'We move around the side of the house,' Ryker said. 'To the car. Slowly.'

Eva nodded again. Ryker held his hand out to her, his feeling of hostility toward her thawing, given the immediate threat of a common enemy. She took his hand.

'Come on,' he said. 'Let's get out of here.'

Chapter 52

Either the Red Cobra was hiding or she'd already scarpered – Ryker didn't see any sign of her as he and Eva cautiously worked their way around the mansion to the front. Ryker hopped onto the driver's seat of the executive Mercedes, and Eva tentatively followed onto the front passenger seat.

As Ryker edged the car along the driveway and onto the road, he wondered what kind of response he was about to receive from the security guards at the outer gates. Had the Red Cobra already killed them on her way in or out? If not, then would they be springing to alert because of the gunshots from the Kozlov residence?

It turned out to be neither. As they approached the exit, Ryker spotted one guard sat inside a patrol Jeep, on the inside of the gates. He was casually reading a newspaper. A second guard was tootling along by his hut on the outside. They barely paid any attention as the Mercedes approached. Ryker could only think that the distance between the gates and the Kozlov house meant neither of the guards had heard any of the commotion and didn't yet suspect a thing.

Ryker slowed the car to a crawl. 'How do we open the gates?'

He looked over at Eva. He could see the doubt in her eyes. He'd rescued her from the clutches of the Red Cobra but did she really want to be driving around with Ryker? She could scream out and get the guards' attention, he realised. But if she did that she'd be putting not just her life at risk but the guards' too. Ryker gave her the chance. In the end she made the right call.

'Here.' She reached into a small compartment within the central armrest and pulled out a key fob. She pressed the button and the gates swung open. The guards both looked up. The windows of the Mercedes were tinted and Ryker doubted the guards would have a good view of who was inside. Eva lowered her window a few inches and casually waved to the men. Ryker could only guess that was normal protocol as the men's only response was to give a cursory smile and wave in return.

'Who *was* that?' Eva asked a couple of minutes later as Ryker steadily weaved the car through the thickening traffic onto the country roads that led back up into the mountains.

'Someone who wants you dead.'

'Me? What did I do?' Eva sounded angry as much as she was surprised or upset.

'You tell me.'

'Where are we going?'

'To get you safe.'

'But... why are you even helping me?'

Ryker thought about that for a moment. 'Because it's the right thing to do.'

And that was the only explanation Ryker could give. He'd never trust Eva. There was a good chance she'd tried to set him up at the bullring, and minutes earlier, she'd screamed that he was a dead man. But then he had been pointing a gun barrel at her skull.

The fact was Ryker didn't know why the Red Cobra would want Eva dead. The only thing Ryker was sure Eva had done wrong was to have an affair with a married man. Hardly an offence punishable by death. Yes, her father was a crook, and she knew far more about what had been happening in Andalusia then she'd let on, but you don't get to choose your parents. For all Ryker so far knew, Eva was nothing more than an observer. Until proven otherwise he would treat her as such.

Ryker took out his mobile phone and made a call to Green. He kept the conversation brief, simply saying that he had someone Green needed to look after and to meet at the hotel where Inspector Cardo had taken a dive.

'You saved my life,' Eva said. Ryker looked over and saw the emotion in her face. She was in shock he knew. For all of her usual confidence and bravado, what she'd witnessed – two men being so savagely killed in front of her – had taken its toll.

'Where's your father?' Ryker asked.

'I don't know,' Eva said looking down.

'You're lying.'

'I'm not! He's... somewhere safe.'

'Why?'

'Because of that mad woman! I told you at the bullring, everyone is on edge, looking over their shoulders – ever since Cardo was attacked. My father has chosen to keep out of sight. He knows he's a target, though he doesn't know why.'

'So why were you in the house still then? Why aren't you somewhere safe like your father?'

'I was supposed to be. That's what we were doing. I had to get my things. We were only there a few minutes. Why is she *doing* this to us?'

'You really have to ask that question?'

'Yes. I do. I've never hurt anybody.'

'Kim Walker? You were sleeping with her husband. I'd say that would hurt.'

'I didn't mean hurt like that. I mean like stabbing people. Spilling their guts on the floor!'

'And what about Sergei? Where is he?'

'Sergei? I haven't a clue. Why would I know that?'

'In Ronda yesterday and then in Malaga this morning, I suddenly found myself staring down gun barrels. And I don't believe in coincidences. Someone wants me dead.'

It was a thought that had struck him as soon as he'd laid eyes on Sergei in Miguel Ramos's home. They'd known Ryker was there. But how?

'That's nothing to do with me! I told you yesterday I didn't set you up. But then you went ahead and attacked me anyway.'

Ryker glanced at Eva's swollen face. He didn't feel even slightly bad for what he'd done.

'Not long ago, I watched Sergei gun down a fifteen-year-old boy. Some great company you've been keeping there.'

'What are you talking about?' Eva was shaking her head. Genuine confusion and shock, Ryker believed.

'If you know where Sergei is, you tell me. Because I'm going to find him, and I'm going to kill him – and anyone who gets in my way.'

Ryker looked over again. Eva stared back.

After that, the journey carried on in silence. They reached the hotel and Ryker pulled the Mercedes into the car park. He parked up and then stepped out from the air-conditioned car into the baking heat. Eva followed and Ryker studied the look in her eyes. 'You know this place.'

'What?'

'How? Why'd you come here?'

'It's somewhere I've been to. The food's good. You should try it.'

'You can't get good food in Marbella?'

'Yes. You can. But that doesn't mean I have to eat there and only there.'

Ryker knew with confidence that there was more to the story than that, but Eva wasn't going to tell him. He'd questioned why Cardo would be staying there. Ryker's guess was the hotel was a hangout for the mob. Good middle ground for them to travel to. Perhaps they held meetings there, or stopped when passing through.

The flippancy in Eva's words, the sudden breakthrough of that natural confidence and charm, even if it was only there for a second, reminded Ryker of exactly whom he was dealing with. Ryker knew he'd never truly be able to read a woman like Eva. As good as he was at spotting an untruth, she was too used to telling lies, to spinning a situation to her advantage. The signs of deceit were too hit and miss. The problem was she lived in a world where she fully believed her own lies.

They walked toward the metal barrier and looked out over the view to the coast.

'Who is your father working for, Eva? I know it's the mafia. Georgians. But give me some names. Do the decent thing. It could save him if I find him first.'

Eva didn't answer the question immediately. Ryker waited.

'It's not like that,' Eva eventually said. 'He's not one of them.'

'Maybe. Maybe not.'

'Please don't hurt him.'

'If he leaves me no choice.'

'He's a good man. Sometimes bad things happen to good people. You must know that?'

'Why was Kim Walker killed?'

Eva looked down at her feet.

'Because of you? The affair?'

'No!' Eva said. 'Not because of that. I didn't do anything.'

'Then what? Did she find out about what Walker and your father were doing?'

'I really don't know.'

'You told me in Ronda that you did. You were about to tell me the reason when your two friends showed up with guns.'

'They aren't my friends.'

'I couldn't give a shit if they are or aren't. Tell me why Kim Walker was killed.'

'Because they found out who she really was.'

'Who's *they?*'

'The Georgians.'

It was the same conclusion Ryker had already come to. Some of the answers Ryker was searching for were certainly falling into place. The hack attack by Miguel Ramos. The profile of Anna Abayev. The Georgians were blackmailing Patrick Walker, extorting money from him. In the midst of that, they'd found out that Kim wasn't who she said she was. When Ramos linked her to the Red Cobra's profile, the mob killed her to settle an old score.

But that still didn't answer who was behind the operation. Or who Kim Walker *really* was. Or why the Red Cobra was now here.

'I'm not part of *that*,' Eva said. 'You have to believe me.'

'Yeah. The problem, Eva, is that I have a hard time believing anything you say.'

The noise of a car engine caught their attention. They turned to see Green's Ford pulling into the car park. He brought the Ford to a stop right by where Eva and Ryker were standing.

'Him?' Eva said.

'He's with Walker. You'll be safe,' Ryker said, seeing the look of concern in Eva's eyes. Her being handed over to the police was probably the last thing her father wanted.

'Patrick hates me.' Eva let out a big sigh.

'Yeah but this is better than the alternative, I'd say.'

Green walked up to them. 'What the hell is going on, Ryker?' He sounded less than impressed.

'Trust me. Keep her safe. The Red Cobra is still out there.'

Ryker made to walk away. Green held out his hand to stop him.

'Where are you going? I'm not a nanny, you know. I'm supposed to be out here investigating a murder, not cooking dinner for rich people.'

Ryker huffed. He was in two minds. He didn't fully trust Green, and he'd never been good at working with others. But he also knew that Green could be of assistance. The problem was Ryker didn't want to draw Green into his murky world. Ryker had never had a problem with the morality of tracking down and killing the bad guys. For many years that's exactly what had been asked of him by the JIA. But Green was a policeman, a detective, someone who lived by rules and laws. Bringing him on board for what was to come would put Green in a position from which there was simply no return.

And men like Sergei? Ryker didn't want him arrested and put into a courtroom. Men like that didn't deserve anything more than they dished out.

'You don't want to be part of this,' Ryker said to Green. 'Trust me on that.'

Green seemed to understand. He stepped back.

'Thank you,' Eva said. She moved up to Ryker and wrapped her arms around him.

Ryker glanced over at Green with an awkward look on his face. When Eva was done hugging him, she reached up and kissed Ryker on his cheek. Green had to hold back his smirk at Ryker's stiff response.

'Such a charmer, Ryker,' Green called out as he turned to head back to his car.

Ryker watched as Eva followed Green to the Ford. Ryker wondered whether he would ever see Eva Kozlov again.

Minutes later, Ryker was back on the road, heading west to Algeciras.

It was time to fight the mob head on.

Chapter 53

The journey to the port city of Algeciras was smooth and untroubled. Ryker made one stop on the way, to collect supplies for the mission ahead. He made a call to Lisa but, as was becoming the norm, it rang out unanswered.

On arriving in Algeciras, Ryker found the address he'd been given by Miguel Ramos using the map on his phone. The building was on the outskirts of the town centre, a small and rundown office block, two stories tall. Similar buildings lay either side; none of them appeared to be occupied.

After waiting for an opportunity where he wouldn't be spotted by the few passersby, Ryker used a torsion wrench and a pick to quickly release the single lock on the ageing door.

He stepped inside and looked around. As he expected from the outside, the building didn't appear to be in use. There was no furniture or fittings. The lights weren't working, suggesting the electric was disconnected. Ryker could only assume the address was used to add authenticity to legal documents drawn up for the mob's operations. The fact there was only two days' worth of mail lying by the front door – judging by the postmarks – suggested routine pick-ups were made.

Ryker didn't hang around. He saw no point. The only person he was likely to come across there would be a simple lackey out on errands.

Back in the car, Ryker plugged the second address into his phone. It turned out it wasn't in Cadiz the city, but a rural location a half hour drive from Algeciras. Ryker soon found himself on twisting country roads heading over the hills and mountains that surrounded the Andalusian coastline.

When he was a mile from the destination, the road turned from tarmac to a simple dirt track covered in thick yellow dust. Ryker took a look at the map on his phone as he drove. He could see no indication of a town or even a village out here on the map; nor were there any signposts indicating what lay ahead. Ryker could only assume the address was a farm of some sort. His mind took him back to the conversation he'd had with Eva at the bullring, about her father's friend owning a ranch where he trained fighting bulls.

If Ryker was heading to a secluded ranch owned by someone who was either connected to, or a member of, the Georgian mafia, he didn't want to announce himself.

He was a little over half a mile away when he spotted another dirt track snaking off to the left of his destination. Ryker took it. He passed over rolling hills and soon came to a small cluster of trees and parked his car. He was in the middle of a valley, hills surrounding him on all sides – a mixture of scrubland, olive farms and grassy fields, yellowed by the lack of water and never-ending sunshine.

Ryker stepped from the car into the intense heat. He grabbed the compact binoculars he'd earlier purchased, and walked away from the car, in the direction of the address he was looking for. He crossed over a wooden fence into a field. The scorched grass underfoot crunched as he walked, almost as if it were frozen.

Ryker kept on alert as he traipsed across the barren field, not just for people, but for animals. He didn't fancy coming head to head with a young *toro bravo* – a Spanish fighting bull.

When he reached the top of the hill, Ryker crouched down and slunk towards an isolated carob tree. From there, he now had an unobstructed view down to his destination, a few hundred yards in the distance.

As he'd expected, it looked like a farm. As well as a large white house there were several outbuildings, including a big corrugated-iron barn. Ryker could see two vehicles parked by the house, a car and a pick-up truck.

Ryker pulled the binoculars up and scoured the area. Both the car and the pick-up truck appeared old and battered, certainly not the type of vehicles he'd seen the Kozlovs driving around in Marbella. Ryker could now see one of the outbuildings was used as stables for horses. He also noticed a young woman – a teenager perhaps – tending to the animals. Other than that, there was no sign of life by the buildings. Ryker swung the binoculars around, searching the rest of the land.

In the distance, beyond the house, he spotted two men on horseback in a field, circling around a horned bull. Ryker watched intently for a few moments. The men taunted the beast, moving around, in, and out, striking the bull with long sticks. Ryker's mind again went back to the conversation with Eva in Ronda. She'd said the bulls chosen for fighting were never put in front of a man until the day they went into the ring. But men on horses wielding sticks? Perhaps that was okay.

A loud and deep grunt caught Ryker's attention. He felt his heart rate increase. He moved the binoculars away from his face and turned his head slowly. Sure enough, fifty yards away was a roaming bull. It was massive, its black coat silken and shining in the bright sunlight. The bull was walking past Ryker, heading toward where he'd come from. Ryker remained still, knowing that any sudden movement would be enough not just to alert the beast but possibly to cause it to charge.

Ryker stared at the bull: at its towering horns weaving in the air, the huge hulk of muscle around its neck and its hind legs shuddering with each step it took. Ryker could feel his heart thudding, so he took long and slow breaths. He had a gun on him; he was sure he could shoot and kill the bull before he came to any harm. Even so, being out in the open and so close to such a fearsome animal was nerve-racking.

When the animal headed over the lip of the hill, Ryker breathed a sigh of relief. He was caught in two minds for a moment. So far he'd seen nothing on the ranch that suggested this was a hangout for the mob. He could go back to his car and get out of there. But what would he do next? Miguel Ramos had found this address through his digging into Empire Holdings. There had to be a connection somewhere, something of interest for Ryker to find.

He'd already made up his mind to move closer to the buildings when the sound of a car engine caught his ear.

Seconds later, a large black luxury saloon car came into view, dust swirling out from behind it. As it parked by the farmhouse, an SUV and a panel van followed it in and parked alongside. The van wasn't the one in which Sergei had escaped from Malaga, this one was blue rather than grey, but it was a similar type.

Ryker pulled the binoculars back up to get a better look. Several men stepped from the vehicles. None appeared to be armed. All wore dark clothes and most of them were big and bulky and menacing. Muscle.

But not all of them. One man was much slighter in height and frame, yet Ryker sensed the danger of the man nonetheless. Sergei.

Chapter 54

Ryker clenched his fist around the binoculars. He was tempted to blast his way down to the farmhouse there and then, take out Sergei and be done with it. But he couldn't. He had to know what was happening. Who the men were and why there were there.

One of the men came over to the black car, opened the back passenger door, and helped out another man. Ryker knew as soon as he laid eyes on the man what he was looking at. The Pakhan. The mob boss.

The boss was in his sixties, possibly seventies. He had wispy white hair, a protruding nose, and a pockmarked face. His grey eyes, set deep in his face, were glasslike. He wore a clean black suit with a white shirt underneath, though the edges of his Vor tattoos – which, Ryker guessed, covered his whole back and torso – were visible above his shirt collar and his cuffs.

The old man hobbled along, supported by a silvery cane in his hand. Ryker debated for a few seconds. He had a gun and enough bullets to take out each of the men who'd just arrived, but that was surely a step too far. He had a beef with Sergei, but Ryker didn't know enough about the rest of the men – what their crimes may be – to go in there all guns blazing. In any case, it was an unnecessarily risky approach.

But he had to do something.

Ryker waited until the men had moved away. All but one of them headed inside the white house. The man who remained outside, the biggest and meanest looking of the lot, stood guard by the front door. But from his lazy and bored manner, Ryker quickly determined the guy wasn't much of a guard. He was a physical deterrent rather than a trained watchman.

Over the next ten minutes, Ryker stealthily moved across the field to within yards of the house, using the natural undulations of the land as well as sporadic trees and the odd cluster of foliage to stay hidden from view. He pulled up alongside a picket fence; then, when the opportunity arose, he jumped the fence and rushed toward the black car.

Ryker came to a stop by the back end of the vehicle. He crouched low and held his breath for a few seconds, listening to the sounds around him. There was no indication anyone had been alerted by his movement.

After a few more seconds, Ryker risked a glance around the back of the car, over to the house. The big guy was still standing there, lazily watching the area in front of him. Ryker pulled his head back in, then reached into his pocket for the new pay-as-you-go mobile phone he'd purchased when he'd stopped en route to Algeciras. He'd charged the phone's battery in the car and had downloaded a free GPS tracking app that would allow him to trace not just the location of the phone but whether it was still or moving, and also its speed and direction of travel. The new phone was now Ryker's own remote tracker, which he could easily follow on the internet browser of his first phone.

Ryker took out the roll of packing tape he'd bought and ripped off two six-inch lengths. Then, moving down closer to the ground, he carefully secured the phone to the underside of the car. It wasn't ideal. The tape would hold the phone in place, but only for so long. And even if the tape held, Ryker would only be able to track the phone as long as the battery had juice.

If he hadn't been hindered by the guy at the door and the possible threat inside the house, Ryker would have found a way into the car and hardwired the phone into the car's electronics so that it remained charged on the car's battery. That simply wasn't possible in the circumstances.

He hoped what he'd done would be good enough.

Ryker was finished here. He peeked under the car and noted that the big guy's shoes remained stationary by the front door. Ryker was about to move off, back the way he'd sneaked in, when he heard banging and voices. Ryker froze and he could do nothing to stop his heart suddenly drumming. He quickly looked under the car again. Several sets of feet were coming from the house. If they headed over to the cars, Ryker only had one option left. He reached down and gripped the Colt, then slowly and carefully pulled it free.

The men were talking, shouting, and laughing. Most of the chat that Ryker could decipher was Russian, but there was a second language too – the distinctive guttural sounds of Georgian. Ryker could barely speak a word of it, but he'd heard the unusual tongue enough times to recognise it.

He stole another glance under the car. He counted seven men in total. They weren't moving, just milling about outside the entrance to the house. Then an eighth pair of feet walked up. The chatter died down as the new arrival spoke, then all the men moved off, away from the cars, towards the stables at the side of the house.

Ryker breathed a long, slow sigh, then he quickly moved away from the car. As soon as he was out of sight, he began his covert walk back through the fields.

Soon after, Ryker looked over the lip of the final hill, feeling relief as he peered down to where he'd earlier parked his car. But his relief was short-lived when he spotted the bull that had previously passed him by obliviously. It didn't look like Ryker would be so lucky a second time.

The bull was loitering casually alongside the fence, at the other side of which was Ryker's car. And there was simply no other way for Ryker to get there – at least not without putting himself in view of the men at the ranch.

Ryker crept forward, his hand at his hip, determined not to use the Colt unless he had to, but wanting to be ready to grab it. The bull spotted Ryker, and both he and the animal stopped moving, twenty yards apart. For nearly a minute, it was stalemate. The bull snorted, grunted, and banged one of its front feet into the dusty ground. Clearly, it was not about to turn and walk away from the confrontation – and Ryker didn't want to stand there all day hoping the animal changed its mind.

Ryker took a step sideways toward the fence. The bull huffed. Ryker took another cautious step. Then another.

And then the bull charged.

All of a sudden, a thousand pounds of snarling flesh and muscle and bone raced toward Ryker. Thoughts crashed through his mind, but other than shooting, there was only one thing to do. Ryker ran. Even though he knew the bull could run far faster than he could, it was the only viable option. He hoped he'd judged the distances correctly.

Ryker sprinted as fast as he could toward the fence. His arms and legs beat frantically as he strained every muscle in his body. He didn't look behind him; he didn't need to – he could hear the heavy and angry panting of the bull, closing in with every step.

The fence was within touching distance. Ryker threw himself at it. His foot caught the lowest rung of wood. He bent at the knee and propelled himself upwards and over. Before he'd even hit the ground in a clumsy, crumpled heap, the bull smashed into the wooden construction. The whole structure shuddered and gave a couple of inches. The bull hit it again, grunting angrily. Ryker had no doubt the animal could tear the whole thing down if it wanted to.

He didn't want to hang around and find out if he was right.

With the bull sniffing and snarling, its beady eyes fixed squarely on its foe, Ryker clambered to his feet and rushed for the car.

Chapter 55

Ryker took the opportunity over the next few hours to rest up and eat, having found a roadside restaurant and bar not far from Algeciras. He kept one eye on his phone's screen the whole time, watching the red dot that represented the location of the mob boss's car. It didn't move during the first three hours following Ryker's hasty departure from the ranch, and he wondered whether the device had been found.

Then, with darkness approaching, there was finally some action. Ryker remained in the bar as he watched the dot moving along the map. It wormed towards the coast, at one point coming to within a mile of where Ryker was sitting, before carrying on towards the city. And there it stopped, in the heart of the city's commercial dockyards.

Which was exactly where Ryker headed.

It was nine p.m. by the time Ryker reached the docks. He scoped out the place where the boss's car had stopped – an industrial warehouse – on a drive-by, before parking his car in a nearby street. He made his way on foot toward the warehouse, taking a twisting route through the dockyards, to avoid being seen, as much as he could.

The docks themselves were a hive of action despite the hour. Giant cranes loomed into the sky lining the front of the port where three massive ships were docked. The cranes, looking like gigantic robots, beavered away with a roaring mechanical whir, removing and stacking large sea containers that clanked and crashed into position. Huge spotlights lit up much of the area with thick white light but there was enough cover from the containers and sporadic low-profile buildings for Ryker to creep about in the darkness unseen.

Moving away from the action to the quieter warehouses that sat alongside, Ryker came back upon the corrugated metal structure he was looking for. The large loading doors at the front were open and the lights inside were on; he caught a glimpse of two parked cars in the space inside – one of them was the boss's.

Beyond the warehouse were a couple of acres of land that were crammed with containers and pallets, forklifts and flatbed trailers. A chain link fence ran around the perimeter. Ryker walked along the pavement by the outer fence, head down. The main entrance had a simple security hut with an in-and-out barrier either side. Easy access. But Ryker kept walking past, not once looking up. He'd already spotted the guard inside the hut.

He kept on going along the pavement, until he came to a spot where the chains in the fence looked like they had come loose. Maybe corroded by a combination of age and weather. Or perhaps they'd been cut? In the darkness, Ryker couldn't be sure. Regardless, he took the opportunity to climb through the broken fence onto the warehouse grounds.

Ryker crept further inwards, moving between containers until he reached the metal face of the warehouse. Now that he was away from the main docks, the area was nearly black. Only the lights at the front of the warehouse were on. He could hear voices within, but could see nothing of what was happening, or how many men there were.

Moving along the edge of the warehouse, Ryker was watchful for any guards who might be doing their rounds. He came across no one. He'd moved around two corners of the warehouse when he came to a stop. On this side, with stacked containers behind him and the water directly beyond, he'd spotted a sliver of light coming from the warehouse wall. A hole no more than an inch in the worn metal surface. A missing rivet perhaps.

Ryker moved up to the light and put his face against the metal. From there he had a near-unobstructed view inside. While the outside of the warehouse was dark and quiet, the inside was buzzing with activity.

Two men stood guard with automatic rifles, one either side of the open doors at the entrance. They were standing back, against the wall, obscured from anyone approaching the front.

Ryker could now see three vehicles parked up inside: the same shiny black saloon car, SUV, and panel van he'd seen at the ranch earlier.

Ryker counted another ten men milling about the place. Other than the two at the doors, none of the others appeared to be armed. Among them was Sergei, but there was no sign of the Pakhan yet. It was clear the men were waiting around for something. But what?

For nearly an hour, Ryker stood there in the darkness. In that time, he twice became spooked when he heard a noise behind him. Both times it turned out to be nothing. Or at least he saw nothing, though he couldn't be certain exactly what the noises had come from.

It was just gone ten p.m. when the heavens opened. Thick rain poured down. The drops clattered and banged on the metal warehouse and the many containers surrounding Ryker. Within seconds he was soaked through. Water poured from his hair, down his brow, and in front of his eyes like a waterfall.

The noise from the torrential downpour would make it easier for Ryker to move with stealth, he realised, but at the same time would make hearing others moving towards him more difficult.

Not long after the rain started, the men inside the warehouse sprang to attention, giving orders and moving into position.

Moments later, Ryker heard the thumping engine noise of a large truck, then the hiss of its air brakes as it came to a stop.

Thirty seconds passed, then the beams of the truck's headlights became visible beyond the open warehouse doors. The truck swung around in the yard then reversed its trailer – a red sea container on top – into the warehouse.

When the whole of the vehicle was inside – water dripping down from its bulk creating large puddles on the floor – two men stepped forward and rolled the warehouse doors closed.

The other men quickly moved into formation. Each of them either drew a handgun or pulled a rifle from an unseen hiding place. All of a sudden, there were a dozen armed men inside the warehouse, crowding around the container.

Two men, rifles over their shoulders, carried a set of metal steps over to the truck's trailer, then another man clambered up and undid the thick clasps on the container before swinging open the rusted doors.

Ryker held back a gasp as he stared at the darkness inside. The man on the top of the steps shouted and held out his hand. A woman timidly walked forward. She was young, maybe early twenties. Her thin clothes were plain and worn. Her skin was streaked with dirt. The look on her face... she was terrified.

The man grabbed her hand and pulled her to him then ushered her down the steps where she was coaxed along by the other men. Then another woman came out of the darkness. And another. Next was a woman with her young baby pressed up against her chest. Then a man with a boy.

Thirty people Ryker counted in total.

Centuries earlier, the proximity of Algeciras to Africa had seen it develop into an important trading location. But the proximity had long been exploited by criminals too. Smuggling. Black market goods. Drugs.

People trafficking.

Ryker looked on as the armed men separated the stowaways into four groups. Families. Single men and women with children. Men. And the largest group – lone females, of which there were sixteen. The armed men moved the groups to different corners of the warehouse. The stowaways looked weary. And scared. Many of them were shaking.

The container doors were closed, then the doors to the warehouse opened before the lorry's engine roared back to life. The lorry was driven away and seconds later, four vans came into the warehouse, each parking up next to one of the groups of people. The armed men shepherded all but the group of lone women into a waiting van. The three filled vans drove away.

Then the warehouse doors were closed again. One of the men with a rifle came over to the black car and opened the back passenger door. And there was the Pakhan. The mob boss.

Ryker gripped the Colt in his hand. What he wanted to do was put a bullet into the boss's head. One shot. Maybe Sergei too. Then run.

But what would that achieve? And could he really kill the old man just like that without even knowing who he was? All the signs were there but still...

The old man, cane in hand, moved over to the group of young women. When he reached them, he stopped and his underlings straightened the women up, moved them into a neat line. Paraded them for the boss. He gave the slightest flick with the cane and one of his men stepped forward and grabbed the chosen woman, twisting her wrist around and pulling on her hair. The woman cried out but no one took any notice, not even the other women, who looked on bewildered.

One of the men helped the Pakhan back into his car. Another shoved the woman in the other side. The men ushered the remaining women into the final waiting van, then lay down their weapons before the warehouse doors were again opened. The van departed and the men stood waiting once more.

If he was going to act, he should do it now, Ryker convinced himself. He stepped back from the hole in the wall and thought through a plan. If he could lure the men outside, into the darkness, he might have a chance.

But then the boss would simply get away. His men would drive him to safety at the first sign of trouble. If Ryker was going to make a move, the boss had to be the first target. He was the one pulling the strings. The one who'd likely ordered Sergei to kill Miguel Ramos. The one who'd had Kim Walker killed. The one who'd been trying to kill Ryker!

Ryker was snapped from his deliberation when above the noise of the driving rain, he heard a faint crunching behind him. Like someone's foot scraping a small stone across the ground.

Ryker spun round and stared into the darkness, his gun pointed out.

Nothing. He could see nothing. Not even the droplets of rain that he knew were cascading down his face right in front of his eyes. It was too dark.

But there was no mistaking the next noise he heard, a second later. A voice.

More than that, it was a voice he recognised.

'Carl,' she said.

The Red Cobra.

Chapter 56

Ryker said nothing. He held up the gun, pointed it out, and twisted himself this way and that as he did his best to scan the blackness ahead.

'Carl, it's me,' she said, her voice nothing more than a whisper, now coming from Ryker's side. 'Over here.'

Ryker stepped back until he felt himself brush against the warehouse metal. It gave him some comfort that wherever the Red Cobra was, she wasn't behind him.

'I won't hurt you,' she said, her voice coming from a different direction again. Ryker spun to the left. Still couldn't see a thing.

'Put down the gun,' she said.

Again the voice had moved. Then Ryker saw her. At least he thought he did. A dark shadow shooting between two containers in front of him. His finger was on the trigger. It was a job to resist the urge to shoot.

'You know what they are now,' she said. 'You've seen what they are. Help me to kill them.'

'Why?' Ryker said, speaking as quietly as he could.

The next second, he felt a rush of air right by him. Saw her. She was sweeping around his side, going for his gun. She was inches away. He ducked, swivelled, and tried to catch her.

She was gone again.

'Carl. I'm not your enemy.'

'Carl's dead.'

'No. He's not,' she said, the direction of her voice again taking Ryker by surprise. 'But those men are.'

'Who are they? The guy with the stick?'

'The Pakhan? Giorgi? You know what he is, you've seen. It's still early. That was one lorry. There'll be five more before the night is through.'

'I'm not going to let that happen,' Ryker said.

'No. Me neither.'

Another flash of movement caught Ryker's eye, off to his right this time. He spun and pointed his gun but saw nothing more of her.

Then all was calm. Still. Quiet. Except for the rain that was still thumping down and the slow thudding of Ryker's heart.

He took several deep breaths.

'Anna?'

Nothing. She was gone.

Or, at least she was no longer by Ryker's side. The harrowing scream of a man moments later, followed by the sound of rapid gunfire, told Ryker exactly where she was.

He spun back round to the warehouse and heard a chorus of shouts from inside. Footsteps moving quickly. The rattling of weapons as the men re-armed.

A car engine starting.

Ryker pushed his eyeball up to the hole in the wall. He spotted a man lying on the floor inside by the open main doors, a large pool of red beneath him. A second man stumbled from the rain back toward the inner sanctum, his hands covered in blood. He collapsed.

Ryker looked over the remaining men. No sign of Sergei. The lights of Giorgi's car flashed on. Ryker couldn't let them get away. He shot into action, racing along the side of the warehouse, his gun at the ready.

He heard more gunshots from inside, more pained cries. The sound of another engine starting. Ryker reached the front of the warehouse and spotted Giorgi's car already out of the warehouse. Its brake lights blinked as it came to a stop at the security barrier that was slowly lifting up.

Ryker opened fire. Aiming for the car's back tyres. He hit both. He turned when he saw another vehicle. The SUV. Ryker fired a single shot at the windscreen, aiming for the driver through the tinted glass. But the bullet bounced away, not even a scratch.

Ryker dove to the ground as the SUV swept passed him. He looked up to see Giorgi's car speeding off the warehouse grounds then accelerating hard when it hit the road outside. The SUV followed on behind. Ryker cursed. Armoured glass. Run flat tyres. Nothing he could do.

He quickly got to his feet and looked around. He could see four men inside the warehouse. Two with handguns, two with rifles. They were cautiously moving toward the exit doors. None had yet spotted Ryker. He could only assume his position had been masked by the darkness, and his gunfire by the rain, the revved engines of the escaping vehicles, and the haphazard firing of the men's own weapons as they desperately tried to shoot at the Red Cobra.

Wherever she now was.

One vehicle remained inside the warehouse. As Ryker set eyes on it, the headlights came on and it shot forward. Ryker could clearly see the face of the driver as it sped toward him. The passenger too. Neither was Sergei. It didn't matter. Ryker had seen enough. Every man left in that place was a target now.

As the van approached, Ryker lifted the Colt and fired two shots. This windscreen wasn't armoured. The bullets blasted through the glass and the cabin filled with blood spatters as the van careened passed Ryker. It swerved violently to the right, nothing more than an involuntary movement from the driver, who Ryker was certain was already dead. If, by chance, he wasn't, the violent crash that ended the van's escape would have finished him off for sure. Ryker watched as the van ploughed head-on into a metal shipping container. The vehicle's front end crushed on impact and sent the heap of metal springing up into the air before it smashed back down.

More gunshots rang out. Bullets whizzed by Ryker's ear. He darted back to the outer wall of the warehouse for cover.

'Nice shooting, Carl,' came the Red Cobra's whispered voice.

Ryker spun round. She was already gone.

The barrel of a rifle poked out from the warehouse doors. Ryker stood still, waited. The man had no other option: he had to come out into the open if he wanted to find Ryker and the Red Cobra. As soon as Ryker spotted an inch of the man's head, he fired another shot. The man crumpled.

A blast of automatic fire rattled the warehouse wall. A series of bullet holes opened up in the metal exterior right where Ryker was standing. He ran for cover over to the nearby containers, bullets ricocheting all around him.

Ryker flung himself to the ground and rolled into a crouch up against the containers. Not even a second later, he was moving quickly around the side, back towards the darkness. And was taken by surprise when he almost walked head-on into the barrel of a handgun.

Luckily, the man holding it was even more shocked than Ryker. That split second cost the man his life. Ryker thrust his fist up and crashed it into the man's nose then fired a single shot as the man reeled backwards.

But the noise of Ryker's attack had given away his position. He took another barrage of fire from the unseen attacker with the rifle, and retreated further into the maze of containers.

The gunfire stopped. Ryker moved quickly and methodically back around to the front. He wasn't going to run and hide. He wanted to take charge and come back on the remaining men from behind.

Ryker heard more screams. Male. He couldn't see where they had come from, but the Red Cobra was certainly still out there. Still on the attack.

There was a moment of silence, of stillness, as the rain died down. For a few seconds, Ryker wondered whether all the men were dead. He darted out from his position and headed back to the warehouse wall. He caught sight of the man with the rifle and, without hesitation, lifted his gun to fire.

Then Ryker saw her. Again, she was nothing more than a shadow as she swept across the man. Just about the only part of her that was clearly visible was the glint of her knife. Ryker opened fire. At both of them. He hit the man, at least once. The Red Cobra? He couldn't be sure. But Ryker soon realised he'd used up the remainder of his bullets. And he didn't have another magazine.

He cagily moved forward, towards the fallen man, his eyes set on the man's rifle. He could neither see nor hear anything of the Red Cobra. Then Ryker stopped.

In front of him, he heard banging. Metal. Ryker continued to inch forward, moving with caution. The sound kept on coming. From the crashed van a few yards ahead.

Suddenly its back doors flew open, and a figure collapsed to the ground. Ryker picked up his pace. The rifle was just a few steps away from him. The figure rolled over. A man. He got to his feet. His face was caught in the light coming from inside the warehouse. Thick, dark blood covered one side of his head, but there was no mistaking who it was. Sergei.

The Vor looked up and Ryker knew he'd been spotted. The smile on Sergei's face told him so.

The fallen man, rifle in his dead hand, was five yards from Ryker. Sergei was the same distance beyond. Ryker knew Sergei had spotted the weapon too. Both men sprang forward. Ryker wanted that rifle, but there was no way he'd get there and fire it before Sergei was on him. In the end, Ryker opted to go for his foe instead.

A good choice because that was Sergei's aim too.

Ryker hurled himself through the air and smacked into Sergei. The two men fell to the ground. Ryker knew he had the size and strength to give him the upper hand – if he could just keep Sergei's attacks at bay. But as he'd expected, Sergei was far from a fighting novice. As the men grappled for control, the Vor delivered quick blows to Ryker's side, then wormed his way out from underneath.

Both men jumped back to their feet and squared off. They side-stepped around an imaginary circle, each waiting for the other to move. Ryker was the one to break the truce. He burst forward, intending on delivering a roundhouse punch that would surely floor Sergei.

But Sergei saw it coming. He feinted then swivelled and swiped Ryker off his feet. Ryker landed on the ground with a thud. He was dazed.

Then he spotted the rifle. Right there next to him.

He reached out for it. Sergei saw what was coming, and he darted over, lifted his boot, and kicked away the rifle. Then he set himself up to finish Ryker off with a heel to the face.

No chance. Ryker grabbed Sergei's leg and bolted, lifting the Vor's foot into the air. The momentum sent Sergei's body tumbling backwards and Ryker threw himself down on top of his enemy once more.

This time he wasn't letting him go. Ryker didn't give Sergei a second to recover. He grabbed Sergei's head and smashed it off the tarmac. There was a loud crack. Ryker did it again and Sergei's eyes rolled. Ryker was set to deliver a third blow that would surely finish Sergei for good when he was distracted by the sound of movement behind him.

The Red Cobra.

Ryker spun, moving off Sergei and into a defensive position. He expected to see the shadow. Perhaps the glint of her knife.

So he was surprised when what he actually saw was the black butt of a rifle, moving quickly towards him.

Not the Red Cobra after all.

But it was too late for Ryker to do anything as the butt smashed into his face.

Chapter 57

Ryker came to when his head jarred against something hard. He opened his eyes. It was dark. Noisy. Another jolt, and his face smashed off a metallic surface just inches away. It took Ryker's battered brain a few moments to calibrate and realise where he was.

The boot of a car.

He couldn't see a thing, could barely move in the cramped space. His wrists were strapped together. His ankles too. Rope? Tape? He had so little room to manoeuvre, he couldn't be sure.

Wherever they were headed, it was one hell of a bumpy road. The car jumped up on its suspension every few seconds. Ryker could do nothing to stop his head and body from bouncing and crashing all over the place. He could only guess from the bumps and the grinding noise of the tyres that they were travelling over a dirt track – back to the ranch where he'd earlier been spying?

Eventually the car came to a stop and the engine went dead. Ryker prepared himself, even though in his hog-tied state he knew he had little chance of launching an immediate counter-attack.

A chance would come though. It had to.

The boot opened and for a couple of seconds, Ryker was blinded by a bright light directly above him. When he finally focussed, he saw it was a spotlight high up on a metal pole. Another industrial yard?

Standing above Ryker were two men. He didn't recognise either. One held a shotgun, the barrel of which he pointed at Ryker's head. The other man reached in, grabbed Ryker under his armpits and half lifted, half dragged Ryker from the car.

The man let go and Ryker thudded to the ground. He tried to look around and figure out where the hell he was. The yard they were in was brightly lit by various spotlights. The fact it was still night told Ryker he hadn't been unconscious long and that they hadn't travelled far. The ground was wet but it wasn't raining anymore. There were a number of cars and vans in the yard. Then Ryker spotted the outline of the white farmhouse. He was at the ranch.

Ryker was grabbed suddenly by his ankles. Someone, maybe more than one man, pulled him. His body flipped over onto his front and his face scraped painfully across the ground as he was dragged along. They moved off the yard and into the large barn that stood alongside the farmhouse.

Ryker heard the clanking of metal, then what sounded like a pulley.

Seconds later, his body was hauled into the air and he was left dangling by his ankles. His body swayed back and forth, his head at least a couple of feet off the ground. Ryker swivelled, looking around the room. It was big, maybe forty feet square. The ground was smooth concrete, and the walls and roof were corrugated metal. It was brightly lit with four large round overhead lamps. He noticed some large silvery troughs, tools, some racking.

He looked up – or down? – at the ceiling. It was lined with hooks and pulleys.

A barn? Or an abattoir perhaps?

Whatever it was, it no longer appeared to be in use. It was too clean, in appearance at least – it smelled old, musty. Some remnants of its previous use.

One of the goons stepped toward Ryker, a glinting metal object in his hand. Ryker flinched as the blade came closer to him, then sighed with relief when he realised it was only a pair of scissors. The man snipped away at Ryker's shirt. Then haphazardly cut down the legs of Ryker's jeans until he was left in just his boxers, socks and shoes.

After that the two men walked away and Ryker was left alone. At least he thought he was. Swinging his body and craning his neck he tried to get as full a view of the room as he could. He certainly couldn't see anyone. And it was quiet. Very quiet.

Ryker looked at his feet. It was rope tying his ankles together. Wedged between his ankles was a large metal hook, the tied rope slung over it. If he could use his strength to lift his torso and grab the chain above the hook, he'd be able to pull the rope free.

But his hands were tied behind his back.

Perhaps if he swung with enough ferocity, the rope on his ankles would loosen. Or maybe even the rope would jump and slip from the hook.

He had to try something.

Ryker swung his body back and forth. It took every ounce of strength he had to build up momentum.

Within a minute or so, his body was moving in a large arc, nearly a full half circle, the air rushing against his face. Every now and then the rope nudged an inch or so in the hook's groove .

A little more and it would come out.

If he could keep it going...

Ryker heard a door open and then the soft sound of footsteps. He turned his head, mid-swing, and saw legs approaching. Four men. Maybe five.

He moved more frantically, twisting his body this way and that. Grunting and groaning and then shouting in both anger and sheer determination.

The roped jumped again. It was agonisingly close to coming free. But the men's feet were edging closer and closer. They were moving casually, no urgency. A contrast to Ryker's frenzied movement.

Ryker gave it everything he had. He thought the rope was about to come free, but it slipped back into position at the last second. Still Ryker kept going. The men were just a few steps away, then...

A man stepped forward. The same one who'd earlier snipped Ryker's clothes away. He reached out and grabbed Ryker as he hurtled toward him. The man stumbled back as he took the moving weight. Then with absolute calm, he brought Ryker to a stop.

So close.

Ryker initially bucked and jolted against the man's strength but Ryker soon went placid. He was huffing, his breathing fast and heavy from the exertion of trying to free himself. His head was spinning from the constant motion. The whole room around him seemed to be swinging still. A wave of nausea passed through him before he regained his focus.

It was only then that Ryker took a proper look over each of the men in front of him. He recognised them all. Two were the goons who'd dragged him from the car, one with a shotgun in his hand, the other holding on to Ryker.

Then there was Sergei, standing back from the other two. Next to him was the old man – the boss – his shinning walking cane in his hand.

The old man spoke. His words were calm and slow, no sign of angst or anger. He was speaking Georgian and Ryker didn't understand any of it.

'He's asking you if you speak Georgian,' Sergei said in English. At least his best attempt at English.

Still, it was something of a surprise. It was the first time Ryker had heard the Vor speak. His voice was gravelly and heartless.

'No,' Ryker said.

Sergei responded to his master. Then said in English, 'But you do speak Russian.'

Ryker didn't respond. Giorgi took a step forward. Sergei matched his stride. The two goons stepped away to the side.

'This place used to be a farm,' Giorgi said in Russian. In the more distinctive tongue, the old man's voice sounded sharper, more clear and confident. A contrast to his doddering appearance. 'Cattle mostly. This room was used to house some of them.'

'You've done a good job of clearing the shit out,' Ryker said. 'Just four lumps left.'

The boss took a moment's pause. Ryker wondered whether the old man would send a goon over to exact punishment for the slur.

No. Whatever Giorgi had planned was still to come.

'But that was many years ago,' the old man said. 'Now I use this room for storage. Mostly we bring the new girls here. Soften them, ready them for trade. Cattle. Like the old days, in a way. I'm also using the land as a ranch for *toro bravo* – Spanish fighting bulls. It's quite an operation.

Bullfighting has becoming a passion of mine. This farm, the land, will once again flourish. How the world changes. You see, the farmer who used to own this place, he had no money. He owed *me* a lot of money. I gave him a simple choice. Give me the land. And everything on it. And I'd go away. A *simple* choice. He didn't take it.'

Giorgi took another step forward. Sergei unbuttoned his shirt. Ryker stared at the swirls of black ink on his skin underneath.

'Instead,' Giorgi said, 'in the middle of the night he walked naked across the whole farm, acres and acres of land, a twelve inch kitchen knife in his hand, and he slaughtered every beast in this place. Bulls, cows, the young too. The floor in here was a sea of blood. It was on the walls, the ceiling. And then, in front of the twitching bodies and the corpses of his livelihood, he took that knife and he cut his own throat. I found him the day after, face down in that sea of red.'

Sergei removed his shirt and threw it to the side. Ryker continued to stare at the tattoos that covered his body. Upside down they looked misshapen and jagged. Or maybe that was the way they were pulled across Sergei's sinewy skin. Sergei wasn't a big guy, but what there was of him was pure muscle, not an ounce of fat anywhere.

'You see,' Giorgi said. 'The farmer thought if he killed the animals, I couldn't take them from him. And if he killed himself, it would make me go away. There would be no way for me to get this land from him: it would pass to his children – a boy and a girl – and I would move on to someone else. They were just ten and eight. His wife, she'd died many years before.'

Sergei took a metal knuckle-duster from his trouser pocket.

'The farmer was wrong,' Giorgi said. 'He should have made the *simple* choice. I killed his son. He died the same way his father did and I buried him out on the farm. I sold his daughter. She killed herself aged fifteen. An overdose. By that point, she was unrecognisable as the sweet young girl I'd first met here.'

Giorgi reached into his pocket. His hand came back out grasping onto a small red book. Ryker's dazed mind took a few seconds to figure out what it was. A passport.

'I don't believe in ghosts,' Giorgi said. 'But this place? I imagine I can still hear the calls and the screams of the animals that night. I can hear the blood spitting and hissing from a hundred necks. I can still smell death in here. It seeps through the blood-stained walls. Can you hear it, Mr Ryker? Can you smell it?'

Giorgi opened the passport and held it up, opened to show the small square picture of Ryker.

'Like the farmer, I'm going to give you a very simple choice too. And I'd advise you take it. I'm going to be asking you some questions. I want you to answer them, truthfully. That is all. Do you understand?'

Ryker pursed his lips. He knew what was coming. He'd been tortured before. Many years earlier, he'd been trained to withstand interrogation, both physical and mental intimidation. That training had been necessary. As an asset for the secretive JIA, Ryker's silence had been an imperative.

The training had worked, to a degree: everyone breaks eventually. Ryker had, at the hands of the Russian FSB – a devastatingly deviant snake of a woman by the name Lena Belenov. Following that a series of events had led to Ryker leaving the JIA and assuming his new identity.

The way he saw it now, he didn't have the same need to hold his silence anymore. His only loyalty was to himself and to Lisa.

Self-preservation.

'I said, do you understand?' the old man asked.

'Yes,' Ryker said. 'I understand.'

Giorgi smiled. Upside down, it made his face look manic.

'Good,' he said. He nodded to Sergei. 'Then let us begin.'

Chapter 58

Ten minutes later, Ryker's vision – through his one remaining good eye – was tinged red from the blood dripping down his body onto his swollen face. The beating from Sergei was relentless. Animalistic. With the knuckle-duster, the Vor pulverised Ryker's gut and chest, back and face.

Ryker was certain ribs were broken, and he was seriously worried about his left eye, which was swollen shut. But he knew what was still to come would likely be much worse than the straight-forward beating Sergei was inflicting.

Sweat droplets rolled down Sergei's face and covered his body. He was panting from the exertion of the pounding he was delivering. Spatters of Ryker's blood added ominous colour to the black ink tattoos that cloaked him.

'Okay. That's enough,' Giorgi said, holding up his hand.

Sergei stopped mid-strike, pulled back his fist and relaxed.

'Get yourself cleaned up,' Giorgi told him. Sergei nodded and walked over to pick up his shirt. Then he left the room. The two goons remained, flanking Ryker. 'First question. Who are you?'

Ryker snorted. He'd tried to laugh but hadn't realised how dazed and detached he'd become. 'I'm James Ryker.'

'But there is no James Ryker.' Giorgi paused. 'Don't forget I have some very talented men at my disposal. We know how to find out about people.'

'Yeah. You use fifteen-year-old kids and then you shoot them.'

'I can only assume you're referring to young Miguel. It was his own fault. His mouth was too big. He had to be silenced. And when we realised you were on to him, it was the only choice we had.'

Giorgi's words made Ryker's brain whir. He again wondered how the mob had known Ryker was on to Ramos. Had Ryker been followed, or bugged?

No, he couldn't believe that was the case. Otherwise they certainly wouldn't have let Ryker travel to Algeciras and attack those men at the warehouse. Most likely Ramos's home was bugged.

'But yes, you're right,' Giorgi said. 'We use talent wherever we see it. Even if it's fifteen-year-old boys. And we've been trying to find out who you are. James Ryker? Nothing. You're not with MI5, or MI6, or the CIA, the FBI, or Interpol. So why are you here?'

This time, Ryker just about managed a mocking laugh. 'To kill you of course.'

And Ryker meant his words. The mission, according to Winter, was to find the Red Cobra, but Ryker was working for himself now. His job – his life – for the JIA had always been about taking out the bad guys. And these guys were definitely bad.

'Kill me?' Giorgi said. 'But what did I do to you? Do we know each other?'

'No. But I've seen enough of who you are.'

'But you know nothing, I suspect, of who I am.'

'It doesn't matter. You're dead. I'm nothing, just a man. You can do what you want to me. But *she's* still out there.'

'Ah. The Red Cobra. I think that's who you mean. Isn't that very exciting. What an enigma that girl is.'

Ryker held his tongue. What was the story that linked the Red Cobra with the mafia boss and Kim Walker?

'Do you know what I hate about life?' Giorgi continued. 'Sometimes the best intentions get you nowhere. In fact sometimes they get you into serious trouble. This all started because I tried to help a friend. Patrick Walker pissed off the wrong man by fucking that little slut Eva. Andrei Kozlov is loyal to me, he's one of us. Walker should have kept his cock to himself.'

'You killed Kim Walker because of the affair?'

'No. I killed Kim Walker because I thought she was the Red Cobra.'

Ryker said nothing.

'Kozlov wanted to punish Walker,' Giorgi said, 'for sullying his daughter like that. And Walker owed me a lot of money. So who was I to say no to Kozlov? I don't know why, but hurting Kim was the punishment he asked for. We weren't going to kill her. But there was a problem, you see. Because like you, James Ryker, Kim Walker didn't really exist.'

'No. She didn't. So you had Miguel Ramos try to find out who she really was.'

'Of course. I mean, I didn't even know Kim or her husband personally. It was Kozlov's territory. But he came to me with the problem. Who was this woman? I helped him. And when we found out–'

'What did she do to you? The Red Cobra?'

Giorgi paused as though building up to answering the question.

'She killed my son,' he said, finally betraying emotion; hurt, sadness. But it didn't last long. This was a man filled with hate and conceit. 'My only son – Alex. She suffocated him in the middle of the night at a home for wounded war veterans. He was a cripple; he had no way to defend himself against an attack like that. He was my only blood in this world. She took everything from me.'

'But Kim Walker wasn't the Red Cobra.'

'It seems not.'

'I came here, to Spain, to find the Red Cobra,' Ryker said. 'To kill her.'

Giorgi paused.

'So you could say we're on the same team,' Ryker added. 'I can help you catch her.'

'No, Ryker. You really can't.'

Ryker was distracted by footsteps. He looked over and saw Sergei coming back into the room. He was dressed but now had a full-length plastic apron covering his front. In his hand was a power drill, a four-inch silver drill-bit protruding from the end. Ryker's heart thudded.

Sergei moved to the side of the room and picked up an electrical extension cable. He casually walked back toward Ryker as he unreeled the cable, then he plugged in the drill and tested it. The drill-bit whizzed round in a blur, the small motor giving out a loud high-pitched whine.

'Techniques such as this have been used since medieval times,' Giorgi said matter-of-factly. 'The prisoner would be hung upside down, much like you. The rush of blood to the brain feeds it with oxygen, which helps to keep you alert. Awake. The prisoner was interrogated. Two men would begin to saw at the groin using a hand saw, four feet long. Slowly they'd cut through the victim, working towards the head. Very effective, I'm sure you'd agree. Very bloody. But not very long lasting.'

Sergei moved forward with the drill. Ryker's heart drummed faster still. He bucked his body, but there was nothing he could do.

'The drill is much better,' Giorgi said. 'Less blood. Less mess. More time to talk.'

One of the goons stepped forward, grabbed a knife from a sheath on his waistband, and slashed at the rope shackling Ryker's wrists together. Ryker's arms fell down by his head. No chance for relief though. The goons promptly took hold of an arm each, giving Ryker no opportunity of freeing himself despite his flailing attempts. The goon on the left forced open Ryker's left hand and held it steady.

'I've found this to be a very effective way of finding out what we need to know,' Giorgi said. 'We start with the hands. Then the feet. Then elbows, knees. Normally by that point we have to change the drill-bit. The bones in the knees are particularly hard and troublesome. After that, though, the rest is easy.'

Sergei pressed on the drill's trigger again. Ryker focused on the blurring drill-bit as it came closer and closer to the palm of his hand.

Then Sergei stopped. He held his hands steady. The tip of the blurring drill was just a quarter of an inch from Ryker's skin. Ryker's whole body, every single muscle, was tense, his teeth gritted. With the blood rushing around him so fast, he felt faint.

Sergei looked over to his master, who gave the slightest of nods. Then Sergei pushed the drill forward.

The drill-bit tore through Ryker's hand and he let out a harrowing scream. The metal eased through and poked out the other side, blood and flesh splashing outwards. Sergei released the trigger and the drill rolled to a stop with lumps of dripping skin and flesh hanging from the end. Then he pressed the button to reverse the rotation and pulled on the trigger again, a wicked grin on his face.

Ryker's scream heightened further as the drill-bit began rotating back and Sergei pulled the tool away, taking more bone and tissue with it.

When the drill was free of Ryker's hand, the goon let go of Ryker's arm. It flopped uselessly by his head. The pain was consuming him. In that moment, Ryker wished he was still the man who could not feel. The robot who'd worked for the JIA for so many years. That man felt no pain. He didn't even recognise the concept. But Ryker did, and the pain was too much.

Ryker's eyes focused on the drill that was dripping with his blood. Then on Sergei, his face smeared red. Still smiling.

'Mr Ryker,' Giorgi said. 'Please think very hard about your answers this time, because I won't ask these questions again. Who do you work for? And why are you here?'

Ryker didn't say a word. Not because he was holding out but because he was too nauseous with pain. Sergei moved across Ryker. Giorgi gave another nod and the drill started up once more. Ryker closed his eyes and clamped down his jaw so hard it felt like his teeth would shatter. He willed something to happen. He wasn't a religious man; he'd seen too many horrors in his life to believe there was a god. Yet he was praying now. Praying for something, anything to intervene.

And it felt like his prayer had been answered when he heard an unexpected clunking noise.

He opened his eyes. Darkness. The lights had been switched off.

Ryker's arm was suddenly freed by the goon who'd been holding it. He heard surprised shouting from Sergei and the men. Movement. Footsteps.

Even in the darkness, Ryker knew what was happening.

The Red Cobra.

Chapter 59

Ryker's body jolted when he heard a gargling scream from a man. One of the goons? The noise was close, yards away, Ryker thought. Then a gunshot rang out. The flash from the muzzle brought the room into view for a split second.

Ryker could have sworn he saw the sweeping shadow of the Red Cobra.

Another scream. A succession of gunshots, the flashes of fire from the guns like strobe lighting.

Panicked shouting. Footsteps. More gunshots. More flashes of light...

Then silence and total darkness once more.

After a few seconds, Ryker realised he was holding his breath and he slowly exhaled, straining for any noise from within the blackened room. He took a sharp inhale of breath and held it in again, feeling the beating of his heart getting faster.

'Aren't you going to thank me?' she said after a few more moments of silence. Her voice was close by.

Ryker said nothing.

A second later, there was a slicing noise and Ryker's body suddenly tumbled to the ground. He landed head first and his back twisted and compressed as the rest of him came down on top. He lay in an uncomfortable heap on the floor for a few seconds as he tried to regain his composure.

The lights flicked back on. Ryker squinted as his eyes got used to the sudden intrusion of brightness. He jumped back when he realised he was staring into the wide-open eyes of one of the goons, a yard away from him. The guy was dead. No doubt about it.

Ryker found the strength to get to his feet. It took a few seconds more for him to properly take his weight on his wobbling legs, and for the spinning in his head to subside.

His whole body was on fire from the beating he'd taken. The pain in his hand was indescribable. It was taking everything Ryker had to keep his focus off it. Now that he was upright, the blood began to drain from his brain. A wave of dizziness washed through him before Ryker felt clarity and lucidity return. He spun round, looking over the room.

The two goons were down. One had a slit neck and a huge pool of blood swept out from underneath his lifeless body, still growing by the second. The other goon had various puncture holes visible in the clothing around his chest. Each hole was seeping thick red blood onto the floor.

But other than the two dead men there was no one else in the room. No Giorgi. No Sergei.

No Red Cobra.

Ryker heard shouting outside. He grimaced as he moved forward and crouched down by the goon with the shotgun. Ryker took the weapon. It was loaded. He quickly searched the body and found a handgun. That was better. He could use it easily with one hand. There was also a spare magazine and a knife. Ryker used the blade to cut a swathe of cloth from the man's shirt which he wrapped around his injured hand. He pulled it as tight as he could. It wouldn't help the pain but would at least limit his blood loss.

Then he was up again, moving quickly – albeit torturously – to the exit, gun held out. Ryker stopped by the door and listened for just a second. Then he slowly pulled down on the handle and inched open the door, unsure exactly what he would be looking out onto.

He saw the yard outside. It was still night. The spotlights that had earlier cast a bright glow onto the area were now switched off. Giorgi's black car was there, its headlights and the dim moonlight the only illumination in the darkened space. The car's engine was idling. The rear passenger door was open.

Movement. Off to his right. Ryker saw three men: Sergei and another man shepherding Giorgi toward the waiting car.

No. Ryker wasn't letting them get away.

But before he could spring into action, there was a flash of silver in the darkness – the Red Cobra making her attack.

Sergei spotted her. He let go of Giorgi and shoved the boss away as the Red Cobra swept past. She slashed her blade across Giorgi's back and the old man fell to his knees. But it wasn't a fatal blow. Sergei's alertness had saved him.

The other underling tried to pick his boss back up. He couldn't manage it on his own. Sergei took some of the weight, half-dragging Giorgi toward the car.

There she was again. Ryker saw her more clearly this time, maybe because he'd been expecting it. But so had Sergei. As the Red Cobra's blade arced through the air, Sergei ducked and swivelled. His left leg extended and he swiped at the Red Cobra's feet. She tumbled to the ground and landed on her back with a thud.

Sergei lunged for her. She swung the blade at him and caught him on the arm. Sergei didn't even flinch. The way he moved, the determination in his eyes, his fearlessness...

It reminded Ryker of the man he used to be. Reminded Ryker of the fight he'd had with the Red Cobra up on the cliff top all those years earlier. And seeing that look in Sergei's eyes... Ryker knew in that moment the Red Cobra was in serious trouble.

Unless he came to her aid.

The whole world before Ryker seemed to slow as thoughts raced through his head. He had the gun. He could shoot Sergei. Could shoot Giorgi too.

Could shoot the Red Cobra.

His orders from Winter had certainly been clear. But for some reason he wasn't sure about that one.

The Red Cobra was becoming desperate. Sergei pummelled her with his fists, his elbows and his forehead. The attack was brutal. In stealth mode the Red Cobra was an ace, but she was no match for Sergei's close combat skills, his strength and raging blows. She feebly swiped at him with the knife, catching him again on the arm. It made no difference. Ryker winced as blow after blow from the Vor rained down on her.

Soon she wasn't moving. Still Sergei didn't stop.

Ryker had seen enough.

He lifted his gun. Pulled the trigger.

Chapter 60

A clicking sound. No shot. The damn gun jammed! Ryker cursed his bad luck. Perhaps blood had flooded the chamber. Maybe it was a dud. Thankfully, none of the other men heard the faint noise. Ryker was still in cover. But he knew he needed to do something.

Giorgi shouted to Sergei. The Vor stopped the savage beating and looked down at the unmoving figure beneath him. He smiled, his chest heaving in and out from exertion.

Giorgi said something else to Sergei in his native tongue. Sergei nodded and got to his feet. He grabbed the Red Cobra by her ankles and dragged her along the dirt, back toward where Ryker was standing.

Ryker had no doubt about Giorgi's intention. The Red Cobra had killed his son. He wanted to kill her – but more than that he wanted to punish her. Much like he'd punished poor Kim Walker, whoever the hell she really was.

Whatever the Red Cobra's crimes, whatever Ryker's orders had been from Winter to kill her on sight, he wasn't about to let a man like Giorgi get his sadistic way.

Ryker slung open the door. It flew wide open and smacked against the side of the building. He burst forward, his battered body running on nothing more than adrenaline.

The noise and sudden movement caught the attention of all three of the men in front of him. But they were all too slow to react. Sergei – hunched down and pulling the Red Cobra, when Ryker threw open the door – had no time to defend himself, and Ryker slammed a knee into the Vor's jaw as he sped past. Sergei's head snapped back and he crumpled, out cold. He wasn't done for good, but Ryker knew he'd bought himself at least a few seconds.

Ryker bent down and grabbed the Red Cobra's knife from the ground, just as Giorgi's guard was pulling a gun toward Ryker's head.

He never got the chance to fire.

Ryker spun around full circle and the blade cut through the flesh on the man's neck like it was a sheet of paper. The single strike from the razor sharp blade damn near took the man's head clean off. Blood hissed and sprayed from the wound as the man keeled over.

Giorgi was stepping back, a bemused look on his withered face. For all his bravado and confidence and devilishness, he was just an old man. His speed of thought, his bodily reactions, were too slow. He let out a pathetic groan as Ryker, still moving in a fluid motion, plunged the tip of the knife into Giorgi's chest.

The mob boss gulped and stared into Ryker's eyes. Ryker stared right back. He pushed the knife further. Pushed as hard as he could. The blade sunk through inches of flesh and Giorgi gargled.

Was he trying to speak? Ryker didn't care. He twisted the blade. Giorgi grimaced and moaned.

Ryker heard a shout from behind him.

'No!'

It was the Red Cobra. Surprise washed over Ryker. But then he realised what her cry meant.

She'd wanted to kill Giorgi herself.

Too late.

Ryker thrust his hand upward. The blade tore through Giorgi's chest. His eyes opened so wide they looked like they might pop. Giorgi crumpled as Ryker pulled out the knife. The mob boss's limp body slid off the end of the blade.

The old man was dead before he hit the dirt.

Ryker didn't hesitate for a second. He spun round again and came eye to eye with the Red Cobra. She was on her feet. Her face streamed blood, much like Ryker's. The two of them together were battered and bruised almost beyond recognition. But both were still in the fight, running on adrenaline and pure survival instinct.

'You killed him,' she spat. Her voice bubbled from the blood in her mouth, her words mumbled because of the bruising that was already covering her face. 'He was mine.'

'I saved you.'

'I didn't need saving.'

Movement from behind the Red Cobra. Sergei.

Ryker hadn't forgotten the Vor was still in the fight. Sergei sprung upright and lurched for the Red Cobra. Ryker threw back his arm and hurled the knife. It somersaulted through the air. The Red Cobra pulled her head to one side – just an inch – as the knife hurtled past.

Sergei wasn't quick enough. Or maybe he was too focused on his target. He was almost within reach of the Red Cobra when the tip of the blade made contact. There was a thudding noise as the fast-moving object sunk into his eye. The momentum of his body carried him forward. The Vor went down in a heap on the ground, right by the Red Cobra's feet, the knife wedged deep in his face.

He wouldn't be getting up again this time, that was for sure.

'You don't need my help?' Ryker said. 'You sure about that?'

Ryker stayed put as the Red Cobra – eyes not once leaving Ryker's gaze – kneeled down and pulled the knife from Sergei's head. There was a squelching sound as she tugged the metal free. A thick mess of blood, brain, and intraocular fluid seeped out of the hole. The Red Cobra straightened up.

'So what now?' Ryker said.

'You want to kill me, don't you?'

Ryker couldn't be sure whether or not she was posing a challenge. Winter's words once again rushed through his head. The JIA commander certainly wanted the Red Cobra dead.

'I heard you talking. To Giorgi. In there,' she said, indicating over her shoulder.

'You were watching?'

'Until I saw the right moment to save you, yes.'

'The right moment?' Ryker held up his bandaged hand. 'Perhaps that could have been before they got the bloody drill.'

The Red Cobra just about managed to laugh. 'Sorry about that... But I don't think you've yet thanked me.'

'Thank you.'

'So you don't want to kill me now?'

'I will if I have to.'

'You don't have to. I don't want to hurt you, Carl.'

'I'm not Carl. Carl Logan is dead.'

'So I heard. Yet here you are.'

'Looking for you, Anna.'

'Didn't you hear? Anna Abayev is dead too.'

'Except she isn't. She's standing right in front of me.'

'No,' the Red Cobra said. 'Anna really is dead.'

Ryker's mind whirred. 'But you're–'

'Catalina. Anna's sister.'

'But you are–'

'The Red Cobra. Yes. I've always been her. The Red Cobra was never Anna.'

Ryker's head was now a confused mess but as the Red Cobra continued, the final pieces of the jigsaw fell quickly into place.

'I was three years older than Anna. When she was sent to Winter's retreat, I stayed with my father, to watch and learn from him. I was so much more like him than Anna. I always had been. Anna was... different. So sweet, innocent and naive. He had to find a way to break through to her. To show her the path to take.'

'Anna killed your father?'

'Yes. She did. After killing those people at Winter's retreat–'

'Giorgi's son.'

'Alex Meskhi. Then she tracked down me and my father to Romania and she killed him too. He deserved it. No, more than that. He wanted it.'

'Why?'

'Because it was time for us to take over his work.'

'But everyone believed Anna to be you – the Red Cobra.'

'There was nothing I could do about that. The murders at Winter's Retreat were well known. Everyone knew it was Anna. Her time there had changed her, but not in the way our father expected. She never wanted to become like us. She just wanted a new life.'

'So she became Kim Walker, and you became the Red Cobra.'

'Yes,' the Red Cobra said. Ryker could see the pain in her eyes.

But he didn't dwell on the revelation. Ryker had spotted his chance to take her down for good. The Red Cobra, Catalina, was too busy thinking, talking. She'd let her guard down, for a split second.

Ryker lunged forward. She moved back into a defensive crouch, ready to counter. Ryker saw it coming. He swivelled, avoiding her arcing blade, and tumbled into her. They plummeted to the ground.

Ryker's good hand gripped the Red Cobra's wrist, keeping her knife at bay. He reached out with his injured hand and flinched in agony as he grabbed her other wrist, pinning her down. A shot of pain coursed through his whole body, making him feel faint.

The position Ryker found himself in was reminiscent of the one he'd been in on that cliff top in Germany. Of the position Sergei had been in moments earlier too. But Ryker was battered, injured. He simply didn't have it in him to control the Red Cobra like he wanted.

And he knew she knew it.

Catalina sprung her counter-attack. In an instant she'd released herself from Ryker's weak grip and slid out from underneath. They spun round and she was on top, the tip of her knife just an inch from Ryker's one open eye. He tensed and strained and held firm with his good hand as best he could.

'It's over, Catalina!' Ryker said through gritted teeth as he fought to keep the knife from penetrating his head.

'No! I told you before. They all have to die.'

'Eva? Patrick? Why? What did they do to you?'

'They were the reason Anna was killed!'

'No!' Ryker said. 'It was Kozlov. Sergei. Giorgi. They're the ones.'

Ryker was about to add *and they're dead.* But were they all?

'Kozlov. Where is he?' he said instead.

Catalina smiled. Or grimaced. Ryker wasn't sure. He knew what the gesture meant. Kozlov was dead all right. It was no loss to the world. But Walker and Eva? Ryker believed they were worth saving. As much as he disliked them, they didn't deserve to die.

'You've had your revenge,' Ryker said. 'It's over. No more.'

He saw the look of doubt creep into her eyes. Deep down, she must know it too.

In a sudden burst of strength, Ryker strained every last sinew in his body. Fighting through the pain, he let out a cry of determination as he lifted up his body, taking the Red Cobra with him. He was on his feet, her body wrapped around him. He slammed her down onto her back, crushing her with his body weight. The blow knocked the wind out of her. He quickly prised the knife from her fingers and pulled the blade up against her throat.

'It's over, Catalina.' He stared at her coldly.

She huffed– anger, sadness, shock? Plenty of fight left in her head, he figured, but none in her body.

She was at Ryker's mercy.

'Remember Berlin?' she said, squirming to get Ryker to release the pressure on her chest to allow her to breathe. He gave her an inch.

'You could have joined me,' Ryker said. 'Instead you killed Gazinsky.'

'Potanin had me,' she said. 'He'd found Anna. He was going to kill her. That's why I had to leave you. That's why I had to kill Gazinsky; it was the only way. Potanin wanted me to kill you too. I thought I could, but –'

'Maybe you should have.'

'Instead I ran. Anna too. She came here for a new life.'

'And you killed Potanin.'

'Yes. Because of you. But that man, Carl Logan, the one I couldn't kill–'

'I told you already. That man is dead.'

Ryker rolled off her and got to his feet. He held out his hand. Catalina looked at it. She took a second before reaching out and grabbing it. Ryker hauled her to her feet. 'I said I'll kill you if I have to. But I don't have to. Walker, Eva, though. They get to live. That's the deal.'

Ryker turned the knife around and held the blade as he pushed the handle out toward Catalina.

She looked down at it.

'No. I don't need that anymore,' she said. 'The Red Cobra is dead too.'

Chapter 61

The sun was coming up over the mountains, casting a warm yellow glow over the ranch, as Ryker drove away in Giorgi's luxury saloon car. He left Catalina Abayev at the scene. He wasn't sure what she'd do next, where she'd go. He hadn't asked because in truth he didn't want to know.

The Red Cobra had long before retired from life as an assassin. A family tradition, something she'd been born into. She'd been off the radar for years for good reason; she'd been in hiding, ever since disobeying Potanin – by not taking out Logan and Mackie – and then killing him. It was only following the murder of her sister, Anna, aka Kim Walker, that the Red Cobra had come back to life.

Now that her vengeance was complete, it was time to retire the moniker for good.

Ryker's first port of call was Walker's villa in Mijas. Green was there, Eva too, along with quite the mini-infantry of armed policemen. Ryker said what he needed to say to Green: he explained what he'd seen happening in the warehouse in Algeciras, and that Kozlov and Giorgi were now gone.

Although shocked, Green looked visibly relieved. As though a weight had been lifted. Perhaps Ryker's previous hunch had been right: Green had been silenced, or at least Kozlov or the Georgians had put pressure on him not to dig into their business. That was fine. Green was a good man. He was simply out of his depth thrust so close to the seedy and dangerous world that had been ruled by Giorgi.

Ryker didn't stay long. He said a cursory goodbye to Walker, who didn't thank Ryker for saving his life. Whatever. Ryker had never cared for the rich man.

He had a more heartfelt goodbye for Eva, who Ryker now felt greater sympathy for. She wasn't all bad – misguided perhaps – and she'd been born into a family entrenched in the criminal underworld. What could she do about that? And that world had just been shattered. Her father was dead – his body had been found at a remote property near Alhaurin where he'd been hiding. Good riddance, Ryker thought.

Eva was angry. Upset. Lost. She needed to find her way in life. It would take time, but perhaps she'd come out the other side of her grief okay. There was hope for her yet, Ryker believed.

Either way, Eva Kozlov wasn't his problem.

After leaving Walker's home, Ryker made a call to Lisa as he headed east back towards Malaga. It wasn't a surprise when the call went straight to voicemail, though at that moment, Ryker could have done with the comfort of hearing her voice. He left her a message to say he would be home soon, then called Winter. The JIA commander had already learned of both the gun battle in Algeciras and the bloody scene up at the ranch in the mountains.

Ridding the world of a scourge like Giorgi was a good thing, both men knew. But they also knew that if you cut an arm off the mafia, another simply grows back. The mob weren't gone for good. Someone would move in to fill Giorgi's shoes. At least Ryker's exploits in Andalusia, the Red Cobra's too for that matter, had blown the Georgian mafia's operations wide open. Maybe Spanish law enforcement could do their jobs now and keep the fight going.

Winter was less pleased about the fate of Catalina Abayev. He'd wanted the Red Cobra dead. Ryker didn't know the details of why Winter felt so strongly about that. He could only assume the Red Cobra had history with the JIA that he didn't know about. Maybe she'd worked against the JIA. Maybe she'd even worked for them. Ryker had tried to recruit the Red Cobra many years earlier but had failed. Perhaps others had been more successful. If so, that meant she knew things that the JIA wanted kept quiet.

To Winter and the JIA, any ex-asset was simply a liability.

Ryker put himself in that boat too. So he certainly wouldn't feel justified in killing Catalina simply because she was no longer on the payroll of the JIA. She was only a threat if she felt threatened herself. Ryker trusted his instinct on that.

'What will you do now?' Winter asked.

'I don't know,' Ryker said, though his natural instinct was that he and Lisa would go on the run once more. A new location. Two new identities. It was the safest thing to do. 'I did what you asked. It's over, Winter.'

'Do you really believe that? No matter how far you run or what you do to hide, deep down you'll always be that man. Carl Logan. You know I can always use a man like that.'

'No,' Ryker said defiantly. 'I'm not him.'

His time in Andalusia had made Ryker question his life. What he'd come to realise was that he'd never escape his past. Some part of that man – the JIA's machine – would always be inside him. But he really wasn't the same person anymore.

For a second or two, his mind took him back to Eva. Then to the Red Cobra. The ranch. Being strung up and tortured. How he'd felt so vulnerable and feeble and... human. He thought of the moment when he'd held a knife against the Red Cobra's neck. The old him would have killed her on the spot. But *he* hadn't.

Because he was no longer that man.

'What am I? I don't know,' Ryker said. 'But I'm not the same. In fact I'm different in many ways. The last few days have taught me that.'

'Then who are you?'

'I'm James,' Ryker said, smiling. 'James Ryker.'

The same day, Ryker was on a plane back home. He'd not yet seen a doctor about his mangled hand, and his body was covered in bruises, cuts and scratches. He needed drugs. He needed rest.

But he wanted to be with Lisa.

By the time Ryker made it back to his home, it was night-time the next day. The connecting flights hadn't been kind to Ryker and he'd spent hours in airports trying his best to catch some much-needed rest on rows of hard metallic chairs. Even if he hadn't been beaten and bruised, he'd have been a groggy mess from the travelling alone.

But as he stepped through the front doorway, into his space, for a moment he suddenly felt alive again.

The feeling didn't last long, though. He'd expected to hear the patter of feet. To have Lisa bound up to him, wrap her arms around him, and sink her head into his chest. It was a moment he'd been longing for for days.

Instead, he was greeted by a dark, cold, silent house. He flipped on the lights.

The open plan room – kitchen, lounge, diner – was spotless, no clothes or mess anywhere. Ryker frowned as he walked through the space and into the bedroom. The bed was made. Everything looked tidy and neat... unused.

Ryker took out his phone. No messages, no missed calls. He dialled Lisa. He heard a buzzing. He moved out of the bedroom, following the noise. There on the coffee table in the lounge was Lisa's vibrating phone.

Ryker killed the call, and felt a sickly, unfamiliar feeling. Was it worry or sorrow or guilt or all three? He painstakingly searched the rest of the house. There was no fresh food or milk in the fridge, nothing to suggest she'd been there recently. All of her clothes and her few belongings appeared to be in place. There was no sign of a struggle, a break-in either.

In a moment of doubt – or was it hope? – Ryker wondered whether maybe she'd walked out on him, run away to start a fresh life on her own. He couldn't fathom why she would do that, but it was surely a better outcome than the other possibility. Could his going to Spain have caused her to leave him?

He moved to the bedroom again, looked in the bedside drawer. Found her passport in the name of Lisa Ryker.

No, she hadn't run, he didn't believe. One way or another, Lisa was in trouble. Winter had already tracked them down, despite their best efforts at hiding. Ryker's only conclusion was that someone else had found them.

And Ryker hadn't even been there to protect her. He felt a flood of guilt. While he'd been busy chasing an old flame through Spain, the love of his life had come to harm.

He didn't know who was responsible or why, but he would do everything he could to find out. To save her.

Ryker quickly moved through the house, collecting the few possessions he needed – weapons, IDs, money. He headed to the front door and opened it, then turned to look back at his home, a place he had truly believed would become his sanctum. *Their* sanctum.

Whatever had happened to Lisa, he knew that dream was gone.

Ryker flicked off the lights and stepped out into the night. He shut the door behind him, and walked away.

61063926R00229

Made in the USA
San Bernardino, CA
13 December 2017